Redemption

T. James Reese

Veritas et Virtute
Media Production

Manufactured in the United States of America

ISBN 978-0615750712

First Edition

There have been so many people who have been a blessing and an encouragement to me during the eight year writing process of the Lucky 13 series, to name them all would fill this page, to name a few would be unfair. So I'll simply say thank you, because you know who you are...

"It may be hard for an egg to turn into a bird: it would be a jolly sight harder for it to learn to fly while remaining an egg. We are like eggs at present. And you cannot go on indefinitely being just an ordinary, decent egg. We must be hatched or go bad."

C.S. Lewis

CONTENTS

1

The swirling wind ripped at their clothing as cool spray showered down on the men, the stormy waters of Lake Michigan colliding with the century-old break wall that stood firm beneath their feet, a bastion of safety amongst the chaos that raged and the death that had followed. Blood coated Gavin's hands, stained his clothes. Delilah laid dead in his arms, her last words haunting him, her revelation ringing in his ears, the name of the Frenchman who had been behind all of Killion's plotting and had arranged for the kidnapping of both Gavin's and Michael's families, a single name: *Laurent*.

Jamie paced carefully on the slippery rocks, his path treacherous as he tried to find a signal on his iPhone, hoping to make a desperate call for help. Michael stood silently still, the mask of Thirteen shrouding his face, his white glowing eyes fixed on the bloody hole where a bullet fired by Killion had pierced the sleeve of his jacket.

"I can't get through," Jamie shouted over the crashing waves.

Gavin nodded as his eyes fell on Michael. He was so angry, but knew that this was not the time or place. They had to get to safety. The truth could wait, for now. They weren't sure how much time had passed, whether it was minutes or hours; they were trapped in a nightmare.

Jamie dropped his phone into his pocket and turned his focus to another matter, still searching for something, but no longer cellular service. Before Killion had killed Delilah with her own gun, he had first fired shots from his own pistol. And then, as part of his ploy, he'd ejected an unfired round from his gun, then tossed the firearm into the tumultuous lake. Jamie scoured the dark stone beneath his feet, praying to find the spent brass casings, maybe even the unfired bullet.

A glint caught his eye. There, in a narrow crevice between the stones, were two empty cases, miraculously caught and protected from the elements. Jamie knelt, scuffing his fingers on the sharp rocks as he fought to retrieve the fired rounds. He stowed the casings in the pocket with his phone and continued the search, hoping to find more.

The unexpected roar of a helicopter came out of nowhere, a blindingly bright spotlight bathing the breakwater in pure, white light. Gavin raised his bloody hand, his pistol firmly grasped, and aimed at the sound.

"Is it Killion?" Jamie cried, using his free hand to block out the intense light, "did he return to finish the job?"

But before Gavin could answer, a loudspeaker screeched above the constant droning of the wind and the beating blades of the craft, "This is the United States Coast Guard. Place your weapons on the ground and stay where you are."

The helicopter drifted in the storm, its spotlight momentarily lifting from the men, allowing them a glimpse of the recognizable orange and white paint that adorned the search and rescue Sikorsky HH-65. Then, suddenly emerging from the darkness, a Coast Guard Defender docked along the wall and four men armed with Mk 14 EBRs hurried from the twenty-five foot vessel, surrounding them, their guns ready.

"Just give me a second to explain," Jamie protested calmly, his hands held above his head in submission. "I'm Chicago PD and there's been a terrible accident."

The officers silently ignored Jamie's plea. One man covered the team as the other three broke off to secure the breakwater. Disarmed, Jamie and Gavin allowed themselves to be restrained by two of the men, their hands zip-tied in front of them. Michael, didn't resist either, still staring at his wound. The fourth man knelt beside Delilah's lifeless body, pressing her jugular as he searched for a pulse.

"No vitals," he announced to his men. "She's dead."

Gavin and Jamie listened as he radioed his findings. They were now standing at an official crime scene. Questions would follow, questions with answers that sounded like lies. Gavin looked down at the blood that coated him, knowing that he appeared to be caught red-handed.

"Let's get them on the boat," the leader said.

Jamie felt a man take hold of his arm as they approached the craft. They'd only taken a few steps when Jamie froze dead in his tracks, the officer caught by surprise. There, just ahead of the gunman's feet was the ejected round, the unfired bullet still in the casing.

"Keep going," the man directed with a shove.

"WHOA!" Jamie exclaimed, throwing himself to the wet ground as he feigned a trip on the uneven rocks, quickly snatching up the bullet in his palm.

"Get up," the stern order came from overhead, the man pulling on Jamie's arm, forcing him to stand.

Again, Jamie continued forward toward the boat. Gavin followed passively behind, not sure of what just happened. Michael, however, still stood in his trance, his gaze fixed on his bloodied sleeve.

"Move, buddy," another officer commanded.

But Michael was unresponsive. The man nudged him in the back with the butt-end of his gun, but Michael failed to move. Angrily, the officer reached up and ripped the mask from Michael's face.

Michael blinked, the bond between him and his mask severed, the searing pain of the bullet wound suddenly realized as he let out a shout. The officer looked at the mask, then the man in front of him, and hesitated before again pressing the stock of his rifle sharply into Michael's spine and guiding him to the boat.

The guards thoroughly searched the men, confiscating the contents found in their pockets. The items were then quickly sorted into individual evidence bags, one for each man, Michael's mask included.

Once the guards had ensured their captives posed no more threat, one of the officers hurried back into the rain, onto the breakwater, and retrieved the men's weapons from where they'd left them on the wet ground. He quickly returned to the boat and racked the guns to ensure the chambers were empty. With that, the Defender eased from the stone wall and then surged away from the lighthouse, it's dark silhouette a ghost in the night, visible only in brief flashes of lightning as the violent storm raged on around them. And soon, the lighthouse was behind them, no longer in sight, now but a stinging memory of their failure.

"Where are they taking us?" Gavin whispered to Jamie, sitting close beside him on the Coast Guard Defender.

We're heading south," Jamie reasoned, "to Calumet Park. There's a Coast Guard station there."

"Do you think they'll listen to us?"

"Would you listen to us?" Jamie grinned.

Gavin once again looked at the blood on his hands. One of the officers had tended to Michael's arm, the bloodied suit jacket lying at his feet, his hands also secured, resting in his lap. The wound looked worse than it actually was, the bullet had only grazed him.

"You've got a point," Gavin smirked.

"Can you contact my lieutenant?" Jamie asked. "As I said, I'm a detective with Chicago PD."

"We'll sort this out with the Captain," the leader replied. "For now, just sit tight...and *shut up*."

They remained silent for a few minutes, listening to the loud motors that surged the boat forward through the rough water. The officers talked quietly amongst themselves, their guns still vigilantly trained on their captives.

"What, did you trip?" Gavin asked, his voice low. "You made quite a scene back there."

"Yeah," Jamie nodded subtly, opening his tightly clenched fist just enough for Gavin to see the 9mm round still clutched in his palm. "It's Killion's."

"So what are you going to do with it?"

"Do?" Jamie whispered. "This just might save our lives."

****

Kayla stared at the clock on the living room wall. She'd hardly slept. Her cell phone sat beside her on the sofa, but it had yet to ring. Jamie was supposed to call. They'd left for the lighthouse nearly five hours earlier. Something must have happened, gone wrong.

Her heart fluttered: she could feel it beating through her chest, hear it echoing in her ears, as her mind raced, imagining all possible scenarios. She pictured her husband floating face down, dead in the water. Tears came to her eyes.

Kayla wiped them away, unaware of the small demon that perched on the back of the couch, its head hovering just above her shoulder, its forked tongue flicking as it hissed soft words of despair into her ear. It grinned in delight at the hopelessness it caused.

"The next time you see your husband," it spoke, "will be to identify his dead, bloated body at the morgue."

****

The waters calmed, the winds subsiding, as the Coast Guard Defender docked in Calumet. The storm, same as the night, was passing.

"Move along," the leader barked, leading the restrained men down off the boat and along the harbor, the front doors to the station visible ahead, awash in the harsh luminescence of the light mounted just above the solid metal frame.

Jamie, Gavin, and Michael followed obediently as they were hustled into the station, then, one-by-one, led to separate rooms for interrogation. They'd had no time to talk, get their stories straight.

"God help us," Gavin whispered, now alone, the door closing firmly behind him.

****

Michael paced about the room in which they'd placed him. The officer had kept his mask, leaving him defenseless. He felt vulnerable, even naked, without its power. Once corralled onto the boat, his jacket had been removed and the sleeve of his now-filthy, blood-stained white dress shirt had been cut to allow access to the bullet wound beneath. Michael loosened his tie and unbuttoned the collar of his shirt, both awkwardly done with his still-bound hands. His hair, as was the rest of him, was tousled, matted from wearing the mask. He suddenly found himself thinking back to five years ago, when Jamie had sat alone in a cell, trapped in the basement of the Tri-Corp building in New York City: Thirteen's prisoner. He remembered how Jamie looked, very similar to how he supposed he himself appeared now. The irony amused him.

The door opened briskly. Apparently he was the first to be questioned. A man, casually dressed and in his mid-forties, entered the room and obligingly removed the restraints from around Michael's wrists, then took the chair opposite Michael at the table. For a moment, they shared silence, each one assessing the other. The man's eyes fell on the bloody gauze wrapped and taped tightly around Michael's left bicep.

"Did the girl do that?" he asked. "Is that why you shot her?"

Michael answered immediately, calmly, "No, I did not shoot her."

"But she *was* shot?" the officer asked, his brow wrinkling theatrically, a pencil scribbling hasty notes on a yellow colored legal pad.

"You sound surprised," Michael replied. "Has no one examined her body yet?"

"It's a crime scene," the man chortled, "you don't just *examine* the body. You've got forensics and detectives, and crime scene specialists who have to do their job first. Hollywood has really messed up peoples' understanding of how this sort of thing actually works. An autopsy will be done to determine the cause of death."

"I see," Michael conceded.

"So back to the point, you say, in fact, she was shot."

"Yes."

"Then if not by you, then who?" the man prodded, acting unconvinced, yet open, his pencil now tapping fervently, distractingly, on the paper in front of him.

"Killion."

"And he's one of the other men with you?"

"No," Michael answered, holding back his growing impatience. "He's the reason we were there."

****

Jamie estimated they'd been at the Coast Guard station for nearly two hours, but he couldn't be sure. Maybe it was two hours, maybe it was four. In the room where he was placed, there was no clock on the wall, no way to gauge the passing of time. His mind raced as he tried to recall every last detail from the previous night. Knowing how he himself would handle such an investigation, the questions he would ask a suspect, Jamie sorted out his thoughts. But he was afraid the odds were against them. What was worse, when they'd been taken on the boat, the guardsmen searched the three friends, confiscating their wallets, cell phones, anything on their persons, including the spent brass casings from Killion's gun. Jamie wondered if they had been properly tagged and catalogued as evidence, something necessary that, if done wrong, could mean the difference between admissible and non-admissible evidence in a hearing.

What if this goes bad, what if we end up on trial? Murder in the first degree!

Killion's unfired round still lingered in his grasp. Jamie dropped it into his pocket, but pulled his hand back sharply, the edge of the plastic restraints cutting into his skin, rubbing his wrists raw.

A firm knock on the door announced the entrance of a portly, square-jawed man. He closed the door behind him and approached the table, placing a notepad, what Jamie recognized as his wallet, flipped open, his detective's shield facing up, and a clear plastic evidence bag, the empty brass visible. He then curtly motioned for Jamie to sit.

"So you're a cop?" the man began, pacing the room and nodding at the badge sitting on the table.

"Detective," Jamie corrected.

"Oh, I see, *Detective*," the man replied sarcastically. "Well let me see if I've got this straight. We've got a dead girl, a guy armed with a bulletproof vest and a pistol with a silencer, a *detective*, and a freak-show in a black mask...sound about right?"

"Sounds like a joke," Jamie stated very matter-of-factly. "We're just missing a priest and a rabbi."

"Funnyman...the *detective* is a funny guy," he mocked, his jaw flinching, "Do I look like I'm laughing!"

Jamie shrugged but uttered no reply.

The investigator continued, "So, *funny guy*, answer me straight so we can get this over with. Who killed the girl, was it you?"

Jamie smirked, this guy was a gem, "Nope, it wasn't me."

"What about these?" the man asked, picking up the sealed evidence bag by its corner and shaking it so that the casings rattled against each other.

"Those are from the *real* killer's gun. Ballistics will find that the discharge burns on the casings are dissimilar from Gavin's and my 9mm's. They'll see when they do test fires for comparison. Also, they'll find slugs imbedded in the outer wall of the boathouse. Those came from these casings."

"Convenient," the man remarked.

"There's one more thing," Jamie explained, extending his arms out toward the investigator, "if you wouldn't mind removing the restraints?"

The man pulled a heavy-duty pocket knife from a clip on his belt, flicked it open, and reluctantly sliced Jamie free, "Don't make me regret this."

"Thank you," Jamie said gratefully, rubbing his tender wrists before motioning towards his pocket. "May I?"

The investigator nodded and Jamie retrieved the unfired round, then placed it down on the table, standing it upright, the distinct hollow-point aimed at the ceiling. His interrogator eyed it for a moment before picking it up for a closer look. He didn't know a lot about ammunition, but, in his limited expertise, he could still tell that this was a unique round, most definitely not from the box of an off-the-shelf retail purchase.

"Where did you get that?"

"This also came from the killer. After firing those rounds at my friend, Michael, he feigned submission, ejecting this bullet from his gun before tossing his weapon into Lake Michigan."

"Interesting," the investigator said, his demeanor softening, "and still a little too convenient. But, I'll make notations and see if we can verify what you've said."

"Thank you."

"So the man you say these rounds belong to, the real killer, who is he?"

"His name is Terrance Killion," Jamie sighed. "He's British, retired Special Forces, ex-MI6. He's a professional killer in the employ of a man we know only as *The Frenchman*."

"That's good," the man laughed, his manner hardening once again, "real good. Sounds like a movie I once saw with Robert De Niro and that French guy, what's his name, Jean..."

"Reno," Jamie prompted.

"Yeah, Jean Reno," he chuckled. "But, I hated that movie and I think you're lying to me. You almost had me convinced that there was another person involved, but then you go over the top, too far as I'm concerned, Detective."

"I'm telling the truth, I swear!" Jamie urged.

****

Gavin shifted uncomfortably in his seat. The room was quiet, empty. He was alone. He wondered what was going on at that moment, if Jamie and Michael were also alone, or if their interrogations had begun. In an odd way, he found himself wishing that perhaps Michael could somehow don his mask and use his power to escape, by any means, but he knew that a violent escape would only make things worse, for him and his family, for all of them.

The fluorescent lights burned brightly overhead. Gavin stared down at the shadow that formed on the table, cast by his bound and bloodied hands. His hair was disheveled, his nerves shot. Only five years ago, this would have been nothing. He'd been investigated before, questioned after the death of a target, a sleepwalker. A detective would ask him some questions and he would answer with a simple *yes* or *no*. Then the phone would ring and the detective's superior would say that the case had been closed, that there was no further reason to investigate. Gavin always assumed it was Joseph making the call, working things out. But after learning that he and Michael, *Thirteen*, had, in a matter of sorts, both been possibly working for Triton, Gavin wondered if the targets he'd hunted so piously were often even sleepwalkers at all, but someone Triton needed eliminated and that is why he was always excused from the interrogations; through Triton's underhanded connections and dealings. The conspiracy grew in his mind. And now, five years later, with both Joseph and Triton gone, there was no one to make the phone call, regardless of the man or his intentions, there was no one to come to his aid.

The door opened, interrupting his thoughts. A slender figured woman entered the room. She appeared to be all business, her chestnut hair pulled back tightly. In silence, she took the chair opposite Gavin at the table and folded her hands gently, staring into his eyes, questioning without questioning, her piercing gaze cutting through to his very soul. Again, he shifted in his seat. He now had another reason to be uncomfortable.

2

The sun crept slowly on the eastern horizon, it's warm orange glow delivering the promise of a new day. But the truth, at that moment, was uncertain. And with the new day came the threat of damnation.

Gavin watched the woman as she curiously stared him down. He was ashamed of the blood on his hands and feared that no one would see past it, but simply pass a guilty verdict on circumstances alone.

"What's your name?" the woman asked calmly, noting how Gavin had begun to shift uncomfortably in his seat.

He hesitated, wondering how much he should tell her, how much Jamie and Michael had already said. What if he said the wrong thing, contradicted his allies with words that would unintentionally become a glaring inconsistency, his death sentence?

"Gavin Dering," he finally replied.

She smirked as he spoke, writing a note on her legal pad. Gavin could only imagine what she must be thinking, and, of course, in his angst, he feared the worst.

"Well then, Gavin Dering," she began softly, "from speaking with your friends, we've learned the *what*. Now we need to figure out the *why*."

Again, Gavin shifted on the hard wooden chair, now as a distraction, to buy time as he thought. The room was quiet other than the sound of his shuffling feet beneath the table.

"My wife was taken from me," he explained, "taken as a ploy to trap me and steal an artifact of unknown value."

"Your wife, what is her name?"

"Ashley," he answered.

Again, she made notations in her notepad before speaking, "Who took your wife, Gavin? Who took Ashley?"

Gavin sat silently, the weight of the culminated events finally realized, the fear of never seeing his beloved again as a free man was suddenly, emphatically real. He felt his eyes begin to well as his heart sank into desperation.

A man I'd never met till last night, a man named Killion. He took her and held her in Los Angeles."

"Los Angeles. And is she still there?" the woman asked, her pen busy.

"She managed to escape," Gavin said. "In Los Angeles, she met Michael's wife, also Killion's hostage. The two of them, as well as Michael's son, managed to escape. As far as I know, they're on their way to Chicago now. I'm praying they're still safe."

The woman listened intently, nodding empathetically as he spoke, "So then, the woman, the one who died, how does she figure in?"

Gavin again looked at the dried blood on his hands. He cleared his throat, controlled his emotions.

"She was hired to kill me, a backup to Killion in case he should fail."

"So she was Killion's partner?"

"In a way. We had arranged to exchange the artifact…"

"Sorry,' she interrupted, "but the artifact you refer to is what?"

"It's an old key."

"A key?"

"Yeah," Gavin answered.

"Hmm," the woman sighed curiously, again scribbling on her notepad. "Thank you for clarification. Please continue."

Gavin collected his thoughts again before finishing what he'd been saying, "We were going to make the exchange when she received word that her grandfather had been murdered.

"So, Gavin, did the exchange go badly? Did she double cross you and you killed her in self defense?"

"Delilah," he replied, "her name was Delilah. And no, I did not kill *her*. She was actually working with us."

The woman now shifted in her seat, "I thought you said Delilah was hired to kill you, why would she make such a turn around, to partner with you?"

"Like I said, another of the men whom Killion murdered was her grandfather. She wanted revenge, so she turned on him. You see, her grandfather was a member of a secretive group of elite who called themselves *The Order*. Among them was a reverend named McNamara, and from my understanding, several senators, congressman, and CEOs as well. If it's not all over the news by now, it will be. Killion killed them all."

"And where did these murders take place?"

"Also in Los Angeles."

"So this man, Killion, murdered a group of people in L.A., then came to Chicago to kill the woman. I follow. So how did you end up at the lighthouse?"

"We wanted to trap Killion, to stop his plan, but we underestimated him," Gavin explained.

"And where is Killion now?" she wondered.

"I don't know. He attacked us from a black, military helicopter then disappeared into the storm after killing Delilah."

They sat for a moment in silence, each staring at the other from their end of the table. Neither blinked.

"And everything you're telling me is true?"

"I swear to it," Gavin nodded.

"Alright, Mr. Dering, allow me some time to confer with my colleagues. I will return," she said, standing and heading out of the room, the door opening briefly, then closing and locking behind her.

****

Kayla began to panic as she sat alone in her living room. The minute hand on the ornate wall clock had ticked past 4:30am, the hours passing terrifyingly fast. She had to do something, she could no longer sit idly, waiting for a phone call that now may never come. Not knowing where else to turn, she frantically searched through the contacts on her iPhone, scanning the names for one in particular, one who she knew could help.

Lieutenant Thomas Walker

She'd found it. She tapped on his name and selected the option to call him. She knew it was early, but was sure that he would be up and readying for a new day.

The phone rang. Kayla waited, trying to calm herself, to steady her voice.

"Hello," a man answered.

"Tom," she replied, happy to hear his voice, "it's Kayla Branson, Jamie's wife. I'm sorry to call so early."

"Oh yeah," he chuckled warmly, "but it's alright. I was up already. So anyway, good morning! How're the kids?"

"They're fine. I'm actually calling about Jamie. I need your help, Tom."

"Of course, Kayla," he said, suddenly concerned. "Is he in some kind of trouble?"

"I don't know for sure," she replied. "I can't go into much detail, but some circumstances arose that forced Jamie to act...*outside*...the law."

"How far outside, Kayla?"

"Far enough that you're the only person I think he would trust."

"Do you know where he is?"

"In a manner of speaking," Kayla sighed. "I know where he was going: the old lighthouse in the harbor, east of the Navy Pier."

"Whatever for?" Tom questioned.

"Trust me when I tell you I can't say."

"Well what do you want me to do?"

"Jamie was supposed to check in with me hours ago, but he hasn't yet," Kayla answered. "Don't go out of your way, just keep your ears open. If you hear about any reports that may involve Jamie, let me know right away."

"I'll do my best, but are you sure you can't tell me more?" he pleaded.

"We were told that if we go to the police, something terrible would happen. If neither of us hear anything before too long, I'll tell you everything."

"Alright, Kayla," the lieutenant conceded. "I'll keep my ear to the ground. We take care of our own. If he's in trouble, I'll vouch for him."

"Thanks, Tom," she said, ending the call.

****

"Normally I'm the *good* cop in these sorts of situations," Jamie taunted, "but I can see you prefer playing the role of *bad* cop. It suits you."

"Why aren't you taking this seriously, Detective?" the man asked angrily.

"Because no matter what I tell you, you won't believe me. If I were on your end of the table, asking the same questions, I don't know that I'd believe any differently."

"Kidnappings, extortion, ransoms…they don't play out like this, not in real life. This isn't Hollywood, Detective. I'm not buying it!"

A gentle knock on the door pulled the interrogator's attention away from Jamie. He turned as the door opened and the woman who'd questioned Gavin entered.

"This is the detective?" she asked.

The man nodded his confirmation as she stared Jamie down.

"I think we're done with our investigation," she said coolly. "Let's let them sit for a bit while we compare their stories."

Again, the interrogator nodded, then gave Jamie a last, angry glare as they exited the room.

Jamie sat alone, the early morning sun bursting through the small gaps between the slats of the retractable blinds that darkened the windows. He knew they were in deep, maybe too deep.

****

The three investigators stood talking in a fourth room in the Coast Guard building, each sharing what they had learned of the prior night's events in the harbor. Each had their own opinion of what the so-claimed truth had revealed.

"I don't know that we're getting anywhere?" Jamie's questioner sighed, his *tough guy* act over, now calm, almost quiet in demeanor.

"I agree," the man who interrogated Michael added. "What they're saying is just too incredible...I mean, espionage, foreign assassins, seriously?"

The woman leaned against the table, a cup of coffee in one hand, the other resting in her pants pocket. She, like the others, was uncertain. But something bothered her: even when considering how incredible the men's stories were, every detail that the detainees had shared matched up. The small differences were there, but more from perspective, rather than deception.

"The hardest part about this," she said, "is the fact that we do have a woman with no ID, no fingerprints in the database, she appears to be foreign, and, pending ballistics, she was allegedly shot with a gun not matching the ones possessed at the time by the men in custody.

16

Furthermore, the important details of each man's statement line up."

"So you believe them?"

She thought for a moment, finishing the last of her coffee, "I say we bug the room, bring all three of them in here, let them talk. They may or may not be telling us the truth, but alone, in confidence, they may say something that'll give them away. Make another pot of coffee for them while I go get a wireless transmitter."

"And then what?"

"We let them sit. While they sweat it out, I'll contact a friend of mine at the bureau. If the deceased is a foreign national, he may know who she is. Prep the room, I'll be back."

∗∗∗∗∗∗∗∗∗∗∗∗

"Wake up, brother," Killion whispered.

"Ugn," Edward grunted as he sat up from where he lay on the hard floor of the helicopter's cargo hold. "What time is it?"

"Nearly five in the morning. We need to go.

"Alright," Edward sighed.

"We have enough fuel to make it to Kings Point, correct?" Killion asked, as his brother entered the cockpit and began his preflight checks.

"I thought we were staying the night at the airfield in Lansing?" Edward replied. "I thought we were heading to Kings Point tomorrow."

A groggy Edward grabbed a headset off the console and sleepily put it on, adjusting the distance of the microphone from his mouth. Killion did the same.

"Change of plans, brother," Killion replied. "We must get as far away as we can, and quickly. The Coast Guard has responded to an emergency in the Chicago harbor. I believe they've found our *friends*. I heard it on the radio scanner just moments ago. The men were taken into custody and are being held at a Coast Guard station just north of here."

"You're sure? I need more sleep, you too."

"No choice," Killion growled over the loudening motor of the helicopter, the rotor overhead spinning brilliantly. "We head to New York now. So tell me, *yes* or *no*: do we have enough fuel to make the trip?"

"Yes, we'll be fine," Edward replied solemnly as he lifted the Blackhawk into the calm, early morning sky.

"*5:03am*," Killion said, noting the time on his luxurious wristwatch. "What's our ETA?"

Edward thought for a moment, quickly calculating the approximate distance and dividing it by their cruise speed, We've got about seven hundred and twenty miles ahead of us and at a steady 150 knots, we'll set down at around zero nine hundred hours."

"Four hours," Killion grinned. "Very well then, Ed, very well."

The brothers' plan, if it truly could be called that, was to capture Triton's key, kill Delilah, and escape. And though they were unsure of the exact timing of said events, they considered what had followed a success. They had the key, Delilah was dead, and now, they were flying over South Bend, following along Route 80 east as they headed for New York State. Once on the ground, a vehicle would be waiting. JFK airport would be only a short drive south. And what was one better, they had intercepted the Coast Guard's radio chatter and knew that they believed the suspects were in custody. Killion and Edward would be out of the country before authorities would even have a chance to look for them, if investigators believed the *suspects'* story at all.

****

Ashley sat behind the wheel of the black Mercedes Benz SUV, her hands tightly wrapped around the wood and leather steering wheel of the vehicle they'd stolen from Edward in Los Angeles, now seemingly forever ago, though only the prior day. After taking turns with Elizabeth and sharing the many hours spent driving since their stop off in Las Vegas, they were finally on the last leg of the trip. The signs denoting Davenport, IA were behind them: they had crossed into Illinois. Now, only three hours on Interstate 88 separated them from reuniting with the men they loved.

****

The woman returned to the office that the investigators had prepared as a holding room. The smell of freshly brewed coffee hung in the air. Quickly, she handed a laptop to one of the men, then a small metal box with a USB cable attached to its rear panel.

"That's the receiver," she said, holding a small wireless pack in her hand. "This is the transmitter. Go to the Captain's office and set up the computer. I'll only be a moment."

The two men headed out, following her instructions. She studied the conference room, searching for an inconspicuous location to plant the device. The outer wall was all windows. The rear wall was home to a large dry-erase board. Behind her was the door, a potted plant next to the frame. On her right was a humble kitchen cart containing the coffee maker and supplies, next to it, a three-foot-tall half-empty bookshelf holding several binders and notepads as well as a small plastic storage box filled with pens and pencils. A long table ran down the center of the room, eight chairs flanking, four on each side, with a ninth at the head. Above was a drop ceiling with integrated fluorescent lights.

Her options were few. She thought first of the planter by the door.

Too KGB.

The ceiling was ruled out as well for fear that the panels may muffle the voices she wanted to hear. The coffee cart was cluttered, but not cluttered enough. However, the bookshelf seemed that it may do.

She chose a black three-ring binder and opened it up. The pages indicated it was some sort of training manual. The woman switched on the transmitter and verified the frequency, then tucked it inside the binder between the cover and the first page and returned it carefully to its place on the shelf. She paused, stepping back to look at it, making sure it wasn't obvious. The binder appeared incapable of closing all the way, but on the shelf, with the other binders pressed close, it was inconspicuous enough.

"You'll tell us the truth," she said, "whether you know it or not."

****

Gavin, Jamie and Michael watched as the door to the office closed. They'd been gathered and moved to a different room. The woman told them to relax as she and the investigators figured things out, that she'd return when they'd had time to discuss the evidence.

Jamie spoke first, "Did they mention anything to you guys about charges?"

Michael and Gavin both shook their heads to say no.

"They can't hold us indefinitely," Michael said.

"According to the NDAA," Gavin countered, "they sure can."

"But we're not terrorists," Jamie reasoned.

"NDAA?" Michael questioned.

"National Defense Authorization Act," Gavin frowned. "The bill allows for the military to indefinitely detain American citizens on suspicions of supporting terrorism."

"Like Jamie said," Michael laughed, "we're not terrorists!"

"Then I guess it depends on their definition of terrorism," Gavin grunted.

"Jamie is a Chicago cop," Michael argued.

"And we were caught red handed," Jamie replied, staring out the window, "with guns in a city where guns are not allowed."

"But you can get us out of this, right?" Michael reasoned.

"It's out of my hands, Michael."

Gavin poured three cups of coffee, setting each one down on the table, "What do they think we're going to do, admit to killing Delilah? That's a lie. And every minute we waste here, Killion gets further away!"

"They've had us in custody for over five hours now, Gavin," Jamie said, glancing at the clock on the wall, then turning to face him, picking up one of the cups of coffee as he spoke, "That's a long time when you have a helicopter at your disposal. For all we know, Killion is already out of the country!"

****

The Coast Guard captain read over the reports collected from the investigators' interviews. The two men sat in silence, listening to the audio being transmitted secretly from the makeshift holding room while the woman placed a call on her cell, the phone raised to her ear.

"I need to speak to him right away," she said. "It's a matter of national security. Yes, I'll hold."

"So what's your gut telling you?" the captain asked.

"I think they're telling the truth," she stated matter-of-factly as she waited to continue her call. "I don't think they did it."

"But it's just too farfetched."

"I agree, but at the moment, there's too much reasonable doubt and furthermore…"

"This is Grier," a deep voice answered abruptly.

"…wait, hold on, Captain…yes, hello? Solomon?"

"Ms. Jacobs," the familiar voice on the phone replied firmly, "it's been a long time."

"Too long, Solomon," she smiled.

"What can I do for you, Monica?"

"I've got an unbelievable case, an investigation that is a little beyond me honestly."

"Go on."

"I have a deceased female, single gunshot wound, early thirties, possibly Israeli, no fingerprints on record, no ID. I also have three men in custody who were found with the body, but swear they had nothing to do with her apparent murder."

"Israeli?" Solomon asked, his voice relaying his interest. "Did the men give you anything to go on, a name?"

"Delilah," the woman replied, "They said her name was Delilah."

"Where did all this take place?"

"Chicago," Monica answered.

There was a moment of silence as the man on the phone paused before answering, "You still working out of the Chicago bureau?"

"I am."

"Where are you holding the men, at the office?"

"No, the Coast Guard station, Calumet Park, you know it?"

"I do. And the deceased, where's her body?" he asked.

"Cook County Hospital."

"Alright," FBI Special Agent Solomon Grier acknowledged, "I'm on my way."

3

Kayla woke with a start, Ethan's wailing cries coming through the baby monitor that sat on the end table beside the couch. She'd dozed off, the sleepless night catching up with her. She looked at the clock: *8:05am.*

She stood and headed for the kitchen, all her worries, all her doubts rushing back to her. This wasn't the first time she'd feared she'd never see Jamie return safely, and after New York, she'd actually prayed that that would've been the last, but as a detective, in Chicago, where the city averages more than a murder per day, she never knew when his investigations would lead him into that *one* building with that *one* suspect that, *for once*, Jamie couldn't outtalk, outsmart. She feared the phone call from Jamie's lieutenant, the one saying that Jamie wouldn't be coming home ever again. That scared Kayla more than anything.

From the cupboard, she retrieved a sippy cup and twisted off the lid, then pulled the milk from the refrigerator and robotically poured. She was in a daze, wandering blindly with eyes wide open.

Ethan's whining would soon wake Marley and she'd have to begin the day, hiding her fear, burying it deep down inside so that her children would never know, never see that mommy was afraid.

Kayla took a deep breath, condemned her sadness, and twisted open the knob on the nursery door. "Good morning, baby," she said to her son, a bright, forced smile stretched across her tired face.

Ethan smiled back, his toothy grin encouraging. She picked him up and laid him down on the changing table, then unzipped his sleeper and prepared a new diaper to replace his soggy one. He pointed at things around the room as she changed him, babbling in his own special language. Kayla secured the diaper and slipped his feet into sweatpants, pulling them up around his waist, his little toes wiggling as she did.

"Mommy," she heard come from Marley's room next door, "Mommy, Mommy."

"Just a minute sweetie," Kayla called out, "I'm changing your brother."

"MOMMY!" her little girl screamed at the top of her lungs, panicked, scared.

Marley continued screaming as Kayla hurriedly dressed Ethan in a t-shirt and picked him up off the changing table. She had no idea why her daughter was acting like this, it worried her as she raced to the adjacent bedroom.

Kayla opened the door . There was little, curly haired Marley, in her pink pajamas, standing on her toy box as she looked down at the front yard, still shouting out for her mother.

"Baby, what's wrong?" Kayla asked, Ethan looking on with confusion from where he was perched on his mother's hip.

Marley turned and looked at her sweetly, her voice now calm and mousy, "There's a car outside, Mommy."

Kayla looked out the window, spotting the black Mercedes SUV idling in the driveway. The vehicle's windows were tinted, but from her angle, she couldn't get a view of the driver anyway.

"Who is it, Mommy?"

"I don't know, Baby," Kayla replied.

Quickly, she carried Ethan back to the nursery and lowered him into his crib, then returned, taking Marley by the hand and leading her to her baby brother's room, "I'm going to leave you in here to play for just a little bit, okay? Watch Ethan for me, please."

Pulling the door shut behind her, Kayla hurried to her bedroom and opened the closet. Her and Jamie's clothes hung neatly in the expansive walk-in. She pushed several of Jamie's suits aside and found his dress blues, next to that, a four-foot tall wooden stand that held his cufflinks, watches, and other miscellaneous men's accessories. In the top drawer, next to where he always kept his badge, was his leather duty holster, a black Beretta 92 safely secured within. She drew the 9mm and ejected the full magazine, then slid it back into the grip and chambered a round.

As she approached the stairs, there was a knock on the door. Her mind was racing, startled by the sound. In her head, Kayla pictured the black Mercedes sedans driven by Triton's Tri-Six, recalled the attempt they made on her life as she was chased on the reservoir road in New York state. Thirteen, Michael, was supposedly the last of the Tri-Six, the others dying in the shootout in the lobby of the Tri-Corp building, killed by Gavin, Ashley and Kayla. Or had he lied? Were there more? Were they here, now, at her very door, ready to exact revenge for their fallen brothers?

Keep calm...breath...

The knock came again. As she stepped cautiously down the stairs, she could see a distorted silhouette through the frosted glass of the front door. She raised the gun, her academy training coming back to her, her motherly instincts replaced with those of a cop.

Kayla paused, planning her next move. Quickly, she slipped through the kitchen and quietly out the rear door that led from the dining room to the patio, scanning the yard for threats. She peered cautiously around the corner of the house, studying the Mercedes in the drive. She could see someone sitting in the passenger seat: a woman she didn't recognize. The driver's seat was empty. Kayla turned and headed back across the yard, stepping over Marley's tricycle, left sitting on the patio, as she approached the opposite corner of the house.

Again she peered around the corner as before, gun ready, expecting a masked Tri-Six, but there was no one. Kayla tiptoed down the narrow stretch that separated their home from the neighbors and knelt as she approached the front of the house. She could hear someone knocking once again.

Hidden by evergreen shrubbery, she remained low, trying to get eyes on the intruder on the porch. Kayla carefully raised her head, peering over the needle-branched top of the bush. She could see someone now, a woman, light brown hair, small frame. Kayla flipped off the Beretta's safety and clicked back the hammer, then raised the pistol and stepped from cover, the woman fixed in her sights.

"You," Kayla ordered calmly, "turn around and keep your hands where I can see them."

The woman whipped around in surprise. Kayla lowered her gun with a relieved smile: it was Ashley.

****

Lieutenant Walker sat at his desk at the precinct, reading over the morning's memos and emails, searching for anything that might be a link to Jamie. There was a double homicide on the west side of the city, but that couldn't be Branson. Armed robbery in the Market District: not Jamie.

Tom perked up in his chair, his eyes widening as he read aloud, *Witness reports of a low-flying helicopter over the harbor, strange lights in the sky near the lighthouse...*

Hurriedly, he picked up the phone and dialed a number, tapping his finger impatiently on the desk as he waited for someone to answer.

"Good morning," he said curtly, "it's Lt. Tom Walker. I need an FAA report on any unusual air traffic patterns last night or early this morning, any reports of unidentified crafts...no, not UFO's...any non-identifying crafts, as in non communicative crafts refusing to verify tail numbers, etcetera. Let me know, thanks."

****

Ashley raced down the porch steps and met her sister in the middle of the front yard, throwing her arms around her, cherishing the familiarity of Kayla's returned embrace. Her escape from Los Angeles had resulted in an arduous, multi-state spanning drive in a stolen Mercedes. She'd been free from her captors, from Killion's grasp, for many hours, but now, in the arms of her sister, she truly felt safe.

"When we heard what happened, when Gavin told us you'd been taken," Kayla whispered, fighting back tears of joy, "I thought I'd never see you again!"

"There was a time when I thought the same," Ashley sighed in relief. "I didn't know where I was, I didn't know why I was there...and, *oh my gosh*...I'm *pregnant*!"

Kayla loosened her hold and looked down at her sister's belly, placing her hand on Ashley's flat stomach, "You sure?"

"It's a long story," Ashley smiled, "but I finally got to take a pregnancy test, and sure enough, I am."

"How far along?"

"Nine weeks, I estimate."

"Well I'm *so* happy for you, Ash, and I'm *so* glad you made it here safe!"

"Definitely," Ashley said grinning, "and I really want to see Gavin, I can't wait to tell him he's going to be a daddy!"

Kayla's smile faded as she pulled away from her little sister. There was no way she could hide her feelings, their happy reunion about to be spoiled by reality.

"Where is he, Kay, is he in the house?" Ashley asked.

"No," Kayla replied, her voice wavering with her uncertainty. "He's with Jamie, Michael, and Delilah. They met Killion last night. They were to exchange the old key taken from Triton's office in order to guarantee all of our safety."

"Delilah?"

"It's complicated, let's go in the house. I have Marley and Ethan holed up in the nursery. I thought you were a Tri-Six. The black Mercedes in the drive reminded me so much of New York," Kayla said, leading her sister towards the porch.

"Oh gosh," Ashley laughed, her eyes falling on the stolen vehicle in the drive, "I almost forgot."

Ashley took her sister by the hand and led her to the black SUV. She motioned for the woman in the passenger seat to get out, that it was okay.

"Meet Elizabeth," Ashley smiled, as the woman stepped from the car and closed the door behind her.

"Yes," Kayla said, awkwardly reaching out to hug the woman, "Michael's wife."

"I am," Elizabeth replied, returning the hug, "and that's Cain in the back."

Kayla looked as the boy peeked out at her sheepishly through the dirtied glass of the backseat's right-hand window. She smiled and waved as he ducked out of view.

"Let's head in," Kayla urged. "I'm sure you're both tired and hungry after the trip. And your son can play with Marley and Ethan."

Elizabeth opened the rear passenger door and helped Cain out, taking his hand and following Ashley and Kayla up the steps to the front door.

"I'm going to run up and get the kids," Kayla said once inside. "There's coffee in the kitchen, juice and milk for Cain in the fridge. I'll be right back."

Ashley poured a half of a cup of coffee as she directed Elizabeth to the cupboard that held the glasses. Kayla returned, Ethan in her arms, finding Cain sipping thirstily at a glass of orange juice as Elizabeth filled a mug with steaming coffee for herself. Marley skipped along behind her mother, her curls bouncing playfully.

Marley froze when she saw Cain. He watched her curiously.

"Mommy," she whispered, hiding behind Kayla's leg, "there's a boy."

Kayla smiled, "He sure is. His name is Cain. Can you say *hello*?

"Hello," Marley said, blushing before racing past him. "Aunt Ashley!"

Marley wrapped herself around Ashley's' legs. Ashley knelt down to hug her niece.

"Come play princess tea party with me, Aunt Ashley," Marley giggled. "I have a tiara and everything, it's so sparkly. I'll show you. Come on!"

"Baby, we have things to talk about first," Kayla said. "Maybe you and

Cain could watch some cartoons this morning while we make breakfast?"

Elizabeth nodded. Cain reluctantly followed the energetic little girl into the living room and watched her turn on the television with the remote. Happy music and goofy cartoon voices filled the room.

"Can you hold Ethan while I get him a sippy cup?" Kayla asked her sister.

Ashley took him and tickled his little, chubby baby belly , making him laugh, "I guess I have to get used to this, you know, holding a baby."

Kayla smirked as she placed a gallon of milk and the carton of eggs she'd taken from the refrigerator onto the counter. She quickly poured the milk into a spill-proof cup and twisted on the spouted lid, then handed it to Ethan who took it happily.

"Is scrambled ok?" Kayla asked as she began preparing breakfast, cracking an egg on the rim of a mixing bowl, the yoke dripping down and settling in the bottom of the basin as she separated the two halves of shell.

"Sure," Ashley answered while Elizabeth said nothing.

Kayla cracked five more eggs, added some milk, and hastily whisked it all into a thick, yellow mixture, set it aside, pulled a large, round frying pan from the cupboard to the right of the oven, then ignited a gas burner on the stove's top. Elizabeth sipped on her coffee anxiously.

"So how was the drive?" Kayla asked as she adjusted the burner to medium heat, coated the pan with cooking spray and then placed it over the flame and readied to pour the eggs.

Ashley thought back to the panicked escape, the stop in Las Vegas, the long drive on the interstate; but all things considered, the rest was like a distant memory compared to the demon which tormented her as she awaited the results of her pregnancy test. She hesitated before answering, not sure if now was the appropriate time to open that can of worms. She wanted to see Gavin. Kayla hid her angst well, but Ashley knew her sister, knew when she was putting on a happy face for the all the world to see. Now was one of those times.

"The drive was alright," Ashley answered, "just long."

Elizabeth nodded, but was still not quite ready to join in the conversation. She was simply glad for some sense of normalcy. Between the cozy feeling of a warm home over a sterile hotel suite and the sound of cartoons happily filling the living room, she was finding herself allowing her guard to fall. She'd trusted Ashley as they escaped, and now, she was certain she could trust Kayla.

"Your sister is an amazing woman," Elizabeth smiled, finally speaking, nodding at Ashley as she opened up. "I believe that Cain and I would surely be dead if it weren't for her bravery. You should be very proud!"

Kayla smiled as she attended to breakfast, listening to Elizabeth's words of praise.

"I could never have imagined doing what she did. She climbed from the balcony of her suite over to mine. We were many stories high and she could have fallen, but she was determined to get us out of that prison. And when she concocted her plan and then attacked Edward and it all worked, well, I just couldn't believe it was true. It was like something *wanted* us to escape, *helped* us, if you understand my meaning?"

"I do," Kayla replied, "but not *something*, I'd say *someone* wanted you to escape, that all this was a part of a larger plan. What is that plan? I have no idea. But thank God you were there for each other and are now here, safe and sound. God obviously has a purpose in His design and He surely hasn't finished with any of us yet."

The three women fell silent, a sudden burst of shared laughter erupting from Cain and Marley in the living room, the funny cartoons more than enough entertainment for the two little new friends. Kayla was thinking about Jamie, worried because she hadn't heard anything, not from her husband, not from the lieutenant, nothing. Ashley could still envision the demon, its words lingering, festering in her soul.

****

Special Agent Solomon Grier took a final walk around Reverend McNamara's tower office. Yellow crime scene tape cordoned off the door to the elevator. Forensic investigators scoured for clues, dusted for prints and studied an odd residue that coated nearly every surface in the room, carefully collecting multiple samples with swabs for testing and analysis.

The victims' bodies had been removed, autopsies pending. Solomon had studied the briefcase device for hours, learning the components, assessing the dispersal system. He'd recognized certain traits, features, inherent to the weapons design, signatures of its creator. The device seemed familiar, yet not. All he knew for certain was that it was homemade and unique in origin, manufactured by a master engineer, and highly effective in its lethality.

In the least, they'd determined that the device was used to release some sort of chemical agent, a weaponized gas. The briefcase was now considered a weapon of mass destruction, classifying the murders as an act of terrorism. That's why Grier had been called. He was the best-of-the-best: the FBI's foremost authority in domestic terrorism. If a bomb exploded, an assassination attempt was made anywhere within the United States, his phone would ring. Tall and well built, Grier, had grown from a young, black Navy recruit, over twenty years ago, into an elite SEAL operator, serving valiantly in Desert Storm and then, post 9/11, offering his skills to the FBI, rising through the ranks quickly. He loved his country and put that passion into his work. An attack on America was an attack on the American people, on him, and he did everything in his power to bring the guilty to justice.

Barring the chemical weapon, the room was clean. A spent 9mm bullet casing was found on the floor of the office and had been bagged and tagged appropriately. And other than the Sig Sauer handgun recovered from Franklin's body outside, there were no other weapons. With the exception of the brutally murdered Mr. Nelson, found lifeless in Franklin's car, there were no other signs of violence: the events all isolated to the Sunrise Chapel.

Agent Grier's report would state these findings as well as the obvious fact that the victims had not only been invited to the crime scene, but were also most likely there to confer on something larger than church matters. That was the question now bothering Solomon the most. The nature of the chemical device proved that the deaths of those in attendance were premeditated; still, why were they there?

He read over the list of victims who'd so far been identified. The elected officials names were recognizable, though not necessarily government elitists. The others were no one important to Solomon. But one name stood out. And now, having received Monica's call from Chicago, he had seemingly more pieces to his already complex puzzle.

"Leroy Klebitz," he read aloud, rubbing his hand quickly back and forth on his shortly-kept hair. "What did you and Delilah get yourselves into?"

****

The phone in Lieutenant Walker's office rang and rang. Anxiously, Tom raced past the rows of detectives desks, coffee cup in hand, and lunged for the handset.

"Lieutenant Walker: homicide," he answered.

There was a pause as he listened to the report coming through the phone.

"Alright," Tom said, "just so I have it straight then: a deceased female, early thirties, three suspects in custody, all male, also thirties, FBI on scene, suspects currently secured at the Calumet Coast Guard?"

Again, Tom Walker grew quiet, listening to the voice on the line.

"But no positive ID's on the suspects?" he asked.

He shook his head and frowned as he received a negative reply, "Okay, thanks for the info. You've helped me greatly. If you hear anything else, call me ASAP. Thanks again."

Tom, the receiver still held to his ear, pressed his finger on the switch to hang up the phone, then quickly dialed the number for Kayla's cell phone. He had to tell her what he'd learned.

****

The Branson house smelled of toast and butter, eggs with cheese, crispy bacon, and freshly brewed coffee. Elizabeth helped Kayla serve the hearty breakfast to the hungry kids. Little Ethan hastily sipped on his spouted cup of milk as he sat in Ashley's arms.

Kayla had yet to explain her concerns over the whereabouts of their husbands. The women, after all they'd been through, seemed so happy to return to a semblance of normalcy and the last thing she wanted to do was rip from their already fragile hearts the prospect of seeing the men they loved safely return.

Cain and Marley picked and nibbled on the food that had been placed in front of them at the table. Though their small tummies grumbled, they wanted nothing more than to return to the cartoons and the toys in the living room: eating with grownups wasn't nearly as fun.

The women ate silently. Excluding the fast food and gas station road-snacks, this was the first real meal that Ashley and Elizabeth had eaten since their brief stop in Las Vegas. Everything was delicious.

Soon, they'd finished, the kids long excused from the table, even Ethan had scampered off to join his older sister and their new friend. Ashley helped clear the table as Kayla loaded the dishwasher. Elizabeth remained seated, staring off distantly at nothing in particular.

"What's on your mind?" Kayla asked, having just placed the last of the dirty plates in the dishwasher and beginning the cleaning cycle.

Elizabeth listened to the swooshing of the washer as it filled with water and prepared to start.

"Well," she began hesitantly, somewhat irritated that the topic had yet to come up, "I was beginning to wonder when I might get to see Michael, I mean, where is he?"

Ashley nodded, she too had been thinking about Gavin. Though seeing her sister was comforting, she wanted nothing more than to feel her husband's arms wrapped tightly around her.

"Okay," Kayla began cautiously, "the thing is, I don't know exactly. I know what the plan *was*, but I haven't heard from them since last night. Jamie was supposed to call me, but..."

"But?" Ashley urged.

"He hasn't."

As she spoke, her cell phone rang to life. All three women stared wide-eyed at the device. Could this be the call they hoped for, saying that the men were all fine, the plan a success?

Kayla looked at her iPhone. The lieutenant was calling.

"Tom," she answered excitedly, the girls listening closely, "have you heard anything about Jamie? Where is he?"

"Slow down, Kayla," he replied. "I have an update for you. It's both good and bad."

"Well, tell me then, Tom, please!"

There was silence as Lieutenant Walker took a deep breath, "Now I can't confirm without a doubt that it's Jamie, but I got a follow-up call, only a few moments ago, telling me that three men had been picked up by the Coast Guard in the early morning hours. The men were found at the lighthouse, exactly where you said Jamie was headed. They were then taken to Calumet, Kayla."

"That sounds like that's them!" Kayla said.

"Sure does, but there's a problem."

"Okay?"

"The men were found with a body, Kayla... a dead woman."

"Delilah..." Kayla gasped aloud.

"The men are suspected of her murder," Lieutenant Walker continued. "They're now in FBI custody."

Kayla bit her lip, her brow furrowed, "Is there anything you can do, Tom?"

"I'm sorry, but this is now a federal investigation, out of my jurisdiction. I can be a character witness at best, but they could face trial, even conviction, Kayla. This is serious."

"What can we do?!"

"Not much at this time, I'm afraid," he sighed. "I'll call you as soon as I hear more, but for now, sit tight. Jamie is smart, he can handle himself. Just pray that there's some evidence that it wasn't him."

4

Gavin stared at the wound on Michael's arm as Jamie paced, stopping every so often to look out the retractable blinds that served as a window dressing for the sterile conference room. The parking lot could be seen in the distance. Perhaps, he hoped, he would see a squad car arriving: the lieutenant coming to their rescue. Maybe Kayla was already working to find them and knew that Tom Walker was a man of integrity, someone they could trust. Regardless, they needed rescuing, someone from outside who could vouch for them.

The men had tried to pass the time as best they could, but waiting so long, with no word, was almost as maddening as the monotonous ticking of the *Seth Thomas* clock that hung on the wall, each movement of the second hand a constant, audible reminder of the ever-growing distance between them and the real killer. Time, it appeared, was not on their side.

"I submitted Killion's bullets as evidence," Jamie announced, turning from the window, his fingers allowing the blinds to snap back in place from where he'd stood peering through them.

"And that will help us how?" Michael chided.

"During the investigation, a ballistics team will test fire all of our guns.

They need to match the weapon that killed Delilah to one of us. Every barrel has a signature, the way combustion burns the casing and the rifling marks the bullet," Jamie explained.

"Like a fingerprint," Gavin added.

"By our testimony," Jamie continued, "the investigators will find the slugs embedded in the brickwork at the base of the lighthouse. When they dig those out, they'll use a microscope and computers to analyze the bullets for these signatures, resulting in a positive match to Killion's pistol."

"Then there's just one problem," Michael reasoned.

"And that is?" Jamie asked, taking a seat in a chair at the table.

"Killion tossed his gun into the lake. The bullet that killed Delilah was fired from her own gun, and, if I'm not mistaken, Killion took that with him when he escaped in the helicopter."

"That could be a problem," Gavin admitted.

Jamie smiled confidently, "But it's not evidence to show that any of us were the one who fired any of those shots. We all took pot-shots at Killion's helicopter as it fled, and I'm sure they'll be able to recover some of those spent casings. The only concrete evidence they'll have is that the rounds *we* fired match *our* guns, everything else is circumstantial. For a conviction, prosecutors would have to prove without a reasonable doubt to a jury that we are the ones directly responsible for Delilah's death."

"But we aren't," Gavin said, "she was with us, one of us. It's Killion: that's our defense."

"It's not our defense, it's the truth," Michael corrected.

"Then let's pray that the ones in charge of this case seek the truth over a conviction. Otherwise," Gavin reasoned, "we may never even have a chance to end things with Killion."

"It would be difficult from a prison cell," Michael agreed.

The three men sat together at the table, their voices falling silent, the hum of the fluorescent bulbs overhead a constant drone, and still, as sure as time itself, the clock ticked away, judging them harshly for poorly laid plans. The longer they waited, the greater was the risk of Killion disappearing. And that would be a danger to all.

****

Ashley crossed her arms as she sat once again at Kayla's dining room table, "I think it's time you tell us everything."

Elizabeth nodded, "Yes. We must know."

Kayla peeked around the corner at the kids, occupied by their toys and cartoons. She knew that all conversations would inevitably lead to this point, she'd only hoped to delay it. But she knew that withholding the truth was a disservice to her sister and to Elizabeth.

She cleared her throat, buying final precious moments before further turning their lives upside down, "Our husbands are in FBI custody. They're the prime suspects in Delilah's murder."

Elizabeth's eyes grew watery. Ashley smacked her open palm on the kitchen table in anger, immediately regretting the outburst as stings pulsed sharply through her fingers.

"We just can't catch a break can we?" she exclaimed, shaking her hand in pain.

"It would seem so," Kayla sighed.

"So *Delilah*, you mentioned her before," Ashley said, "how does she play into all this?"

"Well," Kayla paused, "you know about Killion. He'd been hired by remnants of Triton's order to kidnap you guys and offer you in exchange for the old key. What you don't know is that another person, the Frenchman, paid Killion to kill The Order's remaining members, in effect dismantling the organization, then complete the deal for the key, killing all of us."

"And Delilah?" Elizabeth asked.

"Delilah was the granddaughter of a member of The Order," Kayla continued. "She was brought in by another man who was working at odds to Killion's plan, a Reverend McNamara. Anyway, she turned on Killion when he murdered her grandfather and then chose to help us. She wanted revenge. Delilah went with Gavin, Jamie, and Michael…apparently she didn't make it."

"That's crazy!" Ashley laughed, not because the story was humorous, but simply so unbelievable.

"Right?" Kayla replied, shaking her head as she raised her coffee mug to her lips.

The women sat in silence, contemplating Delilah and her tragic end. Even with their husbands now missing, they pitied her, a seemingly wasted life. Without even knowing the woman, Ashley and Elizabeth mourned her passing. She was a part of this, even if only for a short time.

"Delilah, O'Donnell, Sgt. Sykes...*Jack*..." Kayla sighed, "there are too many to remember. How many more will die because of Triton's legacy?"

Elizabeth shifted uncomfortably, "My father really was a monster wasn't he?"

Kayla and Ashley glanced cautiously at each other.

"I didn't mean anything by that, Elizabeth," Kayla apologized.

"But he was," she continued, "and, Michael, how many people did he kill?"

"As Michael?" Kayla thought. "None that I'm aware of, but as Thirteen? Well, lots."

"And my father? Michael did kill him didn't he?"

Again, Ashley and Kayla looked at each other, their memories from five years ago still vivid.

"He did," Ashley replied. "We were there just after. We saw his body and..."

"And?"

"That's all," Kayla concluded, ending the difficult conversation.

"It was for the best," Elizabeth answered remorsefully. "And I didn't marry Thirteen, I married Michael. What's done is done, the past is the past."

"But this won't be done, not till our husbands are home safe," Ashley said.

Kayla's cell suddenly rang. She quickly reached for it and answered without really looking at screen.

"Tom?"

"No, Kay, it's Jake."

"Are you expecting a call from Lt. Walker?" he asked.

"Actually, yes. I was going to call you at some point today. We may need your help."

"Is it Jamie?"

"Yeah...how..."

"Did I know?" he replied, finishing her question. "I was just visited by an FBI agent. My boat was seized by the Coast Guard and was apparently used in a crime last night. They'd followed the registration back to me. What's going on?"

"It's a long story, Jake," she said, "but we could really use your help if you're able."

"Who's Jake?" Elizabeth asked quietly.

"He's our brother," Ashley smiled. "His family lives here in Chicago too. He's a cop."

"I'll help as much as I can," he offered. "I'm at the station now. Should I just talk to Tom?"

"That would be great, Jake. Thank you so much!"

"Alright, Kay. I'll catch up with Tom and see if there's anything I can do."

"Okay," Kayla said, ending the call and setting her phone back down on the table. "Jake's going to talk to Tom Walker and see if they can find our husbands, maybe communicate with them, I hope."

"So is everyone in your family law enforcement?" Elizabeth mused. "You were a detective in New York, correct? And your husband as well? Ashley said your brother Jake is also a Chicago police officer."

"Yep," Kayla smiled. "Our dad is retired from the Pittsburgh police department and our late brother Jack was also an officer, killed in the line of duty."

"This all sort of began with him actually," Ashley said, goose bumps trailing up and down her arms as she thought about the circumstances and the events in New York City. "In a strange way, our family has been connected to Triton for decades."

"How odd," Elizabeth smirked curiously.

"Indeed," Ashley agreed.

****

"I don't know how much longer I can sit around knowing Killion is on the loose!" Gavin exclaimed, mentally and physically exhausted, his frustration getting the best of him. "I mean, seriously! They either need to charge us formally or follow our leads and get the real killer. What if he's gone after our families?"

"Whoa," Jamie urged, "keep it together!"

"How can you say that?" Gavin argued. "What if he had kidnapped Kayla, what if things were reversed? I don't believe you'd think any differently than me."

"That might be true, but that's not the case," Jamie reasoned. "We need to remain cool, under control. We're under extreme scrutiny right now, and yes, the stress is getting to me too, but we have to get through this."

Michael stood and placed his hand on Gavin's shoulder: a gesture of condolence, "I agree with Jamie. You'll have your chance to get Killion."

Gavin huffed, his arms crossed angrily, "You have a lot of room to talk, Michael *Laurent*."

"Now's not the time," Jamie intervened, dogging Gavin with a pointed, wagging finger.

"Maybe it is?" Michael relented. "I owe you guys an explanation. And, seeing as we're not going anywhere for a while, perhaps now is a better time than any other?"

"Fine, then," Jamie said, pulling a chair out from the table to sit, its four feet screeching against the white and blue speckled, vinyl-tiled floor. "If you want to get into this now, let's hear it."

"It all started centuries ago, in France, during the Holy Wars, the Crusades." Michael spoke softly, cryptically, his voice ghoulish as he narrated an unknown history. "At that time, events were set in motion that cannot be undone. That was where Triton's legacy began and, in a way, our legacies as well: the future we would come to inherit."

"Hold on," Gavin said, "I've heard this story before, from Joseph."

"Not this story," Michael grinned. "His side of things perhaps, but not *this* story."

"Please continue," Jamie said apologetically.

Michael nodded before speaking again, "A French nobleman by the name of Hugues de Payens assembled eight knights, creating an order that came to be known as the Knights Templar. Together, the nine knights set out for Jerusalem, making the Temple Mount their base of operations. Historians agree on the identities of eight of the men, Payens included. But the ninth is undocumented, unknown. Speculation says he may have been Count Hugh of Champagne, though that is not true. This man purposefully kept himself from the annals of time. This man adopted the name *Triton* from the Greek mythos."

"So Dr. Maurice Triton wasn't really *Dr. Maurice Triton?*" Jamie questioned.

"Yes and no," Michael explained. "Every so many years, Triton had to reinvent himself, adapt to the progression of the world around him. If he remained the same man for too long, suspicions may have been aroused and he would have had to begin all over. The one constant was his use of the surname Triton. His guise, first name included, changed countless times, but he was always Triton."

"Why that name," Gavin wondered, "why Triton?"

"There are several reasons I believe he chose the name," Michael continued. "First, is the origin of the name itself. The Greek god Triton was a messenger of the sea, a herald. In the Bible's book of Revelation, the thirteenth chapter, the beast from the sea is the antichrist. I think he saw a connection between the two and declared himself a herald of Armageddon. Second, according to mythology, the name could be pluralized as a host of

Tritones, daemons of the sea, daemon being Greek, the root of the latter understood translation of demon in the New Testament. And this leads to the third, the duality in the concept of the character Triton: half man, half fish: two creatures combined in the same person, a metaphor for the demon living within the host, the two halves essential to carry out, as a whole, his plan of such grandiose design."

"Wow," Gavin mused. "You've really thought this through."

"There are other interesting similarities as well, like the god-Triton's use of a trident, a three pointed spear, and the man-Triton's use of the Tri-Six as a weapon, in effect his own host of Tritones, three groups of six who carried out his plans, eighteen masked men: his figurative trident."

"And then there's the beard," Gavin chided, "or at least in *Walt Disney's* version of *The Little Mermaid*."

"I guess that would make Elizabeth my own *Ariel*, the daughter of Triton who fell in love with a man and left the sea forever."

The three men laughed for a moment. It was nice, to escape, to find a moment of brevity in the midst of their uncertain fate.

"Anyway, back to Triton's first Order," Jamie said. "Were they really Templar Knights?"

"Some of them were, others were pilgrims who had become seduced by the riches the Templars had amassed and, in the poverty that also plagued the Middle Ages, sold their souls for silver and gold. We're talking about a time period in which most people were illiterate and books like the Bible could only be shared by priests. The soldiers who fought in the Crusades were told that it was God's will by men who claimed to be put in their position by God. To claim or interpret otherwise would have been heresy. For years, Triton acted in the interests of the Templars, fighting with them, organizing, helping them establish their banks and financial practices; all the while, secretly building his own private army. Eventually, he cut ties with the Templars, returning to France with his vast wealth,. His army went with him, working his land, farming, guarding his castle. To people on the outside, he appeared loyal to his subjects, a caring provider. Where serfs were typically subjected to poverty and abuse, those who lived on his land were healthy and strong, plague free. He saw to their prosperity and they worshiped him as a god.

"It was from this first Order, that the legacy I came to inherit was forged. My forefathers pledged their allegiance to Triton, became his personal guards. They protected his keep, his wealth. They handled his most delicate and deceitful tasks. In the end, they were the blunt instruments of their murderous master. It would appear that I am the first of my line to realize the truth. My father's loyalty to Triton was unwavering. I was not a son to *Monsieur Emeric Laurent*, I was born with one purpose: to serve Triton as my father before me, and his father before him, and so on…an heir to the Laurent namesake and nothing else."

Michael grew quiet, staring blankly at the faux-wood-grained laminate top on the long folding table. Jamie exhaled loudly, trying to imagine a childhood like Michael's. His own had been quite difficult, but believing that one had not been born, but bred as a servant, a killer; that was nearly unfathomable.

Gavin, after all he'd learned of Michael in the last several days, the uneasy partnership that had turned into a surprise friendship, the common hope they'd shared in finding their loved ones safe and sound, this was still difficult to relate, and yet, in a way, Michael, like Gavin, was an orphan. And though Michael knew his father, he was raised seemingly without a father's love.

"So," Gavin asked, the silence growing uncomfortable as the three men contemplated Michael's words, "Laurent, the one named by Delilah as the Frenchman, is indeed your father?"

Michael hesitated, then nodded with regret.

"Then it's true that your father arranged the kidnapping of his own daughter-in-law and grandson?" Gavin continued.

"Yes."

"And also took Ashley from me?"

"Yes."

"So how do you feel about this?" Jamie wondered. "Do you think your father will be satisfied, meaning, is he still a threat? Do you believe that the birds that attacked Kayla and stole the real key did it under your father's control?"

"My father was most definitely behind the ravens, whether he sent them or not, is not a question. Again, it's what I would have done. And the only other person I know of that my father would have trusted to use such power is dead."

"How do you know that?" Jamie questioned.

"I was there when it happened."

Gavin furrowed his brow and leaned forward, his voice intense, curious, "Who was he, Michael?"

"His name was Sebastian," Michael replied, "Sebastian Anton Laurent, my brother, that is mon jumeau."

"*Mon jumeau?*" Gavin repeated. "What does that mean?"

Michael leaned back in his chair, his arms crossed, his gaze falling nowhere in particular.

"It's French," he replied. "French for *my twin.*"

5

The beating of the Sikorsky's rotors echoed off the busy Bronx streets below. Edward continued piloting the Blackwawk east as Killion confirmed their final preparations, his thumbs quickly tapping away, typing a response to a text message on his cell phone's *QWERTY* touch-screen keyboard.

"It's all set then," Killion said into the microphone of his flight headset. "There's a large clearing in the northwest end of Kings Point Park. That's where we'll land."

Edward nodded his understanding.

"A car is already waiting for us. From there, we make for JFK. I confirmed with the Frenchman; a private jet is fueled and ready. The NATO travel orders he procured will fast-track us through security at the airport and we'll be on our way to Paris."

Again, Edward nodded, this time accompanied by a coy smile.

Soon, they approached the East River. Killion removed his headset and left the cockpit for the cargo hold. The equipment that the brothers had used over the course of their mission was contained in neatly stacked olive drab, mil-spec crates which were then secured tightly to the floor of the hold by ratcheting straps.

He loosened the strap on the pallet nearest him and flipped open the airtight lid of the container that sat on top of the stack. Killion then removed the briefcase he'd taken from the trunk of Franklin's car and set it down on the edge of the crate. The locks clicked as he pressed the switches with his thumbs, a smile stretching ear-to-ear as he opened the case and looked at the perfectly wrapped stacks of bills. Satisfied, he pulled Delilah's Sig Sauer from beneath his suit coat and laid it on top of the small fortune. The locks again clicked as he closed the briefcase and turned his attention to Edward's laptop. Killion removed this from the crate as well and then replaced the lid, once-again tightening the strap before he turned to another weapons case that sat by itself on the other end of the hull.

The helicopter jolted as it slowed and began its decent. Killion needed to hurry. As with the other crate, he loosened the strap and removed the lid. Inside, he found a small handheld device which looked much like a key fob for a car, but with only a single red button. He quickly unwound a series of silver metal pins wrapped in green and yellow wire that, once straightened, strung the metal pins together like a strand of decorative Christmas lights. Those, he then connected to a small black box which had been hard-wired to the positive and negative terminals of a motorcycle battery. At the bottom of the case were two-dozen blocks of M112 C-4, roughly thirty pounds of plastic explosives.

Killion took the C-4 and spaced it out from one end of the cargo hold to the other, the last one placed at the entrance to the cockpit. He then paused to look out the window. They were now below the tree line. He methodically inserted the blast caps into the blocks and, lastly, flipped a small switch on the box wired to the battery. The vibrant glow of a red LED marked the device as being armed, the light reflecting devilishly in Killion's eyes. He looked down at the remote he'd placed alongside the laptop and briefcase filled with money: a similar light was illuminated on the detonator.

"We're all set," he shouted at his brother as the helicopter touched down and the rotors began to slow.

Edward removed his headset, hastily tossing it on the console, and grabbed his laptop, then took hold of the cargo bay door's handle and slid it open. He spotted a tall, slender man dressed in a black suit, smoking a cigarette, his eyes hidden beneath darkly tinted sunglasses as he leaned against a metallic charcoal-gray Suburban parked at the edge of the clearing. Edward dropped down onto the grass, Killion close behind him, the briefcase full of money tightly clasped in his hand. The brothers hurried to the waiting SUV.

As they approached, the man flicked his cigarette to the ground and climbed into the vehicle, taking the driver's seat and turning the ignition. The powerful V-8 rumbled to life as Killion and Edward climbed into the back seat and closed the doors behind them. Dust and small stones kicked up as they roared away from the helicopter, the rear wheels of the SUV finding little resistance on the gravel path.

Killion looked down at the remote in his hand, the red button glowing and ready. Grinning at his brother, the Blackhawk far behind them as they neared the cover of the trees, he pressed the switch.

Within milliseconds, fire scorched the ground as the craft exploded, the metal skin shredded by the fury of expanding gases as the C-4 ignited with a deafening boom. The helicopter's frame twisted and launched into the air, smashing back to earth in a mangled pile of flaming shrapnel and debris. A plume of black smoke billowed from the wreckage, all visible to the driver in his rear view mirror as they passed beneath the trees, disappearing into the protective cover of the dense woods.

"And that is that," Killion smirked, not once looking back.

"A shame, really," Edward said matter-of-factly.

"What's that?"

"I rather liked that heli."

"Indeed," Killion replied, "did the job right well, in fact it reminded me of the good days…"

"I'd say these are bloody good days," Edward smiled, winking with a nod at Franklin's briefcase.

"And there's more to be had," Killion said, reaching into the pocket of his trousers and finding the key, then proudly displaying it in his open hand. "Once we deliver this to the Frenchman, we'll buy you one that's proper, bespoken and much nicer than that pile we left behind."

"Blimey, we could buy the Queen's Crown Jewels," Edward laughed.

"That we could, brother."

The SUV cruised down the Cross Island Parkway, quickly overtaking other cars and swerving in and out of the southbound lanes. Horns honked in angry disapproval. Killion stared out the window wistfully, their successes replaying in his head as a pair of fire trucks roared in the opposite direction, sirens blaring, followed closely by three more emergency vehicles responding to the blast,. They'd pulled it off, disassembled The Order and recovered the Frenchman's artifact.

Soon, road signs announced Jamaica, New York. The airport was near, as was their final step to freedom. Once in the air, they were untouchable.

****

Special Agent Solomon Grier stood outside arrivals at Chicago O'Hare, pacing as he waited for his ride. The flight took only a little over four hours. His mind still raced, analyzing the crime scene in Los Angeles, the clues fitting together like an abstract puzzle. Now in Chicago, he knew where he'd start.

A black, unmarked sedan pulled sharply to the curb. Grier opened the passenger door and jumped into the car.

"Good morning, sir," the driver smiled.

Grier nodded at the young Quantico grad as the car steered into traffic, "It's good to be back in Chicago, kid."

"I was told to pick you up," he said, "but I don't know where I'm taking you."

"Cook County Hospital," Grier answered, staring out the window as the sedan exited the airport loop and they began the drive to Chicago's Near West Side.

"You know, it's the Stroger Hospital now," the driver laughed, "since, like, 2002! When was the last time you were here?"

"Before 2002 then, I guess," Grier smiled.

The car travelled east on I-90, pacing with the busy late-morning traffic. Solomon soaked in the sights and sounds: returning to Chicago was, in a way, returning home. Though not born there, his family moved to the city when he was young, his father a professor of political theory at The University of Chicago. From there, after nearly twenty years, his family moved once more, to Washington DC, again following his father's career as it led to Georgetown. But Chicago always felt like home.

They soon left the intestate and followed Ashland to Harrison before finding the hospital on the right. Grier looked up at the John H. Stroger Jr. building as the car came to a stop. The design was beautiful by today's architectural standards. Grier believed the glass and metalwork looked fresh, indicative of a hospital and the professional treatment provided within, yet in its streamlined sterility, he noted that it lacked the history that accompanied the old Cook County Hospital's grand Beaux-Arts design. The old Cook County was a symbol of the Near West Side and, in many ways, Chicago in general.

"I won't be long," Grier explained as he stepped from the sedan. "Find a place to park."

"Are you going in to talk to someone?"

"In a manner of speaking," Grier replied solemnly.

****

Gavin, Jamie and Michael were startled by a sudden, firm knock on the room's guarded door. The door swung upon as one of the interrogators entered the room. Was this perhaps questioning: round two?

"With all that coffee you guys have been drinking, we figured you could use a restroom break," the stout man chuckled gruffly. "We go one at a time."

The men shifted in their chairs, suddenly aware of their ready-to-burst bladders. They'd been so distracted, they didn't even stop to think of such simple things.

"You guys care if I go first?" Jamie spoke up.

"Go ahead," Gavin said. "I think you drank more coffee than either of us."

Michael nodded in agreement and Jamie headed out with the man, the door locking behind them as they exited. Exhausted, Gavin laid his head down on his crossed arms where they rested on the table. Michael wished he could rest, but an agitation had been brewing deep inside of him. He was growing more and more anxious and uncomfortable. Sure, the restroom called to him as it did the others, but this was something different, like a parasite crawling just beneath his skin, causing an itch he just couldn't scratch.

The room was dead silent. His mind began to wander, wander far beyond the fear and hopelessness upon which it had for so long lingered. Michael's imagination suddenly came alive, whirring with the intensity of complex machinations, his fingers rhythmically tapping a symphony on the table's top.

What if I could get my mask? he thought. *When it's my turn to go, I can overpower the guard and then take control. With my mask, I can set us free. I'm sure it's close by; in fact, I know it is..I can feel its power!*

Michael smirked, the plan so easy, so simple. How could he fail?

Gavin stirred, drifting in and out of consciousness. He wasn't sure if he was awake or asleep, and that fact alone, he argued within himself, could mean that he was dreaming. But he too was feeling a power, something he hadn't sensed in years; since New York and his days as a demon hunter. Alone now, just him and Michael, Gavin was certain he heard a voice whispering, low and serpentine.

"This is your chance," it hissed. "Find your mask and kill them, kill them all. We miss you, Thirteen. Come back and *play*."

****

Jamie followed the man down the hall. He recognized the layout, having studied their path as they were first led to their holding rooms. There, on the right, was the room he was first placed in. That meant that just around the corner was the door he'd noted as being marked *Captain*.

They rounded the corner and sure enough, there was the office, the door sitting open. Jamie kept his head down as they approached. Peripherally, he could see the people watching him as they passed. He counted four for sure. There was a man in a uniform he assumed was the Coast Guard captain himself. The woman who'd interrogated Gavin was also present. Two other men were unrecognized, but they had the distinct look of FBI about them. All had looked up as they passed, except for one of the possible federal agents. Upon his ears was a set of noise-cancelling headphones, the line running down from them and into the speaker outlet on a laptop.

Jamie recognized the auxiliary boxes accompanying the computer immediately. He'd used them many times before as a detective. It was a basic surveillance setup, wireless, portable. He shook his head in disbelief. How could he have been so stupid?

The man led Jamie into the restroom then turned his back, providing semi-privacy, as Jamie stepped up to the urinal and unzipped his pants. He really had been stupid. Of course the room had been bugged.

****

Gavin couldn't believe it. He could actually feel the presence of the demon in the room. He concentrated on the energy that made its presence known. Was there more than one? He couldn't be sure, but the harder he concentrated, it seemed that it was likely that two or three demons now spoke.

Had he removed himself so far from his past life? Gavin felt a sense of shame. In his better days, he would have known, felt, even seen the demons without prompting. That shame quickly turned to guilt as he realized how, over the course of the last five years, as he'd tried harder to assimilate into a normal life, a career, he'd found himself less inclined to read the Bible daily, even weekly, trusting in the knowledge of Gods' word that he could still easily recall as enough. His job had required open work availability, which meant frequent shifts on the weekends. He'd given up attending church on Sundays because he knew he needed his career, to be a good husband, and someday, Lord willing, a good father.

His adoptive parents had raised him to work hard and that he should someday get married, hold down a steady job, and buy a house: the American dream. If only it were that easy. Gavin realized he'd become a domesticated animal. Once so quick to praise God's name and look to Him for guidance, he had now become a slave to money and society's tenants of success.

God help me, he prayed.

****

The door opened. Jamie returned. Gavin raised his head; but before he could speak, Michael was on his feet and headed out the door. There was

51

no time for protest. Michael was gone.

"Jamie, we've got to stop him," Gavin blurted.

There was no verbal answer from his brother-in-law. Jamie emphatically raised his index finger and pressed it against his lips as a signal to keep quiet. He glanced around the room for any way he could communicate. The table was empty. There were no markers resting on the sill of the dry erase board.

Jamie's eyes fell on the bookcase filled with binders and notebooks, a basket of miscellaneous writing utensils with them. He quickly grabbed a legal pad and the first pen he could get his hands on. As he did, the haste with which he'd removed the items from the shelf upset the binders, sending them toppling to the floor, the one with the hidden microphone and transmitter flipping open, revealing their investigators' trickery.

"They've been listening this whole time!" Jamie exclaimed after picking up the small black box and flipping the unit's power switch to *off*.

****

"Hey," the man with the headphones cried, "we just lost signal. There was a…a loud shuffling sound…then, silence."

"We'd better get in there!" Special Agent Monica Jacobs replied as she and the other agent jumped up from their chairs and checked their guns.

"Wait a second," the captain argued. "You can't really expect to need your guns. The men are unarmed!"

"And suspected of murder," she spat back. "We don't know what these men are capable of."

"Hold on, hold on…" the man with the headphones urged. "Signal is back. Maybe it was just some interference. I can hear them talking."

With a sigh of relief, Monica Jacobs holstered her gun and sat back down in her seat. *False alarm*, she thought.

****

52

Michael stood at the urinal as demonic voices echoed in his head. He closed his eyes as tightly as possible, focusing all his will against the urge to turn and snap the neck of the agent who stood watchfully, waiting for him to finish. With his guard dead, he could return to the main office and, using the gun from the dead agent's holster, kill the rest of their captors, recover the mask and be free. He burned with anger, envisioning each move, beginning with the first strike.

Quietly, he zipped up his pants and turned, the soles of his expensive dress shoes slick and silent against the cold tile floor. The man guarding him was still facing the other way, his back to Michael.

Michael eased up close behind the unsuspecting man, his hands ready to clasp him by the throat. A quick twist and he would be one step closer to freedom.

"Do it…do it…" the voices demanded. "DO IT!"

****

"So the equipment is up and running fine now?" Monica Jacobs asked in confirmation.

"It sure is," the man monitoring the equipment smiled.

"Can you tell what they're talking about?" she asked.

"Well, I'm not sure exactly…"he replied hesitantly, trailing off as he concentrated.

"How so?" the captain chimed in.

"They're speaking softly, like they're talking to someone else, almost like…"

"Like what?" Monica interjected.

"Almost like they're praying."

****

"And, Lord God," Gavin pleaded, "whatever is going on in his head, the demons, the temptations, bring Michael peace. Jesus, we beg you bring him peace. Calm him, send angels of mercy to envelop him."

"Lord Jesus, give him strength," Jamie continued, "strength to endure, to overcome. Lord, we bind the evil spirits that are plaguing Michael now in the name of Jesus."

"We know that our enemy is not flesh and blood, and we know that You fight for us. Please, Lord God, fight now for Michael. In Jesus' name," Gavin concluded, "amen."

"Amen," Jamie agreed.

****

A light, whiter and brighter than any that Michael had ever seen, flashed vividly in the confines of the small men's room. The mirrors reflected the blast of energy as did the polished plumbing fixtures. The guard stood in shock blinking, rubbing his eyes, Technicolor spots dancing in his vision.

Michael found himself on the floor, knocked to the ground, prostrate before the power of the Almighty. His vision was not blurred. The whispers had gone, the plague of evil abated. Before him stood an angel, strong, undeniable.

Not a word was uttered. He only stood there, towering over Michael. And then, as quickly as it had happened, the angel was gone.

"What the heck?!" the FBI agent exclaimed, giving his head a final shake as the spots cleared.

His attention was instantly drawn to the sound of crying. There, on the hard floor of the Calumet Coast Guard men's room, sat Michael, slumped on his knees, his face buried in his hands, as he sobbed a confession to God for all his sins."

****

Solomon Grier stepped up to a neatly organized, unattended desk just through the door that led him into the hospital's morgue.

"Can I help you?" a woman asked from over his shoulder.

Grier turned towards the sound of her pretty voice, a sad smile raising the corner of his mouth, his badge flipped open in his hand, "I'm Special Agent Grier, FBI I'm here about a body that was brought in for autopsy. Is the medical examiner available?"

"One moment," she said, stepping around the desk and picking up the phone, her thin manicured finger pressing an extension. "Dr. Crosby, an Agent Grier with the FBI is here to see you. Alright, I'll let him know."

She smiled and sat down at the desk, "Help yourself to coffee if you like, Agent Grier. Dr. Crosby will be with you shortly."

Shortly, however, was an understatement. After the passing of nearly ten minutes and many agonizing glances at the face of his expensive diving watch, Dr. Crosby finally appeared at the door. He was an older gentleman, eccentric hair, Einstein-ish and frantic. He also smiled with an aloofness that reflected his less-than-social work with the recently deceased.

"Right this way, Mr. Grier," the doctor said.

Solomon followed the man down the corridor and into a well-air conditioned room. An examination table sat in the middle of the room, a body covered with a white sheet lay on the table. Large lamps with bright bulbs for illuminating intricate details hung from above the table. Rolling carts filled with devilish, torture-like tools flanked the doctor's work space.

"Is this her?" Grier asked, slowly approaching the sheet.

"You'll be the first positive ID we have for her if she is indeed who we think she is."

Grier nodded and the doctor pulled back the sheet revealing her face. His stomach churned at the sight. She was older than when they'd last worked together, but it was definitely Delilah. Her beautiful olive skin had paled, her plump lips now bluish, cold. Her black hair outlined her face. He wanted so badly for her to open her big brown eyes so that he could look into them one more time.

"It's her," Solomon said softly.

"I want to show you something," the doctor said, matter-of-factly, as he pulled the sheet further back, revealing more of her body.

Grier looked away for a moment, unnerved at the sight of her cold, naked body. She was such a dear friend, a war ally, making it all the more difficult to look at her like this, now a medical *thing*.

"I haven't begun the internal examination yet, Mr. Grier, but look here," Dr. Crosby said pointing across her neck and collar bone. "There's ante-mortem bruising across the jugular. It's on her wrist too. She was definitely grabbed or held by someone quite firmly."

Grier studied the bruises briefly, imagining her last moments alive. How did it all play out? Was she scared? Powerless? Who could do this to her? She was a killer, cold and calculating.

"And here," the doctor continued, now gesturing to the gunshot wound in her right rib cage, just beneath her breast. The gun was fired up close, the muzzle pressed into her side as it was fired. The bullet shattered these ribs here as it entered, the splinters puncturing her lung. The bullet then travelled through the lung, struck the rear of the aorta, before piercing the other lung and lodging in her left shoulder."

"How do you know that without having done the internal exam?" Grier questioned.

"I've seen many shootings, Mr. Grier. Sadly Chicago is well known for its gang violence. Based on the positioning of the entry wound, the angle of entry, and some irregularities and swelling in her shoulder, I believe my exam will be in agreement."

Solomon Grier's jaw flinched as he took a final look at his old friend. She had done her share of killing, but it was honorable, or at least the killing that he knew of. But their days together in special forces were long since over. Perhaps her life had taken a less honorable turn.

"Thank you, doctor," he said, turning to head out, leaving Delilah, the examination room, and the past behind.

6

Terrance Killion, fortune-holding briefcase in hand, stepped alongside his brother as they exited the black SUV that had brought them to their final terminus in the United States. The vehicle had followed the loop around the sprawling international airport and had dropped them curbside at the JFK general aviation buildings. A private jet was waiting for them, fueled and ready to fly the eight hours to Charles de Gaulle. The driver nodded to them as they exited the SUV.

"I assume you'll use the utmost discretion in referring to today's events," Killion stated, looking into the vehicle. "If you are indeed in the employ of the same man as myself, then I know I mustn't stress the importance of *discretion*."

"No, sir," the driver confirmed.

Killion smiled at his brother coyly as the SUV raced off.

"There it is, brother," Killion said looking over at the Dassault Falcon 900 that awaited their departure for transcontinental skies.

"Wish I could give it a go," Edward replied looking up at the trijet's unique S-duct central engine.

"You said you wanted to sleep, now's your chance," Killion laughed. "Besides, what would the RAF gents think of you flying a plane built by *Frenchies?*"

"They'd have a laugh alright."

The brothers climbed the airplane ladder and entered the large white craft, noting the flashy corporate logo accompanied by the name *Tri-Corp* emblazoned on the side of the hull. Killion winked at the beautiful stewardess who led them aboard as they passed.

"What or who do you suppose Tri-Corp is?" Edward asked, taking a seat by the window, settling into the fine, plush leather and buckling in for takeoff.

Killion looked down at an already prepared dry martini, sans olive, just the way he preferred, then back at the buxom blonde in her tight short skirt who now went about sealing up the jet, "As long as they pay cash and their service is as good as it looks, I don't have a bloody care."

****

Kayla, Ashley and Elizabeth loaded the last of the breakfast plates into the dishwasher and took the kids out to the backyard to play in the warm mid-morning sun. Their conversation had strayed from the serious matters at hand and the women allowed the children to romp and shout, a fitting distraction.

"So how are you feeling," Kayla asked Ashley as they sat beneath a large umbrella that shaded its coordinating table and chair set, "any pregnancy symptoms?"

Ashley sighed, already hungry after only just finishing breakfast earlier that very hour, "I feel really gassy, and crampy, but not really crampy…and *hungry*, but I have no appetite. I keep thinking that pizza sounds so good, but I swear, if I see a single slice of greasy pepperoni, I'll barf all over this patio."

Kayla and Elizabeth both laughed. They'd been there before.

Marley screamed with delight as Cain chased her around the manicured garden. Ethan did his best to hobble along behind, his little legs working hard in the recently trimmed grass.

"Well it sounds like you are coming along just as you should," Kayla said.

Elizabeth looked at Ashley with urging eyes. Kayla picked up on the cue.

"Is there something else?" Kayla wondered.

The demonic words had haunted her since they'd left that McDonald's the previous day. She'd done all she could to push the fear aside, but it was still there, lingering in her thoughts.

"Yesterday, after I took the pregnancy test and finally had a moment for it all to sink in," Ashley explained, "I saw a vision or an apparition, something dark, demonic. It reminded me of the dreams I used to have Kayla, even before New York: the nightmares I had as a child."

"The dreams in New York were caused by Triton. And your childhood nightmares were just your imagination," Kayla said.

"Kay, you of all people, should know how that affected me growing up," she reasoned, her voice falling to an embarrassed hush as she went on. "I mean, seriously, I wet the bed till I was eight!"

"Mom and dad had you talk with that church counselor…what was her name? Oh, I can't remember," Kayla frowned. "Anyway, she believed they were nothing more than nightmares. You got so stressed out over those dreams, I remember, Ash."

"And then they stopped, when I was around eleven or twelve," Ashley continued. "I didn't have a nightmare like that till New York."

"So what did the *demon* say?" Kayla asked.

"Basically, in short," Ashley said sadly, "my baby is a blessing and a curse. It called the baby a life that brings death."

"What does that mean?"

"I don't think it means anything," Elizabeth spoke up. "I think it was just an act to instill fear."

"Well regardless," Ashley shrugged, tears forming in her eyes as her lower lip began to quiver, "I'm scared. I don't want anything to happen to this baby."

Kayla reached over and took her sister's hand, "Everything is in God's will. Remember that. Nothing happens without His knowledge and you know that all things work together for good, for those who love the Lord, even the bad things. There's always purpose, there's always hope."

"Yeah, I know," Ashley acknowledged, wiping her eyes as she smiled with new assurance, "and it's not like I'm wetting the bed again. But you know, about two years ago, I sleepily asked Gavin for a glass of water in the middle of the night. He grumpily obliged. The next morning we woke and found the empty glass on the floor, the carpet soaked. Apparently I knocked it from the nightstand as I slept. That night he came home from work with a pink sippy cup for me."

The women shared a hearty laugh before the ringing of Kayla's cell phone interrupted their fun.

"Tom!" Kayla nearly shouted, answering the call. "What have you heard?"

" I just got off the phone with someone from the FBI named Monica Jacobs. She was inquiring about Jamie. He and two other men are being held at the Calumet Coast Guard station. So my lead was right. I'm heading there now to sort all this out."

"Are they alright?" Kayla pressed.

"They're fine, Kayla. I'll let you know when I know more."

"Thanks, Tom," she smiled as the call ended.

****

The door closed briskly behind Michael as he reentered the room. Gavin and Jamie looked on inquisitively. He'd been gone a long time and now returned in a miserable state, his eyes red, his nostrils inflamed, his face flushed and sweaty.

"What happened?!" Gavin exclaimed.

Jamie quickly motioned for Michael to hold up as he scribbled on the top page of the yellow legal pad. *We're bugged*, was scrawled hastily as a cautionary warning.

Michael nodded, still pulling himself together, "I was compelled by voices to use the restroom break as a means of... *escape*. I couldn't fight the urge, it was too strong. But as I was about to make my move, there was a blast of light, knocked me to the ground, blinded the FBI agent."

"Go on," Gavin encouraged.

"I swear on my life that I saw an angel. He was huge, beautiful, armored in silver and royal blue plates, a sword at his side."

"Wow," Jamie whispered in awe of the experience.

"What happened next is the real mystery," Michael continued. "My heart broke in that moment, looking up at God's warrior. I not only regretted my acceptance of the plan to kill the guard, but all the things I did in allegiance to Triton, my father, my family. It's like a burden that can't be relieved. Even now, I find it hard to breath under its weight."

"This is amazing," Gavin replied. "I was so sure you were going to do something we'd all regret. I heard the voices here in this room as I slept. When you left and Jamie returned, we prayed for you."

"Then the angel was the answer to that prayer. I would not have stopped on my own. There would have only been death to follow."

****

Monica Jacobs listened intently as the men's voices came across the wire, the computer recording every word of the conversation. Her team, the captain included, listened as well.

"Did you see anything in there?" Jacobs asked the man.

He thought briefly, recalling the strange events, "There was a really bright light, like flash from a camera, only much, much brighter. I lost vision for a minute, everything was blurry."

"And did he try to attack you?" she continued.

"To the best of my knowledge, no. When I regained my vision, Michael was crumpled over on the floor, tears and all...a hot mess!"

A knock on the door's open frame pulled their attention away from the laptop's screen. Agent Grier had arrived.

"Solomon!" Jacobs smiled as she motioned for him to enter, turning with an outstretched hand in greeting.

"Monica," he said, taking her hand, "good to see you. Gentleman, I'm Agent Grier."

The captain nodded as did the other investigators. Grier had an intimidating air about him. The way he walked, moved, his gestures: he had a confidence that most men envied and most women adored. Yes, Grier was now the man in charge, his alpha status established without a single spoken word. Grier had that effect.

"What do we know so far?" he asked, his firm grip loosening on Monica's soft hand as he talked, their reunion over sooner than she'd have liked.

"We've got them wired up," the stout interrogator offered proudly, pointing at their makeshift surveillance setup.

"Good, good…audio is good," Grier said aloud, more to himself than to the investigators, as he stared at the screen. "And our guests, how have they acted so far?"

"If you mean guilty," Monica asked, "then, no. Other than a few strange occurrences, these guys seem on the level."

"Occurrences?" he wondered.

"Well, we've all been at this for hours. From what these guys are saying, they haven't slept in over a day. We're all feeling it, exhaustion, you follow? So little things are getting to us," Monica said with a tone of admittance.

"There are no *little things*," Ms. Jacobs.

She smiled slightly, curiously, at his unexpected admonishment.

"I need to talk to these guys," Solomon continued. "Anything else I need to know?"

The man who questioned Jamie spoke up, "Well, the detective, Jamie Branson, is a real smart mouthed know-it-all. The guy with all the tattoos, Gavin Dering, *daring*, I think is how you say it; anyways, he's calm, in a nervous sort of way, you follow?. The third guy is just…strange. His name's Michael, Michael Laurent. He had some kind of breakdown, or episode, or…*something*…in the bathroom."

"Yeah," the captain added, "when my men took them aboard their ship, they found this on him."

The captain tossed a wrinkled wad of balled up black cloth on the table. Grier cocked his head to the side and looked at inquisitively before reaching out to touch it.

His fingers tingled as he took hold of the cloth. He carefully stretched the fabric, studying the strange stitching as the cloth's ambiguous shape began to appear as he worked it out in his head. There, with a final twist followed by a tug to straighten it out, Grier caught the full impression. In all his confidence, his machismo, insecurity and doubt crept into his mind. The face was now clear: two black, empty slits for eyes and a devilish grin stitched across the wickedly cut mouth…a mask.

"What's this all about?" he managed to ask, hoping that his reaction had not been obvious.

"Guy was wearing it when we found them," the captain explained, "something to create fear, maybe? We figured you'd seen stuff like this before."

"Yes, but not quite. Ski masks and bandanas are one thing. This is…well, something entirely different."

They all shared in an indelible silence.

Monica Jacobs finally spoke, "They also claim they're innocent."

"Innocent till proven guilty," Grier replied, again with an authoritative wit. "If they didn't do it, then who did?"

"They called him Killion."

Grier paused, his reaction, this time, very obvious.

"You said Killion?" he pondered.

"Yeah," Monica answered. "You know who they're talking about?"

"Maybe…"

Again, stubborn silence followed.

"Anything else?" Grier asked.

Their blank expressions were more of an answer than Solomon needed, "Monica, show me where you put the men. I'm going to talk to them."

She did just that, leading him down the hall and around the corner, stopping outside the locked and guarded office door.

"What are their names again?" he asked as they stopped.

"Um," she thought quickly, "Jamie Branson, Gavin Dering, Michael Laurent."

"And where's the bug?"

"Why?"

"I don't want to inadvertently look at it," he explained. "The last thing I want is for them to find out there's a wire in the room. They may not tell me anything."

"Oh," Ms. Jacobs nodded. "It's hidden on the book shelf, inside the flap of a binder."

"Perfect," Grier smiled, reaching for the door's knob as the Coast Guard officer stepped aside. "And one more thing: it's good to see you, Monica."

She blushed as he disappeared through the door. Most definitely, Solomon Grier was the man in charge.

****

Jamie, Michael and Gavin looked up at the tall, well-built African American man that now stood before them, a new face, a new investigator. He, in turn, looked deeply at each one of them, staring them in the eyes, peering into their souls: a tactic to establish dominance, to be sure. But, it was working.

Grier nonchalantly tossed the mask onto the center of the table, but said nothing. Instead, he headed straight for the coffee maker and poured a cup. Then after setting it down on the table, he strangely searched the bookshelf, found the transmission device, and flipped the power off, placing the wire right in front of Jamie.

"Now that we can speak privately," he said, loosening his tie before taking a seat with the men at the table, "I'm Special Agent Solomon Grier. I'm with the FBI's domestic terrorism task force. All I want to know is what happened, no bull, just the truth."

The men looked at each other around the table, each one unsure of this Agent Grier. Jamie thought back to New York, to Dimitri and Jones, Tri-Six assassins posing as FBI: O'Donnell's murderers. This didn't sit well with him.

"Alright," Grier smirked, "the silent treatment: I can accept that. I know I'm just another badge, another observer here to dissect you're story under a microscope. But you all told the other agents that you're innocent, so why tighten up now?"

Michael stared at his mask, right there, within arm's reach. All he had to do now was take it, snatch it up and reclaim his power. They could be free. Gavin, too, stared at the mask. He'd prayed so fervently that God would intervene, give Michael strength, but now the greatest weapon of his greatest enemy had been hand delivered and sat right there in front of the men, beckoning to its master, calling for death and chaos.

"You, with the tattoos," Grier continued unwaveringly, "That dried blood on your hands, that's the dead girl's?"

"Her name was Delilah," Gavin said, his sad eyes falling from the mask of Thirteen to his own stained hands.

"Oh, I see. So how did it get there, *Delilah's* blood?"

Gavin looked up slowly, "After she was shot, I held her in my arms, felt her body shake and jolt as the last of her life fled from her, listened to her blood-filled coughs as she struggled for her final breath. That's how it *got* there, Agent Grier."

Solomon moved his gaze off into the corner. He could tell Gavin was deeply wounded by Delilah's death. The truth in his voice was certain, the pain evident in his bitter emotion.

"I believe you, Mr. Dering," Solomon said sternly. "But, I need details. Do you swear that everything you told the other agents is the truth, exactly as it happened?"

"Absolutely," Jamie nodded.

"Then can I ask you three for your trust?" Solomon continued.

Gavin and Jamie looked at one another, finding approval in each other's eyes. Michael still stared at Thirteen's mask.

"What is it, Agent Grier?" Gavin asked.

"Start by calling me Solomon, "he requested coolly. "Now, I want you to know that this situation is very personal for me, more than you can imagine."

"How so?" Jamie wondered.

Solomon again stared off at nothing in particular, "Delilah was a good friend, from my past. For years, she was a member of the only family I had."

Gavin and Jamie leaned forward in anxious anticipation. Michael, too, gave Grier his attention.

"I don't know what you guys heard of Delilah's past, and, frankly, I don't care. I cannot, for certain reasons of national security, give details on what we did, but I can tell you that she was like a sister to me. Before I was recruited into the FBI, I was in the Navy, a SEAL. Me and another frogman, a good friend of mine who I met during SQT at Benning in Georgia, a real *Joe Navy*, had the honor of participating in a clandestine UN command with operatives from the CIA, British SAS and Military Intelligence, Israeli Special Forces, French Special Operations Command, and Canadian Princess Patricia's. We worked in smaller groups as part of the larger whole, often times even paired down to a single spotter and shooter, depending on the mission. Delilah was the only woman in the twelve soldier group. We lost four men during a firefight in Afghanistan when a contact went sideways, tried to lead us into a Taliban trap. But eight of us made it out. That was the end of the road for two more. We were down to six team members: Myself, Delilah, my buddy, a French commando, and two MI6 operatives."

"Did you say *MI6?*" Jamie interrupted.

"I'll get to that," Solomon assured, continuing on. "Several of us, the French commando, my buddy and myself included, were a little older, had served during the Gulf War. The others who volunteered were younger, though not by much."

"But the MI6 agents," Jamie interjected once more, "care to share their names?"

"Alright, fine," Solomon smiled. "We'll skip ahead. Arthur Blackwood is a name I'm sure you don't recognize; however, I suppose you have heard of Terrance Killion. That is who you say killed Delilah, correct?"

"Yes!" Gavin nearly shouted. "So you have a history with Killion?"

"We served as part of that covert team for seven years, before the joint force disbanded. Killion and Delilah had become lovers, nearly got them killed in Asia. But after that, I never heard from him. Delilah kept in touch, occasional encrypted emails, but after they broke things off, she went dark as well. I always had my assumptions: Killion left MI6 and went rogue, a mercenary for hire. I feared Delilah had done the same. Now I'm sure she did."

Solomon paused. The men held their breath, unsure of what he might say next.

"The last twenty-four hours have been difficult for me, apparently for you guys as well," Grier said reluctantly. "Yesterday I looked upon the lifeless body of an old man, also a friend, Leroy Klebitz: Delilah's grandfather, shot in the chest by another man found dead outside the very building where he gassed an entire office full of would-be world leaders in Los Angeles. Then this morning, I identified Delilah for the medical examiner at Cook County Hospital. And here it's been Terrance behind it all."

"Well Killion is on the run," Gavin said. "He thinks we're taking the fall."

"That's not going to happen," Solomon replied. "You're free men. But I have to ask, how did you get involved with Killion, and Delilah for that matter?"

Jamie, Gavin and Michael shared a collective sigh upon hearing that they were clear of all charges in Delilah's death. For what they hoped would be the last time, the three of them chronicled the previous days' events for Grier, the abductions, the cat-and-mouse game, attempted assassinations and double-crosses. If he weren't who he was, Solomon would have been as likely as Monica to have been dismissive of their claims. But it was all true, every word.

"Someday I'm going to write a book about all this," Gavin laughed as they concluded.

"Better make it a series," Jamie advised.

"Oh yeah, like Star Wars," Gavin imagined. "I love trilogies."

Grier also shared in their laughter. He could see the weight lifted off the men, see their hope restored.

"So what's the next move?" Jamie asked as the smiles subsided and reality returned. "Killion has a half-day head start on us. He's heading to France to deliver the fake key to the Frenchman. "

"For all we know, my father already has the real one," Michael reasoned. "We need to stop my father. If he and Triton were right, then that key is indeed powerful. I say we head to Paris. From there we can track him down and end this."

"Well Killion needs to pay for what he's done," Gavin argued.

"And he'll be in France too," Jamie reminded.

Solomon had fallen silent, listening to the trio deliberate, "I want Killion as much as you do. Delilah deserves justice."

"What will you do?" Jamie asked Grier.

"I'll make a few calls to old friends, men who will mourn Delilah's untimely passing. We'll take care of Killion. Our interests are similar. My friends will help you deal with the Frenchman as well. But this is completely off the books. I'll close my investigation as another unsolvable. I have a cabinet full of dead cases and lost leads in my office in DC. I'll bury this file when we bury Killion. I have your contact information, Jamie. I'll be in touch as soon as I know more. Give me a day, maybe two. You're free to go."

Solomon Grier stood and straightened up his tie, then nodded at the three men before knocking on the door, signaling for it to be opened by the guard. The door did not close after Grier left the room. Instead, they were greeted by a face familiar only to Jamie: Tom Walker, Chicago PD.

"Jamie, thank God!" Tom said as entered. "I was told in passing that you guys are free to leave. Kayla has been worried sick. She called me first thing in the morning and told me you were in trouble, but this is nothing like I expected."

"Yeah, it was a little harry there, but, like you said," Jamie grinned, "thank God!"

"Come on, I've got my car outside. I can take you straight home," Tom offered. "I already signed papers releasing your private effects and weapons, already loaded in the trunk."

"They let you sign the papers for us, Tom?" Jamie questioned.

"I think they're glad to see you go. Those Feds will be scratching their heads for a while on this one."

"You know what, Tom," Jamie remembered, "my BMW is parked at Diversey Harbor. If you could just take us there..."

"What about the john boat?" Gavin thought.

"I've arranged for that to be picked up as well," Tom added. "I take it you have a trailer at Diversey too?"

"Yeah," Jamie confirmed.

"Consider it taken care of," Tom replied. "Now let's go. I'm sure you're ready to see your family."

7

Kayla screamed giddily as she opened the front door, leaping into Jamie's arms, her lips locking with his, the previous nights stress escaping in the joyful tears that now streaked her face. Ashley followed close behind, pushing past her sister to find Gavin. She pressed against him, her arms wrapped around his neck, sobbing, the thick stubble on his chin rough against her soft cheek. Elizabeth stood behind her new friends, their joyous reunions blocking her path to Michael.

"Sorry," Elizabeth said, trying awkwardly to squeeze out the door frame, "but if I could just…"

She gently pushed past Gavin and Ashley, managing finally to reach Michael, taking his outstretched hand.

"You're okay?"

"I am," Michael smiled.

"It's your father isn't it, he's the Frenchman?"

"Yes."

"Well, you *knew* all along that this could happen," Elizabeth whispered. "When you chose to kill my father, there was always the risk that your father might become as much of a threat to our security. What will you do?"

Michael looked at the other two couples, then kissed Elizabeth on her forehead, "I'm going to kill him."

She nodded and rested her head wearily on his shoulder, "How is it that you were wounded? Did you not have your mask?"

"I'm not sure what happened," he replied honestly. "Perhaps my power is lessening the further my mind strays from evil thoughts. The mask has but one master: me. I will do better next time."

"Let's head inside," Jamie finally urged, lowering Kayla back down, her feet again firmly planted on the wooden planks of the porch. "I want to see the kids, and eat...what do we have, Kay?"

As the group left the world and all its problems outside, Gavin lingered. Ashley's beautifully pale, slim fingers rested in his ruddy, blood stained palms. Ashley's gaze followed her husband's down to where he stared somberly at the death he'd brought home to them.

"It's hers," Gavin sighed, "Delilah's. She died in my arms, Ash. She had chosen to help us, help us get Killion so that I could save you, but we failed her. We couldn't stop Killion."

"But you will," Ashley encouraged, "you will! Let's head upstairs, you can take a shower. I'll help you clean up."

"I need just a little time alone," Gavin said, "to process everything, talk to God."

Ashley bit her lip to hide the disappointed frown that surfaced at his words, "Well, I have something I really need to talk to you about."

"We have a lot to talk about," he agreed. "Just give me twenty minutes and then I'm all yours."

Ashley turned reluctantly and headed in to meet everyone else in the kitchen. Gavin, allowing a teasing smirk to break his soberness, swatted her backside playfully as he turned towards the stairs and made his way to the bathroom.

****

The restroom was where he remembered it to be. He looked around at the room, noting the change of shower curtain since their last visit to the Branson home. He neither approved nor disapproved of the pattern, but recognized it as changed. Change. So much had changed! Oh how he'd longed for his old life, the life of a demon hunter: running and gunning, killing sleepwalkers and living in the shadows, a *holy ghost*. And yet, that was no life to offer Ashley, his love, his best friend.

Gavin looked at himself in the large mirror that hung above the dark, granite-topped double sink of the bathroom's vanity. Peeling off the bloodstained clothing, he looked at his tattoo-covered arms. They were the same as before, during his previous, thrilling life. They remained unchanged, a reminder of the permanence of the decisions he had made, derived from the permanence of his faith in Jesus Christ. He'd marked himself in such a way, that regardless of his words, his body was a living, breathing testimony of what he knew in his heart, believed with all his might. But even in that assurance, he struggled. Not with his faith, but with himself, the anger that he now harbored and allowed to consume him. What was God's plan in all this? Did God really want Delilah dead? He allowed it, let Killion pull that trigger. But what kind of God allows such tragedy?

"Stop it," he said aloud softly, his piercing eyes boring into the same fiery eyes that stared back from his reflection. "Just stop. Who am I to question God?"

And then, a thought came to him, words clear and true. In God's perfect timing, his own timing was imperfect. What that meant, Gavin wasn't completely sure. But as he interpreted it, Delilah, considering all the dangerous missions on which she'd embarked, the combat wounds she'd sustained and recovered from, even near suicide, God did not allow her to die, so that she would be just what Gavin, Michael, and Jamie needed, at the right time. And not just the right time for them, but the right time for her too. At the same time she'd found something to live for, redemption from the darkness of the life she rejected with her last breath.

Delilah was not a victim of Killion or an ill-timed God, no, she was right where she needed to be and right when God needed her there. And, though it made no sense in his own understanding, it brought comfort.

Gavin still stared at himself, watched as his brow furrowed with new determination. The corners of his mouth curled up as he smiled. Of one thing, he was sure: even if they could not win, God could. That was all the hope he needed.

He looked at the scruff on his face. Though it had only been days since his last shave, he was well on his way to a beard, something he thought of as part of the *old* Gavin, but now, it seemed fitting. He then inspected his thick, dark hair, running his fingers through the disheveled, unwashed mess.

Gavin knew just what he'd do. He checked the cabinet beneath the sink but found nothing but cleaning supplies. The drawers, too, held only normal bathroom odds-and-ends, not what he was looking for.

There, in the reflection, built into the wall in the corner of the room, at the faucet-end of the shower, was a linen closet. He turned and swung open the cabinet door. The lower half was a hamper. The top held extra towels and washcloths, toilet tissue, and an electric hair trimming kit hidden away in a small plastic bin which he reached for immediately. He sorted the contents quickly, found the length of attachment he needed, and plugged the two-pronged cord into an outlet next to the vanity.

Again, Gavin stared at his reflection and, as a gesture of self-reclamation, raised the electric razor that buzzed loudly in his hand, then began the work for which it was made. He watched as large clumps of hair fell into the sink, the 3/8ths inch guide ensuring a short, even cut, till finally he was finished.

Gavin smiled at the dark pile before him, pleased with his expression of a return to his *old* ways, the Gavin he once was now standing before him. He found himself humming a melody as he flipped on the shower and finished undressing. At first, the tune was almost involuntary, definitely not deliberate, but as the notes came to him and he heard them aloud, he realized it was a hymn, *Amazing Grace*.

There, alone in the shower, stripped naked before God, Gavin washed Delilah's blood from his hands, the red remnants of her life swirling around the drain, thinning in the streams of hot water that ran down his body, he made the words to that song, the third and fourth verses in particular, a prayer:

Through many dangers, toils, and snares,
I have already come;
'tis Grace hath brought me safe thus far,
and grace will lead me home.

The Lord has promised good to me,
His word my hope secures;
He will my shield and portion be,
as long as life endures.

****

Terrance Killion's eyes slowly opened as he woke with a start, turbulence shaking the sleek jet as they crossed mid-Atlantic. He looked to the seat across the cabin where his brother still slept, undisturbed by the trembling of the plane. He looked ahead and spotted the pretty young stewardess sitting near the cockpit's entrance, her smooth, slender legs smartly crossed, a fashion magazine open in her lap as she skimmed the pages.

"Excuse me, love," Killion called out.

"I'm so sorry, sir," she replied, quickly closing the magazine and making herself available to serve. "How may I assist you?"

"How long have I been out?" he asked with a smile.

"Nearly five hours, sir."

"Please," Killion said, again with a smile, "call me Terry."

She noticed his eyes as they wandered from her own and down her neck till they settled on her breasts, "Excuse me, Terry."

"My pardon, *Missi*, I was simply reading your nametag.

She blushed, feeling silly that she had assumed he was being indecent when he must have been looking innocently, "I thought you were looking at my, well…you know. Oh, I'm sorry."

Killion let her continue, enjoying her awkward position..

"I'm so embarrassed," she admitted.

"Don't be, love," he winked.

"Well, thank you, Terry," the stewardess replied, her cheeks flushed, her neck red as well.

Killion feigned a sigh of discomfort and shifted in his seat as turbulence once again rocked the craft.

"Are you alright?" she asked, reaching for his empty martini glass as she planned to mix him another drink.

"It's just the turbulence, Missi. I hate flying."

"Is there anything I can do for you then, Terry, to make you more comfortable? Perhaps another drink?"

She took the stemmed glass in her hand as he reached out and softly touched her wrist, caressing the spot where the overly starched cuff of her sleeve met her delicate skin, "I think there's something you could do that would make me more than comfortable."

Killion stood and embraced her, forcing his lips against hers, meeting no resistance as she closed her eyes and melted in his firm grip. The longer he held her, the more she desired him, though she was unsure why. But his passion, his touch, was unrivaled and she gave herself to him. She led Killion to the plane's small bathroom, undressing as the door closed behind them.

Moments later, Edward was awoken by the moans and giggles that meant only one thing. He closed his eyes once more, noting that, as expected, neither his brother nor the stewardess were in sight, though thanks to their less-than-subtle lusty exclamations, he was certain of where they could be found.

My dear Terrance, Edward thought to himself as he drifted back to sleep, *always on the job.*

****

Solomon Grier stood at the end of the Navy Pier staring out east over the Chicago Harbor. Sail boats cruised in the still-choppy water from the previous night's storm. Now, white clouds decorated the picture-perfect blue sky. He would have truly enjoyed the history of this place, the Navy

Pier, where pilots trained for carrier missions during World War II, had he not been focused on the lighthouse that stood in the distance, the place where Delilah was murdered.

His cellular phone was raised to his ear. He hoped the man on the other end would be available. But he had dialed a special line, reserved for special occasions, secure, clean, private.

"*Ello?*" a male voice, British, replied after several rings.

"Arthur," Grier smiled, his sunglass-shaded eyes still settled on the red roof across the harbor.

"Oi, Sully boy, is that you?"

"It's me, Arthur."

The Brit laughed over the line, "It's been a bloody long time, mate. How's the Bureau treating you?"

"I'm sure just as good as MI6 treated you, old friend."

"A right bit better, I hope, Sully," Arthur Blackwood replied. "I've done much better for myself with my chair kicked back, my feet firmly planted on the edge of my desk, and the latest edition in my hands. Retirement is wonderful, mate, truly!"

"You really expect me to believe you're retired?" Solomon said, allowing a smile."

"Right you are, Sully."

"No, no," Grier laughed. "Men like us don't retire. We're in too deep. There's no quitting what we know, what we've seen and done."

"Lager has done me right, mate," Arthur laughed. "Helps me forget."

"Is that so? How's the pub?"

"We've got live music every weekend, cold beer to go round, the finest whiskey this side of the dip, and the highest stakes backroom game in all the Queen's land. My pub is the bleeding Monte Carlo. Oi, and the *girls*...you should come out, mate. You'd love the scene!"

"I could use a vacation, but not now. Too much on my plate," Solomon admitted.

"So what is it then?" Arther asked. "What made you give me a ring? Haven't heard from you in ages and then, here you are, on my *special* tele."

"Have you been in contact with Belesur?"

"Jean Luc? Not in months. I buy cases of wine from his vineyard in Marseilles for the pub, but I haven't spoken to him recently? What's up, Sully?"

"Are you alone?"

"I am. I'm in my office, second floor of my fine establishment, preparing for a crooked night of cards with London's best. You sound serious, Solomon. You alright, mate?"

"It's Killion," Solomon sneered. "He finally crossed the line."

"What are on about?"

"Delilah, Art. She's dead."

There was a pause, silence, before Grier had to hold his phone away from his ear. Cockney curses and the loud, violent crashes of apparently breakable items in Blackwood's office roared from the handset's speaker.

"Arthur, you there?"

"So we're going to kill him right?" came the reply, perfectly cool and calm, not a hint of the rage caged within the old boxer, turned soldier, turned entrepreneur.

"I can't be involved, not beyond conversation. But you, Jean Luc, you two can do it…for Delilah. Are you still connected?"

"I couldn't cover illicit gambling if I wasn't, mate, not with the scores I take."

"This can't be sloppy though, Arthur. No London mob."

"Me? Sloppy? Oi!" Blackwood chuckled.

"You know what I mean. There's more at stake than just revenge."

"How so?"

"It involves civilians…kidnapping…blackmail…" Solomon hesitated, "It's big, Arthur."

"And just how did common folk come to bear the wrath of the mighty Killion?"

"It's a long story," Solomon explained, "but their next move is Paris. Killion should be there too, or at least they believe so."

"And you trust the words of a couple of Yanks? Tell them to stay stateside. Jean Luc and I will handle this. They'll just get in our way. I'm not for having inexperienced blokes getting plugged on my watch. Killion requires caution. He's a scary chap."

"No, these guys…you'll like them. Civilian or not, they can handle themselves. Trust me.

"Trust you? Bloody hell! Alright," Arthur sighed, "but if anyone of these Yanks die, it's on you. It's on *YOU!*"

"Fair enough, Arthur."

"So what's the plan then?"

"I'll leave that up to you and Jean Luc. This op will most definitely require a level of fluidity and you'll have to manage it in the field. For now, see if Jean Luc can arrange a safe-house in Paris. From there, it's up to you. I don't care how it's done, just do it. I'll set up the flights on our end and call you in forty-eight hours with their schedule including ETA in Paris. Call Jean Luc, be ready!"

****

The Branson's kitchen fell quiet as they all heard Gavin's footfalls on the oak stairs. Ashley felt as though she'd been holding her breath the entire time he'd been upstairs. She wanted to tell him so badly.

"Hey, bro," Gavin smiled at Jamie, entering the room in a white cotton v-necked shirt and blue jeans, his bare feet slapping on the hardwood floors, "I borrowed some clothes, hope you don't mind.

He met unblinking eyes, the group taken aback by his unexpected change of physical appearance, everyone fixed on his hair. Ashley grinned. With the stubble and buzz cut, he looked just as he had five years ago, when they'd first met, fallen in love.

"No problem," Jamie answered, handing his brother-in-law a mug of hot coffee. "I was going to offer anyway."

"If it's alright," Michael interjected, "I would like to wash up as well, change the dressing on my arm. Do you have anything that I might be able to wear as well?"

Jamie nodded and led the way upstairs, Michael following, Elizabeth coming along too, wanting to help tend to her husband's surprising wound. Kayla looked at Ashley and winked.

"I'm going to go check on the kids," she said. "You two need to catch up."

Gavin wrapped his arms around Ashley as she reached up and rubbed her hand across the top of his buzzed head. They laughed, then kissed.

"There was a moment, a *brief* moment, when I was afraid I'd never see you again," Gavin admitted. "I was so afraid I'd lost you."

Ashley rested her head against his chest as she spoke, "I learned a lot from you, like how to take care of myself. Things you probably don't even think you taught me, I picked up. What I didn't know, I improvised."

"Thank God for that," he said, his lips touching her soft hair, her familiar scent comforting as he held her, kissed the top of her head.

"Gavin," she hesitated, there's something you should know, something I have to tell you."

"What?" he asked curiously, taking her by the shoulders and moving her a step back so that he could look her in her big eyes. "You alright?"

Ashley bit her lip as she stared up at her husband, gazing deeply into

Gavin's eyes. She took his hands in hers, their fingers intertwined. She knew she was blushing, she felt the glowing warmth all through her as she flushed. Gavin, too, stared into her eyes, her beautiful doe eyes. He examined every delicate feature of her pretty face, her soft round nose, her reddening cheeks, her pink, soft lips.

"Ashley, what is it?"

She smiled, safe, secure...in love.

"I'm pregnant."

8

Storm clouds draped heavily across the western French countryside. Thunder claps boomed over the rolling hills and through the lush valleys. Lightning flashed as a fierce wind ripped through the trees, tearing still-green leaves from their heavy branches as nature unleashed its wrath on the small commune of Les Trois-Moutiers.

The weather was no less harsh an hour's walk north of the village, where the ruin of a once-glorious chateau stood ominous beneath the blackened sky. The grounds were overgrown, a forest overtaking the landscape that had been so delicately designed. Hail stormed down upon the castle sending chaotic ripples across the circular moat that guarded the estate, reached only by a narrow, archaic stone bridge from the entrance to the grounds. Nature and time reclaimed much of the chateau's interior. Rogue trees and shrubs grew up amongst the fallen, crumbled stone, a symbol in itself of duality: the organic and inorganic, the living and the dead. The castle's gothic towers now stood dilapidated, a crumbling reminder of past grandeur. A bell still hung proudly in one of the them, teetering ever so slightly in the heavy winds, clinging to the last hope of former glory.

Only one building remained in restorable condition, a jewel amongst the decaying stone bones: the chapel. There, a slender, bearded old man lingered at the marble alter, staring up solemnly at the remarkably unbroken stained-glass windows. Pigeons cooed from where they nested in the ceiling above. Thunder shook the estate, rattling the beautifully colored glass. But from within the shadows cast eerily by the flickering of the old man's candle, movement crept. Whispers echoed off the walls. A faint scratching of claws on stone came from nowhere in particular. It, like the sound of the rain pelting the rooftop, soothed the old man, like music for his old soul.

"How long have you been standing there?" he finally asked, his gaze never trailing from the stained-glass.

"Only a little while," a man's gravelly voice replied from the shadows.

Lightning flashed, briefly illuminating the chapel, revealing the hooded figure that lingered at the entrance.

"And what do you bring me, my son?" the Frenchman asked softly.

The man approached the altar, his right fist clenched as his left hand threw back the hood, his striking face now fully visible, his jet-black hair long and tangled, "I bring you Triton's key."

The Frenchman looked down at his son's open palm, the remarkably unassuming relic finally his. After all his years of faithful service, enduring all of Triton's bragging, he was now the master of the manor. The power hidden away within the crumbling walls of the chateau was at his fingertips and he would finally know all the secrets that Triton had guarded so selfishly.

"You are a blessing to me, Sebastian," the Frenchman smiled, taking the key from his son's hand, then clutching the antique to his chest. "Now, come."

The two made their way across the estate, the ground slippery beneath their feet as the rain continued on, an unrelenting deluge. After a hundred yards or so, they crossed the stone bridge and pushed through the tall, creaking, double wooden doors that led to the forest within. Birds scattered from the trees that loomed in the courtyard as the men passed beneath the slick, rain-laden branches. Beyond, in a great hall opposite the castle's entrance, candle light glowed ominously in the ghostly place.

"Has the assembly begun?" Sebastian questioned, a grin cracking at the thought of progress towards their goal.

"Not many," the Frenchman answered, "but enough. Many important men share our cause. And, they will bring more like-minded believers into the fold as we take control of the powers that be. The assassin, Killion, did his job. The Order within the United States is dead. You have seen to the destruction of Triton's last supporters here in Europe. The old Order has passed away. It is time for a new order, an order that will see peace and prosperity delivered to all nations. And we, my son, are the ushers of that New World Order."

They continued across the courtyard till they were close enough to the hall as to now hear the voices emanating from within. It sounded markedly more like a boisterous evening at a fine gentleman's club than an assembly of global dignitaries and CEOs.

"Father," Sebastian sighed with discouragement, "They are drunk."

"Better with wine, than power," came the wise reply. "As presidents and parliaments and kings and emperors are all drunk on their accomplishments and glories, their wars and conquests, we shall embody their demise. There is one who will rise to lead us all, my son. And we must do *everything* we can to ensure he is welcomed by all. The time has come for a high chancellor who will lead all peoples of every nation, every tongue. Triton wanted that for himself. But we, my son, *we* will deliver that hope to the people of the world."

"And it begins with The Collective," Sebastian said, opening the door to the once-grand hall.

The laughter and jesting stopped immediately upon the arrival of the Frenchman. Those who gathered knew they were here for more than fine, aged wine. The time had come for business.

"Gentleman," he smiled, recalling how Triton himself spoke in such a way, his strong voice demanding an audience's attention, "tonight we make history. For the last three decades, a plan has been in place, secretly orchestrated by a select few. No longer does that responsibility rest in the hands of self-righteous elite. No, we now control the destiny of the world."

The Frenchman looked up and down the long table, studying the men's faces in the flickering, soft orange glow as the candles slowly burned. Tonight would be the night he measured just how far his new partners were willing to go in order to bring peace to the world.

"How's the computer business?" he asked, nodding at a skinny man in an exquisite suit, thick-framed glasses resting on the wide bridge of his nose.

"Sales were down this last quarter, a response to the boom of the tablet market," the CEO admitted. "Every PC manufacturer and their grandma has a new touch screen offering, so we're doing everything we can to stay ahead of the curve."

"And you," the Frenchman said, turning to another gentleman, this one stouter, with a bushy mustache and eyebrows to match, "did the FDA approve your new *wonder* drug? What was it, that heart medication, Athera-*something?*"

"*Atherostatin,*" he replied happily. "It's the greatest HMG inhibitor ever introduced by science and will revolutionize cholesterol treatments, dramatically reducing heart attacks worldwide!"

"Did you rehearse that?" Laurent smiled.

The heavyset man chuckled, "It's in the literature. We just published new marketing, guess the words are stuck in my head."

"Well you don't have to sell me on the idea. If this drug can be offered to the masses for less than its competitors and in so doing, greatly affect their profitability, Tri-Corp is more than pleased to be a part of your fine pharmaceutical program."

The man nodded in thanks and returned to his glass of wine, lifting it off the table in salute. The rest of the room followed suit, raising their glasses to their new leader, the Frenchman: Emeric Laurent

"I am pleased with those of you who accepted my invitation to this evenings affair. Certainly you are all here because we are a brotherhood."

The room nodded, the men at the table once more raising their glasses high.

"And as all true brotherhoods, we must take an oath, a surrender to the will and greater good of the assembly under which we meet. Tonight, we will take that oath." Laurent decreed fervently.

He turned to Sebastian and gestured towards another man, young, dressed as a butler, who stood in the corner, waiting to serve his purpose and fill the next empty glass with more *vin rouge riche.*

"You, garcon, bring in the machine. Sebastian, retrieve the virgin from the cellar."

The young man disappeared into the next chamber. Sebastian obeyed his father's order and headed for the dungeon-like lower level of the chateau. The cellar was dark, musty. Moss grew on the rocks. The old wine racks, though half rotten and decayed, once again served their purpose, bottles finding themselves delicately displayed wherever the wood had strength to hold the weight. Sebastian passed the wine and another small alcove used for storage, restoration supplies stacked neatly by day-contractors. A narrow corridor led him to a small, makeshift bedroom. A cot, reminiscent of second world war bunker fair, sat against the wall, a hand-filled straw mattress added for comfort. The sheets and pillow case were clean, nicer than expected in such a place. Candles burned on an old metal plate, the wax rolling down the candles' sides and collecting in a pool at their bases, hardening as it cooled. That plate sat on a rickety wooden table that also held bottles of purified water, saltine crackers, and a small wedge of cheese. Bites had clearly been nibbled from the cheese, but not by scavenging mice.

A young girl, no older than fifteen, her large, curious eyes not daring to look up at her captor, sat with her back against a heavy wooden door at the opposite end of the small space. When she'd been taken in the cover of night from her parents' nearby farm, her night clothes were all she had. Upon arrival to the estate, she was stripped and bathed, her humble, flowered nightdress ceremoniously replaced by an elegant, white sleep gown, the sheer material draping loosely on her small frame, the gown meant to be filled out by a matured woman. Instead of focusing on Sebastian, she played with the soft lace that hemmed the bottom of the gown.

"Come, ma petit fille," he smiled, reaching down to take her small hand in his large palm.

As he lifted her up from the dirty floor, his eyes fell on the needle marks that tarnished the perfect complexion of her arm's soft skin. Three injection points, three nights of drugging.

"Now hold still, chere," Sebastian frowned, quickly filling a syringe with fluid from a small glass vial he carried in his pocket, knowing now that he was about to add a fourth wound.

He cleaned her inner arm with an alcohol wipe, then pierced her young skin with the hollow needle. The girl's eyelids strained from the sudden pain, then drooped over her large, perfect green eyes as her muscles relaxed, removing any fight she may have tried to muster.

"I am very sorry," Sebastian whispered, his thumb putting pressure on the injection sight to quell the bleeding.

****

The men gathered around the table as the young concierge labored to squeeze the large machine through an only slightly larger doorframe. Its steel-band wheels were round, once, but their now dented and bent surface struggled against the uneven, old stone floor.

The machine was indeed just that: a wood and metal frame, exposed and rusted nuts and bolts holding together each hand-hewn piece. A rustic seat sat between the two old wheels, but there was little backrest to speak of. The rear of the machine was something from the imagination of a sadist. On the surface, it appeared Frankenstein-ish, mad. But it was deliberate in design, its visual impact uncompromising. On the rear, a heavy crank was connected to two sets of interlocking cogs, the first operating a basic, leather-wrapped pump inside a glass cylinder. Tubing, more modern, obvious replacements of what was surely long since rotted away, connected the crude vacuum system to another empty glass cylinder and a bizarre contraption that appeared to raise and lower on the seat's back in correlation to perhaps the differing height of whomever was unfortunate enough to be sitting in the machine. The second gearing turned an elementary copper coil which reminded the onlookers of early Edison prototypes. Wires coupled the electric generator to the adjustable back device, connecting at nearly the same place as the rubber hosing. A tension spring mechanism attached to a metal fulcrum and disappeared into a small box where the rubber hose and wiring led. This seemed to be activated by a trigger of sorts linked next to the hand crank that operated the raising and lowering of the diabolical little box. From the front, two small holes, roughly two inches apart could be seen in the design of the adjustable back piece, but their purpose was beyond the minds of those who gathered at the Frenchman's call. Lastly, leather straps and metal buckles on the armrests and leg braces ensured the necessary restraint of the machine's victim, for no one would willingly subjugate themselves to such a thing as this, this devilish torture.

"Mon Dieu!" one of the men in attendance blasphemed at the sight. "Monsieur Laurent, what is this all about?"

Emeric smiled as shock and awe overwhelmed the members of The Collective, "This is the device we will use for the blood oath. After this, we will truly be brothers and, more importantly, united in our cause. You see gentleman, there's no turning back from this oath."

The concierge brought the machine to rest and closed the locks on the wheels, giving them a firm shake to be sure they were immobilized, as Sebastian returned with the innocent young girl. The men in the room now had something else to hold their interest.

"Is she really a virgin?" the computer magnate questioned, his eyes narrowing as he focused on her long blonde hair, the golden strands shimmering in the warm candles' glow.

"Indeed," Laurent nodded. "She is very valuable to me."

"So," another man, an Asian automotive executive asked, "her innocence, being untouched by a man, that makes her blood more powerful or something?"

"Most definitely not," Laurent answered, his lips curling devilishly as he spoke. "But it is important. I have a much greater use for her yet, a use which requires someone...pure."

"No doubt our host likes to get his jollies," an Englishman laughed, his chuckle shared about the table. "What a tart, she is."

Laurent sighed and looked at Sebastian, recalling his son's disgust at the men's drunkenness, "To business then."

Sebastian led the girl to the machine as the room fell silent. Emeric raised her gown so as to expose the bare small of her back as she was gently guided into the seat. The wood was rough against her legs, but her mind was unaware of the fact, her drug-induced stupor leaving her nothing more than a numb wanderer in an unfamiliar world. Her wrists and ankles were carefully secured in the restraints, the coarse leather rubbing her skin red and raw.

Laurent nodded sternly at his son and they switched places, Sebastian ready to operate the machine, Emeric now kneeling to lower himself face to face with the girl.

"Ma beaute...je suis tellement desole," the Frenchman whispered to her. "I am so sorry."

He kissed the top of her blonde head as Sebastian adjusted the height of the box, lowering it to align with her spine just below her kidneys, then began turning the crank that operated the machine. A small switch blocked the pump gearing from starting as an ominous, electric crackle came from the generator. Blue sparks flickered, charging something within the small box. A smell similar to a hot soldering gun or curling iron permeated the air.

Sebastian continued to operate the crank while he reached for the small box's trigger mechanism. With a sudden, mechanical click, two sharp, hollow cones plunged into her back, narrowly missing her spine on either side, the electrical current coursing through the copper metal cauterizing the entry points. A less pronounced, secondary click marked the ejection of the cone's inner hypodermic needles, one plunging into the abdominal aorta, the other into the inferior vena cava. He then flipped the switch allowing the pump to begin cycling. Almost instantly, the tubes leading from the box shuddered as they transferred her blood into the empty glass cylinder, the bottom and sides spattered in red as the flow continued.

"Just a little more my dear," Laurent encouraged. "We need only a pint for the oath."

The room was deathly quiet. If it weren't for the constant cycling of the pump, there would have been no sound whatsoever. Sebastian monitored the cylinder of blood, noting the level and time. Emeric checked her pulse.

"We are finished," he told his son.

Sebastian slowed the crank, then turned off the pump. He twisted a knob on the right-hand side of the box and the cones retracted, the needles returning to the box. Laurent quickly checked the small of her back. Only two small wounds remained, perfectly reclosed, not a drop of her precious blood wasted.

"Well done," the Frenchman again whispered as assurance. "Sebastian, see her to her room and make sure she eats. She will be weak."

"Yes, father."

Sebastian loosed the restraints that held the girl as the servant carefully removed the blood-filled glass cylinder from the machine and slowly began pouring a small amount into each of the men's empty wine glasses. Laurent waited for his glass to be filled, then raised the blood symbolically over his head.

"Is this all necessary?" one of the men asked with a thick German accent, his upper lip shrouded by his gray, wiry mustache. "I speak of this...*machine*...the blood of a virgin, even this oath. Could we not have made due with a simple syringe and vial, the way a hospital would draw blood from a patient? Why the torture?"

Laurent smiled, allowing his arm to lower slightly as he answered, "Because, mon ami, as it is said, *the devil is in the details*. This machine was Trtion's, as was the process; something he perfected long ago. When? I do not know for certain, so do not ask further. But, this *torture* is part of the process. It is necessary for us to accomplish our goal."

"But you said that you were not desiring power in the way that Triton desired power!" the German reminded.

"Indeed," Laurent confirmed. "I do not envision myself the ruler of the world, only the conduit by which the ruler ascends. That does not mean I disagree with Triton's methods; in fact, I very much agree with his methods, for they were extremely effective. If it were not for the empire he built for himself, this meeting now, here in this most ordained place, would never be possible."

The table was silent. Either they agreed unanimously or they feared too greatly to question the Frenchman further. Once more, the girl well cared for, Sebastian entered the crumbling room, taking his place at his father's side and also lifting his glass in obedience.

"I'm sorry, sir," an Australian finally dared, "but I just don't know that I can do this, drink her blood I mean. I believe whole heartedly that what we are doing will finally bring peace to the world, end hunger, cure disease, but, well, I guess what I'm trying to say is that this just doesn't feel right."

"We've come this far," the Frenchman urged. "There's no turning back now. The blood oath is only the beginning, but it *is* the *beginning*. After this, everything else will fall into place. This is a matter of faith, not *feeling*."

The Australian thought for a moment, then slid back his chair and stood, "Then I'm sorry, sir. Though I believe, I just don't have enough faith."

Laurent stared at him, his eyes not harsh and burning like Triton's would have been, but soft, pitying, "If this is how you truly feel, mon ami, you are excused from The Collective."

The man nodded, "Laurent, you have been more than gracious. I wish you, all of you, the best of luck and wish you prosperous as well."

The table gave him its full attention as he turned, the Australian's back now facing them, and headed slowly towards the door. Laurent wordlessly nodded at his son. Sebastian reached beneath his long black trench coat and drew a 9mm Sig Sauer SP 2022, clicking the hammer back with his thumb. In one motion, Sebastian raised the gun and fired smoothly, the bullet slamming into the back of the Australian's head, spattering the wall in organic mess, as the ball ammo exploded through his forehead.

"Is anyone else inclined to deny their faith?" Laurent asked, regretful of the Australian's decision.

In unison, the remaining men raised their glasses without hesitation, their eyes forced away from the death they'd just witnesses. Their faith, through fear, was now emboldened.

Laurent closed his eyes firmly, his brow furrowed in deep, strained reverence as he spoke, "With this blood, we confirm our oath. That in partaking of this unholy communion, we will see, what before, we could not see, believe what we could not believe, and do what we could not do. We, as brothers, commit to the plan, even unto death, and surrender to the will of the powers that will guide us."

His eyes flicked open and he stared out at The Collective, his gaze purposefully meeting each one of the members, reading their commitment. They, as before, stared back, almost unblinkingly, unsure of which was truly worse: this oath or immediate death.

"For the *one* who is to come," Laurent toasted. "The *one* who will be wounded and healed, the *one* who will finally bring true peace and order to the World."

Laurent drank, the warm, metallic-tasting blood passing effortlessly over his tongue and down his throat. The Collective followed, slowly, reluctantly, gagging as they forced themselves to swallow the thick red human cocktail. Sebastian drank as well, savoring the sweetness of his father's words, Triton's legacy now their legacy. He stood beside his father, the empty glass in one hand, the gun in the other. Surely this was a moment to be proud.

9

Gavin had hardly spoken the rest of the day. Slowly, the reunited group drifted into the laziness of the hot, late summer afternoon, the prior day's happenings, Delilah's death, only a vague haunting as they all tried to dwell on happier things.

Ashley curled up snugly beneath Gavin's colorfully tattooed arm as they cuddled on the bench seat of the Branson's backyard patio-swing, her legs tucked up onto the comfortable cushion as they swayed, back and forth, watching the sun's orange glow break intermittently through the trees, silhouetting the branches, the green leaves glowing brightly, displaying their photosynthetic translucence. The present moment stood in such stark contrast to the despair that was their existence only hours ago. Had they forgotten already?

"Congratulations, daddy," Jamie winked, passing by the couple as he marched about the yard, Marley sitting high on his shoulders, squealing with delight as Cain followed closely behind, brandishing a dirty stick in his hand: a double for whatever his young imagination intended it to be.

"Thanks, Gavin grinned.

In his mind, he replayed his angst over Ashley's disappearance; and now, knowing how much more he could have lost if her attempt to escape had ended differently, well...he didn't even want to consider the thought. He silently thanked God for the moment he now shared with his wife, the slowly setting sun a reminder that tomorrow, the sun would rise once again, bathing a new day in the hope of its light.

He rested his hand on Ashley's still-flat belly and thanked God for the blessing that grew inside her. In the last week, he had regained his faith, reunited with his wife, and been surprised with greater news than he could have ever expected. There was just so much for which to be truly thankful.

There was a serene normalcy: watching the kids play with Jamie, Kayla and Elizabeth talking over iced teas, Michael tending to the hotdogs and corn that sizzled on the large smoker grill, the distinct smell of charcoal in the air. Somewhere in the neighborhood, a lawnmower rumbled, echoing off the houses. This was like any other summer afternoon, all they needed was some baseball and apple pie and this would pass for perfect, Norman Rockwell approved Americana.

FBI Special Agent Grier had told the three men to wait for his call. And that was exactly what they would do, savoring every moment they could now share in peace, as temporary as it may be. Killion was still out there...somewhere...and the key surely delivered into dangerous hands. But allowing their thoughts to linger on facts they simply could not change offered no hope. And that could not be afforded.

****

The wheels on the Tri-Corp jet screeched against the tarmac in smoky protest as the plane landed at Paris Charles de Gaulle International Airport. Killion had long since returned from his bathroom fling, the stewardess blushing every time their eyes met. He wouldn't soon forget the joys hidden beneath her professional flight attire.

As expected, a black Mercedes awaited them as they descended the steps from the plane. They had little luggage and quickly found themselves on the A1 Autoroute, *l'autoroute du Nord*, and on their way to their prearranged apartment that would serve as their safe-house as long as they wished. Soon, Killion would deliver the key to the Frenchman and add to his already astounding earnings.

What would normally have been a thirty-five minute drive was cut down to only twenty-five, their flight arrival at approximately 2:00am of great benefit. They crossed over the river Seine on the Turnelle bridge ahead of schedule, Notre Dame standing within view. The phone in their apartment was meant to ring at 3:00am sharp: instructions for their rendezvous with the Frenchman.

Killion looked at his watch and chuckled aloud, "I forgot to set my Omega. We're here brother, but the time was left in the States."

Edward smirked sleepily. The flight across the Atlantic still wasn't enough rest for him after days of sleepless grinding. All he wanted was a nice, soft pillow to cuddle up with.

"Driver," Killion called up to the front seats, "what's the proper time?"

"2:32 in the morning, monsieur."

"Perfect," Killion smiled. "We've plenty of time for a drink!"

Soon the driver stopped on the boulevard in front of their building, not far from the rail station at Montparnasse and Rue de Rennes. The Killion brothers climbed out of the SUV's backseat and into the warm Parisian summer night. The city's lights glowed warmly, illuminating rooftops, beckoning the curious to explore. To the northwest, the Eiffel tower stood resolute, its steelwork climbing high into the dark sky, spotlights ensuring the renowned monument could be seen for miles.

They exited the vehicle and headed beyond the ornate façade of the building that would, for the time being, serve as their home, their safe house. The elevator carried the two men to the top floor. Edward followed his brother down the hall till they stopped, Terrance trying a key he'd removed from his pocket on the door's lock.

With a grin, the elder Killion swung open the door. The apartment was a simple flat, nothing too fancy, but the view out the tall windows on the far side of the space was breathtaking, the lights, imagery, and cityscape incredible.

The brothers entered through a decent-enough, well-stocked kitchen and placed their luggage on a large square coffee table placed conveniently between two nice couches that stood as the center entertainment area of the main room. Doors on either side of the flat led to smallish, city-sized bedrooms. A tiny bathroom stood just off the kitchen.

"Maybe we should throw a party?" Terrance smiled at his brother, heading to the kitchen in search of wine or scotch. "We could fit a fair few French birds in this place."

"Come off it, mate," Edward sighed. "We've been in Paris five minutes and all you can think about is who you can let in your knickers!"

"Oi!" Killion laughed, handing his brother a glass tumbler filled half-full of liquor. "The stewardess wore the knickers, mate, well, till I took the lovelies off her! And, you'll bloody well thank me when you've got a girl in your arms. This is it, brother. We've done the *big* job, the score we've always wanted. We had money before, but now…we never need work again!"

Killion sat down on the couch, sinking into its soft cushions before sipping once more on his drink, then setting it down next to the briefcase on the coffee table. He flipped open the latches, then the lid, snorting in the imaginary scent of millions in US currency as he opened the case, marveled by their profit.

They finished their drinks in silence, Killion staring at the money, Edward at the city lights. Two brothers: so similar, and yet, different.

The bell on the apartment's phone chimed where it hung on the wall between the bathroom and kitchen. Killion raced to answer, knowing who would be on the other end of the line.

"Bonjour,…oui…c'st moi," Killion said, each phrase an answer to the voice's questions on the other end. "Oui. Je comprends…au revoir."

"Was that the Frenchman?" Edward asked, watching as Terrance returned the phone to its cradle.

"Not personally, but in a manner of speaking. A car will arrive tomorrow morning…9:00am sharp…a black Mercedes, same as what picked us up tonight. We are to enter the sedan promptly, unarmed, and we will be taken to meet the Frenchman."

"Unarmed?" Edward questioned. "But why? Does he think we might take the money and then his life?"

"There have been so many double-crosses at this point, brother, that even I can hardly keep track, and double-crosses are my bag! We'll be fine. All the Frenchman wants is power. We've done a good job for him: knowing that, he may call on us again for future exploits."

"You sure, Terry?"

"Positive," Killion nodded. "Now is most definitely *not* the time to bite the hand that feeds."

****

Kayla and Elizabeth successfully managed to get all the children to bed. The sun had succumbed to the nature of time, having descended beyond the horizon, giving way to a star-filled, moonlit night. With the passing of the day came closure to the events of the lighthouse. Dawn would bring a new day, and with it, a new challenge: find Killion and end the Frenchman's madness.

With the kids fast asleep, the grownups reveled in the peacefulness of a rather typical, boring evening in. Only miles away, the Chicago nightlife roared, but here, in the once-again secure Branson home, the three couples watched a movie on the large flat-screen television that graced the wall of the family room in their finely-finished basement. The screen bathed the darkened room in Technicolor glory, images from Hitchcock's 1954 classic, *Rear Window*, reflecting in the six-person-audience's eyes, nosey James Stewart and Grace Kelly enticing them to snoop along through voyeurism's binoculars as they speculated the murder of his neighbor, one poor Mrs. Thorwood.

"I could watch this movie over and over," Ashley smiled, happily nibbling at butter-flavored microwave popcorn.

"Me too," Gavin agreed, "and anything by Alfred Hitchcock really. The way he used the technology of his day to enact the driving scenes in his movies, the perfect timing of prerecorded backing scenery and small effects like dirt kicking up as the drunk Cary Grant's car veered off the road in *North By Northwest*, for example, just shows how passionate he was about the little things that affix realism and immersion. Simply brilliant!"

"And ahead of its time," Ashley added.

"Wow," Kayla laughed. "So which of you is Siskel and who is Ebert?"

"Shut up," Ashley teased back.

The night continued on. After another hour, the movie ended and they discussed sleeping arrangements. Kayla ran the empty bowls used to serve the popcorn back upstairs to the kitchen and returned with blankets and pillows for Michael and Elizabeth. The Laurents had chosen to sleep on the giant sectional sofas in the family room, allowing Gavin and the pregnant Ashley the comfort of the queen bed in the Branson's second-floor guest room.

Michael nodded at their friends as they headed upstairs. Elizabeth bid them goodnight. A half-bath adjoined the laundry area, the door standing ajar at the far end of the room. Though there was no shower, Michael used the space to change the bloodied bandage on his arm. Elizabeth helped him with the dressing. The wound wasn't nearly as bad as expected and now burned only a little. The bleeding had long subsided and, though raw, the beginnings of the healing process could be seen in the scabbing that had already begun to shield the new skin that would soon grow beneath.

"How fortunate it was just a graze," Elizabeth said, kissing her husband's bare, muscular shoulder as they stared at their reflections in the mirror.

"Indeed," Michael replied softly.

"What is it?"

Michael stared at her in the mirror, "This injury should never have been possible. I was wearing the mask. You know as well as I do that it should have made me impervious to a simple bullet."

"It was five years ago that you last wore the mask, perhaps the bond has weakened?" Elizabeth pondered. "Maybe it will just take time."

Again, Michael paused, "Maybe it's because I don't believe like I used to? Maybe it's me that has weakened and not the mask at all?"

"Do you need the mask to confront your father?"

"I don't know, honestly. At this point it may not matter. Mask or no, we must stop Emeric."

"I've never heard you call him by his first name," Elizabeth frowned. "Do you no longer respect him as your father?"

"He quit being a father to me years ago, when I became the monster that Triton wanted me to be. I wore the mask, same as my father, but where he controlled it, I believe the mask truly controlled me."

"He's still your father. You owe him that respect."

"Really, Liz? That's hard to hear, especially coming from you. Wasn't it

96

your idea that I kill Triton rather than just walk away?"

"It was your father's idea and we needed the money, Michael."

"We already had more than enough."

"You and I both know that no one just *walks away* from Triton. He was my father…ruthless…evil…but still my father. I loved and hated him."

Michael turned as Elizabeth finished securing the clean gauze around his arm with medical tape, "How similar our fathers are…"

"And yet how different," Elizabeth smiled, ending their conversation with a kiss.

****

Ashley returned from the shower, snuggly wrapped in one of her sister's comfy bathrobes, her hair still wet, her skin rosy from the hot water. Gavin had been talking to Jamie in the hallway outside the guestroom, their voices lowered to hushed whispers, but the kids were sound asleep and Kayla assured the men that they needn't worry about waking them.

"Can I get you anything else?" Kayla asked as Gavin and Ashley headed for their room.

"We're good," Ashley grinned. "That shower felt amazing after all that's happened. I feel like I washed away the bad memories."

"Alright then," Kayla smiled, taking Jamie by the hand, "goodnight."

Gavin closed the door behind them. He'd found a lavender scented candle-in-a-jar and lit it, thinking it would help her relax. Ashley flicked the light switch off and brushed past her husband. The two stood in the soft flickering radiance of the candle's burning glow.

"I was so afraid I wouldn't see you again," Gavin sighed, cherishing the sight of his beautiful wife.

"Me too," she admitted. "But here we are…together."

"I missed you *so* much, Ash!"

Ashley bit her lip teasingly as she slowly loosened the soft belt on the white, cotton robe, "I missed you too, babe."

The robe slipped off her shoulders and onto the floor. They stepped towards each other and kissed, their passion unrivalled by any other emotion. Her skin was so warm, soft to his touch.

Ashley grabbed his shirt and helped him pull it off, the two only pausing from each other's lips long enough to get the collar over his head, as he quickly unbuttoned his jeans and slipped out of the borrowed clothes.

She giggled as their bodies collided, their lips meeting once again, "We can't be too loud!"

"Oh I can be quiet," Gavin whispered, leading her to the bed and pulling back the covers.

Again, Ashley giggled, catching herself and pursing her lips to muffle the sound. They disappeared beneath the cool sheets, leaving their fear and angst outside, thankful for each other's love as they embraced.

****

Kayla laid on her back in bed, vacantly staring up into the darkness, watching as the quickly spinning blades of the ceiling fan blurred, allowing the dim moonlight that shown in through their master bedroom's windows to dance playfully on the ceiling. Jamie was somewhere between sleep and awake, his heart heavy, his mind racing as he tried desperately to imagine anything other than the previous day's nightmares. His arm rested heavily across her stomach as he curled up next to his wife.

"Are you asleep?" she asked.

Jamie mumbled a reply. Whether it was yes or no, Kayla was unsure, but she continued on, whether he was listening or not. She needed to talk.

"Do you really think chasing after Killion and the Frenchman is actually a good idea?"

"No," he replied after a moment, his speech slow and groggy, "but it's necessary."

"But we're all together now, all alive," Kayla reasoned. "Do we really need to keep fighting? So what if the Frenchman has the key? So what if Killion escaped? There are other people who can handle this situation."

Again, there was a drawn out pause before Jamie shifted in bed, his hand caressing her playfully as he spoke, "I believe there's a reason we were involved, both now and most definitely five years ago. Call it chance, or fate, or even preordination. But certainly, whether we like it or not, our destiny and that of the key seem to be intertwined. Aren't there questions you still ask yourself about New York, about Triton, even the sacrifice that started it all…even *why* your sister was targeted by Triton in the first place?"

"You're right," she admitted, feeling his fingers softly trace the outline of her hipbones. "I still think about it sometimes, even the puncture marks found on the victims' lower backs in that musty, dark basement. We never did get an answer."

"And maybe we never will. That's what frustrates me the most."

"So let's say we go to France, we manage to find Michael's father, what next? Do we kill him?" Kayla questioned. "When Triton died, we thought it was over, the story had ended. Then Thirteen ended up being the real threat. And again, we thought he died as the hospital crumbled to pieces in the blast. But here we are, five years later, Thirteen sleeping in our basement! Say we kill the Frenchman, what then? Who next? Does it end or are we trapped in this battle for the rest of our lives? What about our kids, Jamie, do they continue the fight? Is this our legacy?"

"Whoa, Kay," Jamie said, raising up onto his elbow, his hand trailing from her hips and calmly touching her cheek, "you're way ahead of everything. I get it, I understand. But Marley and Ethan are why I need to go to Paris, why I need to do all I can to finish this, why I…"

"We," Kayla interjected. "*We* go to Paris, why *we* do all we can to finish this."

"No way I'm risking your life as well and leaving our kids in the US while we travel thousands of miles away and do who knows what! I mean, if you go, who'll watch the kids?"

"I think we should all go: you and I, Gavin and Ashley, Michael and Elizabeth. We're all a part of this, now…and five years ago. You said it yourself."

Jamie flopped back down onto his pillow, "And the kids?"

"We take them to mom and dad's. They'll be safe there."

"Pittsburgh. We're going to fly to our possible deaths in France and you think we should leave the kids in Pittsburgh?"

"Dad was a cop for forty years. He's tough, resilient. Remember how scared you were to meet him?"

Jamie blushed, his smirk barely visible in the moon's soft white glow, "You have a point. What about Ashley though, being pregnant and all. Should she fly? She and Gavin have so much at stake."

"We all do."

They laid in silence, together, but feeling alone. Kayla rolled over tightly against him, stretching her left leg across both of his, her head resting on his chest. He wrapped his left arm up under her, holding her close, his right hand clasping around the fingers of her left hand, feeling her wedding ring.

"I made a promise to you five years ago," Jamie said, tears forming in his eyes, "for better or for worse. This is clearly what's meant by *worse*. I just don't want to lose you, Kay."

"You won't," she promised.

"How do you know?"

"I just do," she said peacefully, snuggling against him, closing her eyes at last, "I just do."

10

Dawn broke over the eastern horizon, the fury of the late-summer sun driving the dark of night into hiding. The trio of couples had slept well in the Branson home, safe, happy to be together and alive.

The rich aroma of fresh brewed coffee and the giggling chatter of the kids lulled Michael from the eloquently bizarre dream that had gripped him for what seemed the entire night, the contributing factors of the nightmare just as confusing as the visions themselves. *But*, he reminded himself, *it was only a dream.*

Elizabeth had already dressed and was busy with Kayla in the kitchen, the two women smiling as they prepared a breakfast feast worthy of kings, or three starving children with an astronomically limitless supply of energy. The three kids, two running ahead, one toddling behind, seemed more than rested from their night's sleep.

Jamie stood in the backyard, the barn-style doors of his red-painted storage shed standing wide open, his beloved lawnmower gassed and ready to lay the unruly, ever-growing grass to waste. On more than one occasion and with an air of extreme, yet unexpected satisfaction, he had told Kayla how much he approved of their living in Chicago over the grass-less New York City bachelor pad he once craved. And, if his words were true, though he openly shared that he despised yard-work, his character believed it made him consider himself more of a man than nearly any other aspect of his life. For indeed, his father never had a lawn to mow, never had trees to trim or shrubs to maintain, no. His father was no gardener, he was a deserter. But having a yard meant responsibility. In his skewed understanding, a home with a well kept landscape meant that someone in the household wanted to present a good impression of the property to neighbors and passers-by, in contrived essence, a good impression of the family within. And Jamie deduced that this *fact* was the definition of his manliness, even in the complexity of the loathe/love relationship. He mowed the yard; therefore, he loved his wife. Simple.

****

Gavin woke, sweat dripping from his brow as his eyes darted about the room, taking in the details, his mind racing to recall where he was. He heard the children's laughter, smelled bacon frying in a pan, a lawn mower rumbled somewhere outside.

"Hey, baby," Ashley said sleepily, rolling over to face him, "you ok?"

He felt the warmth of her naked skin press against his and smiled, it was only a dream, a stark, vividly hopeless dream.

"Yeah," he laughed. "I just had the craziest dream."

"About?"

"About you…and…the baby."

"Oh?" Ashley questioned, raising up on her elbows, then sitting up completely and moving back towards the pillows, coming to rest upright against the darkly-stained wooden headboard. "What kind of dream?"

Gavin rolled over and stared at her belly. He gently caressed the area around her navel, imagining how she would change in ten more weeks, then twenty, thirty weeks, up to birth: a large, round, beautifully feminine and miraculous pregnant belly, the skin taught and firm, a little life moving and kicking within.

"That tickles," she smiled, his finger traipsing around her small bellybutton.

"Sorry, Ash," he said, lost in thought.

"So are you going to tell me about your dream? You seemed upset when you woke."

Gavin hesitated, afraid of what she would think. The dream had most definitely brought him fear, but he knew he needed to tell her the truth.

"In my dream," he began, "we were in a hospital delivery room. You were in labor and I was standing beside the bed, your hand in mine, as you pushed."

"Oh gosh," Ashley grimaced. "I'm not ready to think about giving birth."

"Yeah," Gavin smiled. "Anyway, the dream was in first-person, so I was looking through my own eyes. There you were, face red, covered with sweat, straining as you pushed. I looked down and I could see your knees tucked up as high as they could go, your feet pressed into the stirrups. The nurse was a real *labor-Nazi*, screaming at you to *PUSH, PUSH, PUSH!* So you did just that: you kept pushing. I felt so bad, I wanted to do something, anything; but, all I could do was time my breathing along with you. I held my breath when you held your breath. I exhaled when you exhaled. I tried to say encouraging things in between. You squeezed my hand till I thought it would fall off!"

Ashley listened as Gavin continued, her imagination perfectly picturing every word, creating the stunning scene within her mind.

"So then, the nurse warped or morphed, or whatever, into the doctor and then said something about crowning and that he could see the baby. I looked down between your legs and saw a little wisp of black as you pushed. I thought, *look at that hair, the baby has jet black hair!* But then, as you continued to push, I realized it wasn't hair. The nurse continued to shout demands for pushing and the doctor continued doing whatever he was supposed to do down there. Anyway, the wisp grew. With each push, more wisp flowed out of you, and then I realized what it really was: a thin black plume of smoke. With a final, huge push, a burst of smoke streamed from your body and spiraled up to the ceiling, billowing out and filling the room. The nurse and doctor both changed again, but were no longer human, now dark and scaly, glowing eyes peering out from behind their medical garb. Their white surgical masks covered their mouths, but I could tell they were speaking. Cries for you to push suddenly became a low, hissing chant. *A blessing and a curse*, they said cruelly. *A blessing and a curse, a blessing and a curse,*

A BLESSING AND A CURSE!"

Ashley shivered uncomfortably, and rightfully so. She grabbed the sheets and pulled them up to cover herself, holding the hem tightly to her chin. Gavin hadn't been told about her experience in the McDonald's restroom after seeing a positive result on the pregnancy test. Those same words, *a blessing and a curse*, were those of the demon that tormented her. This seemed impossible!

"I hadn't had a chance to tell you," she said with a shudder, recalling the horrid memory, "but, while Elizabeth and I were on the road, just after taking the pregnancy test and finding out that I was indeed pregnant, a demon appeared and screamed a phrase in Latin, *Vos portare vitae, vita fert multo mortem, benedictionem et maledictionem*. Elizabeth and I worked out the translation. Between the two of us, what we know in French and Spanish, we managed to make sense of the demon's words."

"Okay?" Gavin whispered. "So what does it mean?"

"You know Latin," she replied, "Joseph taught you right?"

"A little...not a lot."

"So tell me what you think it said? Tell me if I'm right?"

Gavin thought for a moment, repeating the words in his head, *Vos portare vitae, vita fert multo mortem, benedictionem et maledictionem*, "You bear or carry life, life that carries, brings, much death, blessing and a curse."

They stared at each other, both physically and mentally stripped bare, their naked state an unspoken metaphor for their obvious vulnerability. Gavin pictured Adam and Eve upon the revelation of their sin against God, how perfect together, one moment naked and unashamed; the next, scrambling to hide their secrets before an omniscient Creator.

"What can we do?" Ashley asked tearfully.

"We can pray."

****

Kayla greeted Ashley and Gavin with cups of coffee as they made their way into the bustling kitchen. Apparently, everyone else had slept more peacefully. For now, after praying, the two felt it best to keep the dream to themselves. They'd turned their concerns over to Christ and that is what mattered. There were still other plans to be made, other challenges to overcome. Why exacerbate an already volatile situation?

The talk at the table was friendly, light, what would be expected while eating bacon and eggs. Jamie had finished with the yard and joined them, his cheeks red from the hot morning sun. But they all knew the normalcy was only meant to be short lived. Soon, they would all face the reality of the road that lay ahead, the inevitability of possible death.

A sharp knock on the front door brought them all back to the present. Who could that be?

Jamie unlocked the door and cautiously turned the knob. His mind was put at ease as Lieutenant Tom Walker stood outside on the porch, a smile on his face, a large, black duffle bag embroidered *CPD* in his hand, the eighteen inch barrel of Jamie's shotgun poking through. The bag zipped only so far in an effort to accommodate the length of the Remington.

"Good morning, Detective," Tom said. "Your brother-in-law's boat was dropped off to him this morning. I brought you your guns."

"Thanks, Boss," Jamie replied, taking hold of the heavy bag.

"I assume those guns aren't appropriately registered in Illinois, so I advise you keep them secure from here on out," he said, nodding at the bag. "I trust you, but I don't know your friends. God knows all we need is another murder in our city. And those aren't junk guns either, so it would assume the company you keep mean business."

"Yes, sir."

"Is everything else okay? Like I said, those are serious guns for serious people. You aren't in any other trouble right? I still don't get why you were out there in the harbor. Is there anything else I can do for you, Jamie?"

"Just approve my LOA request. I need a couple of weeks to, you know, wrap this whole thing up and get past what happened. Just, no questions, alright Tom?"

"I'm not dumb," the lieutenant grinned, "neither are you. I won't ask any more questions as long as you don't do anything else stupid, got me?"

"Loud and clear, sir."

"Alright, LOA approved. I'll sign the paperwork tomorrow. Just promise me you'll be safe, you and that pretty wife of yours. Don't leave your beautiful kids to mourn you."

"I won't," Jamie promised, fighting back the lump in his throat. "I'll see you at the precinct in a couple of weeks. Thanks again, Tom, for everything."

"You bet, kid."

Jamie closed the door and marched the heavy, bulging bag back to the others, setting it down on the just-cleared table, "We've got our stuff back."

"My HK," Gavin smiled, unzipping the bag, exploring the contents within.

He found his gun, but paused, spotting the wrinkled, balled up cloth that laid beneath it. Gavin retrieved the gun, then pulled out Thirteen's mask, staring at the stitched grin.

"Here," he said shaking his head to clear the bizarre blank numbness that had overcome him, then handing the mask to Michael. "Your .50 cal's are in there too."

"Thanks," Michael replied, clenching the balled-up cloth.

As he did, Cain's voice hit his ears. Michael turned and watched his son as he chased little Marley Branson. He thought of his father, Emeric Laurent: the Frenchman. He considered the legacy that had been passed on to him, the mask included. How he wished that this legacy would not in turn be passed on to his son. Cain did not deserve to inherit the wickedness that he was entitled to as heir to the Laurent namesake. No. This was the end of the lineage, a new line would begin. Of that, Michael was sure.

****

Solomon Grier sat at alone in a secluded back booth at a diner on the outskirts of Chicago. He remembered this restaurant from his younger days, remembered their excellent French toast. So there he sat, sipping on his third top-off of coffee. An empty plate had been pushed to the side, a pool of leftover syrup developing a film over its sticky surface as it sat. The French toast was as he remembered: excellent.

He scoured through news articles using an app on his iPhone, making mental notes of current world events, mapping them together in his head. The complexity of what he imagined was staggering. His thoughts were like a giant map, globe-spanning, yellow push pins marking locations, red yarn connecting similar incidents, strung one to the next. And for Special Agent Grier, this was how the world worked. Nothing was by chance, everything had purpose. Whether it was a secret or not was his concern. His experience in the military taught him that things are not always as they seem. His time at the FBI confirmed the fact.

Solomon turned off his phone's screen and set it down on the table, again sipping his coffee. The problem he now faced was the thing that infuriated him most of all. Right there, in the midst of the red yarn, was a peg, a peg with only one connection. The string tied it to Los Angeles: the Sunrise Chapel, Killion's attack on Reverend McNamara's office. The two events shared no other links. So why Killion and why now?

He ran his hand quickly back and forth over his short, neatly trimmed hair. All he could do was wait. He knew he'd receive answers in time, but patience, after the murder of a friend, was something Agent Grier lacked. If all went well, those answers would soon be coming from Killion himself.

****

Killion stirred. It wouldn't be long till morning. He'd drank most of the scotch himself, Edward long since asleep on the couch. He sat up in the comfortable armchair and rubbed his eyes.

Outside, the city grew restless as well. Lovers walked the streets without purpose, only glad to have someone there to hold their hand and share in the sights and sounds. Others were already beginning their day, readying for work, for classes at the universities. A distinct, French police siren wailed somewhere in the predawn.

Slowly, in the dark, Killion found the restroom, succumbing to the urge, his body reminding him of just how much he drank. The flush of the toilet woke his brother in the common room.

"Is it time?" he asked groggily.

"What?" Killion called out over the noise of the water that rushed from the tap and splashed over his hands, then into the sink's basin.

"Is it *time?*"

"No. We have several more hours. You can sleep or we can slip out for an early tea, or latte if you prefer?"

"Oi, brother...sleep."

"Right you are then," Killion agreed, flopping back down in the oversized chair and allowing himself to drift away once more into dreams.

****

Morning had slipped into midday without event. Now, approaching early afternoon, Kayla was growing anxious. They all were, whether they admitted it or not. Reality would soon hit when they would receive the call from Grier: the call confirming that the trip to France was a go. He'd said he would make certain arrangements, provide assistance as much as possible. But they themselves had yet to work out the details, like who was actually going and what precautions they would follow.

"We all know this conversation has been coming," Kayla began, "and we took yesterday to relax, feel a sense of normalcy return. But, we knew from the moment we were all reunited: there's still work to be done. We need to decide, right here and now, what our plan is, or in the least, who's going and who's staying!"

"It'll be the three of us," Gavin stated, "me, Jamie and Michael. I'm not putting anyone else in harm's way."

"Yeah right!" Ashley laughed. "I was already in harm's way and I managed. This will take *all* of us to finish. We've been a part of this since the beginning, for the last five years even. And, I'm not missing a chance to see Paris!"

"You're pregnant!" Gavin argued. "No way am I risking your life or the baby's!"

Michael sat in silence as Jamie interjected, "Look, Gavin, I know it's not what you want to hear, but she's right. Ashley does have a point. Fate or God's will brought us together five years ago in New York City. Fate kept us together and brought us here, now. There's something divine behind all this, even the evil. Perhaps we have been called by God to overcome, to rise up against this evil. I think God planned for all of us to play a part. In the end, we aren't choosing who goes because God has already chosen. Harm's way is not ours to control or challenge. Do you remember that night five years ago, the night before we attacked Thirteen at the hospital? I was an empty mess! I needed pain pills just to make it through the day and I drank myself to sleep at night. But you and Kayla and Ashley showed me that there was hope. I saw in you that I wasn't alone. You brought me before God, broken, lost. You set my path straight. It's because of you that I'm here now."

Gavin thought deeply upon Jamie's impassioned words before he answered, "It wasn't me, Jamie. It was the Holy Spirit, guiding you, convicting you, forcing you to face your weaknesses and cast them to Christ."

"You're right," Jamie agreed, "it was the Holy Spirit. But God put you in my life when I needed saving. Kayla, our relationship, the goodness I envied in her, only cracked the ice that kept my heart cold as stone. The Holy Spirit, through you, broke that bondage, broke me deep down inside. Jesus set me free from my bondage, but He used you. Don't ever forget that."

Michael nearly cracked a smile, his eyes twinkling as he heard Jamie's testimony. What Jamie was saying, rang true in his own life. Though he was already aware of the emptiness his life had brought, his marriage, his child: these where placed in his life with purpose. For all the evil that had been unleashed upon the earth through the mask of Thirteen, he, Michael, had been allowed blessings, blessings far beyond what a sinner, a killer, deserved. Perhaps his heart was being prepared, he too being broken in his core, opening the way for salvation's redemption.

Elizabeth also felt these same strange feelings, like waking from a long, cold winter's slumber, when the air is crisp and the comforting warmth of bed beckons, holds so soundly. Yet waking is a step of faith. To live dreams rather than simply dream, to walk with eyes open in truth, perhaps she was finally awake!

For Michael and Elizabeth, little of their time was ever spent around Christians. They laughed at the idea of church: hopeless, sad people clinging to fairytales, slaves to a fictitious God, not strong enough to make it on their own esteem so they use the guise of religion as a crutch. Indeed, Michael knew there was a God, he'd been taught so as a child, then trained, indoctrinated even, to believe that he, in Triton's service, was injecting needed chaos into God's perfect social experiment. Though, he never understood why. And even worse was the fact that angered him the most:

why didn't God simply strike him, Thirteen, down? If God cared so much for the world, then why would He allow so much evil, someone as evil as Thirteen, to exist? But in Michael's short time with Gavin, he realized something. Maybe, just like for Jamie, Gavin was the catalyst to something greater, not for himself, but for those whose company he kept?

And in all this, Michael, Thirteen, a servant of darkness, a carrier of evil will, came to realize that this planet, its inhabitants, is not a cosmic social experiment where God stands back and allows evil and hate and despair. No, God is not uninvolved at all, not even hindered by subtlety. God shouts in a thundering voice that shakes mountains, rattles the very foundations of the earth. It is not God who truly allows evil, but mankind: His beloved creation. For every choice that man makes, there are repercussions. God does not allow evil to persist, but he allows consequences for mans' actions, mans' choices. And the further man has strayed from truth, from the thoughts that follow after God's own heart, the consequences have worsened.

But, for the first time, Michael saw what had been hidden from him, what his father, his grandfather, and generations before them had missed. There is no choice between good and evil, only a choice in whether to believe or not believe. For in that decision, the recognition that God's love is so abounding, so everlasting, so complete, that Jesus himself, God's son, died to save all mankind and offer redemption, true, pure forgiveness, that was the choice. Through Christ's redemption, Jamie was freed of mental torture and a dependency on something he'd made his god: drugs. Through Christ's redemption, Jamie was made whole, clean, new. Through Christ's redemption, Jamie was still a sinner, still capable of terrible things if he would choose them, but his heart was changed. He now sought after the things of God, not the things of man. The choice to believe: that is what God allows. Man then, in turn, allows good or evil.

Michael pondered all this as the discussion of who would head to Paris continued on without him. He, same as his wife, had finally woken.

"Okay," Gavin said, "*if*, Kayla, you and Ashley want to come along, what about the kids?"

"We'll leave them with mom and dad," Kayla reasoned. "Dad is retired Pittsburgh PD. He has guns, training, and friends! Plus, their home is pretty secluded, well hidden."

"Dad *is* a bit of an off-the-grid kind of guy!" Ashley smiled.

"What do you think, Elizabeth?" Kayla continued.

"I..." she hesitated, "would be of no use to you. I've never even fired a gun. And, if it came to that, I'd only get in the way. I'd be a risk to all of you. I would like to stay with the children."

"And you think this is best?" Gavin asked Jamie.

"I do. We all have experience, not just police experience, but we've been here before, battling spiritually, I mean."

"Michael?" Gavin wondered.

Michael seemed startled, his thoughts somewhere else, "Um, yeah. I agree, Elizabeth has no experience. I've seen the four of you work together first hand. Together, we have a good chance of ending this."

"Chance?" Jamie replied.

"Look," Michael explained. "My father is strong. He surrounds himself with others who are strong and he manipulates everyone he comes in contact with. I never once saw my father fight. My time with him in France was peaceful. But I know there's a monster there, lurking just beneath the surface. When we awaken that monster, we must strike fast and true."

"So he's a sleepwalker, like Triton?" Ashley asked.

"No, not in the same sense. When I say *monster*, I don't mean a physical manifestation or demonic possession. I mean he's capable of anything. That is why he's so scary. His connections are endless, his network a spider's web, tangled and dangerous at every step."

The group sat in silence, once more considering their doom. Michael was right, the Frenchman should not be approached without skillful preparation...and prayer.

"Then it's decided," Gavin announced, knowing further debate would only raise more questions and doubt. "Elizabeth will stay with the kids at our parents' home in PA. Michael, Jamie, Kayla, and Ashley: we five will accept Grier's help and head to Paris. We *will* stop the Frenchman...*and* Killion will pay for what he's done."

11

"So Jean Luc is in?" Grier asked, smiling as he talked into his cell phone.

"He is," Arthur Blackwood confirmed. "He's been out of the business for while now, but he's still one of the best."

"Alright, Art. I'll let the Americans know you two will be able to help them with everything. And again, I'll call you with flight times and any additional details."

"Right, mate."

"Killion will follow old habits," Grier continued. "He's just completed a big job here in the states, he'll be laying low. He'll be difficult to find."

"Was his brother on the job as well?"

"My sources tell me yes."

Blackwood chuckled, "Then there's our answer. Edward is our *in*. We get the brother, we get Killion."

"And you think Edward won't be hiding out with Killion?"

"Oh no, mate…I'm sure of it. But he's no pro. The kid's a computer nut, hacker sort; a good pilot if I recall, but sloppy. No, he's our ticket to Killion. Just one catch…"

"Yeah?"

"I've never seen him."

"It's your show," Grier replied. "Just keep it quiet and keep it clean."

"I can promise you one thing, Sully," Blackwood grunted. "Killion killed Delilah. She was one of us: a mate. You don't kill your mates. That's bad form. When I find Killion, it'll be quiet…but it won't be clean."

****

Kayla leaned against the granite kitchen counter top, her iPhone raised to her ear. The time had come to move forward.

"Hi, mom," Kayla smiled as her mother's warm voice answered the call. "I'm good, yep…kids too, and Jamie. How about you guys? Uh, huh. Good. Hey, mom…can I talk to dad?"

Shuffling could be heard through the phone's speaker as Mrs. Rose set the phone down and called out for her husband, "Walter, it's Kay on the phone. Walter…"

"I'm coming, Evelyn," came the reply.

Again, more shuffling. Kayla couldn't help but smile.

"Kay? You there? It's dad," he said into the phone, adjusting the positioning of his glasses where they'd slipped down on the bridge of his nose as he spoke.

"Hey, dad. What are you up to?"

"I was in the basement, working on my trains., Kay. I just got a new engine, a real beaut. "

"That's great, dad. I bet it is."

"Oh sure, Kay. It's a blue diesel with yellow accents, a thick, wide yellow stripe up its side. I just finished touching up a few spots where the factory paint didn't line up."

"Oh yeah?" she smiled.

"Yep," he beamed proudly. "But I bet you didn't call your old man just to talk about HO trains, what is it, hunny?"

"Well…" Kayla paused, "do you remember what happened in New York, five years ago?"

"How could I forget," he sighed. "Both of my baby girls fell in love *and* then nearly died as they got caught up in something I'm still not sure I fully understand."

"It's kind of like that…*again*, dad. We're all ok, I promise, but we have to do something or this will never go away. New York will haunt us the rest of our lives, maybe even follow Marley and Ethan. Jamie and I can't let that happen."

Walter Rose sighed, rubbing his brow as he weighed his daughter's words, "What about your sister…is she wrapped up in this too?"

"Of course, dad. We all are. And Triton's evil has touched another family as well, their young son included. We have to end this, dad."

"This man, Triton. He took a son away from me, nearly killed my daughters. You say he's dead, but that that didn't end it all? What makes you think that this time you will? How many people are you and your sister going to have to kill to be free of your past?"

"Dad, it's not like that."

"Then how is it, Kay? Tell me?"

"I don't know. I just…*I just*…"

"What, Kay? You just *what*?"

"I need you to take the kids for a while, a week or so. There's a woman, Elizabeth, and her son, Cain. They all need your help, your protection."

Walter shrugged, "Does she have a husband?"

"Yeah, dad."

"Then tell him to take care of his wife like a good husband should!"

"Don't be so stubborn, dad," Kayla pleaded. "Her husband is coming with us. He was there when this all started and he's going to help us finish it., once and for all."

"So what's your plan?" he conceded.

"I'll tell you when we get to Pennsylvania. We're flying into Pittsburgh tomorrow."

"And then, Kay, what next?"

"We fight, dad. We end this!"

****

Solomon Grier thanked the young FBI driver for the ride and headed into Chicago O'Hare. Regardless of his findings, he hadn't planned on staying in the city long. The reports pertaining to the Los Angeles incident had been filed and now, Grier knew he needed to be at his DC office. Too much time had been spent in Chicago already and not being there *officially* meant unwanted answers would need provided to unwanted questions that would be asked.

He purchased his ticket and found a seat in the domestic terminal. Through the large windows, he could see the sun's orange glow as it had already begun its descent into the western horizon. It was time to make the call. Grier dialed Jamie's phone number and waited for his answer.

"James Branson," he said as Jamie picked up.

"Agent Grier."

"My associates are a go."

"That's great news," Jamie replied.

"Have you all decided what you're doing? When should I book you for Paris. I need to let my man know when you'll be flying in."

"We need to take our kids to my in-laws' home in Pittsburgh first, then we can make a flight to Paris."

"Is your in-laws' secure?"

"Yeah, dad is retired law enforcement. He's well equipped and if anything happens, he'll have the entire department backing him up."

"And when are you leaving for Pittsburgh?"

"We booked the flight today online," Jamie explained. "We're leaving at 8:00am tomorrow morning."

"Then I'll book your tickets out of Pittsburgh International for tomorrow night. I'll text you the exact departure time. My man will be awaiting your arrival at Charles de Gaulle airport."

"You don't have to pay for our tickets, Solomon. We've got it."

"Accept them as my thanks. Three tickets to Paris are the least I can do if it means Killion answers for what he's done."

"There's five of us going."

"Very well then, five tickets, still more than worth the cost."

Jamie wasn't sure how to respond. His silence was confirmation of the plan.

"Five tickets to Paris. I'll text you the departure info: time, gate, all you'll need to know. From there, you fly to Paris. Arthur Blackwood will be waiting. Goodbye, Mr. Branson."

****

Jamie stared at the phone's brightly illuminated touch screen as it went black. Kayla and Elizabeth had accepted the challenge of bathing three rambunctious kids in preparation for bedtime and had long since taken the children upstairs to the readied, bubble-filled tub. Gavin, Ashley, and Michael remained in the kitchen, listening as Jamie spoke with Solomon Grier.

"So it's settled then?" Michael asked. "We have Grier's support?"

"We do. It sounds like his contacts can *do* or *get* us anything we need."

"Perfect," Gavin replied. "The sooner we deal with Killion and the

116

Frenchman, the better. Every day they're alive, they gain the advantage, stepping ever closer to using that key for what must be its intended purpose. They must be stopped."

"Right," Jamie nodded. "Should we consider what we need to take with us?"

"Well, we won't be able to take our guns. We'll have to have Grier's people set us up over there," Gavin said.

"Yeah, I know," Jamie grinned. "I was thinking more like clothing."

"No," Michael interjected. "We must travel light, only what we need to get us to France. We'll purchase clothing, supplies, anything else once there. We'll also arrange a vehicle once in Paris, maybe two. Mobility and discretion will be our greatest allies. I am happy that Grier is behind us, but I trust his men will be able to help us only so far along. The time will come where we must bear the weight of this ourselves."

"Then I'll pack for the kids," Jamie agreed. "Perhaps Elizabeth can borrow some things from Kayla. I'll see you guys in the morning."

Michael nodded and headed for the basement as Jamie made his way towards the second floor. Gavin, now left alone, stood in the affliction of his anger. He brewed a cup of coffee, added some vanilla caramel creamer from the fridge and left the quiet kitchen for the summer sounds found on the patio. Cicadas chattered shrilly from the tall trees in the backyard. The sun had nearly set. A mosquito buzzed near his ear, causing him to swat erratically, still missing the tiny insect that longed for a juicy snack.

Gavin's thoughts were as unpredictable as his ill-attempted extermination. His dark dream lingered, Ashley's own demonic experience as well, the curious words haunting him. Then there were the images of Delilah's dead body and, though his hands were clean, he could still see her dried blood clinging to his skin.

"It's time we talked," a voice whispered softly from the shadows of the Branson's garden.

Gavin squinted into the dark, trying desperately to find the source of the voice. Whoever it was sounded familiar, yet not exactly as he remembered. Could it truly be?

"Joseph?" Gavin questioned, spotting a peculiar silhouette amongst the hydrangeas.

The shape moved, stepping slowly into the soft light of the 40 watt bulbs used in the patio's decorative, house-mounted lanterns. Gavin raced towards the shadow and threw his arms around the old man as his face came into the light.

"I never thought I'd see you again!" Gavin smiled.

Joseph returned the embrace., happy to reveal himself once more to his prodigy, "It's been too long, my friend."

"Where are your monk's robes?" Gavin asked, looking at the finely fitted tan suit his old teacher wore.

"I traded them in," Joseph laughed.

"So why are you here?"

"Come with me," Joseph said, looking up at the house, lights glowing from behind pulled blinds, "into the shadows. I do not wish for anyone else to see me."

Gavin followed without hesitation, "Okay, Joseph. So what's going on?"

"Let me ask the same of you. I've always remained close and I know what you are facing, but I want to hear it direct from you."

"Ashley is pregnant. But I'm scared."

"First off, congratulations! Secondly, of what are you afraid?"

"A demon appeared to Ashley and told her the baby was a blessing and a curse."

"As they are," Joseph winked. "They are the greatest blessing, a gift of Heaven and a reminder of the complexity and purpose of God's creation. But also a curse, in the middle of the night, when they are hungry or wet and require the attention of already sleepless mommy and daddy. I'm joking of course."

"No, I get it," Gavin frowned. "I just figured you'd take this more seriously. I haven't seen or heard from you in five years and now you're here, making light of a prophecy concerning my baby!"

"Prophecy?" Joseph laughed. "Tell me, when has an angel or demon ever prophesied? Hmm? Nothing coming to mind? How about in scripture then? Show me where an angel delivered a word of truth in its own power and not a message sent from God Himself?"

Gavin rolled his eyes. He knew where Joseph was going.

"Anything?" Joseph asked. "The demon did not prophecy. It did just what it was commanded: deliver a message. In this case, one of fear and doubt. We angels do not know the mind of God, nor do demons know Satan's. We only serve."

"So you're saying there's nothing wrong with the baby?" Gavin pushed. "And that Ashley will deliver safely, that they'll both be okay?"

"You know I don't know that anymore than you do. Only God knows these things. Tell me, who do you think you are to question Him?"

"I wasn't questioning God or His power," Gavin blurted in defense.

"But you believed in your dream, right? You believed in the words spoken to Ashley, did you not?"

"I did, do…whatever."

"Then you have already questioned God," Joseph reasoned. "In believing in the Devil's deception, you give those words power. You've inadvertently placed faith, merit, in the words coming straight from the mouth of the ultimate liar, Satan himself."

"But I know that God is greater and that He can save our baby."

"Then you should have nothing to worry about. The fear of the Lord is the beginning of knowledge, not the fear of the Devil. Some trust in chariots and some in horses, but we will remember the name of the Lord our God, understand?"

"Yeah, thanks," Gavin sighed. "Now I'll have that song stuck in my head all night."

"It's the least I could do, my friend."

The reunited companions stood in silence, the sun now gone, marking the end to another day.

"So is this why you came to me?" Gavin asked. "I would be foolish to assume you don't know about the Frenchman, about what we're planning to do."

"I know, Gavin," Joseph assured. "As I said, I've always remained close. Do not worry about the baby. Keep faith. As for the Frenchman, I can tell you that he plans on unleashing an army, opening the gates of Hell and loosing a demonic scourge upon the earth. He believes it is time for the antichrist to rise, to subvert the world into submission under one ruler, one government."

"He thinks he's the antichrist?!" Gavin exclaimed.

"No, but he believes he knows who that man is and wants to see him ascend to power."

"So this is why you're here: to warn me about the end times?"

"Heavens no," Joseph laughed. "But know that we, meaning a host of warriors, are at the ready should the Frenchman succeed in his plan. The demons will come and, as you well know, only we angels can fight them. I came to ask you about the death of the woman, Delilah, and about how far you will go for revenge?"

"It's not about revenge," Gavin said, "it's about right and wrong."

"So then, my friend, if you find Killion and take his life, will it restore Delilah? Will she live once more?"

"Of course not."

"I see. So then you'll teach the wicked Killion a lesson by sending him to an early, albeit well-deserved, grave?"

"I guess so."

"And," Joseph continued, "this will make you feel better about her death and somehow relieve you of the guilt you've suffered by not trusting God to restore to you your wife when she had been taken away, or that He would protect you as you suffered at Delilah's mercy before her change of heart? Or how about now, having enough faith that God will deal with the Frenchman in His timing, and simply taking Ashley and walking away? Must it end in death?"

"I don't know," Gavin admitted. "I really don't. So just tell me what to do!"

"All I can tell you is that a time will come when you must choose between your own devices and that of God's to protect what you care for most. Pray you will know when the time comes. Otherwise, whether you choose to fight or walk away, know that we angels are ready to stave off the evil that *will* follow as a consequence of the Frenchman's actions."

"So are you saying that we don't have to fight the Frenchman?" Gavin asked. "Isn't this what you trained me to do when you taught me as a demon hunter?"

"Indeed, it is similar, but not the same. Sleepwalkers and demons are one thing. However, the Frenchman is just a man, no demon possession, nothing. He's not a host for an evil spirit like Triton was, he is just deceived. If you kill him, it will only end his life. That is what the Bible refers to as murder. The same goes for Killion. His death will be murder. And you, my friend, are no murderer."

Gavin had nothing to say. He understood Joseph completely, knew he was right. Now he felt ashamed.

"If you know what's going on," Gavin said, changing the subject, "then you know who is working with me, who has helped me get this far."

"I do," Joseph nodded. "Thirteen."

"We call him Michael."

"Yes. Ironic isn't it that one of your greatest enemies would, in turn, become one of your greatest friends? The mysteries of God's plan never cease to astound me. But beware…he relies on you more than he would ever admit."

"How so?"

"He was injured at the lighthouse, was he not?"

"Yes."

"And he *was* wearing his mask, correct?"

"Again, yes," Gavin answered.

"He is losing his power," Joseph smiled, "and you, my friend, are responsible."

"What are you talking about?"

Joseph's smile grew into a proud, exaggerated beaming, "Because, in you, as Thirteen has spent more and more time with you, he has seen Jesus. Michael cannot serve two masters, both Jesus and his mask; therefore, he's conflicted. He too will have to choose between his own devices and those of God's! Exciting isn't it?"

Gavin nodded, his thoughts no longer about the deceptive words alluding to his unborn child, but on the hope that Michael had come to see the truth of Jesus Christ. Joseph reached out and firmly grasped Gavin by his shoulders.

"It has been so wonderful to see you, my friend," he said. "Know that I will remain close."

"I will," Gavin replied. "But what will you do now?"

"Now? It's a beautiful night. I think I'll go for a walk, maybe help someone change a flat tire, let them entertain an angel unaware," Joseph winked.

"You're not going to spread your wings?"

"And take off this lovely suit? I don't think so. Farewell, my friend."

"Goodbye," Gavin smiled, watching as Joseph, his mentor, an angel, faded into the night.

12

Edward Killion sat up sleepily. The early morning sun flooded the streets of Paris with the hope of a new day. He lumbered to the window and looked out at the majestic scene. The Eiffel tower stood as an imposing centerpiece in his view. Cars honked and hurried down the boulevard as commuters worked their way to the metro. But Paris was not his home. The sights and sounds made him miss London all the more. He couldn't wait for this job to be finished.

"Are you up then, brother?" Terrance laughed, stepping from the bathroom in nothing but a towel wrapped tightly about his hips.

As he did, a tea pot came to boil on the stovetop, whistling loudly as steam escaped. Edward acted startled and was left embarrassed by the fact.

"It's only the kettle, Ed," Killion teased. "Should I pour you a cup?"

"Yes, please," Edward replied. "And two sugars if you have it."

"Right. Two sugars."

Killion stirred the tea with a spoon, then placed it on the kitchen counter. Edward excepted the cup thankfully and the two brothers stood in front of the large window, sipping on their morning beverage.

"You're awfully chipper this morning, Terry," Edward remarked. "What, did you sneak a girl in here after I nodded off?"

"No, Ed…though that sounds like it would have been a bloody good idea. I'm just rather looking forward to collecting from the Frenchman."

"I see, brother. What are you going to do when we've finished then, Terry?"

"I haven't thought about it really. I suppose I'll buy an estate, maybe a stable and horses, the yacht I've always dreamed of. How about you, Ed?"

"I'll start a garage that specializes in restoring classic cars. We'll buy 'em, sell 'em, even trade. Oi! I'll get the Aston Martin I've always wanted."

"The DB5?" Killion smiled.

"In blooming silver, just like James Bond drove, but without the ejector seat and machine guns of course."

"You know you don't have to own a garage to by the Aston?"

"Yeah, but if I don't do something with my hands, I'll go crazy. I need to be productive," Edward explained.

Killion understood, smiling as a group of college girls made their way to the nearby university, "I know what I'll be doing with my hands."

"Sod off," Edward laughed.

"Suit yourself," Killion replied, nudging his younger brother playfully with his elbow. "You keep your bloody James Bond car and leave the girls to me. I'm getting dressed. Our ride should be here within the hour."

Edward agreed. He finished his tea and set the cup down on the window's ledge. Perhaps, once this was all over with, he could get what he wanted most: out from beneath his brother's shadow.

****

"Do you think Killion knows his key is a fake?" Sebastian asked as he followed along beside his father, a tray with toast, jam, and coffee balanced effortlessly on his outstretched hand.

"I do not think so," the elder Laurent replied. "Killion relies too much on what he knows, not giving a second thought to the unknown."

The Frenchman opened the door that blocked their path. Within, the young girl stirred in her bed as they entered.

"Bonjour, mon amour," he whispered sweetly. "I have brought you a small breakfast."

The girl sat up groggily, trace remnants of the drug still running its course.

"There should be no rain today, ma fille precieuse. Perhaps we can walk in the garden?"

"Oui," she replied softly.

"I also bought you some new clothes, something to wear other than your nightdress. They are in the bags, the ones sitting over there in the corner," Laurent pointed. "If you would care for a bath, let me know."

Again, the girl replied yes. Sebastian and the Frenchman left the room so that she could eat and dress in peace. She was confused by her host, the room in which she was kept. The drugs made it all the more blurry as she tried to recall how she even arrived in his care. But he seemed like a nice, kind old man. Memories of her family were just that: memories. They were not painful; in fact, she didn't seem to want to return. The thought crossed her mind that she indeed had chosen to leave her parents farm. Perhaps the old man had found her aimlessly walking along the road and offered food and shelter? She looked down at the puncture marks in her arm.

Am I sick? she wondered.

As she ate the toast, she tried to remember why the younger man had injected her. Was it a vaccine? What happened after that? There was a room, with candles...a dinner perhaps. Maybe she'd eaten a delightfully elegant supper with the old man? Her thoughts were too jumbled to decipher completely.

She crunched down on the last bite of toast and sipped her coffee. The girl wanted now to see what fine things her host had brought her. Excitedly, like Christmas morning, she tore through the bags, sorting the contents onto the bed. There was a pair of dark blue denim jeans, tall brown leather riding boots with buckles at the top of the calf, several cute t-shirts, lace underwear, socks, a pair of red flats, and lastly, a beautiful antique white linen sundress covered in softly colored flowers. Hues of mustard, oxblood, and cornflower blue petals graced the olive tinted stems and leaves that wound in an intricately playful pattern on the dress. She loved it.

The girl quickly removed the sheer night clothes and slipped gratefully into one of the pairs of new underwear. She readied to pull the sundress down over her head when she paused, a sharp pain in her lower back causing her to do so. She did her best to twist awkwardly, hoping to see what might be wrong as she felt along her back. Her fingers hit the tender spot and her eyes grew wide with the pain.

She could feel the two small wounds. Now aware of them, they burned. But how did they get there? Had she fallen, scraped her back? She tried to remember, but she simply could not.

The sundress fit her budding frame perfectly. She looked down at her small, bare feet, then up at her slender legs, the hem of the dress falling just above her round knees. Thin straps held the dress at her shoulders, her blonde hair falling to meet them wistfully. She wished so badly she had a mirror. The riding boots were decidedly better paired with the jeans so she slipped her toes into the pretty red flats, once more admiring the fit of the clothing.

Happy, like in a dream, she spun on her toes, the dress flowing playfully as she laughed, her petite voice echoing in the small, stone room. Just outside the door, the Frenchman smiled, listening to her joy, envious of her youthfulness.

"Are you dressed?" he asked, knocking softly on the door.

"I am," the girl laughed.

"Then we shall go for that walk."

****

The black Mercedes arrived just as expected. The Killion brothers left their flat and climbed into the backseat of the sedan.

"Do you have it?" the driver asked, his eyes shaded by darkly tinted sunglasses.

"Have what, mate?" Killion toyed.

"The key, *mate*," the man replied mockingly, his English marred by his heavy French accent.

"I wouldn't have come to Paris if I didn't."

"Then we're set," the driver said, pulling away from the curb. "We've got about three hours travel ahead of us. Get comfortable. It's a long drive."

****

The Frenchman escorted the girl through the crumbling chateau and out into the warmth of the morning sun. She squinted in the glorious light, her young face exhibiting her happiness. She walked beside Laurent, her arm wrapped around his.

Her eyes lit up as they circled the house, following along the border of the castle's moat: the garden beyond was blooming, full of rich red and white roses, bright yellow tulips, stunning purple orchids.

"C'est magnifique!" she exclaimed, drunk with the indulgent scent of the garden.

"Oui, le plus incroyable," he agreed, "most incredible indeed."

The drug she'd been repeatedly given, as hoped, delivered a unique side affect. Though it was a simple sedative, for a girl such as this, a *dreamer*, it lessened her sense of reality and allowed for her to dream while awake. In a sense, she was travelling between spiritual and physical planes, the past present, and future aligning into one blended vision, aligning what was, is, and is to come. He had, without the help of the demonic realm, created a psychotropic sleepwalker.

Laurent marveled at the weed entangled vista. Though random wildflowers sprouted amongst the overgrown brush, thistles and thorns ruled the landscape. If she was indeed envisioning beautifully manicured flowerbeds, then it meant that Laurent was right: this young girl was the dreamer he needed, necessary to his plan. For she would be capable of seeing what no other eyes could see.

He turned his attention back to the decrepit, once-beautiful, still-captivating structure of the chateau. There was no future for this place, no restoration that could truly save its walls and towers from their fate; a fate so cruelly implemented by the unforgiving passage of time. If the girl truly saw flowers and gardens, then it was a vision of the chateau's glorious past, before age, weather, and fire touched it with their wrath. And if the girl truly saw the past, then she was most capable indeed. She was meant to open *the* door, Triton's door, rusted, worn, and mated to the old key. Laurent was sure of this!

****

The landmarks of Paris disappeared from Killion's sight as the black sedan travelled south on the E5 in the direction of Orleans, traversing the somewhat-congested thoroughfare in haste.

"So where are we headed then?" Killion asked of the driver from the backseat., watching out the side window as they passed exit signs for Orly airport.

"Monsieur Laurent is the master of a great property. *That* is where we are headed," the man replied gruffly. "As I said before, the ride is long, a little over three hundred kilometers. Relax, enjoy the view. When we reach Tours, I'll drive you past the cathedral and the basilica, if you'd like."

"Two old churches," Killion sighed, "how lovely. Only, I can hardly wait."

"What is it you Englishmen say...*chin up, chap*...no?" the driver snorted as he laughed. "From Tours, it's only another hour. It will pass before you know it. Laurent, he has good wine too."

Edward rode in silence. He was less concerned with where they were going and how long the trip would take. He simply wanted to be done. The dangers of the lives they lived were exciting, something he would surely miss. But he now had the money to do whatever he wanted. If that meant never again firing a gun, he would be completely satisfied with that outcome. After all, killing was his brother's sport, not his own. He would be happy with a woman, just one woman, the rest of his life. The years of unrewarding complicacy spawned as party to the elder Killion's lust for carnality and death had left him alone and now ever so jaded, a fact which he wished dearly to rectify. But his brother had promised him that this was their last job, the one that would set them up for the rest of their lives. Edward wanted to believe so with every fiber of his miserable being.

"The Frenchman, he will be there, in person? And he will have our money as well, I presume," Killion wondered.

"Absolutely, monsieur," the driver assured. "He is most gracious of your particular talents and ability to elude certain questioning authorities. Laurent said you did such a fine job for him in Los Angeles. I'm sure your reward will be great, mon ami."

"Undeniably," Killion smiled, once more returning his attention to the quickly passing road signs and markers.

****

Michael couldn't sleep. Even with his eyes closed tight, his mind forced him to see and question. There was a battle going on inside of him. Somewhere in his subconscious, he stood face-to-face, toe-to-toe, with Thirteen. They stared into each other's eyes, challenging one another: the mortal and the monster.

His imagination filled the landscape with sprawling, sandy dunes, the wind arid, the sun sweltering. Hot wind blew furiously, whipping spirals of sand up around the two figures mercilessly as they encountered one another.

"What would you have me do?" Michael shouted over the howling wind.

Thirteen stood indignant, "I would have you be a man, hold to your convictions, claim your legacy!"

"But what if my convictions have changed?" Michael argued.

"Then you're pathetic," Thirteen scoffed from behind his hideous mask. "You have such a gift, a power that all would be envious of."

"How so?"

"For one, you can nearly fly! Also," Thirteen reminded, "my mask makes you immortal. I think the majority of people would love to be the possessor of power that would exempted them from the chains of death."

"What if I do not possess the power, but the power possesses me?" Michael reasoned. "When I wear the mask, I am not myself, I am you."

"And that's a negative because?"

"Because when I'm you, I forget who I am, what I have...I forget about love,' Michael admitted.

"Who are you?" Thirteen laughed. "I remember when we reveled in chaos, the world around us ours to manipulate and twist to our ambitions. What a blessing!"

"Blessing? You think this power is a blessing?" Michael growled. "It's a curse! It has haunted my family for more generations than I can count. My forefathers were blinded by what you call a *blessing*, but I am changing that mistake. Cain will not share in the same life of desperate servitude."

"And who would you serve if you didn't serve yourself, who greater than you?" Thirteen asked. "Seriously, who would you serve? God?"

"Perhaps."

Thirteen threw his head back in laughter, "What on earth would God really want with you, a murderer and psychopath? Even if you chose to serve Him, He wouldn't want you! You're nothing without my mask, nothing!"

"Maybe, maybe not."

"Are you kidding me? Do you even realize what you're saying? You'd have been dead a decade ago if it weren't for me! Do you remember when Triton said you were too weak, told your father that you could never be me? He tried to convince *dear old dad* that the Laurent line had been broken by your pathetic weakness, but father pushed you, encouraged you more than I ever would have. When everyone, me included, thought that father was wasting his time, you, Michael Laurent, surprised your greatest critics and became a mighty warrior, powerful beyond what even Triton himself imagined. And now, you would walk away from that power to serve God? The very God whose lies about His son have tricked millions into false hope of deliverance and redemption? You poor soul..."

"If they were lies, then why did Triton fight for so long against the will of God?"

"Because," Thirteen laughed once more, "it's good fun!"

Michael fumed.

"And can you honestly say that you believe in a fairytale claiming that Jesus Christ, God's *only begotten son*, died on a cross at the hands of the

Romans, was buried in a tomb…pronounced dead, of course…and then managed to rise again, as if from slumber, only three short days later?"

"You say that like it's too unbelievable, when the things I've done with your mask would by some be considered miraculous in and of themselves," Michael rebuked. "You and I very well know that Jesus death *was* real and that God's love *is* real. How many demons have we seen cast out in His name, seen destroyed by His angels? To question the truth of Jesus Christ is stupidity in its simplest form."

"So why are you thinking this now, after thirty-five years of breathing in this world's hate and simply giving the world what it deserves? What has made you abandon your legacy, your power?"

"Truth."

"Truth? Oh Michael, poor, poor Michael," Thirteen mocked, "have you been set free?"

"Free indeed."

"Well then," Thirteen conceded, "what's done is done. I can't believe I'm saying this, but if you're sure of…this *truth*…then I'm happy for you. I can't stop you from living a newfound life of piety and service to God. You *must* follow your convictions and be the man who you ought to be. All you need to do now is leave the mask with me, leave it behind, forget *all* about it. After all, now that you have *God*, you don't *need* the mask anymore, right? After all, His *grace is sufficient*…"

Michael looked on, his resolute jaw softening, his eyes no longer burning with determination, "I have use for it just a little while longer."

"Is that so?" Thirteen grinned.

"Once I've defeated father and destroyed the key, Tritons plot with it, I will have no need for the mask."

"Then, sadly," Thirteen chuckled, "I do not believe you are truly free."

****

"I never thanked you," the pretty young girl smiled, her arms still entwined with Laurent's.

"For what, dear child?"

"For my beautiful clothes," she laughed. "This dress, it is so feminine, so lovely. I don't deserve something this grownup."

"It is but a simple thing," Laurent sighed. "And you deserve so much more, mon cher. You are special."

"Oh, but this place," she squealed in delight, "the wonderful flowers, the beautiful chateau...*you*...I think I'm falling in love?"

"With me?" he chuckled. "I am but a humble old man. I could nearly be your grandfather. I am no one to love."

"But you care for me, protect me, dote such lovely gifts," the girl said, her hand clutched adamantly to her chest, "you must love me as well, no?"

Laurent stopped her where they stood, placing his hands on her bare arms and looking her in the eyes, "Indeed, I love you, mon cher, but not in the way you think. I am fifty years your elder. If, perhaps, I was much, much younger, then we could be lovers, like when I met my wife in my youth, but you are too precious for a man such as I to touch. I will not spoil such a sweet young flower."

Her lips curled into a pout, her eyes longing.

"You remind me very much of my wife when she was your age, when we first met, God rest her. She was an American, on holiday in France. I trampled her petals without regard, I'll never forget. But we were so close in age. You, mon cher, are like the daughter she and I dreamed of, but never had. I do love you, my dear, and let's just leave it at that.

13

As indirectly promised, the overeager driver made sure his route to the Frenchman included the renowned landmarks of the city of Tours. The Killion brothers feigned enthusiasm at the sight of old buildings that did little to arouse their interest in the man's birthplace. Honestly, how could a few ancient buildings compare to the massive fortune that awaited them? The unwanted loitering simply drew out the time, made the anticipation of meeting with the Frenchman all the more harrowing.

"Shall we be on then?" Killion urged, the driver excusing himself from the car and returning with a hot coffee.

"Merci beaucoup," the driver said as he returned. "But I cannot pass that shop without purchasing coffee. It is the best in all of France, I assure you. Perhaps you would reconsider? I can still go get you some, if you like?"

"No, let's just get on with it."

"Que vous le souhaitez, my friend," he laughed, starting the car and pulling away from the café.

The last hour of the drive, same as the rural scenery, passed quickly. Soon, the car turned left off the main road and parked in a large, gravel courtyard, the tiny stones crunching beneath the weight of the sedan.

"Follow me," the driver ordered, exiting the car.

He led the brothers across the courtyard and to the small stone overpass that bridged the chateau's primeval moat, the water beneath dark and murky. They followed compliantly, looking down at the tranquil, cloudy water as they crossed.

"This property seems to be quite old," Edward mused, following his brother and their guide through the tall double doors that marked the entrance into the macabre den of the Frenchman.

"Indeed," a voice echoed in answer from somewhere within.

Edward shot his brother a look. Killion nodded in silent understanding. There was a feeling in the air, an inherent level of creepiness, that could not be explained, as if the place were charged with static, a high presence of ionic energy in the dank atmosphere.

"This house is very old," the voice continued, growing louder as they navigated the scattered rubble in the open, middle court of the chateau, continuing closer to the dim hall across the way. "Thirteenth century, to be precise."

The driver led them into the room, beckoning courteously for the brothers to pass, "After you."

The voice was undeniable, soft, yet strong. Killion had heard it several times, speaking to him from behind the veil of cellular communication. The face was as expected, but the stature did not meet Killion's expectations. The Frenchman was more humble than he ever could have imagined, at least humble for a man who possessed nearly unrivaled power and sway in the world's courts.

"It's a pleasure to speak to you in person," Killion gushed, bowing in a show of respect.

"And you," Laurent smiled.

The door to the room slammed shut loudly, echoing throughout the ancient corridors. Both Terrance and Edward relayed their sudden shock. Before either man could protest, hands groped their bodies, searching beneath their clothing. Sebastian and the driver frisked them for weapons.

"What's this about?" Killion grunted smugly. "You don't trust us?"

"Oh, but I do," Laurent replied, watching as his son and servant verified the men were unarmed. "I trust you to be predictable. After all, what is a professional without his gun?"

"Apparently *unprofessional*, it would seem," Killion acknowledged, knowing that he hid nothing on his person. "And too trusting of his host."

"You have nothing to fear from me," Laurent encouraged. "This is simply a matter of protocol."

Sebastian and the driver finished their search with satisfactory results. Certainly, Killion had told the truth: the brothers were unarmed.

"To business then?" Killion said, adjusting the fit of his suit coat now that their prying was complete.

Laurent nodded at his son. Sebastian reached behind a small bush that had grown right up through the floor, its trunk forcing the mason work apart, its sprawling roots causing the old stone to crack. Removing a large, black canvas duffle bag, Sebastian tossed it loudly onto the table, unzipped the opening and spread the mouth of the bag wide for Killion and Edward to inspect.

Killion swallowed deep, forcing back his excitement. The contents of the bag were more than double what he'd received in Franklin's briefcase.

"All there?" he questioned.

"It appears that you do not trust me either," Laurent laughed. "I wish you no ill will, the money is all there: thirty-seven million, seventy-eight thousand, two hundred and ninety Euros…I rounded up…the equivalent of fifty million US dollars."

Terrance approached the bag and inspected the contents. Well pleased, he removed his wallet from his back pocket, flipped open the billfold, and withdrew the old key from amongst the paper money.

"As promised," he said haughtily, extending the key to Laurent.

"Not exactly," the Frenchman winked. "Follow me please."

Killion glared uneasily at his brother. What was this all about?

Sebastian's firm nudge sent the two hesitant men on course. Laurent led them down a flight of winding stone steps and into a small corridor lined with small wine cellars branching to the left and right.

"This way, please," Laurent continued on.

They followed to what seemed the midway point of the corridor and turned into a small alcove. The Frenchman knocked politely on the half-rotten, wooden door that blocked their path.

"It is I, mon cher," he announced.

The door opened, the young girl eager to accompany Laurent. He took her hand and the group moved across her makeshift chamber, stopped once more by another wooden door, this one much heavier, firmly held by strong iron hinges and locks.

"Go ahead," Laurent urged.

"With what?" Killion asked in confusion, the dead-end less of a question in his mind than the mysterious, beautiful young girl living amidst the well-aged wine bottles in the cellar.

"The key, *Triton's key*," Laurent explained. "I cannot wait to see it used for its purpose."

"This key unlocks that door?" Killion mused.

Laurent chuckled and muttered something under his breath in French, "That would be silly, mon ami. The door is unlocked. In my possession, there is a skeleton key that operates all the locks, all the doors within this place…all except one. Please, enter."

The heavy door creaked open, the hinges laboring against age and rust. What little light that existed flooded in through the open doorway, the shadows cast by Killion and the others concealing whatever the already pitch-black room hid.

"Here," Laurent said, pushing past Killion and flicking a match, the small orange flame igniting a candle's wick.

The candle stood on the corner of a small wooden pulpit, the center of which held an ancient leather-bound text. The cover was remarkably intricate. Scrollwork and numerals marked the bulky tome. The pages were yellowed and mildewed.

With only a small glow coming from the candle, the room was too large to mark its boundaries. Edward, certain his eyes were playing tricks on him, could have sworn he saw a set of blinking eyes in the distance, on his left, then, seconds later, again on the right.

In the center of the room stood a curious, solitary door, no walls adjoined to the frame. Killion approached the door cautiously, though why, he did not know. It only seemed as if he should.

The candle's flickering glow did little to illuminate beyond the door, but in its light, Killion studied the frame, following it down to where it met the floor, large iron brackets securing it firmly to the hand-fitted stone blocks on which he stood.

Slowly, he reached out and touched the door frame, expecting it to be dry and termite ridden. But the wood was solid and oddly damp. Killion sniffed his fingers, inhaling the oddly sweet aroma, like roses and vanilla.

"What is this?" he wondered.

Laurent smiled, "This is the end of your task. Please, use the key, open the door."

Killion retrieved the old key from his pants pocket, stared at it momentarily, then hastily slipped it cleanly into the rusting lock on the strange door. He glanced over his shoulder, Edward looking on, waiting for his brother with bated breath. Killion nodded and returned his attention to the door. Confidently, he twisted the key, but nothing happened. The lock was obstinate, solid. Again, he tried, but the key would not turn.

"What's wrong with it?" he asked angrily, turning to Laurent, his hand still clinging to the key where it rested in the lock.

"Isn't it obvious?" the Frenchman said.

"No, it's not," Killion barked. "Why isn't Triton's key working?"

"Because, Monsieur Killion, that is not *Triton's key*!"

Sebastian reached beneath his trench coat and removed his Sig Sauer 9mm, focusing the front sight on Killion's chest. The driver did the same, pulling a pistol and pressing it into the back of Edward's head, the hammer clicking back ominously.

"There's no way," Killion shouted. "This key came from *them*! They traded it for their lives. I took it from Delilah, right before I ended her life!"

"Then you ended her life for naught," Laurent scolded. "They tricked you, mon ami. They gave you a fake!"

"Not possible," Killion argued.

"And how is that so?"

"Because…there's simply no way. Why would they risk the lives of their loved ones for a fake?" Killion reasoned.

"Perhaps they assumed you wouldn't know the difference and that you would return it to me?" Laurent answered. "And perhaps, upon this exact scenario playing out, I would, in anger of your failure, kill you?"

Sebastian now clicked back the hammer on his automatic, his aim still true and steady.

"You seem to act as if you knew this would happen. What are you playing at?" Killion demanded.

"That's the real question," the Frenchman admitted. "You see, I already knew that the key you would bring me would not work. For, you see, while you were busy with Franklin and his Order, while you played cat and mouse with Delilah and her new friends, Sebastian retrieved the *true* key from the Branson's home. The fact that you did such a fantastic job distracting them is why I have decided to let you live. Come."

The Killion brothers were led at gunpoint back up to the great hall, then told to look at the black bag on the table as Laurent spoke. Sebastian and the driver remained vigilant, their pistols ready should either of their guests try anything stupid.

"As I said earlier, the money is all there, but now, you see…and certainly you understand in lieu of present circumstances…not all *the* money is *your* money."

Killion's jaw flinched in anger. Edward shrunk inward, his dream of freedom from his brother's grasp violently ripped from him.

"I will generously allow each of you five million Euros," the Frenchman explicated. "You will then disappear with the money and *never* speak of this place or what has transpired. I expect you to leave France expediently and never set foot again in my proud country. What's more, I assume you will return to London, but I know of your private estate on Cyprus, Monsieur Killion. My eyes and ears are far reaching, have no bounds. If I learn that you have even hinted of our arrangement, you will most assuredly join your beloved Delilah in death."

Killion burned inside. Sebastian smiled coyly.

"Do we have an accord?" Laurent asked firmly.

"We have a sodding accord," Killion confirmed.

"Very good choice, mon ami. Here is what I will have you do. The sedan in which you were brought, drive that back to Paris. Obviously, we know precisely where your safe-house is. The Mercedes has a GPS tracker: deviate from the course or arrive to your destination later than expected, and the car will detonate. Upon arrival at your apartment, you will clear out your belongings, then drive to Charles de Gaulle. There will be a pair of one-way tickets to London Heathrow waiting for you. Leave the car in the parking section, and again, we'll know its location, board that plane and never look back. Once in London, you are free to live out your lives however you deem fit. Any questions?"

"How much time do we have to do all this?" Edward asked.

"You are approximately three hours from Paris, then another forty-five minutes from the airport. With possible traffic conditions factored in, plus time to collect your effects, I believe six hours will suffice. Anything else?"

"No," Killion growled.

"Then I bid you adieu, Monsieur Killion," Laurent nodded, his hand motioning politely towards the exit.

****

"Their flight will arrive at Charles de Gaulle at 8:35am your time, the day after next," Solomon Grier informed Arthur Blackwood via his secure line.

"I'll be there at 8:00am," Arthur chuckled, "just to be safe. Knowing Jean Luc, he'll have us there at 7:00am anyway, watching for traps and suspicious folk. A mysterious blighter he is."

"His suspicions are almost always right," Grier reminded. "He's one of the best for a reason."

"Yeah, well…I don't think the man has slept more than three hours a night for the last decade, always clothed, a gun in his hand…there's suspicious and then there's paranoid! Belesur, friend as he may be, is most definitely the latter: paranoid."

"After the things we did, in the cover of darkness, unbeknownst to the world, striking from the shadows, killing and disappearing with the breeze, I don't blame him. Jean Luc was a religious man, probably still is. Some people say *for God and country*, I don't think he ever reconciled that. He did his duty without question, but prayed for forgiveness even while the enemies blood was still sticky on his hands. That's enough to drive any man mad, especially after twenty years of covert actions. If it weren't for Jean Luc, I may never have found God."

"Hey, mate...you know where I found God, right?" Blackwood asked, his voice already tinged with laughter. "At the bottom of an empty pint. So I kept drinking, just to see Him again each time I finished."

"You're rotten in so many ways," Grier sighed. "I can't even have a serious conversation with you without then having you make light of a man's convictions."

"Oi, I'm just having a laugh. It's how I deal with things. You know that, mate."

"I do."

"You used to laugh," Arthur pointed out. "What happened?"

Grier grew quiet, "Delilah died, Art. That's what happened."

"Alright then," Arthur replied. "We get the sod who did it. We get Killion. By God, we will be his judges, jury, and executioners. How's that for religious conviction?"

"I don't think you get it completely," Solomon laughed, "but it's a novel idea. Spend a little more time with Jean Luc and you might."

"Ten years worth of bloody missions at the man's side did teach me a thing or two."

"Are you going to make another joke?"

"No, seriously. Jean Luc, if he weren't so proficient with a weapon, would have made an excellent priest or monk, or whatever religious men go off and do."

"So?"

"I'm just saying that he made an impression, that's all."

"Good then," Solomon chuckled. "As for Paris, and Killion, it's in your hands now. Keep me posted. When the job is done, you let me know."

"Indeed, Sully. As always, a pleasure. Goodbye."

****

"Who the bloody hell does the Frenchman think he is?" Killion growled as he sat behind the wheel of the black Mercedes, racing along the country road, heading back to Paris.

"At least he didn't kill us," Edward acknowledged.

"But only ten million Euros? He's a greedy bugger! We did the job and he owes us. It's bad business it is!"

"We've got Franklin's money and with what the Frenchman did pay, we can live without a worry. Be thankful, brother."

"And what do you suppose we should do then, follow the Frenchman's orders? Leave France?" Killion barked. "I have half a mind to go back there and kill the bloody old fool!"

"Yeah?" Edward replied. "Well then, listen to the other half of your brain and sort it out first. Doing something rash will only get us both killed. Do what you want, but from now on, count me out."

"What's that, little brother?"

"I said count me out. I'm done, done with plotting and looting and killing and hiding, just done."

"You make us sound like bloody pirates!" Killion laughed.

"Seriously, I'm done. When we get back to London, that's it. I want my share and that's that."

Killion glared at his brother. Was he truly serious?

"So what, you'll take your money and open your ruddy garage, is that it?" Killion mocked. "You'll buy, sell, trade? Sounds bloody boring, brother."

"What do you care what I do with my life?!" Edward snapped back.

"I just want you to be happy, little brother."

"Then it's the first time," Edward said. "I've followed you, looked up to you my entire life. All I wanted was for you to look at me as capable, like one of your old mates from the war. And what did I get? I'll tell you! I got drug into all your little games. We were never partners, you used me all along."

Killion softened. His brother's words were so sharp, rang so true. But his anger with Laurent was too great. Revenge was all he could think about.

"Are you even listening?" Edward asked.

"I am."

"Well from here on out, Terry. We're no longer partners…simply brothers."

"And what's that mean?"

"It *means* that if you want to go after the Frenchman, you're on your own. When we get back to Paris, we're splitting up the money and taking the tickets to London. Once there, you can decide whether returning to France is worth your life. But if you decide to kill the Frenchman, you won't have my help; you *are* on your *own!*"

14

Kayla sat anxiously in her seat as the A319 airliner began its slow taxi away from the gate and onto the runway. She leaned forward as much as her seatbelt would allow, reaching to the seat ahead, her hand finding Jamie's shoulder where he sat, sharing the three-seat row with Gavin and Ashley. Marley sat to her right, in the window seat, trying desperately to see what was outside the plane. Ethan played between them, more interested in the toy Kayla had provided than anything else, even the roar of the turbofan engines.

The whole travel situation had become exacerbated by Kayla's decision to bring Ethan's car seat. After all, she reasoned it would be safer to fly if he was properly buckled and having the car seat would also make the shuttle trip from Pittsburgh International to her parents more legal than the toddler simply sitting on *mommy's lap*. This meant that, on top of all other preparations, Jamie had to remove the seat from Kayla's car, carry it through the airport, and finally battle with the plane's stubborn seatbelt to ensure proper fit before then battling to get Ethan into the seat ahead of takeoff.

What an ordeal, he had said in no unexaggerated terms. Kayla smiled as she recalled his words, his frustrated huffs as annoying as they were funny. She looked down two rows and across the aisle to where Michael, Elizabeth and Cain sat. Everyone was settled and everything felt fine. But still, Kayla was nervous. It wasn't the impending flight, or possible turbulence that worried her. No, this was the first time they'd flown with their kids. Who knew what was in store for them at twenty-three thousand feet.

Before she knew it, the plane was in the air and they were on their way to Pittsburgh, one step closer to Paris. The flight was a very short hour. They seemed to land only after just taking off. At one point Kayla thought she heard Gavin joking that he could see his and Ashley's house as they flew over North East Ohio. But the plane arrived in Pittsburgh without event. Even the children had behaved wonderfully.

Now, they all stood at the foot of the driveway leading up to the Rose family's large rural home on the outskirts of Robinson Township, PA, watching as the shuttle van left on its return trip to the airport. Gavin and Michael carried what little luggage they'd brought. Jamie followed behind, lugging Ethan's car seat, as they headed for the impressive wrap-around front porch. Walter and Evelyn Rose were waiting for them, sipping coffee from colorful mugs as they swung slowly on their whitewashed porch swing.

"Oh my goodness!" Evelyn exclaimed as Marley raced up the wooden steps.

She stood and hugged her granddaughter, then reached out to softly touch Ethan's red cheeks. Kayla set him down and they all took turns hugging, and exchanging greetings. The Rose's introduction to the Laurent family was short and sweet.

"Who's hungry?" Grandpa Walt, as the kids called him, belted out. "I've got the griddle going, The hotcakes are hot, the eggs are scrambled, and the bacon is extra crispy!"

They all nodded enthusiastically and followed Walter and Evelyn into the house. The kids immediately scoured the expansive lower-level rooms for toys while the grownups caught up on things.

"How was the flight?" Evelyn asked with a warm smile. "Did the kids do ok?"

"They did, mom," Kayla answered. "Hardly made a peep!"

"And Ashley," Evelyn continued. "I haven't heard from you in a while. How's the museum work?"

"It's great," Ashley said, her eyes wandering into the distance.

"And what else should I know?" the grandmother asked with a perceptive wink.

"Oh," Ashley suddenly felt a little sheepish, happy but embarrassed. "There is something else!"

"Well go on," Evelyn smiled, placing her hands on her daughter's belly, "or do I have to wait for the baby to tell me herself."

"Her?" Ashley laughed.

"Call it *motherly intuition*, and I'll take that as confirmation. Congratulations, sweetie," Evelyn continued. "You hear that Walter, you're going to be a grandpa *again*."

"Heavens…you mean little Ashley?" Walter gushed, flipping a pancake and setting down the spatula so he could properly hug his daughter, then give Gavin an awkward and unexpected high-five. "Well done, *daddy*."

Jamie laughed and nudged his stunned brother-in-law, "You guys have been married for five years now. We're all adults and they know you have sex."

Everyone followed in happy laughter. Ashley's news was truly worth celebrating: a new life amongst the death they'd only so recently witnessed. Michael soaked in the atmosphere. Was this what a real family was like? When Elizabeth gave birth to Cain, Michael informed his father, but only as a formality. There was no joy on the other end of the line when he'd made the long distance call to France, only the prospect of another Laurent bound to Triton's legacy. Elizabeth, too, was happy. She felt safe in this place, with Walter and Evelyn. And though she didn't know why, every moment that passed reassured her that they were in good company. The Rose's simply had a way about them. Kayla had been right. This was the right thing to do.

"So do you know when you're leaving then?" Walter asked as they ate the delicious farm-fresh breakfast.

"Not yet, dad," Jamie answered. "I'm waiting on a message, with specifics, but I was told it would be tonight."

"And this is really what you want to do, chase this man and this key to Europe?"

"We have to," Gavin confirmed. "Otherwise, this might never end. I can't have that hanging over all of our children."

"All because of New York?' Walter questioned.

"All because of Jack," Kayla reminded. "What we went through in New York was only a continuation of what he went through, dad. Gavin is right: this could go on forever if we refuse to act."

"And what if you fail?" Evelyn chimed in. "What if the Frenchman wins? What happens to the kids?"

"You guys would become their legal guardians," Jamie answered.

"What do you think, Michael?" Walter prompted. "You've been pretty quiet this whole time. You don't strike me as shy. Do my kids have a chance?"

Michael looked around the table, everyone's eyes fixed on him in turn. He wasn't sure exactly what to say, he'd simply enjoyed feeling so normal for once.

"There won't be any need for talk like that," he promised, "because we're all coming back. We'll take care of each other, as a family, just like you all have always done. We'll be fine!"

"You're a bold man," Walter laughed. "I like that. You're right: you'll all be just fine."

A bleep from Jamie's phone announced the arrival of a new text message. He quickly dug into his jeans pocket and removed the phone, swiping the touch screen and reading the message.

"*6:35pm. Delta. Terminal C. Tickets waiting at the gate. Good luck,*" Jamie read aloud for everyone to hear.

"Well, now we have a time," Gavin added. "And France is what, six hours ahead of us?"

"Yes," Michael answered.

"And how long is the flight?" Gavin continued.

"Eight hours or so," Michael confirmed.

"Then we know when we should be arriving," Ashley smiled.

"You sure know a lot about France?" Walter chuckled.

"I should. I was born there," Michael explained.

"But you have no accent?"

Michael smiled, remembering his mother's kind face, "My mom was American. I was schooled in America and commuted home to France for the summers. But I am fluent. I lived with my father for several years after I graduated from university, but moved to the States for a job. That's how I met my wife, Elizabeth."

"And what happened to your mother?" Evelyn asked curiously.

"She died when I was away, my first year of grad school. I dropped out and moved back to France to be with my father. But he didn't need my support."

"Well I'm sorry to hear that," Evelyn sighed, tossing her used napkin onto the table and then slowly standing to begin cleaning up the dishes. "Come along, Walter. Help me clean up. Let the kids talk about their plan."

"So what time is it now," Ashley asked.

"Almost noon," Jamie said, looking at his watch.

"Today is going by way too fast!" she exclaimed.

"We have to be back at the airport in about six hours," Jamie continued. "Are we sticking with the *'we don't have a plan'* plan?"

"I think we'll figure it out once we meet with Grier's men," Gavin replied. "Our plans never seemed to work in Chicago, let's not push this. If we're patient, things might play out better than we could arrange."

"I hope so," Kayla said. "Ugh…only six hours. How will I ever say goodbye to the kids?"

"I know it's going to be tough," Jamie admitted, reaching across the table to take hold of her hands reassuringly. "It's all a matter of faith now."

"I'll be here," Elizabeth smiled, "and your parents are wonderful. Everything will be fine."

"*Fine…*" Ashley repeated. "We've said that word what seems like a dozen times in the last hour and a half. How can we be so sure?"

"Like Jamie said," Gavin grinned, looking his pregnant wife in the eyes, "now we walk by faith. The time for sight is long gone."

"I want to spend as much time with Marley and Ethan as I can before we leave," Kayla said, leaving the table and heading out to the enclosed porch where the kids were playing with old, age-worn metal dump trucks and faded wooden building blocks.

Elizabeth followed. And soon, the rest of the table did as well. With such little time left before their flight, it seemed right to spend it as a family, focusing not on what lay ahead, but rather on all for which they could be thankful.

The next few hours passed quickly, the house filled with laughter and the sounds of happy children. But Walter had grown restless. True, he hadn't seen his grandchildren since last Christmas and having both his daughters home was like the old days, but he was unsettled and not sure why.

"James, Gavin," the gray-haired man said suddenly, almost gruffly, "you boys: give me a hand out back will you?"

The men followed their father-in-law respectfully. Whether it was his age, or the cop left in him, or the fact that he was the father of their wives, made them exceedingly compliant, especially under *his* roof.

"What do you need, dad?" Gavin asked as the three men exited onto the rear porch and stepped down towards the immaculate garden full of homegrown corn, juicy red tomatoes, multicolored peppers, and assorted herbs.

"Look over there," Walter smiled pointing to another section of garden, orange painted stakes driven into the ground at each of its corners, marking the boundaries of his newest expansion. "Carrots, potatoes, green beans: they're all doing great. Even the lettuce is flourishing. I don't know what's in the soil, but, by God, anything grows!"

They stopped for a moment so Walter could inspect something on a plant, but what exactly, they did not know. He then stood abruptly and marched in the direction of his appropriately painted red barn, really just an extra large wooden shed, but big enough to keep all sorts of gardening tools and supplies, even park his wide-deck John Deere riding mower and various pull-behind accessories. To the buildings immediate left was the chicken coop, the birds clucking and strutting as the men approached the wire fencing.

"You boys know that the eggs we had this morning came right out of that hen house there?" Walter asked with a chuckle. "You won't get much fresher than that!"

He unlocked the shed, swung the tall, wide red doors open and disappeared inside, returning quickly with a well-used shovel. Handing it to Jamie, he and Gavin looked on questioningly. What was Walter up to?

"Come on then," their father-in-law ordered. "We've got work to do."

****

Killion parked the black Mercedes. He exited the car and glared at Edward to do the same. Their disagreement had lasted nearly the entire return drive from Laurent's chateau. Each man had given, defended, and swore to stand true to their argument, Killion pleading to stay, Edward promising to leave.

Upon reaching their apartment, the atmosphere was no different. Edward gathered up his computer and miscellaneous devices. Killion leaned against the kitchenette counter, pouring a glass of whiskey.

"There's no point in leaving without me, brother," Killion urged. "I won't be the one who's alone, you'll be. Can you handle that? Being all alone?"

"Shut up," Edward ordered disdainfully. "I'm so tired of your games. I'm simply done, with all of it. Just give me my cut and we can end this sodding fight!"

"I know what this is all about," Killion laughed. "You're still angry that you got bested by a little girl. She did beat you rather well. But I admit, your face is looking a bit better, but just a bit."

"She snuck up on me in the dark and bludgeoned me with a bloody table lamp. I'd like to see what you would look like after that kind of blow!"

"Relax," Killion replied, finishing the whiskey and pouring another. "I've got a lovely idea. Why don't we do a proper pub crawl, like we used to back in London. We'll hit all the finest liquor establishments that Paris has to offer, get bloody pissed, bring a couple of young libertines back to this apartment and entirely forget about the Frenchman all together! What do you say?"

"I think it's a rotten idea, brother. And I know you too well. All the French whores in all of Paris would never make you forget about Laurent and his double cross. You want revenge, nothing more. In fact, I bet your real hope is to get me so bleeding plastered that I can't even walk, then you go on your bloody crusade of vengeance and kill the whole lot, any man who's ever associated with the Frenchman. Tell me I'm wrong!"

"You are very wrong indeed. Getting drunk is a fantastic plan. In fact," Killion said, knocking back his second drink and again pouring more whiskey, "I'm already started. Come on and catch up, Ed."

Killion quickly gulped his third shot and readied to pour another for himself, but also took another tumbler from the overhead cabinet and poured one for his brother as well. Edward was furious. Why wasn't his brother taking him seriously? He'd had enough.

Edward raced across the room and leapt in the air, his knuckles curled, fist raised, jaw resolute, as he crashed down on his half-cocked, unsuspecting brother. Edward's fist collided with Terrance's nose with an awful *pop,* followed immediately by a heavy flow of blood from both nostrils. The brothers collapsed to the tiled kitchen floor.

"What are you doing?!" Killion gasped, tasting the metallic bite of blood on his tongue as it gushed down over his lips and onto his shirt.

Edward began laughing hysterically. His fingers ached and his brother was a sight. The brave and powerful Killion, reduced to tears on the floor of their makeshift hideaway, cramped between two sets of cabinets, blood all over his face and hands, had finally felt his younger brother's wrath. Edward thought it was wonderful, and oh so freeing. And Killion, though his face throbbed and his blood boiled, he to, for some odd reason, found himself beginning to laugh as well. Edward reached up onto the counter for a towel, then the bottle of whiskey. He tossed the towel to Killion, then took a long swig from the bottle, the strong liquor burning his throat as he swallowed.

"So what's your bloody plan," Edward asked.

Killion wiped his face and pressed the towel against his nose, his head tilted back to help stop the bleeding, "For now, we get blooming pissed. As for the Frenchman, it's simple really. We know exactly where he is. And better, I counted no more than three, him included. That's fantastic odds for men of our talents."

"What about the girl?"

"She was what, fifteen at best? What could she possibly do?! I say we ditch the car, procure weaponry and a new *base of operations*. We have cash, so no need to get noticed. He'll never know what hit him."

"Do you have any old connections here?" Edward wondered, taking another drink.

"What, in Paris? Not really, not anymore...pass that over here, will you?" he said, reaching for the now half-empty bottle. "Back in the military days, one of our group was a *Frenchie*. But I haven't seen him since we all parted ways."

"Can you make contact? Maybe he can help?"

"I doubt it. The man was a loner, super religious, I tell you. He's probably a monk now or a member of the Vatican guard. He'd be of no use."

"What then?"

"Paris is just like London, dear brother," Killion grinned, dry blood crusting his nostrils, the soaked, once-white towel at his side. "The pubs will serve two purposes, well three actually. We can drink away our sorrows, catch a bird or two, maybe *three*, and drop hints of our need to connect with this beautiful city's seedy underworld."

"Just like that?" Edward questioned, taking back the bottle for another swig.

"Just like that."

****

Michael had been watching the minutes tick by on the Rose's country-styled clock that hung on their wall in the well-appointed family room. He sat comfortably next to Elizabeth, his arm draped across her shoulders, his other hand holding hers in her lap. But he too, like Walter, was growing ever more restless as the second hand swept in constant clockwise circles, signifying time, once passed, that he could never again regain.

"Excuse me," he whispered to Elizabeth. "I need to stand."

He un-entangled himself from his wife and paced near the large, stone fireplace that looked well suited for warmth on snowy, cold Pennsylvania winter nights. Kayla returned, having managed to lay both Marley and Ethan down for mid-day naps. Ashley, dozing off, was curled up beside her mother on another couch opposite where Elizabeth sat. Cain still fiddled with one of the old toys.

"Son," Michael called.

Cain, kneeling as he played, jumped up and ran to his father.

"Come here a minute, please. Outside," Michael said, leading them back through the kitchen, into the vast living room and out the front door.

They sat down on the porch swing and stared off nowhere in particular. Overhead, being only a few short miles from the Pittsburgh airport, in and outbound jet traffic could be heard in the distance. They watched a 777 circle above on approach.

"I wanted to make sure we spent a little time together before I have to go," Michael said softly.

"Why do you have to leave?" Cain asked sweetly, his voice so young and pure.

"There are matters at hand that must be resolved," Michael explained, "and, in time, you will come to understand why. What I leave to do will set you free of a fate that has followed the men in our family for generations."

"What do you mean?"

Michael smiled, looking down at his young son, "There's a saying, *the sins of the father*. That is what I'm amending, something that no other Laurent before me could do. But it is what is truly right, what *must* be done."

"Will you see grandpa where you're going?"

"I will indeed."

Cain stopped and thought, his legs swinging inches above the porch below, "What's grandpa like?"

"My father is a man of many qualities, some admirable, son. He's also a man of dualities. Do you know what that means?"

"No," Cain said, shaking his head, processing the new word. "What's a *du-al-i-ty*?"

"It's two things naturally in conflict with one another, in this case, all within something consisting itself of those two parts. For example: your grandfather is humble, but proud, fearsome, yet gentle. Understand?"

"I think so."

"My father is a great man, but also foolish. This too, you will come to understand, just like you'll come to understand that I myself have been quite foolish, taking for granted what matters most to me. But now, after having nearly lost you and your mother, I have woken from my foolishness."

"Does that mean you love me?" Cain asked, looking up, his big questioning eyes searching his father.

"Absolutely and unequivocally, with all my heart," Michael smiled.

****

"Here's good," Walter decided as they stood beneath the shade of tall apple and pear trees.

"And what are we doing?" Jamie asked curiously.

"Dig a hole."

"How deep?"

"I'll let you know once you've started," Walter answered mysteriously.

Jamie thrust the spaded end of the shovel hard into the dirt, kicking down on it with his foot, then scooping out the first lump of crumbling earth. Gavin watched, apparently helping Walter supervise Jamie's work. This continued, Jamie digging ever deeper, Gavin and Walter ever watching.

"That'll do," Walter finally said, the whole a good two feet deep by one foot wide.

"I'm glad," Jamie said, his ungloved hands already growing red and sore from the shovel's handle.

"You know a hard day's work in the field wouldn't hurt you," Walter said with a wink, his hand reaching into his pants pocket and returning with two small, folded pieces of white paper and two green golf pencils. "Each

153

of you now, write everything you're afraid of losing, but also everything you know you need to give up. You follow?"

Gavin and Jamie nodded, taking the paper and pencils, and began scribbling out words, phrases...whatever came to mind. Walter stood in silence, listening to the faint, distinct scratching of lead on paper as he marveled at his two sons-in-law. Their lists took several minutes, each man pausing briefly to consider the assigned topics. This pleased Walter: it meant that the young men were not simply writing, but thinking. When they finished, he picked the shovel up from where Jamie had let it fall and leaned on it, a city cop doing his best to pose like a country boy.

"Do you want to read them?" Gavin asked.

"Nope," Walter smiled, handing Gavin the shovel. "Now fold your papers up and drop them in the hole. James dug, Gavin you bury 'em."

Walter and Jamie watched as Gavin poured the dirt back into the hole, the slips listing their secret convictions disappearing into the earth. When finished, Walter took hold of the shovel and leaned it against the trunk of a nearby fruit tree, then took hold of one of each of his sons' hands and asked them to do the same, forming a ring around the disturbed ground at their feet.

"Pray with me," he led.

Jamie and Gavin closed their eyes. Walter did the same.

"Lord God," he began, "You are so great. Your hands shaped the mountains, formed the valleys. Your voice gave light, brought life. Through Your son, Christ Jesus, we have forgiveness. Today, these boys each planted a seed in Your earth, Lord God. Let that seed grow in thought and mind, reminding them over and again of Your ever abundant blessings and Your undeserved mercy. Lord, help them as they move forward. Guide their steps and keep them keen to what You would have them do, not what their own hearts tell. We all know that the troubles of this world are fleeting, because You have already overcome. But that can be lost when in the midst of battle, when the darkness seems greatest. But You, Lord God, are the light that shines in the darkness. May Your light illuminate their path. In Jesus most holy, precious, and powerful name..."

"Amen," the three men said in unison.

They stood there in silence, still holding hands, bonded by the power of prayer. This moment was so unexpected, but more amazing then could have been imagined and was precisely what Gavin and Jamie needed.

"I still believe that I couldn't have given my beautiful daughters to any two men more deserving than you two," Walter smiled, releasing his grasp on their hands only to now take firm grip of both their shoulders. "I know that what you go to do is an enormous burden and I know you fear for the lives of Kayla and Ashley, but I'm also proud that you are letting them be a part of this. Would I prefer to see you all stay here? Of course. Why would I want any of you risking your lives? But the fact that you are together, family, with a common goal and bond, God will reward that faithfulness, rest assured. In the end, you can only be responsible for your part. Whatever happens in Paris will be God's will, whether we like the outcome or not."

Walter left the two men, taking hold of the shovel and heading back towards the shed. Jamie and Gavin followed solemnly, mulling over his vastly profound words.

"The hour is at hand," Walter announced. "It's time for you all to go. Take that plane, fly to Paris, and end this, once and for all!"

Gavin and Jamie nodded. Walter locked the shed and they returned to the house. Their goodbyes were short and teary-eyed. But the time had come. A honk in the driveway announced the airport shuttle's arrival. They loaded into the van, waiving and wiping away tears, leaving the children in the loving care of Walter, Evelyn, and Elizabeth.

Their tickets were waiting for them, the plan already in motion. They fought off the fear that this might be the last time they see their families and swallowed the lumps of possible inevitability that choked them. Indeed, Paris, and whatever else, lay ahead. Their journey was no longer their own as an uneasy, unspoken thought came to the five companions. The outcome of their venture, whether success or failure followed, could impact the entire world. And that was a staggering notion.

15

The Killion brothers finished concocting their plan, as well as the whiskey. And, besides consuming more alcohol and enjoying the company of loose women, the rest of their plot was quite simple. They were currently initiating phase one: create fear and doubt.

In their drunken state, they managed to navigate, albeit dangerously and at great risk, the busy, winding streets of Paris and leave the explosive-rigged car in a city parking lot, hidden amongst other like-colored vehicles, sure it wouldn't draw attention till the promised fireworks ensued.

This would accomplish two things, or at least they hoped. First, if the car was left at the airport, the GPS location confirming the fact, Laurent might believe the men to have followed his command and fled back to London. But if the car exploded far from its appointed destination, there was hope of Laurent developing a nagging fear; fear that the great Killion was scorned and would deliver retribution. Second, would be the act of creating doubt. The reserved tickets would never be picked up, another part of the Frenchman's clear instructions. If the tickets were never picked up, then the Killion brothers could be anywhere, even stalking Laurent on his own dark and shadowy grounds. Fear and doubt.

After this bold accomplishment, the inebriated brothers were ready for phase two: alcohol and girls. And Killion knew exactly where to start, a quaint bar down a back street, connected by an old, graffiti marred alleyway: a haunt from his old days, when drinks with brothers in arms quenched the horrific nightmares of a secret war.

****

A charcoal Range Rover pulled sharply to the curb, stopping quickly in front of an aging building in Montmartre, found in the 18th district of Paris. Arthur Blackwood looked down at the hastily scribbled address on the bar napkin he held in his hand, then back up at the small, cinderblock warehouse fronted with a dent-ridden automatic garage door. This was the place. He exited the car and was immediately pleased with the volume of constant, noisy traffic. They could do whatever they wanted inside and not be heard.

Arthur quickly surveyed the surrounding buildings, the one Jean Luc had arranged ending up a superb location. There was nothing garish, nothing hinting of a secret operation. The first floor of the old building, from what he could gather, must have once been used as a shipping and receiving warehouse for a local business or individual. The steel garage door was joined by a steel security door just a few feet to its right. Arthur pounded on the door then stepped back, allowing for his whole self to be seen through the door's small security peep. As he did, he scanned the second floor. Large, frosted plate windows stretched from one corner of the building to the other.

The door opened inward. Arthur was met with outstretched arms, a brotherly hug from Jean Luc Belesur. The two men were an odd pair to say the least, as any passerby would have seen. Blackwood, though stocky, well built, but quite fit, stood at roughly five and a half feet tall. He was bald, which fit his attitude perfectly. Arthur's broad, sharp jaw was always clean shaven, a nod to the sophisticated London ladies whose company he kept. Jean Luc was thin, muscular, but by no means a heavyweight. Swirling black, but graying, locks stood high on the top of his towering head, accenting and even exaggerating his stature at 6'4." Belesur's face was long, covered with a peppered stubble that betrayed his age and his nose was slightly crooked from a rather ugly bout in his youth. The one thing these men, separated by almost twelve inches in height, shared in common was their eyes, both dark, gloomy, having borne witness to the atrocities of war and the secrets they vowed to keep. Even still, there was a sparkle, a faint hope. Standing, embracing as old friends, they shared that twinkle.

"Hello, Arthur," Belesur smiled. "It has been too long."

"Agreed," Blackwood replied.

"Come, let's head inside. We have much to discuss."

Arthur followed Jean Luc into the small warehouse and, as old habits dictated, found himself once again in the thick of a secret war. The long, open space had been staged as a base of operations. An eight foot folding table held two large flat screen monitors, their wires leading to a black twenty-four space rack case filled with various audio and surveillance equipment as well as a networking system supported by two computer towers. A keyboard and mouse sat in front of each monitor. Jean Luc had apparently been working at one of the stations, a cup of still-hot coffee was placed politely on a saucer next to the keyboard, beside that, an aptly placed Beretta 92 with a silencer attached to its barrel. On his direct left, a white cargo van was parked in front of the garage door, the sliding door on the side of the vehicle standing open. Wooden crates stamped with the Belesur winery mark were visible in the cargo area.

"Now that you are here," Jean Luc smiled, locking the door behind them as they talked, "you can help me unload my shipment. We'll stack them right over there."

Blackwood followed and helped move the heavy crates, placing them where Jean Luc had specified, right alongside one of the four steel I-beams that supported the floor above.

"These seem a bit heavy for bottled spirits?" Arthur huffed, lifting another crate from the side of the van.

"That's because they are not all wine," Jean Luc winked. "The first couple, yes. But the remaining six are care packages for our guests. Here, help me with the last one. It's very heavy."

The final crate took both men, straining heavily to manage its weight.

"This is ammunition," Belesur sighed beads of sweat on his brow, relieved to set the crate down separate from the rest.

"You never cease to amaze, Jean!"

"The Americans will be satisfied. I can't imagine anything they might need beyond what I have provided, excepting perhaps an RPG," Belesur chuckled.

Their hands sore, muscles burning, the old friends left the boxes behind and walked towards the monitors. Arthur glanced over the open windows on the screen, but saw nothing of interest.

"So how are we going to find him, find Killion?" Arthur questioned.

"I fear this will not be a hi-tech operation, and not simple either. We should pray for luck," Jean Luc advised.

"Can you pray for a thing such as luck?" Arthur grinned.

"Perhaps, no. But it couldn't hurt.."

They laughed, then stood in silence, staring blankly at the computer screens.

"You have any more of that coffee?" Arthur finally asked.

"I do, upstairs, in our communal living quarters. Not much privacy, but it will do. There's ample room for seven. The coffee is on the kitchen counter.

Arthur nodded his thanks and headed beyond the table of equipment, to the far side of the room where a flight of worn wooden steps disappeared to the flat upstairs. Reaching the top step, he spotted the kitchen area and, more importantly, the coffee pot right away. The opposite side of the room looked to be where the toilet could be found. The space in between was occupied by full-size military cots, complete with OD green, wool blankets and overly firm pillows. An ancient, dusty sofa was accompanied by a mismatched ensemble of pieced together furniture, all encircling a cheap coffee table littered with brick-a-brac. He quickly found a mug and poured himself a full cup, then returned to his friend back down on the first floor.

"It's quite homey up there," Blackwood joked.

"Do you think so?" Jean Luc wondered. "I wanted the Americans to feel comfortable here."

"I'm kidding you, mate," Arthur laughed. "Where did you find that trash?"

"Most of it was up there," the ageing French commando admitted. "This warehouse is owned by a friend of mine, a restaurateur who owns a place not far from here. He's stored useless things in this space for as long as I've known him. So, he agreed to set us up here in exchange for free wine to serve his patrons."

"Can he keep his mouth shut?"

"He has no reason not to," Jean Luc said, taking a sip of his coffee.

"So back to Killion…where do we begin?"

"Well, I've made calls to many of my contacts within the city. If they see anything odd, they'll let me know right away. None of them would know him by face or even name, but they would recognize an Englishman who seemed out of place. And, with the description I've given them, he shouldn't be missed."

"So why the computers? If we're going old school, then what do we need them for?"

"It's a long shot," Jean Luc explained, "but if Killion would perhaps pop up on the grid, I have processes working constantly to ping major resources such as credit card transactions, track passports in and out of countries, even cellular traffic, all in search of references to Killion. If his name is attached to anything, the programs automatically track the information and categorize it, then sort it through filters to determine its relevance. I've already had nearly a thousand hits on the last name alone in just the last twenty-four hours, but none are conclusive. The odds of an exact match of Terrance Killion are extremely slim, considering the fact that we must also assume that he may not even be operating as Killion, but perhaps using an alias."

"I agree, Killion was always good at accents, often using just his voice as a disguise and he could disappear into a crowd like few I've ever seen. Now I know why you suggested *praying* for luck."

"Right. In the meantime, we must keep our eyes and ears open, utilize our resources, and not allow him to know we are in Paris. The last thing we want to do is become the hunted."

"Absolutely," Arthur said. "I'm going to go back out, drive a bit. I want to familiarize myself with the roads and locals. Maybe I'll even get a little lucky and stumble across the blighter!"

Jean Luc laughed.

"Any way," Arthur continued, "do you have a pistol for me then as well?"

"Oui," Jean Luc replied, looking away from the monitor and motioning towards a specific crate. "I wasn't sure what the Americans' experience or taste in weapons would be, so I brought a little bit of everything. There are more Berettas like mine, Sigs, HKs, Glocks, even Colt 1911s. Like I said, a bit of everything. Oh, and suppressors as well."

"Very good, mate," Blackwood said, prying open the lid and smiling as he saw the firearms, neatly packed in straw to appear as innocent freight at first glance.

He chose a stainless steel Colt .45, but held off on a suppressor. However, an extra magazine suited him. That, he dropped into his pants pocket, the gun tucked away in the back of his trousers, concealed beneath his suit coat.

"I'll be back in a few hours, you've got my mobile number. Give us a ring if you need me," he announced, turning and heading out to his SUV.

****

Killion leaned against the bar, a drink in hand. He put forth his best effort to seem less drunk than he really was, but he wasn't doing as well as he thought. Edward sat on the stool next to him, staring at the incredible collection of empty shot glasses they'd amassed.

"I'm off to the loo," Edward said loudly over the music.

Killion watched his brother stagger off in the direction of the lavatories, hoping his brother had the good sense of mind to, in the least, enter the men's room. Now, he stood by himself, surveying the regulars as they came and went, managing to hone in on some of their private conversations, listening for any opportunities to determine a mark.

His attention was drawn to a couple at a table to his right. Their exchange had turned to a quarrel and the man stormed out, leaving the woman in tears.

And Bob's your uncle, Killion thought with a smile.

"Barkeep," Killion said in remarkable control, lucidness suddenly, as if at will, overpowering his drunken state, "the young lady over there, what's she drinking?"

The man behind the counter looked at him oddly, then cast a glance at the wine glass on her table, "It is a merlot, monsieur."

"Then let's have another shall we?"

The bar tender obliged, pouring more dark red wine into a new glass and placing it in front of Killion.

"Merci," Killion said without looking at the man.

He stood and strutted over to the girl's table, setting the full glass down next to her near-empty one, "Bonjour, love. Parlez-vous Anglais?"

"Oui, a little," she smiled, wiping away her tears, embarrassed by the scene she and her boyfriend had made. "I'm Polly."

"A pleasure, Polly. You can call me Terrance.

****

Sebastian stared at the tracking application on his phone. The Mercedes in which the Killion brothers had left the estate was off target and running late. He marched through the crumbling chateau and down the stairs. Laughter shared by his father and the young girl could be heard from the floor above.

"Father," Sebastian said impatiently, knocking on the closed door to the girl's quarters before entering. "Sorry to interrupt."

Laurent and the girl sat an arm's length apart on her makeshift bed, telling funny stories. Him reminiscing on his youth, her trying to be as grown up as she could.

"You're fine, my son. But you seem agitated. Are you alright?"

"It's Killion," Sebastian explained. "The car hasn't moved in the last hour."

"Is it on course?"

"Far from it, father. I tracked their movement. They spent longer than I would have expected at their apartment and, when they finally left, it was not in the direction of de Gaulle. I believe they are still in Paris."

"And how long since the car last moved?" Laurent questioned, his brow furrowed in thought.

"An hour."

Laurent hesitated to answer. He was confused, having been sure he instilled the proper fear in the Killion brothers, giving them reason to flee.

"Alright then," the Frenchman decided. "Blow the car."

Sebastian tapped on the small red dot where it appeared as a beacon on the digital map. A message box appeared, asking if he wanted to continue. Again he tapped the screen, immediately sending a wireless message to the phone used as a trigger for the device, detonating the bricks of C4 planted beneath the black Mercedes' hood.

****

Arthur Blackwood jammed his foot down on the Range Rover's brakes as chaos erupted in the street ahead. Vehicles crashed into one another as panicked drivers swerved and skidded in reaction to the giant fireball that erupted just off the side of the street. Pedestrians fought to stand, knocked over and wounded by the blast and flying debris.

He parked and raced from the SUV, realizing as he made it closer to the explosion's center, that aside from the random, shredded car parts, human limbs were also part of the devastated wreckage. Whether they were in the car that detonated - targets of the attack - or innocent bystanders sadly caught in a madman's ruthless game would be difficult to tell.

Paris was not typically a mark for terrorists, so what had he witnessed? A woman was laying on her side, clutching her arm, beside her, a man who was charred on his entire right side. She stared at his lifeless, bloodied face, her mouth shaped into a horrified scream, but there was no sound escaping.

Arthur helped her to her feet, leading the shocked woman away from the gore. She didn't even seem to realize that he was there, his arm around her waist, helping her limp to safety.

Regardless of what seemed to have happened, Arthur knew one thing: the explosion was no accident at all, it was most definitely deliberate. The question of who and why was the real mystery.

****

"Did you hear that?" Killion asked excitedly, knowing indeed that it was the sound of a Mercedes Benz, only three blocks away, being blown to kingdom come.

"How could I not have!" Polly replied. "The whole bar shook!"

"Quelle horreur! Une bombe a explosé," they heard a man shout from outside the front door. "Il s'agit d'une attaque terroriste!"

"What did he say, Polly?!" Killion asked.

"He said it was terrorists!" she cried. "Someone detonated a bomb!"

"This is awful. We must go quickly. Do you have a car?" he pressed.

"Oui, it's parked around the corner, a silver Renault."

"Then let's hurry," Killion urged, taking her by the arm.

Edward returned from the restroom just in time to catch the nod his brother intended for him. He then did his best to act confused, having missed the excitement.

"What's everybody on about?" Edward asked the bartender.

"There was some kind of attack," the man answered. "Maybe terrorists?"

"Bloody hell!" Edward exclaimed. "It's times like this I wish I had a sodding gun, I tell you."

"I agree, monsieur."

"But where to get one?" Edward mused. "Pour me another whiskey, mate. This one will be my last."

"Oui, monsieur."

"You didn't happen to see where my brother went did you?"

"A man, I believe your brother, left just after the bombing, with a young woman."

"I see," Edward answered, pulling a large folded stack of Euros from his pocket. "I'll pay for his drinks as well then."

The man behind the counter eyed the money, hiding his excitement, believing he might take advantage of the unsuspecting drunk, "That's a lot of money, monsieur. I would be careful who sees you with that. This is not the safest of neighborhoods."

"All the more reason to have a gun then, wouldn't you say, mate," Edward smiled, peeling two fifty euro notes from the stack and tossing them on the counter next to all the empty glasses. "Keep the change."

He spun around on the stool and nonchalantly walked to the door, seeing for the first time the panic and fear that crippled the streets outside. Rescue vehicles and police were now on the scene.

"Hold on, monsieur," the bartender called out, his voice quickly falling to a whisper as he continued. "If you are serious about what you said, about protecting yourself, I have something for you."

Edward stopped and looked cautiously around the now empty café. He turned and headed back to the bar, the man leaning across the counter, his hand lying flat on its wooden top.

"Call the number," he winked, slowly sliding his hand back to reveal a pack of matches, the café's name printed on the flap.

Edward picked up the matches and flipped them open. A telephone number was scribbled on the inside.

"Thanks for the tip, mate," Edward smiled, once again turning towards the door.

****

Arthur managed to get back to his SUV and force his way through the traffic, speeding away as emergency vehicles passed him going the opposite direction, their sirens wailing as they raced to the blast site. His phone was raised to his ear. Jean Luc was on the other end.

"You said an explosion?" Belesur questioned.

"Yeah, a big one. Cars don't just blow up at random. That was staged."

"For what purpose?"

"I haven't the foggiest," Blackwood grunted.

"Could it be Killion?"

"To what end?" Arthur asked. "There's nothing in that location that seems a logical target for terrorists, let alone Killion. The Arc de Triomph is close. Maybe it was a message, you know…showing how easy an attack could be?"

"Then why not target the landmark itself?" Jean Luc reasoned. "Even so, that's not Killion, not his style."

"Maybe it was just random?" Arthur considered.

"Perhaps…perhaps. Regardless, we will keep our ear to the ground," Jean Luc said. "My contacts may learn more about what happened, acquire leads from internal government sources. Regardless, Killion or not, there's someone very dangerous in this city, someone capable of terrible things."

"True, mate," Blackwood replied. "I'll see you soon. I'm on my way back to the warehouse now."

"Alright, Arthur…and be safe."

16

"I've had a wonderful time with you, love," Killion smiled, sitting in the passenger seat of the young woman's car.

"Me too, Terry," she replied.

The sun had set on Paris. Without a doubt, the afternoon following the blast had passed quickly. Many of the most famous attractions had been placed on lockdown and guarded dearly for fear that another attack might follow. Now, Killion and the girl, Polly, sat parked near the Seine, the Eiffel Tower stretching high above them into the glowing Parisian night.

"Do you think there really are terrorists in the city?" she asked, watching an armed patrol in the courtyard at the tower's base.

"I fear the worst," Killion whispered, leaning in closer to her, his hand settling naturally on her thigh. "Tell me, Polly. Do you have a safe place to go this evening?"

"But of course, Terry. I have an apartment, near the university where I study."

"Do you share it with your ruddy awful boyfriend?"

"No," she laughed. "He abhors school and it's too close for him, makes him feel like he's *living* and *learning* in the same place. I live with a girlfriend."

"A girlfriend?!" Killion smiled sweetly, teasingly, his hand moving ever slightly higher, carefully, strategically.

"Not like that, Terry," Polly blushed. "She is my best friend. We are like sisters."

"You got me excited," he whispered, going in for the kill, placing his lips on the warm, soft skin of her neck.

"She...my friend...*Oh, Terry*...she went home to...to..." she moaned, giving in to his passionate advancement, his lust-filled kisses driving her mad as his wandering hand disappeared beneath her skirt.

"Where did she go, love?" he whispered, his touch more intoxicating than the two bottles of wine they'd shared that night.

"Avignon, to...Avignon...to visit family for the summer."

"Then we should hurry to your place," he encouraged, pulling his hand away, sitting upright in his seat.

She sat staring at him wide-eyed, wanting more, her cheeks and neck flushed rosily, her arousal unsatisfied. Polly started the car. She couldn't wait to get this mysterious man home.

****

Edward sat patiently, drink in hand, at the cabaret, Villa d' Este, watching the show, but not really enjoying the entertainment. Hopefully soon, he would get a call or text message from his brother. The plan was to arrange a place to stay, then procure weapons. Edward had the connection he needed, a link to the Parisian black market. He trusted that Terrance would fulfill his task: vehicle and lodging.

A beautifully costumed woman sang wonderfully from the stage, her strong voice seducing the crowd as her risqué backup singers danced provocatively, allowing the imaginations of both men and woman alike to ponder the many pleasures this show had to offer. But Edward was too distracted to enjoy the performance. He couldn't hope his brother's call would come any sooner.

****

"I can't stare at this bloody screen a moment longer," Arthur said rubbing his weary eyes, backing the metal folding chair away from the surveillance table, its feet screeching on the cement floor. "The Americans will be here in the morning. I'm going to get some sleep."

"Go ahead," Jean Luc replied. "I don't sleep much as it is. I will continue to watch for leads, you rest."

Blackwood nodded and patted his old friend on the shoulder as he stood and headed up to a cot. The night was still young, but morning would arrive soon, bringing with it the Americans and another day of searching for Killion. He took off his suit coat and laid it over the back of the sofa, then removed his shoes, slipping them beneath the cot. Next, he removed the 1911 pistol and extra magazine, placing them beside his shoes, at arm's reach.

Sleep came quickly. Arthur drifted off, thinking of terrorist attacks and unconnected dots. The sooner they found Killion, the better.

****

Michael gazed out the window of the Boeing 777, the ocean passing silently thirty-five thousand feet beneath the giant craft. His friends, as did most of the other passengers, slept, the flight cruising in the dark night. He watched clouds pass, the moon's brilliant glow shimmering, defining their soft edges and shape. Somewhere in France, under the same stark white moon, was his father; and with his father, his destiny.

Without warning, the plane shook violently; and then again, harder and longer. There was a sudden, bright flash that poured in through every open window, filled the cabin with pure, brilliant, blinding light, followed immediately by the ear-shattering boom of thunder. And then, more turbulence.

But oddly, there was no panic. The passengers continued to sleep or read, or whatever they'd been doing just as if nothing had happened, as if they weren't flying through a hellish storm. But just as with the first lightening strike, a second came unexpectedly, this one flashing longer. And that was when Michael saw... *him*.

Michael stood quickly, unsure on his feet as the plane rocked in the gusting wind. The flash illuminated the figure for only mere seconds, but he knew without a doubt who it was. Another flash, and again he saw the figure, now more defined, now drawing closer.

He left his row and began hesitantly up the aisle towards the front of the plane, to the shadowy specter that confused him so. Each step was a struggle, both from near-paralyzing fear and the jarring movement of the weather-tossed jet, his mind churning with horrid possibilities as he tried his best to keep his feet firmly planted. There was no way he saw what he thought he had, simply impossible. And why was no one else on the plane reacting to the storm, to the haunting figure lurking in the darkness?

"There's nowhere to run now, Michael," the familiar voice spoke softly, his voice a mysterious, taunting. "But of course you knew you'd have to face me eventually."

Michael searched in the darkness, his eyes hoping for a glimpse of the voice's origin, but he couldn't place it in the long cabin. He'd seen the figure up ahead, but the voice seemed to float, linger, coming from everywhere and nowhere.

"Show yourself!" Michael demanded.

Lightning flashed again, blurring his vision. But, Michael managed to spot the figure once more. Now, he was certain, there was no question. The figure's posture, arrogance, was unmistakable. And if that wasn't enough, the black suit paired with the black mask was undeniable. Thirteen's white eyes now glowed, Michael focusing in on them, watching them seemingly float in the darkness, now growing larger as Thirteen closed the gap between them.

'How is this possible?" Michael shouted, catching himself against the seat to his right as the plane rocked violently.

Thirteen walked effortlessly, perfectly balanced and unaffected by the fierce, tossing movements, "Isn't it obvious? It is because, though I am you, *you* are not *me*."

Michael righted himself, his knee aching from having been slammed into the hard metal of the seat's frame. He and Thirteen now stood face-to-face.

"What do you mean? How can you be me, but I am not you?"

"Bizarre, is it not?" Thirteen mused, his wicked mask displaying the grin that most surely was shared on his face beneath. "It's like looking in a mirror. But I would suppose we are now *through the looking glass*, as it were."

"Answer my question!" Michael ordered.

"Come now, Michael. That's no way to speak to such an old friend. Who would you be without me?"

"How can *you* be *me*, but *I'm* not *you*? How is that possible?"

"It's simple really. You became me through your actions, by killing and stealing and lying and deceiving. But I existed long before you. I am more than just a mask, you see. I am the realization of all your greatest hopes and dreams, your passions, *everything*. Therefore, without *my* power, you are nothing. Without me, you are a weak, insignificant, worthless, inadequate human, no different than any other pathetic soul on this plane."

Michael stared at Thirteen, frozen in the reality that the power he thought was truly his to control was able to now stand as its own host, separate from himself and his bond to the demonic mask.

"But you need me?" Michael questioned.

"Please!" Thirteen laughed. "What on earth would I really need your mortal sack of flesh for? My power is eternal. I have been here since the fall of man. I assure you, I will be here long after your wretched life has ended."

"I don't believe you. I'm special," Michael argued.

"I made you special, Michael. I did, not you, not anyone else…it was *me*!"

Michael didn't respond. He was too angry; so angry, in fact, that he decided he only had one option. He reached within his pocket and removed his mask, pulling it down over his face. A rush of energy coursed through him, leaving his fingers tingling. Immediately, Michael felt as light as air. The turbulence no longer rattling him.

"Now it's truly like looking in a mirror," Thirteen laughed.

"Indeed," Thirteen replied, clenching his fingers into fists.

The Thirteen who was Michael threw himself headlong into the imposter Thirteen, slamming his fist against the masked pretender's jaw. Thirteen flew backwards from the impact, slamming hard into the floor in the narrow aisle. Michael leapt into the air, his knee thrust forward, driving into Thirteen's chest.

"Is this really what you want, Michael?" Thirteen questioned, fighting back, pounding Michael in the face, sending him toppling backwards.

Michael stood quickly, resolutely, "I don't believe I have a choice."

"What about all the passengers on this flight, do you not care for their lives? If we fight, they all will die."

Michael glanced around the cabin, looking through the bright white eyes of his mask. There was no movement, complete, silent, stillness. His gaze fell upon Gavin and Ashley, then Kayla and Jamie. Did he dare risk their lives in a battle of egos?

"We settle this," Michael decided, "right here, right now."

"So be it," Thirteen answered.

For a brief moment, there was an absolute calm. And then, chaos.

The two Thirteen's lunged at one another, a flurry of fists as they punched and jabbed at the other, knowing all the same tricks, all the same moves. They battled relentlessly, battering the cabin of the jet as much as they did each other. Every misplaced attack resulted in damage to the plane. Seats broke. Innocent bystanders flailed uncontrollably, displaced from where they sat comatose. Luggage spilled from the overhead compartments.

"Happy now?" Thirteen taunted.

"Not till you're dead."

"Then you'll have a very unhappy life because you cannot kill me."

Michael thrust forward, his fist sharply finding Thirteen's face. A follow up strike beneath the chin sent Thirteen smashing into the roof of the plane. Again, Michael attacked. Thirteen blocked the punch and took hold of Michael's arm, wrenching it before swinging him like a ragdoll, sending Michael flying into the outer wall of the cabin, the impact shattering the window as the skin of the plane bent and buckled, then began to peel away. Emergency lights flashed as oxygen masks dropped down above all the unaware passengers. The cabin depressurized quickly, small items from scattered luggage, as well as passengers and debris, being sucked out the growing hole in the plane's side.

With a jolt, the jetliner began to lose altitude, spontaneously dropping thousands of feet, spiraling into an uncontrollable nosedive as the plane raced towards the dooming waters below. The velocity caused the wings to rip from the hull, shredding even more of the plane as it plummeted downward, a trail of wreckage following behind the ill-fated jet. Inside, bodies tumbled and bounced, Michael and Thirteen included, as if trapped in a merciless snow globe of death.

Thirteen laughed loudly, pleased by the series of events. Michael clung desperately to a headrest, dizzied by the corkscrew trajectory.

"I told you so," Thirteen ridiculed. "And I know you're definitely not happy now!"

Michael closed his eyes sadly, knowing the battered remains of the plane were only seconds from smashing into the ocean, the passengers a total loss, "Oh, God…*PLEASE NO!*"

****

Edward's phone buzzed where it sat on the tabletop at the cabaret. The brightly lit screen displayed a new text message. It was from Terrance.

"At last," me muttered as he read the address and the following instructions telling him to stop at a pharmacy and pick up sleeping pills and foam earplugs. "What are you up to?"

He left money on the table to cover his drinks and began the hunt for a drug store, maybe a convenience store, that would be open at such a late – *or early* – hour. But after walking several blocks, he came across a shop that seemed a likely candidate.

The search was short. He found both the sleeping pills, the label warning that the contents were exceptionally potent *and* highly addictive, as well as the earplugs. Now to find his destination.

****

Michael opened his eyes slowly. His face hurt and his body ached. He couldn't be more confused. The plane was still safely in the air, the fuselage intact. Rain pelted the outside of the jet, streaking across the windows. It was all a dream.

He looked down at his clenched fist, his mask firmly grasped, his knuckles whitened and tense. Indeed, just a dream. But then, why was he in pain?

"Sir," a soft voice spoke from behind him.

Michael turned to see who it was, finding a stewardess approaching with a glass of water.

"That must have been some nightmare you were having," she said wide-eyed. "I was afraid I was going to have to wake you! You were tossing and mumbling, Mr. Laurent."

"How...?" he said, taking the water from her.

"...Do I know your name?" she smiled. "I checked your seat on the manifest. No worries, sir. We'll be landing soon."

He thanked her for the water and loosened his grip on the black cloth, adjusting it so that he could see the stitching. Even like this, resting on his leg, he realized just how terrible the mask was, the fear inherent in its design. Michael studied the stitching. What he'd always thought of as random and haphazard, a device of intimidation, was truly purposeful, defining the chaotic power borne within. He was sickened by it, sickened that, for so long, he'd chosen to hide behind it, finding himself more at home beneath its restricting material than living life as himself: Michael Laurent. Perhaps the mask was not the monster, perhaps he was.

But his thoughts fell on Thirteen's words, that he, Michael, was Thirteen, but that Thirteen was not Michael, was separate and self reliant. Their relationship, which he had assumed symbiotic was actually a choice on his own part. He, having been convinced of his weakness, had gained power from the mask, but the mask had gained nothing. Evil existed in the world, whether or not Michael wore the mask.

And in that realization, Michael found an odd peace. If he had *chosen* to be Thirteen, then he could ultimately *choose* to end the tie. There truly was hope of redemption.

★★★★★★★★★★★★

The climb up three flights of stairs was relatively exhausting. Edward had drank too much alcohol and slept too little. And, three flights of stairs after covering several square kilometers of Paris on foot, meant that he was ready to rest. But at last, he'd arrived.

Edward stood in front of the entrance to the apartment, staring at the unit number on the door as he knocked lightly. There was no reply, so he knocked a bit louder, though only slightly.

"Hello there, brother," Killion said, opening the door. "Come on then."

Shirtless, Killion's pants were pulled on, though not buttoned, his belt hanging loosely, unbuckled. His bare feet slapped against the wooden floor as he walked.

"You got what I asked for?" he asked.

"Yeah, Terry," Edward confirmed, handing the shopping bag to his brother. "What do you need them for?"

"For her," he said, nodding towards the bedroom.

Edward looked through the open door, seeing the young women sprawled naked on the bed, sleeping half-covered by a white sheet, "Why not just kill her, isn't that what you do?"

"We have to be careful now, brother," Killion smiled. "For one, we don't have any weapons. Also, if we want the Frenchman to believe we are dead or, in the least, gone, we must not put ourselves in a position where we can be found out. We'll keep her drugged. That way, we have her apartment as ours, as well as her car. If I simply killed her, we couldn't keep her here. And, if I dump the body, we risk her being identified and then, of course, the investigation that would follow. We need her alive, at least till we've finished with Laurent."

"Makes sense," Edward admitted, breaking into a yawn. "Is there just the one bed?"

"No," Terrance explained, gesturing towards another door, this one closed. "That's her roommate's. She's home for break from college. Have at it."

"Where are you sleeping then?" Edward asked as he headed towards the unoccupied room.

"With her," the elder brother winked. "Get some rest. We've got work to do tomorrow."

"Oh, I almost forgot."

"Yeah, Ed?" Killion asked.

"Here," Edward said, pulling the matchbook from his pocket and holding it up so his brother could see the phone number written on the flap, "I think I found a source for firearms."

"Good job!" Killion smiled. "Now turn in, Ed."

Edward disappeared behind the door. Killion returned to the young women, dropping his pants to the floor and crawling into bed beside her, her skin warm and soft to the touch. This was a satisfactory arrangement indeed.

17

The sun had long since risen, bathing the iconic streets and landmarks of Paris with its warmth. Early morning gave way to rush hour. Traffic clogged the main roads. At Charles de Gaul Airport, the group's plane had only just touched down, precisely on time. The five companions had picked up their luggage and been processed into the country.

As Solomon Grier had promised, a vehicle was waiting for them. Arthur Blackwood welcomed them to France. Jean Luc remained vigilant behind the wheel of the large, white, seven-passenger Land Rover Defender, scanning the area from behind his darkly tinted, round-framed sunglasses.

"You must be the Americans," Arthur smiled.

"We are," Jamie answered, his hand outstretched to greet Solomon's contact. "I'm James Branson, call me Jamie. This is my wife Kayla, her sister Ashley. Beside her is her husband, Gavin Dering. On the end is Michael Laurent."

"Arthur Blackwood," he replied, shaking each person's hand in turn. That's Jean Luc in the car. He's arranged almost everything. We can talk more in the wagon. Come along then."

"Bienvenue à Paris, mes amis," Jean Luc smiled as the five climbed into the back of the Land Rover. "Welcome to Paris."

The vehicle pulled away from arrivals and merged into traffic, beginning the trek to Montmartre. The group was enamored by the sights, especially Ashley. She could hardly wait to look upon all the art and history that lay ahead. Michael; however, was not. He'd seen it all before.

"Is this your first time in Paris, my friends?" Jean Luc asked as they drove.

"It is," Gavin answered for the group.

"Then perhaps, once you are settled in...if time allows of course...I can show you some of what makes Paris so special."

"That would be great!" Ashley replied happily.

"But we need to locate the Frenchman first, find out where he is," Gavin interjected. "Once we know where he is, we should be able to determine what areas would be safe for us to visit. The last thing we want to do is stumble out in front of him and give ourselves away. We'd lose every tactical advantage."

"The first place we'll look is my old family home in Vigny. It's a small chateau, but it's where I grew up, a far stretch from the farm where my father was born. There's a secret room. I found it as a boy and was lost to my family for half a day till my father found me. After that, I was never allowed in his study. But I believe that hidden chamber may be the best place to begin. From there, if we do not find him, then we may have some difficulty." Michael reasoned.

"So your father is the Frenchman you're looking for?" Arthur chuckled.

"Yeah," Michael sighed.

"So what about Killion?" Kayla asked. "Any luck so far? Do you know where he might be?"

"Nothing yet," Arthur answered. "But Jean Luc knows all the right people. If Killion is indeed in this city, we'll find him. Never you worry."

"Well if we can," Ashley said, still thinking about the attractions, "I want to see the Eiffel Tower and the Louvre. Oh, and Notre Dame for sure! I guess I really just want to see it all. I can't believe we're in Paris!"

"Ashley is an artist,' Gavin explained. "She does restorations at a museum back home."

"Then you will love Montmartre, mon cher," Jean Luc said. "Picasso lived in a studio just a block from where we are staying. The whole neighborhood is known as a haven for artists. How fitting."

The passengers grew quiet, the rest of the drive passing with occasional excited awes from Ashley as she recognized various landmarks or commented on random architecture. They soon arrived at the warehouse.

"I'll drop you off here," Jean Luc said. "Go on in with Arthur. There's little room to park here plus I do not want this vehicle to draw unwanted attention. I will park it down the street and meet you all inside. Then, we'll make plans."

Arthur opened the door and led them inside, quickly closing it behind them, ensuring to lock the bolt, "He'll only be a moment. We'll all be sleeping upstairs. There's a small kitchen and a loo, nothing special, but it'll do. Once we've got everything figured out, there's a lovely pub just up the way. We could talk over a couple of pints."

"Well I'm definitely using the restroom," Ashley announced.

"I'll come with you," Kayla decided, following her pregnant sister up the stairs.

There was a firm knock on the door, two quick raps followed by a pause and then a final thud. Then, they heard the lock turn. Jean Luc entered, quickly relocking the door and removing his sunglasses.

"Alright then, has Arthur given you the tour?" he asked, scratching his stubble-covered chin.

"We've got the general layout," Gavin answered. "The girls already headed upstairs."

"Good," Jean Luc nodded. "To business then, please."

Gavin, Jamie, and Michael were directed to some folding chairs and they promptly settled in near the table of computer hardware. The screens blipped and flashed with lines of text:; hits and possible matches returned through the filters in an effort to weed the needle that was Killion from the veritable, digital haystack. Other open windows on the monitor displayed, in real-time, the points of interest from the text as glowing orb-like markers on an interactive map of Europe. Clickable and zoom-able down to the last detail, the map was powered by tracking satellites, hacked by the venerable Jean Luc Belesur.

"Where did you get a hold of this technology?" Jamie wondered. "You don't secretly work for the NSA do you?"

"Among the many satellites that congest our atmosphere, there are nondescript ones, government ones, long since replaced by newer, more expensive versions. But some of these satellites still have enough fuel and, with the proper source code, can be activated and controlled," Belesur explained. "I'm connected to two units we used frequently during our dark days."

"The *dark days* are what he calls our time spent on tour with Solomon and dear old Killion," Arthur added.

"Solomon didn't really tell us what it was you guys did. Delilah hinted, but nothing concrete," Gavin asked. "What did you guys really do? I mean, *really* do? It sounds like you operated on your own orders and with technology like this, was it sanctioned? Seriously, what squad would be given access to their own spy satellites, without controls, checks, or balances?"

Arthur eyed Jean Luc. They were both sworn to secrecy, as were Solomon and Delilah.

"If Sully or Delilah told you anything at all," Arthur smiled, "then you already know too much."

"Is this one of those *you could tell me, but you'd have to kill me* situations?" Gavin joked.

"That's a little too cliché, don't you think," Arthur replied. "But what I will say is this: in regards to matters concerning our pasts, mate, ignorance truly is bliss."

"Fair enough," Jamie conceded. "So where do we begin? We have two fish to fry, Killion and the Frenchman."

"Well, first then," Jean Luc recommended, "let us take inventory of what we have and what we might need."

"I for one, would love a new suit," Michael spoke up, having been silent through most of their exchange. "No offense Jamie, but I'm not really a khakis and t-shirt kind of guy."

Jamie smiled. Michael continued.

"So I suggest we update our wardrobe, all of us. You too, Gavin. We're in Paris now, not New York or Chicago. It may be necessary to gain access to exclusive locations where *casual attire* is simply not acceptable."

"Hey," Gavin countered with a laugh, "I used to own a suit, well jacket at least, but it was great: tweed with brown leather patches on the elbows."

"Right," Michael continued, "Well no more retro-sheik. I'm imagining you in gray."

"You're the expert," Gavin smiled.

"Alright then," Jean Luc interrupted. "So besides clothing, is there anything else we will need?"

"Guns?" Gavin asked.

"Look over there, in those crates," Jean Luc directed. "I believe these should do the job."

Gavin stood and approached the first crate, the one filled with ammunition. He popped open the top and immediately broke into a large grin. Bulk cases in the hundreds filled the crate: 9mm NATO, .45 ACP, 5.56x45mm, 7.62x51mm, and 7.62x39mm. He turned to the next crate, the handguns. Again, he smiled, like a kid on Christmas, listing the choices as he perused the pistols. There were Colt 1911's, Beretta 92's, Glock 17's, Sig Sauer 226's, HK USP's in 9mm and 45 caliber, and silencers as well. Gavin withdrew a compact USP 9mm and a proper suppressor, clearing the chamber before twisting the can onto the threaded barrel.

"I found my sidearm," he announced triumphantly.

"Is that the 9mm or the .45?" Jean Luc smiled.

"The 9mm."

"You know," Jean Luc bragged. "HK does not make a threaded barrel for the compact 9mm, only the .45 ACP. That is a custom match barrel, mon ami, very rare."

Gavin nodded his approval and continued on to the last two boxes. If he'd been excited about the handguns, then what he found next was a dream. He pried open the lid with a crowbar that lay beside the stacks of crates. Jean Luc had not opened this one yet. Pushing aside the hay that covered the top, he spotted an assortment of rifles and SMG's. He moved aside the AK-47's and M16's, took pause to admire a select-fire HK G3, smiled as he handled an MP5, but it was the suppressed HK UMP 45 at the bottom that he was after. Again, he cleared the gun and function checked the controls and charging handle, cycling the bolt.

"So we're covered for guns," Gavin said happily, almost greedily.

"I'm glad you appreciate my offerings," Jean Luc replied. "You and I share a deep love of guns. We are friends indeed!"

"We'll arm up and do what we can today," Arthur continued, bringing the conversation back to their actual purpose. "I suggest we work as two teams. I'll head up one, Jean Luc the other. We can cover more ground that way and look less suspicious than seven nutters scouring the streets for Killion."

"I want to go to Vigny today," Michael said. "It's important we find my father. Killion is of little importance now. We must reacquire the key."

"I'll go with you," Gavin volunteered. "How about you, Arthur, are you in?"

"I'm game."

"Then I'll take Jamie and the girls," Jean Luc continued. "It will give Ashley a chance to see the sights of Paris while I can check in on some of my contacts."

"Sounds like a plan then," Jamie agreed. "Let's get moving."

****

Jamie stepped from the fitting room at the Michael Kors on Rue Saint Honoré, admiring his reflection in the mirror, adjusting the fit of the navy suit he'd chosen. Michael had immediately selected a black suit and tie. Gavin reluctantly went with charcoal, admitting that Michael had been right about the color and, now seeing himself dressed in the fine clothing, the look was growing on him.

"I need some sunglasses, silver aviators, to go with this suit," Gavin laughed posing in front of the men. "I feel like James Bond!"

"But I didn't think you liked suits?" Jamie reminded.

"Eh, I guess I just didn't know I did," Gavin shrugged.

"You lot are worse than girls," Arthur laughed.

"Maybe," Gavin smiled.

"It looks like you gents are handsomely outfitted. How's a bout we be on our way then?" Arthur replied.

Michael paid for the three men's entire purchase, which also included white button-down shirts, smart ties, appropriate dress socks and polished leather shoes, and, lastly, Gavin's choice sunglasses. Proudly, they stepped from the haute designer storefront and returned to Arthur's Range Rover, their old clothes stuffed into large gold emblazoned shopping bags.

"We'll stop back at the warehouse for arms, then we're off for Vigny," Arthur planned.

"Are you expecting trouble?" Jamie wondered.

Arthur Blackwood smiled as he started the SUV and shifted into gear, "Always."

****

Kayla and Ashley finished their eggs, toast, and strong, black coffee. They'd kindly made enough for Jean Luc as well. He'd happily taken the breakfast and enjoyed eating in front of the glowing monitors of his computer station.

"Is it weird that we're in Paris, the fashion capitol of the world, and it's our husbands that are out shopping for new clothes?" Kayla asked with a smirk as she rinsed their plates in the stainless steel sink.

"A bit," Ashley laughed. "But we'll have our chance while we're out with Jean Luc. We'll drag Jamie through some trendy boutiques. I want a summer dress for sure!"

"Oh that will just torture Jamie...I can't wait!"

"Yeah," Ashley winked.

"So how are you feeling today?" Kayla wondered, finishing with the dishes, tossing the now-damp towel she'd used for drying onto the counter. "Any more nausea?"

"I'm better now that I ate."

"That's good. I remember I was so sick with Ethan, Marley not so much," Kayla recalled. "But by around sixteen weeks or so, it had passed."

Ashley looked down at her stomach, "I just can't believe there's a baby inside of me. It's so surreal."

"Just wait. Another month from now, you probably won't fit in those jeans anymore," Kayla teased.

"That soon?!"

"Maybe two months. But you'll be surprised how quickly baby, *and tummy*, grow!"

The familiar, secret knock echoed through the lower level and up the stairs, followed by the clunky opening and closing of the heavy steel door.

"They're back," Ashley said. "I wonder if they actually got Gavin in a suit?"

"Only one way to find out," Kayla grinned.

They headed downstairs. Ashley whistled flirtatiously at Gavin, looking him up and down in his sharp, charcoal jacket and slacks.

"Yeah, yeah," he answered.

"Seriously," Ashley said. "You look dashing!"

"Dashing? What, are you from like the roaring 1920's now?"

"Shut up and accept the compliment," Ashley ordered, leaning in close to her scruffy, yet well-dressed husband for a kiss.

"Alright," he sighed, kissing back.

"Well, now that you got the girl, *Mr. Bond*, we should get a move on," Arthur said, interrupting their moment. "Grab your guns and we're off."

Gavin slipped his arms out of the suit jacket and handed it to Ashley, then found a long, vertical leather shoulder holster amongst Jean Luc's ample supplies. Though meant for a long barreled revolver, it was perfect for the compact USP, allowing carry of the weapon with the silencer still attached. And what was better, the fit of the jacket did a surprising job of covering the rig, leaving little trace of the firearm beneath.

Jamie picked up a Beretta 92. Though there were many guns to choose from, he'd carried a police-issue 92 for most of his career. His familiarity with the gun made it the perfect choice. He backed his belt out several loops and then fed the belt through the narrow channels of a leather holster, then back through the pants loops, re-buckling his belt comfortably which pulled the holster tight to his right side. He checked the 9mm bullets in the magazine, then chambered a round, flipping the safety downward to de-cock the hammer before securing the gun in his holster.

Michael missed his .50 caliber Desert Eagles, but a matching pair of stainless tactical 1911 .45's would suffice. He found two separate shoulder holsters, one left hand and one right, swapping the right-handed holster's spare magazine pouches for the left-handed holster, creating a double-gun rig, one for each side. It, like Gavin's shoulder holster, fit well beneath his suit jacket. He then returned to the Michael Kors bag of borrowed clothing and pulled his mask from amongst the neatly folded articles inside, tucking the mask into the inner pocket of his jacket.

"Alright, lads," Arthur directed, looking at Gavin and Michael, "it's best we be off."

Gavin kissed Ashley once more and then turned to Jamie, "Look after her alright?"

"Of course," Jamie replied, slapping Gavin firmly on the shoulder.

"That's it then," Arthur said, nodding confidently at Jean Luc. "We'll return in a few hours."

The three men headed back out to Arthur's gray Range Rover. Vigny was a relatively short drive, the commune being only forty minutes northwest of Paris. The only question that remained was what they might find upon arrival?

****

"Is she alright then?" Edward asked, sipping on a steaming cup of hot tea as his brother emerged from the girl's bedroom.

"Aye," Killion smiled, buttoning his dress shirt and tucking it into his pants. "I slipped a triple dose of sleeping pills into her morning coffee and she was out like a light."

"So what did you need the earplugs for?"

Killion smirked, pouring himself some tea from the pot on the stovetop, "They were for you, so that you could sleep whilst she and I had a go."

"Sod off," Edward grunted.

"Calm down, brother. It's just a joke. I wanted them in case her apartment was in a noisy area, help make sure she remained undisturbed."

"Whatever you say, Terry."

"So what did you find out about weapons?" Killion asked pointedly.

"I got us the number. You give it a ring."

"What is it, a bloody underground or resistance? The French love that sort of thing."

"Not sure," Edward explained. "But the bar man was happy to oblige when he saw my bankroll. He must have assumed I was legit and could afford whatever they had to offer."

"Then let's have it," Killion said, reaching for the book of matches as he took out his phone.

He dialed quickly. The phone rang on the other end.

"What's happening?" Edward asked in a hissing whisper.

"Shut it, it's still ringing."

"Allô?" a gruff voice answered in French, the line abuzz with an obscuring static.

"I'm here," Killion replied.

"Parlez-vous Français?" the man questioned.

"Un peu," Killion replied. "Only a little."

"Heureusement pour vous, je parle Anglais, monsieur."

"Sorry, I don't know what you said. You mean to say you speak English?"

"Oui, mon ami. Where did you get this number?"

"It was written on the inner flap of a match pack," Killion answered boldly. "I'm in town on business and there's been a complication. And now I'm shopping for a solution, but there's not a boutique in all of *gay Paris* that can provide me with what I require. You follow?"

"And what is it that you require, monsieur?"

"I'll know it when I see it. I have fifteen thousand Euros in hand at present. Where can I find you?"

There was a long pause before the voice returned, "Paris, the 17th arrondissement. Rue Davy: across the street from the De Bordeaux Hotel. Look for a window with a red sign hanging within. Knock twice on the door. Come alone."

The phone went dead.

"It seems a bit dodgy," Killion admitted, "but I don't think we have another choice."

"Alright then," Edward agreed. "I'm driving."

18

During the drive to Vigny, Gavin and Michael told Arthur their entire story, all the events of the previous week that had led them to this exact point: a small commune in northern France. The Brit was amused to say the least, though he still had trouble understanding Michael's relationship with his father; primarily, who Emeric Laurent truly was and just what his insidious plan entailed.

"And this is all about some bloody old key?" Blackwood contemplated.

"Yes," Michael replied. "But again, its purpose is still a mystery."

"Well it must do something wonderful if kidnapping and murder are reasonable sources to attain said relic," Arthur grimaced, trying to understand what could possibly be so special about what sounded to be nothing more than a trinket, albeit one shrouded in colorful myth. "I'd rather like to see this bauble now."

"We're almost there," Michael announced. "Up here, there's a drive on the left. Follow it. You'll see the break in the trees.

Arthur did as Michael instructed. The Range Rover rounded onto the gravel drive and travelled along beneath the shadows of the tall trees that lined the pathway. The drive suddenly opened into a clearing and they could see what Michael had described as a *small* chateau. The castle was brilliant indeed and Michael had been too modest, the multi-pinnacled roof rising strikingly above the three level, stone manor.

"You grew up here?" Gavin asked in awe.

"I did, till I left for America."

"How could you leave this?" Arthur laughed. "It's fit for an emperor!"

"I followed the orders of my father, left to fulfill the duties of the legacy that had been passed on to me. This is the first I've returned in years and, if it were up to me, I wouldn't be here now. But fate has a way of directing us exactly where we do not want to go."

Arthur stopped the SUV near the main entrance into the great hall, "Doesn't look like there's anyone here. Does your father have this whole place to himself?"

"If my brother is still alive, then this is where I'm certain he would live. Also, my father had butlers and maids, cooks, stable hands, a gardener; everything that would be appropriate for a property such as this."

The three men exited the vehicle and stepped up to the solid wood door. Arthur reached out to examine the wood, get an idea of what exactly they were up against.

"I don't suppose you have a key?" he said.

"No," Michael answered, reaching into his jacket and bringing out his mask.

Gavin and Arthur watched as he pulled the black cloth onto his head, stretching it down over his face. Then, Michael, now Thirteen, leaned back and kicked the door mightily, sending it swinging open violently, the locks broken and tattered.

"How in the bloody hell did you do that?" Arthur exclaimed, watching as Michael headed into the chateau, Gavin following, his suppressed pistol raised and ready.

"In time, Arthur," Michael replied softly. "Father's study is on the second floor. Let's go."

The house was eerily quiet. For such a spacious property, they hadn't seen any signs of occupation. Thirteen led the way upstairs, then down a long corridor, rooms splitting off on either side of the hallway.

"We're almost there," Michael whispered.

Ahead, they entered an enormous two story library. The men stood on the edge of the balcony, looking down over the lower level from behind the banister. Across from them was a peninsula-like level that extended out into the room, large enough for a magnificent desk. Matching staircases spiraled down to the floor below from both sides. The balcony on which they stood wrapped around the room, allowing them access to the study area from the second floor.

"Come on," Michael urged.

They made their way to the desk and froze. The luxuriously upholstered swiveling chair had been facing away from them; but now, they saw that the high-backed seat was occupied. An older man, late seventies by his hair and complexion, dressed in a fine black suit with matching bowtie, was fast asleep in the chair, an old book resting open in his lap.

"Is this him?" Gavin asked confused, the unassuming old man obviously a non-threat.

Thirteen shook his head no.

"Then who is it?" Arthur wondered, his 1911 trained on the chair.

"Aubert!" Thirteen shouted.

The old man woke, startled at the sound of his name. His eyes fell on Arthur and the gun pointed at his face. There was a moment where he was ready to fight the intruder, but then a look of intense fear overcame him.

"Mon Dieu!" he cried. "C'est impossible…c'est vous."

Aubert then promptly passed out, slumping over in the chair.

"Now what was that all about?!" Arthur exclaimed.

"I have that *affect* on people," Thirteen answered, looking over his shoulder, his head cocked to the side.

"So if he's not your father, then who is he?" Gavin wondered, his gun now lowered at his side.

"Aubert here is the head butler. I've known him since I was a boy."

"What should we do with him?" Arthur asked.

"He'll be fine. We won't be long now," Thirteen said, removing a drawer from the right hand side of the desk and then feeling around the edge of the inner frame.

A faint click could be heard as Thirteen found the hidden switch. And then, a louder clunk, the sound of weights and pulleys moving in the outside wall of the peninsula. Gavin looked down over the railing. A section of wall, the rich wooden paneling, had recessed slightly.

"Is that a secret door?" he asked.

"That's the *secret room*, Gavin."

They hurried down the spiral stairs, stopping at the trick wall. Thirteen pushed and the door swung quietly, opening the way to the dark, dusty space. Inside, they found old wooden shelves full of dried out leather-bound books, the pages fragile and yellow from age and candle smoke. Bizarre, ritualistic odds and ends cluttered the small room, piled on shelves not already storing books, stacked on the rickety, half-rotten table that occupied the center of the chamber. An old quill and ink well stood next to a series of beakers and tubing, a sure sign of experimentations.

"Is it here?" Arthur whispered, feeling as though he should have some form of reverence for this unholy place. "The key?"

"I don't see it," Thirteen growled.

"Honestly," Gavin said in disbelief, "this room reminds me so much of the one we discovered in Triton's office five years ago, right before we found him dead."

"My father and Triton used the rooms for a similar purpose. You could say my father was imitating him, or emulating, or even both."

"Well if the key isn't here, is there anything that will tell us where he's gone?" Arthur said, shuffling through the mess of dust-covered manuscripts and parchment.

"I remember a large book, very heavy. The cover was detailed, marked with archaic symbols of the occult. It sat right there," Thirteen pointed to the far side from where they stood, "on a pedestal or alter. They're both gone. But, like the key, I do not know where."

"So maybe they are used together?" Gavin reasoned. "Does the key open a lock or something on the book? Maybe that's what it was for."

"The book had no lock. I would have remembered."

"Then we came out here, nearly scared an old man to death, for nothing." Arthur scoffed.

"It wasn't a total loss," Thirteen reasoned. "For at least we know where my father is not!"

"Yeah, well look at the cup however you like, half-empty or half-full, the bloke still isn't any closer to being found."

"Why don't we wait for the butler to wake. We can question him, find out what he knows," Gavin offered.

"Aubert is of no use to us. If he was important, my father would have taken him along. He won't have a clue where to find him or the key for that matter. The truth is…" Michael trailed off, distracted.

Something had caught his eye. On the table, amongst the muddle, was a small silver ring, a strange, flowery rococo crest engraved on an oval, Latin script extending the rest of the way around the band. The crest looked like an A overlaid on a V, or perhaps it was two V's, one inverted, a small dash in the middle. Regardless, the symbol was a mystery, yet strangely familiar.

"I feel like I've seen this crest, in my youth," Thirteen said in disbelief, "but I could not tell you where!"

"What does the script say?" Gavin pondered curiously.

"Non est verum nisi prospectum" Thirteen read aloud, then translated. "There is no truth only perspective."

"Which means?" Arthur laughed.

"There's no *real* truth. What is true is only because you see or think of it as true, or better said, what I think is truth, may not be truth to you."

"In other words, everything is a lie?" Gavin questioned.

"That could be assumed," Thirteen said. "For whatever is not truth would most certainly be a lie."

The three men stood in momentary silence, contemplating the ring and its meaning. In the main hall, outside the library, the passing of the previous hour was announced by the loud chiming of a highly ornate grandfather clock.

"What should we do then?" Gavin asked.

"I suppose we should head back," Thirteen answered, staring at the ring as he grasped it between his thumb and index finger. "Perhaps the symbol still has more to tell us."

They left the library, Aubert still resting unconscious in the chair, and exited the house, climbing into the Range Rover. Michael removed his mask, tucking it away in his jacket, quickly straightening his tussled hair. Gavin was disappointed. He'd hoped they'd be leaving with enlightenment, not more questions. But regardless, if the ring did offer any information, then perhaps they'd caught a break.

Arthur sped off, the time now past three in the afternoon. He hadn't heard from Jean Luc, which was a good thing, meaning they'd not come across any trouble in Paris. Maybe his old friend had a lead of his own?

****

Edward maneuvered the silver Renault sedan into a parking space on the Rue Davy, the De Bordeaux Hotel on their left. On the right, a row of shops fronted the street. The brothers carefully searched every window, every door, looking for the mark showing that they had the right place.

"There," Killion pointed, spotting the red sign they'd been told to find. "Keep it running. I won't be long."

Killion exited the car and casually strutted around the hood then onto the sidewalk. He first walked past the marked window, pretending to look in the shops, searching for whatever he hoped people might assume an innocent man would browse for on a beautiful day in Paris. Satisfied that no one on the sidewalk was paying him any mind, he returned to the as-described window, then took hold of the door's handle, knocking twice firmly before entering.

A bell dinged overhead as he entered. Killion's nostrils were immediately assaulted by a multitude of scented candles and their non-coexisting odors that battled for his sensory attention. He'd never seen so many candles and all different sorts too. Candles in jars, candles in stands, on plates, kits to make candles, packages of wax, wicks, dyes…he was in a crafting nightmare.

"Bonjour, monsieur," a gentle forties-something lady smiled kindly. "Comment pourrais-je vous aider?"

"Je parle seulement Anglais. English?"

"Oui, monsieur," she smiled sweetly, "I speak English."

"I called and spoke with a man. Is he here now?"

"May I ask what about?"

Killion looked around the small shop, homey and welcoming to decorators, "Guns."

"That's a funny thing to request in a candle store, monsieur."

"I thought so much," Killion smiled, tipping his head. "Good day, madame."

"Wait!" she said, calmly. "This way."

Killion turned and looked at her with distrust as she gestured for him to follow through a back door. He could see the narrow hallway beyond, disappearing around a corner. But they needed a gun and he knew he had no other choice.

The hallway stopped at a flight of old wooden stairs leading down, the building's basement level at the bottom, a reinforced steel door just beyond the last step. The woman pointed that he was supposed to continue on, apparently alone.

"Knock twice, only twice," she explained. "Two knocks, heavy and clearly apart from one another. Then, wait."

She squeezed past him in the constricted corridor and headed back to the store's front. After hearing her instructions to knock on *this* door, he felt a little embarrassed that he'd knocked at the main entrance, believing that that was the door which the man on the phone had meant. Killion paused, studying the setup. The hall was secluded, no other doors, no windows…no escape. A discreet security camera hung above the door, focused on the spot where a visitor would stand to seek entrance to the mystery beyond. But he hadn't come this far to only turn around now.

Killion tried the first step, the dry wood creaking beneath his weight. No surprises, no trapdoors. He continued on to the bottom and stood in front of the heavy, rusting and pitted door, glancing up at the small camera, his face reflected in the lens. Careful to follow the woman's precise instructions, he knocked twice, firm and defined. Now, Killion waited.

The answer was not immediate, nor polite, when the door finally opened. A burly man reached out with hairy arms, taking hold of Killion by his suit jacket, then pulled him roughly inside.

"Check him," a voice spoke, crackling from an intercom speaker.

Immediately, Killion was groped and manhandled, every inch of him scrutinized. He looked up, another camera was watching the scene from above yet another security door. The guard looked up at the camera, nodding to confirm their visitor was unarmed and the familiar voice, the same voice Killion recognized from his phone conversation, allowed entry to the next room, the lock on the door remotely buzzing so that it could be opened.

Killion entered the next room, dark, windowless as before, belowground. There a man sat half hidden in the shadows, tilted back on the rear legs of his chair, his black booted feet elevated, resting on a small table, a sawed-off double-barrel shotgun aimed at Killion as he entered. Beyond the man was a room, completely filled with contraband arms, a dim light hanging overhead, a locked chain link entryway between Killion and the fenced-in guns.

"Let me see your money and I'll tell you what you can buy," the man explained.

Killion slowly reached in his jacket pocket and removed the thick, folded stack of Euros secured in a nickel-plated clip. He then tossed it to the man.

"As I said, fifteen thousand."

"I supposed you were lying when we spoke on the phone," the man admitted, dropping the chair down on all four legs and leaning into the light, revealing his aged, bearded face. "You show me what you would like to purchase, monsieur, and I'll decide if we have an accord."

The man supported the short barrels of the shotgun with his forearm as he stood and retrieved the key from one of the oversized cargo pockets of his drab green khakis, "Entrer, mon ami."

Killion stepped through the unlocked gate. Perusing the many options, the various rifles, machine guns, sub-guns, pistols, and even rocket propelled grenade launchers.

"Do you have ammunition for all this?" Killion questioned.

"I do. Now, choose."

He returned his attention to the guns. His options were endless, but Killion was driven by sensibility and practicality, preferring the familiar. He selected two Sig Sauer P226 9mm pistols, mated with thread-on silencers, placing those on the table, then returning for a final look. The full-size rifles were too large. He wanted to deal with the Frenchman up close, sniping was not acceptable for the message he wanted to deliver. An AK-47 found its way off of its wall mounts and into his hands. Killion played with the folding stock, raised it to his shoulder and sighted the assault rifle. But it too was larger than he wanted. MP5's were decidedly too cliché. Killion wanted something unique, as compact and lethal as possible. He found that in the FNH P90 5.7mm bullpup. Testing the ambidextrous bolt handle and magazine release, this was unquestionably the weapon for the job.

"I'll take this too," he said firmly. "I want additional magazines for the pistols and three more fifty-rounders for this one as well. Also, one hundred rounds of 147gr 9mm and two hundred rounds of 5.7x28mm will do fine."

The French gunrunner obliged, gathering the requested ammunition and magazines. As the man did, Killion quickly ejected the magazine of one of the pistols and tucked it away in his pocket. The dealer returned. Killion picked up one of the boxes of 9mm and opened the flap on the end of the box, then partially sliding the tray from the box, revealing the brass-cased rounds for inspection. He took one, rolling it between his fingers.

"Is there something wrong with the bullets, monsieur?"

"Absolutely not," Killion grinned. "Now how about a duffle bag or something to carry this lot?"

Again, the man obliged, once more turning his back towards Killion, "Un moment."

"Now about the cost of these fine weapons," Killion said loudly, distractingly, as he quickly pulled the magazine from his pocket and pressed the single round into it, then snatched the 226 from the table.

In a fast series of motions, Killion slammed the magazine into the frame and racked the slide, feeding the bullet into the chamber, the hammer remaining cocked and ready from working the action. The French man turned slowly, stunned by Killion's treacherous move. But before the dealer could face him, Killion rushed forward, pressing the round suppressor against the back of the man's hirsute head.

"Name your price, mon ami," he wimpered.

Killion paused dramatically, the tip of his finger ready on the trigger, "Free of charge sounds right."

He pulled the trigger, the action of the gun as it operated louder than the actual shot. The French man slumped forward against the chain link cage, then down to the floor, settling in a bloody mess of sticky human tissue.

"Glad you concur," Killion said haughtily, taking the black canvas bag from the man's dead grip and filling it up with his illicit goods.

Killion finished with the bag, then ejected the empty magazine from the pistol. He loaded five more rounds into it and then chambered one, double checked the fit of the suppressor, then lifted the bag onto his shoulder and crept up to the door through which he'd entered. He spotted a light switch on the wall and flicked it downward. The room was immediately pitch black. Killion took hold of the knob and allowed the door to open, hiding behind it as light from the hall outside shone in.

"Bernard?" the guard in the hallway questioned, the room beyond dark and silent. "Êtes-vous bien?"

There was no reply. The guard pulled a small .380 pistol from a hidden holster and slowly investigated. As soon as the man was beyond the door, Killion aimed and fired, the suppressed gunshot nothing but a soft pop.

"I almost forgot," Killion said aloud, stepping over the second body and returning to the dealer to retrieve his fifteen thousand Euros.

Guns and money in hand, Killion climbed up the steps to the main floor. He peeked around the corner: the coast was clear. The front door was visible and the shop empty.

Killion ignored the woman's words as he hurried across the sales floor. She shouted a curse, swearing she would call the police.

"Not a word, love," he demanded, turning back, the silenced pistol trained on her as he stepped out the door.

He heard her shrill scream as he escaped to the waiting car, the frame-mounted entrance bell happily jingling once again as the door swung shut behind him. Edward was ready, had kept the engine running. Killion jumped in and they sped off.

"How'd we do, Terry?" Edward asked, glancing down at the bloodstained bag.

Killion grinned, dropping the suppressed Sig into the canvas duffle and holding up the unspent stack of currency, "I extended an offer and the sodding fool accepted."

"You didn't kill them did you?!!"

"Of course I did, Ed. But you explained it perfectly last night: killing is what I do. Are you surprised? We got the guns *and* kept the money. I fail to see the problem."

"The fact that you don't see the problem, that *is* the problem. Now there's a trail. There was a security camera on the front of the building. It watched you enter, watched you leave. There will be timestamps and evidence, everything!"

"Besides the Frenchman, no one knows us in Paris," Killion argued. "It was a bloody job-well-done."

"Whatever you say, big brother," Edward chided, "whatever you say."

****

Jean Luc circled the Land Rover around the Arc de Triumph, one of the landmarks on Ashley's short-list of must-see attractions. And, apart from satisfying Ashley's artistic adventure, it allowed Jamie and Kayla to familiarize themselves with the city and its layout. They'd visited Notre Dame and walked along the Seine. The Eiffel Tower, looming in the distance, was their next destination.

"This is a dream come true!" Ashley sighed as the white SUV

meandered through traffic. "I just wish Gavin was with me, that we weren't here for any other reason than as tourists."

A cell phone rang loudly in the quiet cabin of the vehicle. Jean Luc reached in his pocket and retrieved his mobile.

"Allô? Oui," he spoke. "When? Just now?! Merci...I'm on my way!"

The Land Rover accelerated swiftly, the powerful turbo engine roaring. Jean Luc's eyes were intense. They were no longer wandering in Paris, driving without exact purpose; something must have gone wrong.

"Who was that?" Jamie asked, his arms extended, bracing himself against the dash as they cornered sharply. "Was that Arthur? Did something happen?"

"That was one of my contacts," Jean Luc explained. "He served in the GIGN with me, a French special operations unit, Groupe d'Intervention de la Gendarmerie Nationale. He now works for the Ministry of the Interior, a specialist with the Police Naitionale."

"Okay?" Kayla urged. "So what did he say?"

"A report just came through, a double homicide in the basement of a shop on Rue Davy in the 17th arrondissement. We're not far. If we hurry, we can see for ourselves. He already informed the police on-scene that he was sending a liaison. My contact said that the woman who found the bodies described a debonair Englishman in his thirties or forties. If we're lucky, we may have a lead to Killion."

19

"You realize we can't return to the girl's apartment, don't you?" Edward fumed as he and his brother sped back to their hideout, racing southwest, away from the arms front. "I'm sure by now that the plates on this car are circulating the city. Every bobby in Paris will be watching for this car."

"Come off it," Killion barked. "There must be hundreds, if not thousands, of silver Renaults in this city. Unless we draw attention to ourselves, it'll take them a good amount of time to find this car."

"You're right. In fact, they'll most likely find the apartment first. They'll run the registration on the plates and find that it belongs to your little misses. That'll do us a lot of good, having the police show up knocking on her door and finding her drugged. Blast it all, she knows your name!"

"She's in college. I bet the car is registered in her parents' names."

"Oh yeah, that's loads better. That would buy us what, half of a day? The police would *still* follow it back to her."

"You know, you're right, Ed," Killion laughed. "We'll head back, gather what we need, take care of the bird, and..."

Killion was cut short as Edward swerved hard to the left, counter steering to control the skid as they narrowly missed a head-on collision with a recklessly driven, huge, white Land Rover Defender, the SUV crossing into their lane to push through the congested traffic on Rue Cardinet.

"He's a bloody berk isn't he!" Edward shouted.

"That would have been really bad!" Killion agreed.

****

"That was close!" Jamie exclaimed as Jean Luc continued on, pushing the Land Rover to its limit. "We nearly hit that Renault!"

"Sorry, my friend," Belesur admitted. "But we must hurry if we are to gather any evidence for ourselves.

The next minutes were harrowing, Jamie, Kayla, and Ashley hanging on as the SUV continued, finally making a right onto Rue Davy.

"Up there," Ashley pointed ahead, spotting two white Citroens, their light bars flashing, *Police* screened on the cars' exteriors.

Jean Luc mounted the curb, stopping the Land Rover in line with the Citroens, "You girls stay here. If anyone asks, you're American dignitaries, guests of the Ministry of the Interior. If they push for papers, tell them that they are at the Place Beauvau, in the care of the préfet de police."

"*Place Beauvau, préfet de police,*" Kayla repeated.

"Come, Jamie. We will have but ten minutes before this place becomes a circus."

Jean Luc stepped from the driver's seat. Jamie followed. A policeman guarded the front door.

"Allô," Jean Luc said curtly, quickly flashing what he intended to be assumed as proper identification and clearance. "Je suis avec le ministère de l'Intérieur. Où sont les corps?"

"Les corps sont dans le sous-sol," the officer explained, gesturing to the rear of the shop, through the door marked *private* beyond the sales counter.

"Merci, officier," Jean Luc nodded politely, Jamie following suit.

The men hurried to the back of the store, passing two more police who questioned the hysterical woman who'd been threatened at gunpoint, she being the part-owner of the illegal front who then found her friends murdered during their exchange with the Englishman. Jamie noted at least three surveillance cameras starting from the one outside, trained on the street and walk below. He pointed at the fourth camera that hung above the door to the secured room as they trotted down the steps.

Jean Luc pulled a penlight from the inner pocket of his jacket, using its narrow beam to scan the dark room. Jamie pulled out his iPhone, utilizing its flashlight app, but also ready to take photos as evidence.

"Here they are," Jean Luc said, shining his light on the dead men. "The first looks to have been shot in the side of the head. What do you think?"

Jamie checked the man's bloody head, the entry wound clear on the right side, just behind the ear, "Looks like the shooter stood in this area, maybe surprised this guy from behind the door, shot him where he stood.

They both inspected the second body, again noting the entry wound. The tissue clinging to the chain links and the amount of damage where the round exited suggested he was shot point blank.

"This wasn't a robbery or a deal gone bad," Jamie deduced, searching the man's pockets, finding a single key on a gaudy ring. "Look. The cage is unlocked, all the weapons still there. This guy still had the key. He wasn't panicked, there was no struggle. He was double crossed."

"I agree," Jean Luc confirmed. "But this wasn't just a bad deal either. This was premeditated, or, in the least, improvised by a professional."

"Why do you say that?" Jamie wondered.

"A common street thug would have carried every piece of hardware he could get his hands on out that door. Whether he would use them or sell them is irrelevant. The fact that they are still here tells me that this man knew exactly what he wanted, nothing more, nothing less. He had no use for the rest of the weapons. A professional would choose only what he needed for a given job and not bother with anything else."

"Good point," Jamie smiled.

They stared for a moment into the cage, studying the plethora of firearms and heavy ordnances. Together, they seemed to have understood the crime scene, come to very supportable conclusions.

"Where do you suppose the camera feeds go?" Jamie questioned. "We need to see what's on the video, if there's still time?"

"Alright. Let's get back up to the shop."

Jamie followed the cable as it ran up the stairwell and down the hall. Continuing on, the black insulated line led them to a computer with a patch box and small monitor beneath the sales counter. Jean Luc quickly rewound the feed and he and Jamie watched the killings on the little screen. The surveillance confirmed their suspicions. The men were most definitely victims of Terrance Killion.

"Take it back a few frames, Jean," Jamie whispered, "right there, where he looks up at the camera. Perfect."

Jamie quickly snapped a few pictures of Killion's face on the security feed with his cell phone. Hopefully one would turn out. For now, this was the best they could do.

"We can run that through the facial recognition software running on the servers that I set up," Jean Luc smiled. "I had no recent images of him. Excellent thinking, mon ami."

"Thanks, now let's see if we can see him leave," Jamie considered.

Jean Luc pressed buttons on the control box till the view from the outside camera appeared. Briefly rewinding, then hitting play just in time to watch Killion stride out the front door, a suppressed pistol in hand, a black bag slung over his shoulder.

"Look," Jamie smiled, "he gets in that silver car. What kind is it?"

"A Renault."

"Ok, a Renault. Too bad we don't have an angle on the plates."

"We have enough," Jean Luc said. "We'll head back to the warehouse. From there, we can find Killion through the traffic cameras. I already opened a backdoor into the network. We should be able to find where he went. But you know, he wasn't driving. There was someone else behind the wheel. I couldn't see who it was though."

"I'm certain that would be his brother," Jamie explained.

Approaching sirens warned them that it was time to go. Jean Luc led the way, Jamie close behind. They thanked the officer at the door as they passed by, then climbed into the Land Rover, excited to share with the girls all that they had discovered.

****

Edward slowed the car cautiously, both he and his brother scanning the sidewalk, building front, and traffic for any sign of surveillance, anything unusual. A white police Citroen drove through the nearby intersection, but he wasn't in a hurry and paid them no mind.

"Park here," Killion instructed. "I'll go back on foot, clear out the apartment, and take care of the girl. If there's barney, you take off, understand?"

"What about you?" Edward asked with concern.

"We've got our phones. I can disappear, then contact you when they all bog off. But they can't catch you with the guns, little brother," Killion replied, reaching into the bag and quickly loading two spare magazines, then ejecting and fully loading the half-empty mag in the 226 he'd used to kill the dealer and his partner. "There's a Sig in here for you if you need it. Save the P90 for the Frenchman."

Killion did the best he could to conceal the silenced pistol beneath his jacket as he walked awkwardly with the elongated weapon. His custom fit holster, meant for exactly this, was in the girl's apartment along with their things. He'd be happier, and more comfortable, once outfitted with his proper gear.

He chose the stairs rather than the old iron-barred elevator, sprinting up them two at a time. Barely winded, he raced down the hall and stopped at the door, listening intently, the gun ready. Slowly and as quietly as possible, Killion unlocked the door and twisted the knob.

"Terry?" a soft female voice whispered hoarsely.

"Yeah, love," he smiled, smoothly hiding the pistol behind his back as he entered.

As he obviously found out, she'd woken, rather recently as her sore voice implied. Her eyes were red, the lids droopy. She looked terrible. She'd wrapped herself in a plush, green bathrobe, white slippers on her feet.

"I was wondering when you'd be up," he continued. "You must have the nastiest hangover in the history of drinking, Polly. You've been asleep since yesterday!"

"Well, this is crazy," she smirked, her head pounding, "but I almost feel like I've been drugged. Funny right?"

"Oh yeah. Who would ever drug someone as sweet as you?"

She poured a cup of coffee from the freshly brewed pot, "You want some?"

"No thanks, love. I had two cups at lunch already. I'm all jitters," Killion teased.

"I wondered where you'd gone?"

"I had business to attend to, but here I am."

She came up to him, her walk slow and drowsy, and reached up, wrapping her free arm around his neck and kissing him softly on the mouth, "I was afraid you'd left me, that I was just a one-night-stand."

"Absolutely not, love."

"Glad to hear you're sticking around, Terry," she said, biting her lip. "I'm going to go take a shower. You can join me if you like."

Killion watched as she entered the bathroom and turned on the water. Steam began to cover the mirror. She looked back at him, her tired, red eyes innocent, yet implying, as she dropped her robe to the floor before stepping into the claw foot tub and adjusting the clear vinyl shower curtain to hold in the water.

Hurriedly, he collected his briefcase of money and Edward's satchel, his laptop inside. Killion slipped out of his jacket and retrieved his special leather holster from where he'd stashed it in his brother's bag. He put his arms through it, then once more donned his suit jacket, the holster perfectly concealed. Now ready, he slung the laptop bag over his head and left shoulder, the strap falling cross-bodied at his chest. Then, briefcase in his left hand, cocked pistol in the right, Killion entered the bathroom.

"Goodbye, love," he whispered, raising the gun and firing through the clear shower curtain.

The girl's body thudded against the curved bottom of the old iron tub. Her blood mixed with the water that rained down over her as she slipped away, red swirls circling the drain, lost to nothingness.

Killion holstered the pistol and threw the keys he'd stolen for her apartment onto the kitchen counter. All he left behind, was the book of matches, flipped open, the arms dealer's phone number clearly visible.

He shot back down the apartment stairs and through the entry hall, then out onto the stoop. The car was gone. Where was Edward? Had there been trouble?

Killion quickly calculated his next move, but was thrown off as a car slammed on its brakes and skidded to a halt in the street just ahead of where he stood, car horns honking in protest to the driver's madness. Killion looked up, happy to see his brother's face behind the wheel of the car, a red Peugeot coupe.

"Get in!" Edward cried out.

Killion raced to the right side door and jumped in, "What happened to the Renault?!"

"I thought it might behoove us to ditch the girl's car for something with which we won't be so easily connected."

"Good show, brother. Let's find a place to hideout then for a bit." Killion said, the Peugeot speeding off, blending into traffic. "Remember, it's a three hour drive to the Frenchman's. And now, it's late afternoon. We have to decide if we want to go after him in the dark or if broad daylight will do us just fine?"

"There's just the old man, his nutter son, and the driver, oh and that strange girl," Edward remembered, "and for what it's worth, that place gave me the creeps. We can handle the lot during the day. Not to be superstitious, or whatever, but I just don't feel comfortable going there at night."

"You have a feeling?" Killion laughed. "When did you get bent? I think we might be quicker at night. Look at the guns I got for us. We'll be the scariest things in the dark."

"So you want to do it tonight?"

"I say we drive down, sneak onto the property. We stick to the shadows, kill them in their sleep and take the money."

"Alright. If you're certain, we'll head south," Edward agreed reluctantly. "We'll stop off in one of those small towns for petrol and a bite to eat. Honestly, I'm famished."

Killion nodded, glad to be moving forward. He glanced at his watch, quickly estimating all the factors, envisioning their success.

"By midnight tonight, we'll be rid of the Frenchman and add nearly twenty-eight million more Euros to our names," Killion smiled. "Be glad, little brother. We're almost done."

"And the girl?" Edward asked, already certain of the answer. "Will she be remembering your name?"

Killion stared ahead, his eyes soft, but cold. Before killing Delilah, there was a part of him, though small and buried away, that hoped and longed to reunite with his lost love, to reconcile their past and make a new future. But when he saw how bitter she'd become, Killion knew, without a doubt, that she was already dead, long before he pulled the trigger on that stormy night in Chicago. Delilah had become a beautiful temptress, dangerous, seductive, but wholly empty. Her heart was a rotten apple, her tormenting memories were the worms that feasted within. And the worst part of it all? Killion knew deep down, that it was him who had slowly been taking her life for all these years. From the moment they separated, to their final, violent embrace, Killion had been a poison in her veins, a plague infesting her mind. She indeed was dead long before Killion stole her life and he, in that moment, riding in the passenger seat of the flaming red Peugeot as it wound through the streets of Paris, came to terms with a fact that had been eating away at him as well, a bitter truth that he was sorely wrong not to admit, but was aware of it every single day since she broke his heart: he too was dead. That is why killing was so easy for Killion. He believed he'd already forfeited his soul.

"The girl won't be remembering anything," Killion said softly. "Of that, I'm sure."

****

Aubert slowly opened his eyes. For a moment, the room was spinning, the shelves of books blurred and twisted in a dizzying array of contrasting colors and confusing lights. But when the sickening motion stopped, the old man found himself right where he remembered. He slowly, awkwardly stood form the leather desk chair as quickly as his weak body would allow, panicked, glancing left and right, haunted by the face he thought he'd never see again: the masked face of Thirteen.

He straightened his suit and raced down the spiral stair case on his left, finding the secret chamber wide open. This wasn't good, not good at all. He rung his hands as he stood frozen with fear, certain that anger and shouts, a fit of rage, would follow, knowing his gracious employer, Emeric Laurent, *the Frenchman*, would not be pleased. Gladly however, nothing seemed disturbed. Aubert closed up the wall and headed for his quarters, cursing the large house and its long corridors, panting for breath as his aged legs ached with every forced step.

The old man knew what he had to do, but feared the reaction he would knowingly receive. He ran his fingers through his thinning, gray hair as he dialed and raised his private line to his ear

"Sebastian?" he said as a voice answered on the other end, "Oui, it's Aubert. Are you with your father?"

"Oui," came the reply.

"I am so sorry to call you," Aubert explained. "If it were any other way, I would never have interrupted your holiday. I know that your father will be most unpleased and again, I'm so sorry for bothering you while you and your father are away."

"Aubert," Sebastian sighed, "what is it? What is wrong?"

"Monsieur Laurent, he is in grave danger!"

"Are you mad?"

"I saw him, he's back."

"Who is back?"

"He's back, Sebastian, *he's* back!"

"*WHO?!*"

"*HIM*! You're brother...*THIRTEEN*! I saw him, Sebastian. He was here, at the house in Vigny, searching for your father!"

On the other end of the line, standing in the crumbling chateau located near Les Trois-Moutiers, Sebastian was answerless. His jaw flinched as his mind raced to catch up with the words he'd just heard. Had his exiled brother returned, the one known as Thirteen? Aubert wouldn't lie, not ever, and especially not about his long removed brother.

"And you are absolutely positive?" Sebastian questioned.

"Complètement!"

"Then I will tell my father that the prodigal son has returned."

20

Jean Luc sat at the warehouse workstation, typing quickly on the wireless keyboard. The prior day, he'd hacked into the Paris police traffic system and vehicle registration database, leaving himself a back door in case they needed it. Time had proven that this was a wise decision. Jamie leaned over his shoulder as the tech savvy Jean Luc Belesur navigated the system, running searches and pulling feeds from the traffic cameras. Ashley and Kayla chatted nervously, reviewing the murders that Jamie and Jean Luc had described.

Gavin, Michael and Arthur only just arrived from their disappointing trip to Vigny. Where Michael expected to find answers, they uncovered nothing, only a dead end. His frustration was obvious; though, with the confidence given by donning the mask of Thirteen gone when not wearing said mask, he buried his thoughts, thinking he might burden his friends. The doubt and anger that haunted him, Michael believed, was better left unsaid.

"So you know it was Killion?" Arthur mused. "He actually let himself be caught on video?"

"Why do you say it that way?" Kayla asked. "You said Killion *let* himself be seen. Are you saying he had any other option?"

"Most definitely. The man is beyond a professional," Arthur explained, "he's a ghost. And ghosts aren't seen unless they want to be."

"In other words, he's sending a message," Kayla concluded.

"Right," Jean Luc confirmed.

"But a message to who?" Ashley questioned. "He doesn't know we're here, right?"

"Would he expect you to be?" Arthur asked.

"I doubt it," Jamie chimed in. "Last we saw him, he was flying away in a helicopter. For all he knows, we've been arrested and thrown in prison without bail on a handful of charges, mainly murder in the first degree."

"Have you had any communication with him?" Arthur continued.

"Nope," Gavin said, shaking his head. "We only knew that he was going to bring the key to Paris, or rather France in general, and deliver it to the Frenchman."

"Then I doubt Killion expects you to have made the trip," Arthur reasoned. "He was sending a message to someone else."

"My father perhaps?" Michael wondered, involving himself in the conversation. If Killion has already been to see the Frenchman and things went as I would expect, meaning a double-cross, then quite possibly, this was a testament, a display, of just how far he's willing to go to exact revenge. My father is a clever man, his greatest asset is his meek demeanor, but believe me, he's a serpent underneath, coiled and ready to strike."

They all fell silent, contemplating Michael's words. Jean Luc continued typing furiously, the key strokes clicking loudly in the quiet space.

"Enfin!" Jean Luc announced excitedly. "I got something."

The group huddled around his chair, looking down at the main computer screen. An image of a silver Renault, its front plate clearly visible. Killion could be seen in the passenger seat, another man behind the wheel.

"That is him!" Jean Luc smiled.

"Yeah, but who's driving?" Arthur asked. "Is that his brother?"

Ashley sighed, reliving her captivity and escape from Los Angeles in her mind. Being the only one of them who had actually seen Killion's brother, she knew right away. His face was still bruised from when she'd brutally attacked him, fighting for her life, allowing herself and Elizabeth the opportunity to get away.

"It certainly is his brother," she said. "That's Edward."

****

"Aubert told you that?" Emeric Laurent confirmed, Sebastian sitting with him, once again in the chapel on the chateau's sprawling grounds.

"Oui, père," Sebastian answered. "Michael is in France, but he is not himself. He is most certainly Thirteen."

"This changes everything," the Frenchman replied.

"But how can this be? I thought you said his power had left him, that the demons were no longer with him?"

"I said what I *thought* to be true, Sebastian…nothing more."

"Do you think he has come to help us, to assist you with your task?"

"I fear not, mon fils," Laurent answered. "I believe he's come because of what we did. He's looking for answers as to why we stole away his wife and my grandchild."

"Then perhaps nothing has changed," Sebastian suggested. "We can continue as planned. You knew he would come. That's part of the plan."

"But it's too soon! I do not know if the girl is ready to open the door."

"Then I will fight him, father."

"If your brother has returned to France with the full power of Thirteen at his command, he'll kill you."

"I'm strong," Sebastian growled. "I understand his power. I have mastered black magic, can conjure whatever I must to defeat him."

"But I'm afraid it's still different. Michael, via the mask he can commune with the spirits in a way that you simply cannot. Where you use their power, Thirteen *is* their power, manifest in flesh, making the flesh impossible to destroy. When he wears that mask, he is like an ancient god, the legends of Greece and Rome. He is Ares, Apollo, Bacchus and, most definitely Hades, god of the underworld!"

"Then what should we do, if you find me incapable of facing my brother?"

"We begin the ritual tonight, at sundown."

"But we will not be able to assemble The Collective in such short notice. After all, that is only hours from now."

"We'll do it without them. The girl will have to be ready. Fate will decide," Laurent grinned.

"You seem happy about this. Am I missing something?"

"Only that chaos is everywhere. The fact that, regardless of how well we plot, how greatly our plan is conceived, we are still at the mercy of destiny! But if doing these things, what I admit is purely evil and horrid when judged in my right mind, opens the way for the one to rise, the one who will bring peace to the earth, end bloodshed and famine, cloth the poor, provide universal care for the sick, then it is all for good, for the betterment of mankind. And that, my son, makes it all worthwhile."

"And you believe in this man, that a single political figure will bend every nation to his whim and gain absolute control of the world through his office?"

"The nations have already set the stage, whether knowingly or not. The rise of the New World Order has been long coming. It has been a delicate process, spanning decades, a joint venture of presidents and parliaments, prime ministers and heads of state. They call it globalism in academia, but it is truly a universal government and universal economy. This man is out there. Even if he himself does not know it yet. In fact, I believe that this man will be earnest in his rise to power, that he seeks true peace for the entire world. What a great day it would be to see Israel and Palestine live as brothers, to see Iran, North Korea, China, Russia and the United States end their silly nuclear posturing! Imagine a world where socialism and democracy were the same thing, a world where communism, true communism was allowed to flourish! Every need would be cared for hunger and homelessness would be cured. Social class stigmas and racism would end. No one would have more than they need, because there would be no need to have more! We could all share in the glorious wealth and promise that this planet has to offer. What we're doing truly is a great thing, my son. And we will press on, we must; for the sake of the world!"

"Then we begin tonight. And soon, if you are right, father, Paris will be the first to fall!"

****

"I've found the address!" Jean Luc announced excitedly. "The vehicle is registered to a Pollyanna Marchand. It's not far."

"Great job," Gavin smiled, patting Belesur on the back.

"Here's the address," Jean Luc said, scribbling on a scrap of paper.

"I'm on my way," Arthur confirmed, looking at the address he now held in his hand.

Jamie grabbed his suit jacket and slipped his arms into the sleeves as Arthur headed for the door, "I'm coming with you."

****

The bright red Peugeot cruised along the roadway. Terrance and Edward Killion pushed the rural speed limit as they headed south west, towards the Frenchman's chateau, hoping to arrive before nightfall. They'd only just passed Orleans, but they were making good time, almost halfway to Les Trois-Moutiers.

"Why don't we stop in Tours for a quick supper?" Edward asked. "That'll put us only an hour away. We need to be at our best and I'm starving."

Killion agreed with a silent nod. He too was hungry.

"So have you decided how we'll do this then?" Edward continued speaking. "Are we going to be all guns and glory or are we going to play in the shadows?"

"We've got the P90, that'll do a lot. Quiet is key, but only to get close. After that, we give that old geezer hell."

"Do you suppose we'll face any real resistance?" Edward wondered. "I mean, honestly, the place isn't nearly fortified. And, we only saw the French bloke, his son, his manservant or whatever he was, and the young girl."

"I don't see how," Killion answered. "We kill anyone who gets in our way, the girl included."

Edward concentrated on the road ahead, the sun slowly continuing its recessing arc into the western sky, "There is one more thing."

"Speak then."

"When the Frenchman took us to the strange room in the chateau's cellar, you remember, the one with the freestanding door?"

"How could I forget, brother?"

"Right, well…when we were down there, I swear I saw two sets of blinking eyes!"

"You superstitious blighter," Killion laughed. "What are you on about?"

"I'm just saying I saw something, that's all."

"Well get it out of your head," Killion ordered. "Nothing will keep us from having our revenge, nothing!"

****

Arthur parked the Range Rover. They were at the address, but the silver Renault was nowhere in sight.

"Let's head in, shall we?" Arthur said stepping from the SUV.

Jamie followed and the two men entered the building, quickly finding the elevator. They had to manually close the metal gates before the lift would allow them to travel up to the floors above.

Arriving on the third floor, Arthur opened the metal doors as quietly as the nearly century old gates would allow, then drew his gun and crept down the hall, reading the apartment numbers that hung on the wall next to each door.

"Here we are," Arthur whispered, leaning up against the wall, his 1911 pistol ready.

Jamie pulled the Beretta from his holster and took a breaching position on the other side of the door. Arthur counted to three, then twisted the knob and pushed open the door. Jamie followed the Englishman through the frame, his aim trained to the right as Arthur covered the left, but the room was empty. Killion didn't appear to be there.

"Hey," Jamie whispered as loudly as possible, "over here."

Arthur quickly joined Jamie, immediately aware of what had drawn his new friend's attention. The sound of running water: someone was in the shower.

They approached the bathroom carefully, first peeking into the empty bedrooms on each side, the sound of water coming from the middle door.

"Oi!" Arthur shouted, rushing towards the bathroom with his gun raised. "Hands where I can see them!"

There was no response. Arthur grunted unhappily as he crossed the threshold into the bathroom.

"I think we found Pollyanna Marchand," he said, looking down upon the dead body, the hot water running out long ago, cold water showering down on her mercilessly.

Jamie came in and pulled back the curtain, sighing as he checked her for a pulse, but finding nothing confirming what he knew at first glance. Her blue eyes stared off blankly into space. Jamie closed them for her respectfully.

Then, just as he was about to stand, he noticed something on her body, a purpled wound on her ribs, just below her left breast, hidden by where her elbow had settled as she died. He lifted her arm away to take a look.

"She was definitely shot," Jamie said, pointing at the mark. "That's the exit wound. Killion must have hit her from the right side and the bullet passed through there."

"So did Killion kill her just so that he could have her car?"

"Well," Jamie answered, "I've been a police officer for a long time. This would be the first carjacking I've ever seen take place in a third floor apartment bathroom. She was clearly aware of his presence, possibly even welcoming him. He shot her in the back."

"I follow," Arthur nodded. "This wasn't just a murder, this was absolutely cold blooded."

"Was Killion always like this?" Jamie asked, standing back up and pulling the clear shower curtain back to provide the dead girl some dignity.

"He was calculated, a bit of a loose cannon so to speak, but never this ruthless. I mean, she's what, nineteen, twenty at best?"

"Sounds right," Jamie agreed.

"But Killion was always the least burdened of us, after a particularly nasty mission, he always seemed to walk away as if he'd immediately forgotten what we'd just been through, what we'd just done. But we killed with purpose, military targets, hard and impenetrable by standard means. We did everything we could to avoid collateral damage, but…there were times where it couldn't be helped. It's a terrible thing you know, watching women and children die because a coward hides amongst them."

"So is that all she is? Collateral damage?"

"In Killion's eyes, yes."

"Tell that to Mr. and Mrs. Marchand," Jamie frowned.

"There is always a cost of war, mate. That's the ugly truth. Trust it coming from someone who's broken his fair share of eggs to make the omelet we're in now."

"You consider yourself responsible for this, indirectly I mean?"

"If you had any idea how many times I saved that blighter's sodding arse, you'd understand. I pulled a bullet from his leg once, with my bare, bloody hands!"

"You can't think like that. Killion has chosen this life. You are not responsible," Jamie encouraged.

"But if I'd just have let him die…"

"Then you would be living with that guilt to this day and we'd only be chasing another killer now. This *is* what it is. Nothing more!"

"Are you a cop or a head-doctor?" Arthur winked.

"I've just been there, seen terrible things, which is why I became a cop. I used to question how God could exist and allow such an evil world, so much pain…death. For the longest time, I believed that scenes like this, looking at Pollyanna Marchand, were evidence that there was no God. But I now understand how God is still here, even in this."

"How could you ever find evidence of a loving God in the murder of an innocent young woman?!"

"Because," Jamie answered, "in finding her, you felt remorse, a sadness for the loss of her life. It proves you're still human, nothing like Killion. It means you can still come back, back from the life you lived. There's forgiveness, there's redemption. God is good, no matter what evil we face, how bad the opposition. God simply *is*."

****

"There's little daylight left," Emeric Laurent said, his voice flourishing with excitement. "Prepare the girl. The ritual will take several hours and there's no time to waste!"

Sebastian nodded, then hurried for the cellar. He descended the stairs quickly and navigated the corridor in moments, stopping at her door. She answered after he knocked lightly.

"Voyons, ma petite fille. il est temps." Sebastian smiled sweetly. "It is time."

He helped her undress from the new clothing that his father had provided, draping her once more in the ceremonial lace gown. Sebastian then took a new needle from his pocket, pulled the vial of sedative, and filled the syringe with the clear drug. He then gently took hold of her arm, finding her vein and plunging the needle in. Her eyes fluttered as the liquid mixed with her blood, coursing through her body, her limbs growing light and warm.

"Now rest," Sebastian said, helping her lie down on the bed. "We will return shortly, and then, we will begin."

Sebastian headed back up stairs, knowing his father would be in the chapel. He traversed the grounds quickly, the sun now hidden by the towering trees, lost behind their green tops. Laurent was found, just as expected, alone, comforted by the sullen flicker of a single candle. He'd pulled a rough, ancient looking robe down over his fine suit. There was another, identical one for Sebastian as well.

"She has been prepared, father."

Laurent nodded, taking hold of the hood and pulling it up over his head, his brow suddenly covered in shadow. Sebastian quickly removed his long, black trench coat and slipped into the old rags his father handed him. He too pulled the hood up and the two stood in silence, staring at the dimly burning candle.

"It is time," the Frenchman whispered, dousing the flame between his forefinger and thumb.

The father and son moved quickly through the shadowy wood that had overtaken the property, standing between them and destiny. The moon glowed in the darkened sky and an owl hooted ominously somewhere in the branches above.

They quickened their pace as their excitement grew, every step drawing them closer to the future, closer to the rise of the greatest leader the world would ever know. And the girl, the precious, young, innocent girl was the real key. Triton's trinket was but a mere prop. The girl was everything, just as before, in New York City, when a young and naïve Ashley Rose was given dreams by Triton himself, drawing her into his world, using her sister and their circumstances to bring her to him, all so that he could use her to open the door.

The process required a youth, no older than eighteen, female, and innocent, never defiled by the lust of a man. She must also have been susceptible to suggestion, someone with an abundance of imagination and an excitable nature. Ashley was all of these, as was the poor French girl. But where Triton failed, Emeric Laurent would succeed. The ceremony would begin and the door to Hell would be opened, unleashing an army of darkness and wrath on all of mankind. And then *he*, the chosen one, the one who would follow after, this evil army would become his to command as he ascended to power out of the multitudes, the antichrist, glorified by all nations.

Emeric led the way as the men hurried down the creaking steps and into the dark cellar. The girl's door was left open. Laurent found her lying on the bed, her eyes glazed, staring off into nothing, lost between a dream and reality.

"Come now," he whispered, taking her by the hand and helping her sit, then stand, finally placing the key in her palm. "And do not let go of this."

Sebastian pushed ahead, opening the door to the inner chamber. As they entered, whispers haunted the room, the air stiflingly warm. Lighting a candle, Laurent led the girl to a precise spot where a circular pattern in the stone floor marked the exact place she should stand.

"The time has come," the Frenchman spoke loudly, his voice bold, echoing in the dark place. "Join us, my servants."

For a moment, there was nothing; but then, there was a stirring. Blinking eyes reflected the warm glow of the candle, arching all around the room, from one side to the other. Sebastian grinned.

Laurent took the candle to a recess in the wall, found to the right of the door through which they entered. A rope hung from the top of the recess, disappearing in the stone work above. Below it was a small pool of liquid, oily and slick. The rope too, revealed by the candle light was covered in the same substance, its end dangling mere inches from the basin.

The Frenchman whispered a quiet prayer, words of incantation, and touched the candle's flame to the small pool of liquid. Fire engulfed the surface of the small stone bowl, igniting the wick-like rope. Laurent watched the flame rise higher and higher, then into the wall when, suddenly, a roar filled the room, a flame crawling in an oil-filled channel that encompassed the entire room, shooting to the left and right above the alcove and meeting somewhere on the other side. The room now glowed red in the firelight, revealing its design: circular, the ceiling higher than expected.

The whispers grew as the light also disclosed the inhabitants of the room, the source of the blinking eyes. People of all ages, sizes, genders, and color stood shoulder to shoulder around the entire chamber. Their eyes glowed like a cat's at night, when light is reflected off the cellular tapetum lucidum within the animal's inner eye. However this was not caused by science. They were humans, genetically incapable of eyeshine, lacking in the necessary cellular structure. No, this was impossible. Even so, there was something stranger still than their animal-like eyes. Their skin, leathery and rough, seemed dried out and dead, like living, breathing corpses. Again, Sebastian smiled at the sight, nearly sixty of them in that circular chamber alone.

As if on cue, moans and grunts echoed from the outer halls as shuffling feet found their way from the side rooms and into the main chamber. All accounted, there was easily a hundred of these creatures, bringing with them the stench of decay.

Laurent nodded at his son, confirming his readiness. The man approached the alter which held the thick, ancient book and the ceremony began. He opened the cover, flipped to the marked page and spoke in a slow, deep growl, Latin flowing from his eloquent tongue. The young girl began to shake violently, her convulsing evidence that she was in the right place, her mind freeing itself from its fleshy prison. Blood trickled from her nose. Her eyes rolled back in her head. The Frenchman began a dark and sinister chant, the words themselves carrying an evil note as he repeated them over and over again, each time louder than before. Sebastian began as well, following his father, his voice immediately followed by an unholy chorus as the creatures joined in as well. The room shook as the chant was now a riot, screams and shouts assaulting the ears, the sound a chaotic, yet rhythmic pulsing, pounding off the heavy stone of the floor, ceiling, and walls. There was now nothing but sound, head-splitting, ear-aching sound, the decibels crushing, beyond dangerous, beyond humanly tolerable. Sebastian reached up, blood now dripping from his own nose. His face shone with a glorious smile and he laughed, still repeating the words, his voice lost amongst all the others.

And then, without any warning, the Frenchman slammed shut the cover of the tome. All at once, the flames extinguished and the voices ceased, the room engulfed in total darkness and absolute silence.

Sebastian strained his eyes to see, his ears ringing. Emeric too, focused intently on the space ahead, where the girl stood.

Her bare feet softly slapped against the stone floor as she slowly paced forward. Though they could not see her in the blackness, they heard the sound of the door jiggle, the key turn the lock, and then...the creaking of the ancient hinges as she pushed it open. Blinding white light blast from within the frame, silhouetting the girl in its radiance. A howling scream, long and shrill emanated from the beyond, her hair and clothing blown back by a horrifying wind.

The young girl collapsed to the floor. And then, nothing.

21

"Did you hear that?!" Killion asked, pausing as they exited the red, stolen Citroen, caught unawares by the strange sound.

"I did, brother!" Edward whispered, fear evident in his voice. "What the bloody hell was that?!"

"I haven't the faintest," Killion replied. "Here, take this Sig Sauer, give the silencer a firm twist to make sure it's secure."

Killion handed his brother the suppressor-equipped pistol as well as some backup magazines. He pulled his pistol from its special shoulder holster, checked its rounds, chambered it, then returned it beneath his suit jacket. Then, Killion pulled the short P90 automatic from the bag, stuck his head through the loop of the gun's single-point sling, and fit a loaded fifty round magazine into the top of the short-barreled select-fire rifle, cocking it dramatically.

"Stay low and follow me," Killion ordered.

The brothers crept as quietly as the gravel parking area would allow, the small stones crunching beneath their feet with every step. They hurried along the perimeter of the small outbuildings that led to the narrow bridge, clinging to the shadows that darkened the buildings' corners. The bridge was the only way across the protective moat, but it was out in the open and they knew that traversing it was a huge risk, being left with but one option: total exposure at their enemy's gate. But in truth, they had no choice.

Killion nudged Edward and began to whisper once more, the two brothers standing at the last corner of the last outbuilding, nothing but open space between them and the chateau, "Once we move from this spot, we don't stop. We run as fast as we can, mindful of our footfalls. We must remain quiet. As soon as we're across the bridge, we flank up on opposite sides of the main door. I'll take the right, you cover the left. Have you got it?"

"Yes," Edward nodded in deep concentration, his brow furrowed for extra measure. "Run to the door, don't stop…got it!"

"And don't fire a bloody shot unless you have to!"

"Right,' Edward understood.

"Are you ready?"

"Terry, about that sound, the scream…"

"Whatever that was doesn't matter. All that matters is Laurent and the money. We kill Laurent and take the money. Kill Laurent, take the money!"

Edward, again, nodded. Killion patted his younger brother's shoulder in an unspoken affirmation of his love. The two stared into each other's eyes as if it might be for the last time, each one wordlessly speaking the things they'd always wished to share, but never seemed to manage in sorry communication marred by brotherly competition and quarrels. But now, in this moment, hiding in the shadows from the moon's white glow, everything made sense. They'd come to terms, shared a silent peace, and knew that there was a chance that this could be their end.

"I'll count to three and then we make like the devil for the front door," Killion grinned.

Edward closed his eyes and mouthed a few short words.

"Did you just pray?" Killion smiled.

Edward shook his head in uncertainty, "I'm not sure. But words just came to me and seemed the right thing to do in the moment."

"Right then," Killion said, returning focus to the mission, the goal: kill Laurent, take the money, "One…two…THREE!"

The race was on as the brothers scrambled across the exposed gravel lot. They managed to the reach the bridge without event, now only a measure of meters separated them from the front door. Killion made it across, but Edward froze midway, his face pale, his eyes focused on the dark and murky water below.

The defensive ring of water that encircled the chateau was bubbling, brewing into a frenzy. It swirled and churned as bubbles popped, breaking at its surface. And then, shapes began to take form, ubiquitous shapes that resembled humans, yet didn't seem *human*. Slowly, a soft yellow glow rose from the depths, recognizable as not one, but two glowing orbs as it came closer.

Then, Edward gasped. The yellow orbs were putrid eyes accompanied by a shark-like toothy grin and a leathery, oval, hairless head. In panic, he raised the pistol and fired into the dark water, the 9mm bullet splashing into the pool. The horrifying face disappeared, but there was no blood, no lifeless body rising to the surface.

"Bloody idiot!" Killion hissed. "What are you doing?!"

Edward did not reply. He still searched the churning water for answers to the questions that now cluttered his mind.

Killion ran to his brother, violently clutching his elbow and dragging him from the trance, "Have you gone mad?!"

But Edward still didn't answer. Killion slapped him full across the face.

Edward blinked, "Oi!"

"What's wrong with you?" Killion asked angrily. "They might have heard your shot! And what were you doing anyway? This isn't exactly the time to go fishing!"

"I saw something in the water!"

"Oh you saw something did you? Like what?"

"A face, brother…an ugly, grotesque…*evil*…face!"

"You seriously expect me to believe you saw a monster out for a midnight swim? You're imagining things," Killion growled.

"But I did see...*something*," Edward argued.

"We'll talk about it later, we have to move on. Now get it together, mate!"

The brothers hurried to the door, taking their places on the left and right of the entrance. Killion nodded, then silently counted off with his fingers. *One...two...*and again, they moved on *three.*

The door was unlocked and it opened easily. They were in.

Moonlight shone down through the crumbled and open ceiling above. Once more, they clung to the shadows, slinking like stalking cats through the weather-devastated structure, the passing of time so evidently unkind to the glorious property.

The brothers, guns ready, found the hall in which they'd met Laurent earlier. There, sleeping with his feet propped up on the table, was their chauffer, Laurent's lackey, next to his feet, the satchel that held the remaining money. Killion let the P90 hang to one side, then quietly pulled his silenced pistol from beneath his jacket, mercilessly executing the man with a well-placed shot to the back of his head.

"Get the bag, brother," he whispered.

Edward nodded and stepped around the bloody chauffer's body slumped dead in the chair, then half unzipped the bag, gazing upon the fortune within and then zipping it back up and slinging it cross-bodied over his shoulder.

"Is it all there?" Killion asked

"Looks like it."

"Alright then. Now for Laurent."

Edward hesitated, the weight of the bag firmly on his shoulder, "We have the money. Why don't we just leave? We can disappear!"

"It's the principal of the matter," Killion replied. "The man broke his promise and did us wrong. I can't live with that. Laurent must die."

Edward stared reluctantly at the path beyond. The steps leading down to the cellar disappeared into blackness while the way to the exit beckoned him, illuminated by the moon, certain and sure, freedom and promise waiting outside.

"What are you waiting for?" Killion muttered. "This way."

Edward looked once more at the dark stairwell, then the brightly lit path to the open, unguarded front doors.

"Come on!" Killion urged.

Reluctantly, he followed Terrance into the darkness, turning his back on hope and facing what he believed was their impending death, all for nothing but the restoration of his brother's wounded pride.

"Do you think they're down there?" Edward asked cautiously.

"If they're not, most likely the girl will be. That was her bedroom, if I'm not mistaken. If Laurent and his son aren't down there, then we'll, in the least, take the girl. You saw the way the old man looked at her. He'll do anything for her."

"So you're saying we kidnap her for ransom?"

"Indeed."

"But we already have the money," Edward questioned. "What would Laurent give in exchange?"

"With a man like Laurent," Killion smiled, glancing back over his shoulder as the brothers squinted to see in the pitch-black dark, "there's always more money."

Edward sighed and continued to follow Killion. There was no arguing with his brother. After a moment of pause to gather themselves, to re-center directionally, they found themselves standing outside the girl's door.

"Alright," Killion whispered, "we go in slowly, quietly. If Laurent is there, we kill him. No conversation, no questions…end of story. If he's not, you grab the girl and we head back to the car. Understood?"

Edward nodded in compliance.

"Good," Killion winked, carefully testing the door and finding it unlocked.

Killion led the way into the girl's room, but she wasn't there. Other than a pile of her clothes lying on the uncomfortable-looking bed and a candle that slowly burned on a small table, the room was empty. This was unexpected. The brothers glared at each other in the flickering candle light, uncertain of their next move. No Laurent, no girl: this wasn't working out they way that Killion had hoped.

"Maybe it's a sign?" Edward pleaded. "Maybe we aren't meant to find Laurent? Let's just take the money and get out of this bloody place!"

"Perhaps you're right, little brother," Killion relented. "Maybe we should just go."

But as they turned to leave, a whisper found its way to their ears, carried by a cool draft that escaped from beneath the door to the strange inner chamber, stopping the men where they stood. They listened, their heads cocked, trying to make sense of what they might have heard; and again, the voice spoke.

"What is that?" Edward wondered.

"Did it come from in there?" Killion questioned, pointing at the heavy wooden door to the curious room beyond.

"Maybe."

"Oh, listen, brother," Killion said, the voice speaking softly once more, leaving him certain of its direction. "It's coming from inside!"

"This might not be the best idea," Edward pointed out. "I mean, after what I saw in the water, this is too weird. Something just isn't right."

"Don't be daft," Killion said. "Come on."

Killion took hold of the centuries-old knob and slowly opened the wooden door. The hinges creaked as the voice grew louder, now distinguishable as two.

"I have a bad feeling about this," Edward warned.

But it was too late. The door was now fully open. And there, in the very center of the room, was the mysterious door to nowhere, the young girl sprawled out on the ground in front of it, Emeric and Sebastian Laurent on either side of her unmoving body.

"Hello, chums," Killion laughed devilishly, his suppressed Sig Sauer pistol raised, pointed at the elder Laurent.

Edward reluctantly took aim as well, his front sight focused on Sebastian, "Keep your hands where we can see them, mate!"

"You shouldn't be here," Laurent growled, his voice deep, sinister, not like before. "You have no business here!"

"Indeed I do," Killion argued. "You think you can make a fool out of me? You tell me the item I bring you is a sodding replica, after all we went through to get it for you? Well that's too bleeding bad, isn't it? You owe us for services rendered, old man."

"I'll give you one last chance," Emeric negotiated. "You can walk out of here alive, both of you. Or…"

"Or what?" Killion barked. "As you can plainly see, you're outgunned."

"Fine," Laurent sighed. "You leave me no choice."

For a moment, Edward took his eyes off of Sebastian and glanced once more around the room. The solitary door in the center of the area stood open. A strange smell lingered in the air. And, if he wasn't going mad, he might have heard an exhale from somewhere over his left shoulder. The room was too dark to see, but he suddenly had an overwhelming realization: perhaps they weren't alone.

"What are you going to do, talk us to death?" Killion mocked. "We're in control here. We make the threats."

Emeric Laurent ignored Killion's brash ignorance as he kneeled next to the young girl, his hand holding hers, her chest faintly displaying her shallow, labored breathing. She was alive, but for how long? Laurent wasn't playing any games. That time was over. There was no turning back.

"Get them," the Frenchman ordered into the darkness.

The room was suddenly filled with chaos as shadowy figures descended upon them, their eyes glowing, their fingers clawing at the brothers. Panicked, Killion struggled to holster his pistol. Though it was something he had done so often and so well, becoming second nature to him; here, in the maddening darkness, vastly outnumbered and with unknown creatures tugging and pulling on him, the length of the suppressor became a major hindrance, slowing him down and nearly allowing him to be overcome. But he managed to tuck the gun away as he fell back, Edward steadying him.

"What are you waiting for?!" Killion shouted at his brother, raising the full-auto P90 bullpup and spraying bursts of fire into the unrelenting wave of groping hands.

Edward did his best to aim, but there were simply too many. And worse, he discovered with every well placed shot to an attackers chest, the round did little but stagger them. These people, or creatures, or *whatever* seemed impervious to their bullets.

The fifty round magazine in Killion's gun was empty, all the bullets spent in mere seconds as he held back on the trigger. He removed it and tossed it aside, fumbling to insert another full magazine into position beneath the upper sight rail. But he finally did, clicking it into place and charging the bolt. Again he fired and again, in only second, the gun ran dry.

"We have to get out of here!" Edward screamed over the snarling of their attackers.

"GO!" Killion replied, letting the P90 hang on its sling, reaching into his jacket for his pistol.

The brothers raced back through the girl's room, slamming the door shut behind them as they did. They turned out into the hall and navigated the narrow, dark corridor, desperately searching for the stairs.

Behind them, the *things* that obeyed Laurent's order smashed through the wooden door, splinters flying as the planks cracked and buckled behind the creatures' fury. The host of monsters flooded into the hall, stumbling over one another as they made chase.

"This is insane!" Edward cried.

"Just keep moving!" Killion demanded, twisting as he ran to fire rounds haphazardly, hoping to slow them down.

But the throng continued. The brothers found the stairs and bound up them as quickly as they could, then raced for the entry hall, dodging tree branches and heavy fallen masonry that littered their route to freedom.

"We're almost there, brother," Edward laughed. "We can get away!"

Just then, only moments from escape, a lunging hand took hold of the duffel bag full of money that slung across Edward's shoulder, pulling him violently backwards, toppling to the floor. The strap on the bag stretched to its limit, the nylon stitching beginning to pop under the stress.

"NO!" Killion screamed, nearly falling over an exposed root that pushed up through a crack in the stone floor.

He turned back for his brother, raising his Sig Sauer and aiming at the mob of grotesque creatures. But his well-aimed shots did nothing. Killion managed to take hold of his brother's arm and, at point blank range, fire into the side of the chaser's head. A black, oily substance splattered on both brothers as the bullet ripped through attacker's skull. Apparently, they realized, they'd discovered the trick: these monsters could only be stopped by shooting them in the head!

By sheer luck, Terrance and Edward had reached the main hall. And what was better, now knowing the secret to killing the creatures, they used their surroundings to their benefit. The door leading into the hall was narrow and tall.

Quickly, they dispatched the attackers who had already made it through. After reloading, both men fired carefully, aiming for their oppositions' heads. One by one, the creatures fell, piling up in the forced bottleneck of the door. Each body fell over the one before it and, with an ever increasing surge of creatures, the dead bodies had plugged the hole, slowing down any who followed after, forcing them to climb or dig their way through the gory roadblock.

"Well done," Killion smiled, wiping the creature's black blood from his face. "Let's get out of here."

****

High above the lights of Paris, on the Eiffel Tower's observation deck, two men stood. They looked out into the night, speaking every so often, their mood light, yet they remained vigilant.

They were tall and slender, athletic, dressed in casual attire, nothing fancy. The men both fit in, yet also stood out against the Parisian backdrop.

"The night seems darker than usual, doesn't it?" the one man asked the other.

"True," he replied.

"What was it we're looking for?" the other man wondered.

"Not sure. But remember, we were told we'd know it when we see it."

The men fell silent, still staring out over the city. The night was not only strangely dark, but also particularly crisp, the air unusually cool for a summer night.

"Do you think it's true what was said," the inquisitive man continued. "that war is coming?"

"I don't know any more than you do. I just do what I'm told. There's no point in interfering with the process. We have to let it unfold and see where it goes. If it means war, then we fight."

Again, the men grew silent, thinking on the words that had been said. Far below, beyond the reach of normal sight, something stirred.

"Hey, look there!" the talkative man persisted. "The river...the water...it's swirling, bubbling!"

They peered down from the Eiffel Tower, trying to comprehend what they were seeing. A large whirlpool began to form in the Seine. And then, without warning, shadowy, winged creatures, bat-like but man-sized, burst from the center of the spiraling pool, dozens, maybe hundreds pouring into the night sky.

"This can't be happening, this *can't* be happening!"

"There's no way, it's too soon, much too soon!"

The two men fell into panic, clinging to the railing, their knuckles turning white, their faces pale at the sight of the demonic legion invading the city of Paris. Was this the war?

Below, cars continued on, unaware of the threat that loomed overhead. Late-night wanderers still strolled hand-in-hand, captivated by Paris' history and charm, paying no notice to the impending doom.

With every passing moment, more and more demons escaped through the watery portal. Now numbering in the thousands, the creatures perched on rooftops, glided above the streets, cackling and whooping excitedly. For too long, they'd moved in small scale, doing Satan's bidding, trying to destabilize the world, but now, summoned forth from Hell, they were ready for pure and utter chaos. The time had finally come.

The two men stepped back from the railing, beyond the demons' view.

They simply could not fathom, even begin to comprehend what they were seeing.

"What should we do?!" the first man asked.

The second man thought briefly, then spoke, "We were told we'd know *it* when we saw *it*, right?"

"Most definitely."

"Then I think we know why we were told to be here, on this very deck, on this very night. It's time."

"For what?"

"Time to get Joseph."

22

Wake up...

Gavin stirred, rolling over onto his side, sleeping with difficulty on the uncomfortable cot. His mind raced, his eyelids fluttering as he dreamed.

Wake up, a voice whispered in his ear.

Again, Gavin rolled, returning to his back. Whatever he was dreaming of seemed to torment him, add to his already agitated state.

Wake up.

His eyes blinked open, his brain trying to separate reality from the nightmare that haunted his sleep. Gavin was certain he heard a voice, a soft whisper in the night, calling him, beckoning him, coaxing him out of slumber. But who was it?

Gavin looked around the room, Ashley sleeping soundly on the cot next to his, the rest of his companions, sleeping quietly as well. He sat up, turning as he did, his socked-feet finding the wood floor. Scratching his beard, he stood. For some reason, he had been woken, and now, wide awake, there was no hope of returning to sleep. And not that he was wanting to anyway, having suffered through a horrible dream.

He walked to the kitchen area, found a clean glass, and filled it with cold water from the tap, careful to only slightly open the faucet so as not to make unnecessary noise and wake anyone else at this early hour. Gavin racked his brain. If everyone was asleep, who called out to him?

Gavin, the voice spoke once more.

He turned, peering into the dark corners of the room, a sour ache growing in the pit of his stomach. Old, familiar feelings of spiritual angst were returning, discernment flooding his thoughts.

Downstairs…

Gavin was certain the voice came from behind him that time. Other than small kitchen cupboards hanging on the wall, there was nothing but the steps to the level below.

"'Downstairs' it is," he mumbled, stepping cautiously, tiptoeing as he went.

He looked down the stairs as best he could, still unsure of whether the voice he heard was real or a remnant of his terrible dream. Either way, he was awake and seeing how everyone else was still asleep, he would investigate. The view to the level below was limited. From the top of the steps, all he could see was the bottom and an area of cement that was only a small portion of the entire floor below. Four steps down, he could see the table of computer equipment. Another three steps and he was almost at the bottom, the entire warehouse in view. And there, pacing a perfect and repeated straight line was a familiar face, an old friend: Joseph.

Joseph was dressed as before, nice suit, polished shoes, but there was something different: his eyes. His soft, kind, comforting eyes were filled with concern, fear even, as he looked up at his apprentice, Gavin hurrying down the last steps to greet him.

"What are you doing here?" Gavin smiled. "Did you come to check on us?"

"Sadly, no," the old, balding man replied. "I received word that something sinister has happened. The world is in grave danger."

"What are you talking about?"

"The key, Gavin. Emeric Laurent…the Frenchman…has used the key!"

"Which means?"

"Peril," Joseph winced, "absolute peril. For an army of demons has been unleashed, the likes of which has not been seen on earth for many centuries."

Gavin stood frozen, his eyes wide and expressive, "So are you saying that Armageddon has come?"

"No this is not Armageddon, this is not the end of the world. But it's close."

"How do you know that it's not?" Gavin pondered.

"Only God knows the timing, my son. Even us angels follow His will."

"Then it could be."

"I highly doubt it. Because, if this was truly Armageddon, I would have been told to let things unfold unhindered, to allow mankind and angel-kind, both holy and fallen, to engage in the last battle for the world. No, I have been asked to intervene, to fight here and now, in Paris, the first city upon which this pestilence has been released. If we can stop this now, then other cities can be saved."

"You just said *we*," Gavin replied. "Do you mean us with you or you and an angelic host of warriors? Because I know we can do nothing to battle a spiritual force other than to pray against it."

"That's true, Gavin. But do you recall the night five years ago, when I vanquished the archdemon that lived within Triton?"

"How could I forget! The two of you fought tirelessly, nearly destroyed the street below the Tri-Corp building. It was epic!"

"Indeed," Joseph nodded, "but I knew that I, an angel, could not strike Triton, a human host. For centuries, I trained men just like you to hunt and kill the host so that I might defeat the demon within. I hoped you would be the man to finally accomplish this seemingly impossible feat. But it was Thirteen, your friend Michael, Triton's own apprentice, who killed him, allowing me access to the archdemon. I said *we* because I meant it. I, and the angels I command, am ready to fight the demons. But you, you and your family must stop the Frenchman. I see it now so clearly. God truly has a wondrous plan for you, Gavin. To think, I trained you to help me chase

Triton, but I was so obsessed with him and him alone, that I forgot that it was not Triton at all, but the spirit within him a spirit of the antichrist. And that spirit, is not of form like a demon, it is of nature, like the holiness of Christ. Only man can battle nature and will. For nature and will are not capable of being struck down with sword or spear, or gun or knife. They are a battlefield within the mind."

"What can I do then," Gavin asked, "if the battle is in the Frenchman's mind?"

"Don't misunderstand. *His* battle is within his mind. Just like your battle for your soul is in your own mind. It is inside your mind that you battle everyday as demons whisper thoughts of hate and lust, greed, envy, selfishness, and more. And there, within your mind, the Holy Spirit fights back, feeding you scripture and hope to defeat the evil thoughts. An angel cannot fight inside your mind, but of course neither can God. He allows you to choose whether you will fight or succumb to temptation. That is a privilege of free will. Therefore…if the Frenchman is unwilling to face himself and recognize that what he is doing is wrong and that his actions, his motivations are of evil intent, then he must be stopped by another means. I cannot strike him down, just as it was with Triton, but you, Gavin, you can. You are that other means!"

"But stopping the Frenchman won't stop the antichrist from coming to power. Armageddon will still happen," Gavin said.

"True. The end is already known. But this is not the time for such things to happen. You must fight the spirit of the antichrist. I will handle the demons."

Gavin thought on Joseph's words, allowed the scope of all he said to sink in. He'd come to Paris knowing that the Frenchman must be stopped. But apparently, they were too late. And now, a demonic plague released upon the city, their purpose had changed. There action was no longer preemptive: this was full out war!

"Is it really as bad as you say?" Gavin asked.

"Close your eyes," Joseph answered. "Take my hands. I'll show you."

Eyes closed, his hand clutching tightly to Joseph's, Gavin felt a sudden rush of tremendous, gripping power. He watched a view from above as, the only way he could describe it, his consciousness left his body, lifting up, leaving Gavin looking down upon himself and Joseph, their feet firmly on the warehouse floor. In seconds, his spirit travelled with Joseph, passing through the building's second floor, leaving Ashley and the others behind to sleep. Then they shot beyond the confines of the warehouse and into the night sky, flying over rooftops, dodging chimneys, till coming to a stop and hovering over a wide boulevard, the Eiffel Tower in full view.

Demons swooped and frolicked, doing all they could to create chaos. They forced stop lights to change at random, sending cars crashing into one another, blocking up the intersections, leaving drivers confused and angry. Fist fights erupted as taxi drivers leapt from their vehicles and argued over who's fault the accident was. From above, demons shouted down insults and foulness, the people below spitting the same words at one another, mirroring the demons who laughed hysterically. There were sudden outbreaks of violence, muggings, even murder as the people involved, under incredible spiritual duress, gave in to the evil whispers and allowed the battle to grow.

"I've never seen anything like this!" Gavin said, nearly laughing because of the sheer ridiculousness of it all, watching as thousands of demons tormented the city.

"And it will only get worse," Joseph replied, pointing at the whirlpool in the Seine River. "The portal must be closed. You must find Laurent."

"Tell me where he is!" Gavin pleaded.

"I do not know. That was not part of what I was told to do. But I have faith that you will find him. Your path will be illuminated, your steps guided. God may even bring the Frenchman to you."

Joseph winked. Gavin opened his eyes, finding himself once again on his back, laying on the uncomfortable cot, instantaneously returned to the second floor of the warehouse, everyone else still sleeping soundly. With the exception of Jean Luc's snoring, the room was quiet.

Now, the game had changed. And, sadly, Gavin had no idea what to do next.

****

"Can you even believe what just happened?" Edward asked, sitting in the driver's seat of the stolen, red Citroen coupe, the pedal to the floor as they raced back to Paris, putting as much distance between them and those creatures as possible.

"I can't. And, if I hadn't been there myself," Killion laughed, "I'd have said that any person telling that story was a bloody liar!"

"Honestly, how does something like that happen? It was like they felt no pain! The more we shot at them, the more they just kept coming. They can't be human!"

"Obviously not, brother. I've never seen anyone or *anything* that bleeds black. So where did they come from? How did the Frenchman control them?"

"No clue," Edward sighed. "And, you've got black on you, right there."

Killion wiped his face where his brother pointed, looking down at the oily substance on his fingertips, "You saw what happened when we shot them in the head. That was the only way to kill them. I just don't understand."

"It was like something out of science-fiction horror, like a zombie movie or something," Edward replied. "But they couldn't have been, am I right? Zombies aren't real."

"I don't know what to think. I'm just happy we made it out alive *and* with the money no less. This is cause for celebration!"

"But what about those monsters?"

"What about them?" Killion asked. "We got what we went for. True, the old man still lives, but what does that matter? We'll drink tonight, forget about whatever those *things* were, and head for London tomorrow; rich beyond our wildest dreams!"

"How can you just let it go at that?" Edward barked. "You drag me back there to retrieve the rest of the money and kill the Frenchman. The whole plan goes Barney and you just forget it all like it never happened? Tell me, brother, when one of those creatures grabbed me and pulled me to the ground, did you come back for me or the money?"

"Don't be stupid. I came back for you."

"And the money? If I'd have dropped the bag would you have gone after it or me?"

"I'd have gone after you. If the opportunity would have been there to get the money as well, then of course I'd go after the money too!"

"Is that so?"

"And what does it even matter, here and now, after the fact? We made it out didn't we, with both the money and our lives?"

"Yes," Edward agreed.

"Then let's celebrate!"

****

Several hours had passed since Joseph had returned Gavin to the warehouse. He'd tried to sleep, but only tossed and turned, the images of the demonic havoc too fresh in his mind.

He heard the sound of someone stirring, then the creak of the cot as they sat up, followed by the shuffling of feet to the quant bathroom in the corner of the room. Moments later, the toilet flushed. Gavin watched Jamie exit, closing the door behind him, yawning widely.

"You can't sleep either?" Jamie whispered, seeing Gavin wide awake.

"Nope. What time is it?"

Jamie looked down at his watch, "Almost 6:00am. The sun will be up soon. Want some coffee?"

Gavin joined Jamie in the small kitchen and they helped each other prepare a pot to brew, one taking care of the water, the other putting a new filter and grounds into the machine. In the distance, the sirens of emergency vehicles wailed. Smoke could be seen rising many blocks away as the darkness of night began to fade. A building burned, the fire but one more event spurred on by the demons' play.

"We need to talk," Gavin said quietly urgency in his eyes, watching as the brewing coffee began to drip down into the clear glass pot, a dark, aromatic stream of pick-me-up.

Jamie nodded and the brothers-in-law waited for the coffee maker to finish. They each took a mug from the cupboard behind them and filled them, then headed down to the lower level where their voices would not bother any of the others.

"So what's up?" Jamie asked, taking a seat in one of the folding chairs at the surveillance table.

Gavin sat as well, placing his mug next to one of the keyboards. Neither man paid any attention to what was on the screens, Jean Luc's algorithms still working and searching, the server's hard drives clicking and whirring as they sorted through hundreds of terabytes of data.

"Last night," Gavin began, "I was woken by a voice. I followed it down here and found Joseph!"

"What?" Jamie laughed. "That's incredible!"

"Not as incredible as what I'm about to tell you."

"Well get on with it then," Jamie smiled excitedly, taking a short sip from his steaming mug.

Gavin explained the sensation of feeling his spirit removed and lifted, leaving his body behind, then travelling to the Eiffel Tower and observing the chaos as it unfolded, emphasizing the whirlpool and his assigned charge of stopping the Frenchman by any means.

"So then Joseph, sort of, dropped you off back here after all that?" Jamie wondered, the words sinking in.

"I guess you could say that. One moment I was there, floating above the street in the middle of all the madness, and then the next, I was back on my cot."

"This is like New York all over again," Jamie mused, "only bigger!"

"Then again, look on the bright side," Gavin encouraged. "At least there aren't any *sleepwalkers* this time."

✱✱✱✱✱✱✱✱✱✱✱✱

Killion and Edward had made it back to the city nearly two hours ago, carefully maneuvering past several groupings of emergency vehicles clustered in the middle of the city. But given their recent escape, they paid little mind to the strangeness of small riots and looting. It was like the whole world had gone mad and to them, this was perfectly normal.

The brothers had chosen to spend what little nighttime that was left swallowing shot after shot, hoping that, in alcohol induced stupor, they would forget about the creatures all together. Perhaps then, the chaos would end.

Drink after drink, they laughed and slapped each other on the back, leaving their worries and doubts to drown in an amber pool of whiskey. Sleep was of little use to them now. When the new day arrived, it would bring with it more alcohol, more back-slapping. As long as they were jolly, the world could burn for all they cared. They had their lives, they had their money. London was calling.

23

The rising sun drove the demons from the ever-brightening sky, sending them searching for refuge till the dark of night would once again cover Paris. Decidedly, they'd created enough chaos for now.

Jamie and Gavin had been joined by the rest of the group, all partaking in rich, darkly roasted French coffee as Gavin retold the events of the prior night once more. Ashley, Kayla and Michael, having lived through and seen so many strange, spiritual things weren't truly surprised by what he shared, though they were discouraged by the added complexity to their purpose. Jean Luc, devout as he was, was somewhat skeptical, remaining silent, digesting Gavin's more than sincere words. Arthur however, found it all too incredible to believe, making his opinion known.

"You all are a loony lot if you nutters expect me to believe that a bunch of demons are out there in the city right now!" Arthur laughed. "I'll help you all with Killion, but that's that. If you all want to play angels and demons and *holy whatever*, be my guest. But you can count me out!"

"It's true," Gavin said earnestly. "I know it sounds crazy and I don't blame you for not believing, but it's true."

"Even if the bloody archbishop of Canterbury walked in here right now and anointed you king of all bloody England, then told you of this fool crusade, I still don't think I'd believe it, end of story."

"You have no idea what kind of powers are truly out there," Michael added solemnly. "There are more than I would care to admit."

"Mon Dieu," Jean Luc sighed. "I need a cigarette."

He reached in his pocket and pulled out a half crumpled blue pack. Jamie was taken aback, speechless at the sight of the familiar cigarettes: *Gitanes*, just like O'Donnell smoked.

"Anyone care to join me outside?" Jean Luc asked, offering to any takers, the pack extended generously in his hand.

"I don't smoke," Jamie replied, "but I'll go with you."

Jean Luc nodded and the two men stepped out the front door.

"Are you sure you do not want one?" Jean Luc asked once more, placing a cigarette between his lips, then returning the pack to his jacket and pulling a small box of matches from another pocket.

Jamie declined as Jean Luc struck the match's head on the side of the tiny cardboard carton, a flame flaring up, consuming the red, phosphorous tip. He then raised the match up to the cigarette, slowly drew in air and exhaled a puff as the cigarette began to burn.

"Is what Gavin said really true, and Michael as well?" Jean Luc asked, taking a long drag on the short and wide, filtered cigarette.

Jamie stood perfectly still, staring blankly at the concrete sidewalk, nearly in tears as the uniquely strong scent of the burning tobacco brought back buried memories of Patrick O'Donnell, Jamie's former NYPD police captain and stand-in father figure. He'd died five years ago, murdered at the hands of two imposter FBI agents, members of Triton's Tri-Six, an eighteen –man guild of assassins. Michael, or rather Thirteen, was ironically the last surviving constituent. Gavin, Ashley, Kayla, and Jamie had seen to that, the four personally responsible for the deaths of the other seventeen as they battled to end Triton's evil plan. And, until only days ago, they believed Thirteen to be dead as well.

"Jamie," Jean Luc said, waving his hand in front of Jamie's face. "Snap out if it, mon ami."

Jamie blinked, shaking off the mist, "Sorry. The cigarettes, their smell: they remind me of an old friend. He smoked the same kind."

"Your friend has good taste," Jean Luc smiled. 'Where is he now?"

"Dead," Jamie frowned. "Five years ago…murdered."

"I am truly sorry," Jean Luc replied. "I would not have asked if I'd have known."

"How could you have?" Jamie said. "Anyway, just smelling the smoke, it's like he's back, like he never died."

"Your memories of this old friend, are they pleasant?"

"Most of them are," Jamie smiled, recalling both the good and the bad times.

"Then I am happy to reacquaint you with this man."

The door opened behind them as Gavin stepped out to get some air.

"Hey guys," he smiled, looking up at the sky, his eyes searching.

"Can you see them now," Jean Luc questioned, the cigarette dangling from his lips., bobbing with every word he spoke. "The demons; are they up there?"

"Not right now," Gavin explained. "Though they were concentrated quite a distance from here. They might be just out of sight."

"If they were there, would we all see them, or just you?" Jean Luc wondered, looking to the sky.

"If you had the gift."

"*Gift?*"

"Yeah," Gavin sighed, "the spiritual gift of discernment. Sometimes, honestly, it's more like a curse."

"I understand such things," Jean Luc said. "Take knowledge for example. It too can be a gift, but also a terrible curse. It is a danger to a man to know too much."

Gavin pondered those words. Jamie still lingered on every whiff of smoke that the slight breeze carried his way, still thinking of O'Donnell.

"Though I think I believe you," Jean Luc said, nearly finished with his cigarette, breaking the silence that lasted for several minutes, "I must agree with Arthur. I am not here for any spiritual war. I am here for Delilah. I will help you find Killion, but that is all. Besides weapons and vehicles, stopping this man you call the Frenchman is in your hands."

"I respect that," Gavin nodded.

Jean Luc tossed the butt on the ground and crushed it under his foot, following Jamie and Gavin as they returned through the door. They were met by Kayla and Ashley, large, excited smiles stretching across their faces. Arthur sat at the computer, staring dumbfounded at one of the screens.

"We got a hit, mate." he said to Jean Luc. "Killion, he's here in Paris. A traffic cam picked him up exiting a car at a pub not far from here. It's a ninety-eight percent positive match against the image taken from the surveillance video at that shop. The computer confirms it! And what's better?"

"Go on," Jean Luc urged.

"This was from this morning, about two hours ago to be precise. We might be able to catch him!"

"You think he's really still there?" Michael questioned.

"I pulled up the feed from the camera that spotted him and reviewed the video back to that time. He and another man park a red coupe and immediately exit the vehicle. It's a bloody miracle that the only available spot on the side of the road was in view of this camera, if only just barely. We could have missed him entirely. Unfortunately, we only managed to get the top of his brother's hair, so still no facial grab on Edward for the recognition software to search and analyze. Anyway, it's a live feed now and I haven't seen them leave."

Jean Luc hurried to a medium sized cardboard box and opened the flaps. Inside was a thick, black cloth hood and ratcheting cargo straps.

"We'll take the van," he said, reaching in his pocket for the keys. "I know the restaurant. We can be there in less than twenty minutes."

"There's two of them," Ashley said. "Edward is with him."

"Well I only have the one hood," Jean Luc replied. "We'll have to make due. Come on!"

They all climbed into the van, armed and ready. Jean Luc used a remote attached to the driver's side visor to open the automatic door, then allowed it to close once again as soon as the rear bumper cleared the entrance. The van sped off towards the west side of the city. Gavin prayed they wouldn't be too late.

****

"Do you think she's alright?" Sebastian asked his father as the two men attended to the young girl, left unconscious by the prior nights ritual.

"She is still breathing," Laurent replied, her hand held in his.

Shortly after Laurent's army of sleepwalkers chased the Killion brothers from the property, Sebastian checked to ensure the grounds were secure, then he and his father carefully moved her from where she'd fallen to the floor, now resting once more on her bed.

"What do you think happened to her, father?"

"It's hard to say. Perhaps the power that she unleashed was simply too strong?"

"Is there anything in the text that would explain her collapse, why she's like this now?" Sebastian continued.

"There is nothing discussed after the ritual itself," Laurent explained. "We weren't even certain that she could channel the energy for sure, but she proved to be the *one*. Now we must wait and see where her destiny lies."

Sebastian understood. He looked down over her, his eyes lingering on her beautiful young face.

"I am amazed that someone so innocent could bear the weight of so much darkness," he mused, watching her soft lips quiver as she breathed.

"That is why she was chosen, my son. Her innocence was the main requirement. A girl with more knowledge, a lust for adulthood and its many pleasures, would have been consumed by the power she controlled and, in that power, surely die."

"Do you believe she was successful? How do we know that she managed to open the gateway?"

"Because, Sebastian, we have faith. And in truth, I believe we witnessed something beyond astonishing. The girl not only opened the gateway, but I think she may have actually become the gateway herself. Meaning, she can now open portals and bridge worlds at any time, no rituals, no rites. She now possesses the power."

Laurent touched her cheek as her eyes fluttered and she inhaled suddenly. He expected her to wake, but she continued on unconscious, settling back into her deep slumber.

****

Jean Luc pulled the white van to a stop. The café was in sight, but they decided to approach with caution, parking a short walk from the front of the building.

"I don't see the car," Gavin said, leaning between the front seats and scanning the parked vehicles.

"Nor do I ," Jean Luc agreed. "I hope we are not too late. But, they had a window to leave and may have while we were driving. We should send someone in to confirm whether Killion is there or not."

"I'll go," Ashley quickly volunteered. "It has to be me. If they are in there, I'm the only one who knows what Edward looks like. I can slip in and out before they see me."

"If you're going, you won't be alone," Gavin said. "I'm going with you."

"I agree that she shouldn't go alone," Arthur interjected, "but Killion will spot you in a heartbeat. He could lose us in a shootout. We have to keep as low a profile as possible."

"Then I'll go too," Kayla decided. "Killion hasn't seen me yet. Neither has Edward. I could sit down right next to them and they wouldn't be the wiser."

The men looked at each other questioningly. Kayla and Ashley were dead set on going.

"You're taking my gun," Jamie finally said, giving in to the girls plan as he reached for the Beretta in its holster.

"No," she replied. "Why don't you and Arthur cover us. We'll poke around. If Ashley sees them, then we'll signal you. If they've gone, then there'll be nothing to worry about anyway."

"I don't know about this," Gavin sighed.

Jean Luc was becoming the binding voice of reason within the group, "I do not think we have any other choice. I agree with the girls: they should be the ones to scout the restaurant. Jamie, you and Arthur can follow behind and guard the entrance. Gavin, Michael, and I will be waiting in the van. If there's a change in plans, we are only seconds away, bringing with us either more firepower or a means of escape."

Kayla slid open the side door of the van, cautiously looking up and down the street before exiting. Jamie climbed out and stood next to her as Arthur stepped from the front passenger seat, tucking the black sack into his back pocket just in case.

"Be careful!" Gavin ordered, giving Ashley a kiss before she joined the others on the sidewalk.

"I will," she said, staring him in the eyes.

"Don't worry," Jamie encouraged, before sliding the door shut, "I'll look after her."

Gavin watched helplessly as Ashley and Kayla started up the sidewalk, their mannerisms revealing an obvious intention to blend in with the surrounding pedestrians. But, he believed, to the casual onlooker, their actions, their gestures, would not be questioned. They were two women out for a day of shopping and fun, stopping at a local restaurant for an early lunch. And of course, Jamie and Arthur were following behind, not too closely, allowing space, but they too managed to blend right in as well.

"Do you really think there's any chance that Killion is still in there?" Gavin asked, the girls now only a few brief steps from the restaurant's entrance. "I mean, considering that the car is gone, there's no reason to believe that he's not long gone."

"I thought you were a man of faith?" Jean Luc questioned.

"I am, but..."

"Then there is no *but*, mon ami. You must simply believe."

****

Ashley glanced back briefly before pushing open the door to the restaurant, hoping to get one last look at her husband, seeing him nod encouragingly, his eyes assuring and strong. She couldn't believe how little fear she felt, though it helped that Kayla was by her side. In a way, she found humor in their current position. Only days ago, she was held captive by Killion and Edward, managed an astonishing escape, and now hunted them, hoping to best them at their own game.

Oh, how the tables have turned, she thought.

The sisters stopped in the entryway, pretending to be interested in the menu; but knowing next to no French, they wouldn't have been able to read it if they wanted to.

"Do you see either of them?" Kayla whispered.

Ashley looked out of the corner of her eye, trying with all her might to appear as though she wasn't scanning the tables of patrons or the bar for the elusive hitman and his brother.

"No, Kay. I don't see them."

Just then, as her heart sank, the door to the men's room slowly opened. There, apparently drunk as he made an awkward attempt to ensure the fly of his pants had indeed been returned to its closed position, was Edward, staggering back to the bar for another drink.

"There!" Ashley nearly shouted, miraculously keeping her voice to a hushed volume.

"At the bar?" Kayla asked.

"Yes! It's Edward."

"What about Killion?"

"I don't see him. Maybe he's still in the restroom?"

Kayla and Ashley continued to wait, watching both Edward and the men's room. But they knew that people were growing aware of their standing in place for so long. This was attention they did not want.

"Let's go back outside," Kayla whispered, "slowly, like we just decided there's nothing her we like."

They left the restaurant as nonchalantly as possible, then headed straight for Jamie and Arthur. Gavin and Jean Luc watched excitedly from their position down the street.

"What's up?" Jamie asked quickly as the girls approached.

"Killion's gone, but Edward is still in there," Ashley explained.

Arthur smiled, "I think I know what to do. Jamie, I want you and Ashley to be ready out here. I'm going to head in and get friendly with Edward, one Brit to another. That'll drive him out into the open. Kayla, you go back to the van and tell Jean Luc that we're doing a *snatch*. He'll know what you mean."

They all nodded, listening as he formulated a plan.

"How will I know him when I go in?" Arthur asked.

"He's the only guy at the bar and he's drunk too," Kayla answered.

"No need for further description then."

"What do you want Jamie and I to do when he leaves?" Ashley wondered.

"I want your face to be the last thing he sees!"

∗∗∗∗∗∗∗∗∗∗∗∗

Arthur strolled confidently into the restaurant as if without a care in the world. He strutted right up to the counter, paying Edward no mind, and loudly ordered a pint of ale, certain to allow his heavy British accent to proudly declare his country of origin. The barman obliged and placed a dark stout beer in front of the Englishman.

"Thanks, mate," Arthur winked.

Edward took the baited hook without question. And seeing as just how much alcohol he'd stomached, his guard was less than effective. Here he was, surrounded by Parisians, and another Londoner just happened to pull out a stool not but two seats away. What luck!

"Oi," Edward stammered with a hiccup, raising his shot glass in salute, "God save the Queen!"

Arthur nodded, his glass raised as well and they drank. Edward slammed his empty shot glass down amongst the collection he'd accumulated.

"It's a little early for a party, wouldn't you say?" Arthur asked with a grin. "Let me guess, it's a woman right?"

"In a manner of speaking," Edward mused.

"So you're here in Paris then, all by your lonesome, just you and a girl? What, did she run off?"

"No, actually. I'm here on business with my brother," Edward explained, a growing annoyance at his present circumstances ever the more evident in his voice. "We're partners. Anyway, we *were* celebrating a deal, a rather mad one if I might add, when he met a girl here in this very restaurant. *I'm taking the car*, he says to me. *We're going to her place for a bit*, he tells me. So now I'm stranded while my dear old brother has a roll with his new bird. Bloody good riddance, if you ask me."

"So you're brother's not around then?"

"Nope, he's probably already got her knickers off by now. It's been almost a half of an hour ago that he left."

"That's too bad," Arthur laughed.

"Why do you care?" Edward asked, his sudden suspicions allowing a sober thought.

"Well because then I could have met two Londoners in Paris!" Arthur covered. "Imagine that! Oi, another drink for my new friend."

The drink was poured and delivered. Edward's suspicion subsided.

"So what's your name, mate?" Arthur asked.

"Edward," the younger Killion brother replied. "And you are?"

Arthur thought quickly and smiled, "Ernest Pennyworth, happy to make your acquaintance."

"Right then, Mr. Pennyworth. What is it you do, what has brought you across the channel?"

"I, too, am on business."

"Fancy that," Edward smiled. "What's in Paris for you?"

"A man," Arthur said, finishing his beer and tossing a euro note on the counter. "I'm looking for someone. A Londoner, a man named Terrance Killion. You wouldn't happen to know him would you, one mate to another?"

Edward had only just raised the shot glass to his mouth, the rim resting on his lower lip as his new friend spoke his brother's name. he swallowed the liquor and then calmly set the glass down.

"And you know," Arthur laughed, slapping his palm sharply on the wooden counter top, the empty glasses rattling in protest, "I remember now. The man I'm looking for has a brother, a brother named Edward. That wouldn't happen to be you now would it?"

Edward's mind raced as he panicked. *Who was this man? What could he do, could he escape? If only Terrance hadn't left him behind!*

"You said Killion did you?" Edward questioned, deciding his only chance was to play dumb. "Never heard of him. My last name is....um...Brewer. Yes, Edward Brewer. Funny coincidence though, my sharing the name Edward with the brother of this Killion fellow. It's a small world after all."

"Funny thing," Arthur smiled, his eyes piercingly cold as he stared Edward down.

"Well, Mr. Pennyworth. It has been a pleasure, but I have to be somewhere else...that's not *here*...at the present moment and I only just remembered, so if you'll pardon me, I'll be off."

Edward hurriedly pulled his wallet from the right rear pocket of his pants and sorted out the proper amount to cover the many shots he'd consumed as well as the tab his brother had left behind. He tried his very hardest to act unsurprised by Arthur's revelation, but he knew that he was, in truth, failing miserably.

"Right then, *Edward Brewer,*" Arthur grinned. "Maybe I'll bump into you again?"

"Good day," Edward replied standing and hurrying for the exit.

He pulled open the front door and made it out to the sidewalk, but froze mid-step. All the color drained from his face as he tried desperately to form recognizable words. Ashley stood right in his path.

"It can't be, there's no bloody way!" Edward shouted.

"Hello Edward" Ashley grinned.

And suddenly, everything went dark, a black cloth sack forced down over his face. Then he felt someone's very firm grip take hold of his arms as he heard the sound of a vehicle's tires screeching to stop. After that, he was lifted and thrown into the back of what he decided must have a been a van before striking his head squarely on the hard metal floor. The last thing he heard was a quartet of excited American voices. And then, Edward Killion, once the captor, now the captive, passed out.

24

Gavin stood on the rooftop of the warehouse, his eyes fixed in the direction of the Eiffel Tower. The time had crept well into the afternoon, evening threatening as the sun continued its unstoppable course through the sky. In the distance, he'd spot an occasional large, black mass gliding in the air, trying hard to determine whether it was just a bird or something more sinister; but whatever it was, it was too far to properly see, leaving him with nothing more than speculation.

With little other options, he prayed silently as he watched the sky. He bound the demons' and their power in heavy, spiritual chains, asking God to intervene, allow His angels to strike the demons down.

Without warning, Gavin grew weak in the knees, completely lightheaded, his vision blurring as his head began to pound. Then, as quickly as the feeling came, it left. He looked to his left and right as he righted himself, gathering his bearings. And then he realized what happened. As he'd prayed, God had allowed a switch in his brain to once more be flipped on. That was the closest thing to which Gavin could compare the feeling. Though it was dizzying and painful in the moment, he was now aware of the world around him he'd once been able to see and interact with daily.

It was then that he also realized why the *switch* that controlled his gift of spiritual discernment was metaphorically turned off. He had done it himself, not intentionally, but he, Gavin, was to blame. After marrying Ashley, he'd done everything he could to live a normal life, to leave demon hunting behind. As he focused more on work and his husbandly duties, providing a home, food, love, he had begun spending less and less time in prayer, reading his Bible infrequently, relying on what he had memorized and learned in his past as enough to carry him into the future.

Gavin had taken God for granted. He'd placed the Creator, Jesus, and the Holy Spirit in a box, compartmentalized and easily stored on a cluttered shelf in his mind. And in doing so, his choice kept God from speaking to him the way he'd grown accustomed. His questioning of God, the distance he felt so greatly, it was all his fault. Now, standing on a small rooftop in Paris, looking out over the city, he realized that God had never stopped talking. He simply could no longer hear Him, having packed God away for a rainy day. Gavin's sobering prayer, the admission of his guilt, had blown the dust off the top of the box, the lid being ripped away like a child tearing through the wrapping of a toy at Christmas. That was the dizzying power that overcame him.

"I wondered when you'd wake up?" a voice spoke from his right.

Gavin turned to find a man leaning against an HVAC unit. His hair was short and golden, his face strong and sincere. He was dressed in armor, a sword at his side. The angel stood upright and Gavin could see the white feathers of his wings reflecting the sunlight.

"Have you been there this whole time?" Gavin asked, amused by the angel's sudden appearance.

"I've been with you for many years, Gavin. You do not recognize me, but I was the one who carried you out of the hospital during the blast, protecting you from the flames. I watched over you after that, guarded you, protected you and your wife from the demons who have come after you over the years."

"I had no idea!" Gavin exclaimed.

"I know and it's alright," the angel answered.

"If you've been protecting us, then why was Ashley kidnapped, why has all of this happened?"

"Because the time had come for you to remember, Gavin. God is ready for you once more. You and Ashley had to go through these events in order to be used once more. No offense, but you had become so comfortable and content in your life that the only way God could get your attention was to allow your life to be turned upside down. And look, here we are, right where God needed you to be. You were created with purpose, Gavin. Never forget that."

"Was it necessary for all this though? Had God just asked me, I would have said yes."

"Would you?" the angel questioned. "If God Himself appeared before you, blazing like the burning bush, and asked you to put your happy life on hold and place yourself in danger, even unto death, and that it would also require Ashley to help you, would you have done it?"

"Of course!" Gavin argued.

"You can say that now, after seeing such things, but imagine beforehand. Don't answer, just think on it."

Gavin knew the angel was right. He needn't bother with reflection.

"So what's the plan? Has Joseph figured out how to stop the demons?"

"We've assembled an army of warriors," the angel said. "We begin fighting tonight at sundown. We will do everything we can to keep them preoccupied. But you must close the gateway. Joseph will speak to you soon."

Gavin nodded and watched as the angel stretched out its wings, then soared into the sky and disappeared. He smiled, now feeling very much like the Gavin of old. God had restored him.

****

"Bloody hell, Ed. Why aren't you picking up?" Killion growled angrily, listening as, for the third time in a row, Edward's phone proceeded to voicemail after ringing unanswered.

Killion, after having spent the middle of the day with a beautiful stranger, had returned to the café where he'd promised to once more meet his brother. He'd had no luck finding Edward inside and he was nowhere to be seen on the boulevard. Killion reasoned that there was a high probability Edward had grown bored waiting and had chosen to perhaps take a walk and enjoy a summer afternoon in Paris, but that didn't explain why he wasn't answering his phone.

Confused and even a little helpless, Killion sat down on a bench and decided to wait for a while, in case his brother would happen to return. But this wasn't like Edward and Killion knew that.

****

Gavin returned from the roof, joining the rest of his companions on the warehouse's main level. He immediately took notice of how quiet everyone was and grew concerned.

"What is it?" he asked.

Ashley looked up at her husband, "It's Edwards phone…it's been ringing now for the last several minutes. The name on the caller ID says *Terry Killion*."

"And no one has answered?" Gavin questioned.

"Not yet," Jamie replied. "We hadn't planned on calling Killion till we'd at least had a chance to speak with his brother."

"So he still hasn't woken?" Gavin said, more rhetorically than a true question. "Let's see if we can't speed things up a bit. Michael, Arthur, Jean Luc, come with me. Jamie, you too; but first, grab a cup of coffee for our guest."

Ashley and Kayla watched as Gavin and the rest of the men headed past the van and disappeared around the corner, the sound of an opening door that led to another room clearly heard. The girls decided to sit at the computer table and wait.

The light to the small storage room was already on as the men entered. There, in the center of the small space was a chair, Edward firmly seated in it, secured in place by two tightly cranked ratchet straps. His head, still shrouded by the black bag, hung low, his chin resting on his chest.

Gavin approached the unconscious man and quickly pulled the bag from his head. Edward didn't react, so Gavin applied a firm smack to his cheek.

Finally, their captive stirred, his eyes blinking slowly, unsure as he adjusted to the light., his vision finally settling on Gavin, "Where am I? Who…who are you?"

"Los Angeles," Gavin replied, "the woman who must be responsible for the bruising on your face, she's my wife."

"Ashley Dering," Edward sighed. "So that would make you *Gavin*?"

"I am."

"And who are the rest of these men then? There was only one other woman in LA. You can't all be husbands."

"Elizabeth is my wife," Michael growled, his eyes burning, the mask stowed in his pocket beckoning, urging for blood.

"I see," Edward replied, looking now towards Arthur's familiar face. "You there, the Englishman, what do you have to do with this?"

"Your brother, Terrance, he and I go way back," Arthur replied, placing a hand on Jean Luc's shoulder. "My friend here and I worked with your brother, had a certain bond. But Killion, he broke his oath to us, all of us, when he killed a member of our brotherhood."

"And who might that be?" Edward grinned. "Bloody Franklin? That fool Nelson fellow? Or perhaps another member of the sodding Order?"

"Delilah," Jean Luc answered.

Edward's grin disappeared, his eyes widening, caught in the sudden realization that he was not a captive of a group of global elitists, old men growing fat while the world starved. No, he was at the mercy of professional killers, much like his brother. And what scared him the most was the knowledge that these mercenaries wanted revenge.

"Blimey!" Edward grunted. "You lot are going to kill me aren't you?"

"Not if you don't give us good reason to, mate," Arthur assured.

"Then what do you want?"

"Two things," Jamie spoke up. "Killion and the Frenchman."

"I'll tell you what," Edward laughed. "The Frenchman is crazy. He's all yours, but the man is surrounded by monsters. I kid you not. They'll tear the flesh right off your bones."

Gavin and Jamie glanced at each other anxiously. Michael looked angry.

"Hang on," Arthur shouted. "Do we look like morons to you? Do you honestly think you're going to scare us off his trail? It won't work."

"What do these *monsters* look like?" Gavin asked.

"You aren't falling for his story are you?" Arthur blubbered, turning to Gavin.

"Just let me ask him!" Gavin continued. "Tell me, Edward. What did they look like?"

Arthur was furious. He shook his head in disbelief, certain they were all crazy.

"Go on," Jamie urged.

Edward lowered his eyes, staring at the floor, as he relived the horrid events in his mind, "Their skin was rough and leathery, their eyes black, void of color yet strangely reflective, their jaws snapped hungrily, and...when we tried to kill them...our attacks were useless. We fired round after round into them, but the bullets did nothing, they wouldn't stop coming after my brother and I, they just kept on us, bleeding black, oily blood everywhere. All we could do was shoot them in the head. That was the only thing that would stop them."

"Sleepwalkers," Michael grunted.

"How many?" Gavin pressed.

"Hundreds," Edward shivered.

"This changes everything," Gavin said in a sulking manner. "We're not prepared for this."

"Later," Jamie promised, turning again to Edward. "Where did this take place? Will you tell us how to find the Frenchman."

"Absolutely."

"And what about Killion?" Jean Luc asked.

"He's all yours too. I'm done with living *his* life. All he cares about is money. He would have left me to die when we were attacked if I hadn't been carrying the money the Frenchman paid us to bring him the key and execute The Order. You'd be setting me free."

"Well then, a deal is a deal," Arthur smiled, unbuckling the straps, allowing Edward to stretch his aching arms. "Jamie's got a coffee for you if you like. And again, I promise, you help us and I'll make sure you walk away very much alive."

"Get me a map of France," Edward demanded, "and something to write with."

Jean Luc nodded and left the room momentarily, returning with a roadmap and ballpoint pen. He unfolded the map and handed it to him.

Edward looked over the roadways briefly, gathering his bearings and locating Paris, "Give me the pen please."

He followed along the southerly route, marking the roadway and denoting the city of Orleans, then from there, heading west by southwest through Blois and Tours. Edward finished off with a heavy circle marking the approximate location of the chateau.

"You'll find the Frenchman on a large estate just before you would reach Les Trois-Moutiers on the Route de Roiffe. The chateau will be on the left. It's in very bad condition, crumbling. Also, encircled in water."

"Is that everything?" Jamie asked.

"All that I know. When will you let me go?"

"Once we have Killion," Gavin confirmed.

****

"What did you find out?" Kayla asked excitedly as the men returned from the storage room, Edward once more locked away, but now left unrestrained.

"He gave us directions to the Frenchman," Jamie grinned.

"And what about Killion?"

"We'll call him from Edward's phone and arrange a meeting. The only thing to decide is what we'll do then."

"Regarding the Frenchman," Gavin said, "there is one problem."

"What's that?" Ashley asked.

"*Sleepwalkers.*"

****

The young, French girl sat up quickly, glistening in sweat as her pulse raced. She'd had a vision, glimpsed the future. Millions upon millions of demons spread all over the globe like a disease, blacking out urban centers and creating panic and chaos at every turn. One by one, the nations fell on bended knee, acknowledging the supremacy of a single man, a glorious leader like none before him, capable of both wondrous and terrible things.

Emeric heard her stir and woke, having fallen asleep in a chair by her side, "Merci! Are you alright, child?"

"Yes, Laurent," she smiled.

She stood and stretched, then turned about the room gracefully, the hem of her lacey dress fanning out as she twirled. The Frenchman looked on in wonder.

"How do you feel?" he asked curiously.

"Lighter than air," she giggled sweetly.

He stood and stopped her in place, softly touching her shoulders as he looked her in the eyes. Something had changed within her, drastically even. Gone was the somewhat introverted farm girl. Her eyes now told a different story, alluring, piercing and captivating, hungry for danger and excitement. A fire burned deep inside, warmed her, moved her. She could not explain it, nor did she seem to remember what she was like before she had opened the door, it was as if she had always just *been*.

"Why are you looking at me like that, my love?" she teased, caressing his cheek seductively, then tickling his chin playfully.

261

"You're only but a girl," he corrected. "This is very unbecoming. What has happened to you?"

"I'm finally alive," she winked. "I want to drink and feast! I want to be loved like a woman, I want riches…and splendor…and, oh, just…everything. I want the world at my feet, you included, my sweet Emeric."

Laurent backed away. What had the ritual done? It was like another soul had replaced her own, one of gluttonous lust. She was only meant to be a small part of the ritual, herself as much of a key as the trinket that was recovered from Triton. But this, this shouldn't have happened. At worst, Laurent expected that she might die, but this…he now wished she had.

"Will you kiss me?" she asked. "You know I've never been kissed before. You should be the one, Emeric. You have brought me to life!"

As she spoke, her eyes grew dark, the softness fading away, succumbing to the evil that controlled her. Her voice was not her own. She was audible in it, yet it sounded like a shrill chorus of many voices, a harmonic song of madness. Indeed, he wished her dead.

****

"So how should we handle Killion?" Jamie asked, their group of seven huddled around the small kitchenette counter on the warehouse's second floor.

"I, for one, think we should let him sweat it out for the night," Arthur suggested. "We should arrange a meet with him in public, broad daylight."

"Why not meet him as soon as possible?" Ashley wondered.

"Like tonight? I agree with Arthur," Jean Luc replied. "we need to be as careful as possible. Killion alone is still very dangerous."

"That's right," Arthur continued, "and we have to keep him under the belief that his brother's life hangs in the balance if he were to risk taking any actions."

"Then you meant what you said?" Gavin asked surprised. "You told Edward that we weren't going to kill him and you were telling the truth."

"I guess I feel sorry for the man," Arthur admittedly a little sheepishly.

"After all, it's his brother that is the real villain. Edward is but a pawn in Killion's game. He may have worked with his brother for the money, but that doesn't place Delilah's blood on his hands. Killion pulled the trigger, he'll be the one to pay. And, aside from the kidnappings of course, from what Jean Luc and I have heard of your story and the group that called themselves The Order, Edward, in assisting his brother, actually helped do the world a favor by ridding it of those elitists. Sure he was still playing for the wrong team, but it worked out alright."

"That's a funny way of looking at it," Kayla laughed, "but I think you're right. He's only dirty because Killion made him so. I don't think he'd have done anything like this if it weren't for his family ties."

Ashley, Gavin, Jamie and Michael all nodded in agreement. Arthur continued formulating the plan.

"So we'll meet Killion in public, someplace with easy access to roadways for a getaway, but far enough away that we can place ourselves as assets between him and any means of escape. Any thoughts, Jean Luc?"

"We need a location that is going to draw people to it, no matter what, someplace touristy. What about the Louvre? The museum would be perfect, it meets all the criteria."

Ashley's eyes sparkled at the thought of visiting the greatest collection of art in all the world, the Mecca for da Vinci purists, home to the Mona Lisa and so much more, "Please tell me I'll have time to see just some the exhibits?"

"We're talking about arranging a meet with one of the most dangerous assassins since the Cold War and you fancy a look at some old paintings?" Arthur jeered.

"I may never get a chance to come back to Paris," she reasoned. "Just give me an hour!"

Jean Luc smiled at Gavin who shrugged his removal from the argument.

"I know there's no talking her out of it. If we're going to the Louvre, I don't think we'll be able to hold her back," Gavin laughed.

"You worry about never having the chance to return to Paris," Arthur pointed out, "but if we botch this up, you'll be worrying that you ever make it out of this city alive."

"He has a point," Jean Luc reasoned.

"You know what, the girls really don't need to be involved in this part of the plan," Jamie urged. "Things might get ugly. And, if Edward was telling the truth about what awaits at the Frenchman's chateau, then I say give Ashley a little time to clear her head. She and Kayla can watch each other and tour the museum while we setup for the meet with Killion. There'll still be five of us, all armed. The fewer our numbers, the easier it will be to hide in plain sight."

"That's true," Gavin acknowledged.

"Fine," Arthur agreed. "What time should we tell Killion to meet?"

"I say noon," Jean Luc thought. "By midday, there should be plenty of people to help us with our cover. Too early, and Killion might easily spot all of us and disappear."

"You know he'll be expecting a trap?" Arthur added.

"Well," Gavin grinned, "that's exactly what he's going to get."

25

Killion hardly allowed his cell phone time to ring, answering as soon as he heard its tone, glancing only briefly at the name that flashed on the screen. Certainly, he'd been waiting for this call all day.

"Ed!" he spoke into the phone, relieved that his brother was finally making contact after apparently wandering off that day. "You had me so worried!"

"You don't know the half of it, mate," Arthur replied.

"Who is this?" Killion demanded, keeping his voice calm and level even though there was a rage boiling within him.

"An old friend."

"Blackwood? Is that you?"

"Aye."

"What have you done with my brother, where's Edward?"

"If you want to see him again, you'll meet me tomorrow, noon, at the statue of the horse and rider that stands in front of the pyramid at the

Louvre. We have a matter that needs discussed. Come alone and unarmed. When you arrive, stand with your hand in the air as if you're waiving at someone. That will be the sign and I'll come to you. If you are not there at precisely twelve o' clock, then the next time you see your brother will be in a coffin, savvy?"

"What is going on, Arthur? What business do we have?"

"Noon or Edward dies."

"Wait!" Killion protested too late, the line going dead as Arthur hung up on his end.

****

"So that's it then?" Jamie asked. "We'll meet Killion and then what?"

"Don't worry yourself with that, mate," Arthur smiled. "We'll deal with him when the time comes."

"As for your Frenchman," Jean Luc said, "if we are to believe Edward, then I am honestly more concerned with him than Killion. You will need all the help you can get."

"That's for all of you to decide then," Arthur stated. "When we've dealt with Killion, I'm going back to London."

"We understand," Kayla answered. "You've done a lot for us already, but we expected to face the Frenchman alone."

"Well I will help in any way I can," Jean Luc offered freely. "There's a curiosity, I admit. I want to see these *sleepwalkers* for myself."

"Bloody mad, the lot of you," Arthur laughed.

They picked at the food they'd set out on the counter, snacks mostly: crackers, sliced cheese, deli meat. Gavin had found a small jar of Dijon mustard in one of the cupboards and that was added to the makeshift meal.

"And how will we deal with Killion then?" Kayla asked.

"Arthur, we'll sort of leave this up to you," Jamie reasoned. "You know Killion, what's the best way to handle this?"

"We'll meet, just myself and one of you."

"I'll do it," Gavin volunteered without hesitation.

"Right then. You and I will meet Killion face to face. We'll take my Rover. Michael, you'll be the driver. There's a road that passes through the plaza. You can hang back there, pulled off to the side. If security were to question you, you speak fluent French, you can give the excuse that you're picking someone up. Jean Luc, how about you drive the van. It's plain, inconspicuous. We'll have you park within view of us on the same ring, that way, you can react as necessary. Jamie, how are you with a scoped rifle?"

"I've hunted deer and coyotes before, I'm an alright shot within two hundred yards."

"You'll be less than half that distance. You'll watch from the back of the van and keep Killion in your crosshairs. If he does anything even remotely peculiar, you take him out."

Jamie nodded, accepting what seemed like a big responsibility.

"The windows in the rear doors of the van are tinted darkly, no one will be able to see you. You can shoot through the glass if need arises. There's a scoped and suppressed .308 bolt gun with the other weapons. But you'll only have five rounds in the magazine, and little to no time to reload."

"What about us?" Kayla asked.

"Stay out of sight. We'll arrive at the museum plenty early, give us a chance to walk through all this and make any necessary changes there in the field. You girls need to take care of each other. If something goes wrong, you two leave the country, forget about the rest of us. Take care of yourselves first. Killion will kill us all."

"That seems harsh," Kayla argued. "We can fight!"

"Ashley is pregnant," Gavin reminded. "I agree. You both need to think about the kids."

Kayla reluctantly agreed. Ashley grew solemn at the thought of the worst happening: Gavin dying, leaving Ashley to raise their baby alone. She didn't know if she could live without her husband.

"So then we just kill him, right there in front of hundreds maybe thousands of people?" Jamie continued. "I don't see how that's going to work?"

"We'll get him in the waiting Range Rover, bring him back here. We'll tell him that if he doesn't come quietly, then Edward is as good as dead," Arthur explained. "He'll follow along."

"Alright then," Gavin urged. "If we all agree that this is the right course, I think we should pray over the plan together, ask God for protection."

Gavin extended his hands at his sides, taking hold of Ashley's. Jamie took hold of his other hand as the circle linked together one by one.

"No offense, but I'll sit this one out," Arthur said, excluding himself from the ring of prayer.

Jamie nodded at Arthur, understanding how difficult and awkward this moment must have been, "I would have been with you once, before my eyes were opened to so much. Are you sure you don't want to be a part of this?"

"I've seen plenty," Arthur grinned. "I'll leave you to your hokey religions and ancient superstitions."

Arthur excluded, they closed their eyes and bowed their heads as Gavin began to pray aloud,

"Lord God, our great redeemer, we have so much to be thankful for: the lives You've given us, our loved ones, the opportunity to care for one another. But here we are, at what seems like the end of an incredible journey, one that has left us with many questions and few answers, but we trust in You. Now, Lord, we ask for protection and guidance, we ask for wisdom and understanding. Lord Jesus, we might be going to our deaths, but only You know how things will unfold. I lift each and every one of us up to you: Jamie, Kayla, Ashley, Michael, Jean Luc, myself…and Arthur. I pray that, when the time comes, we follow You and not instinct. That we seek Your will and not our own. In the end, Lord God, it is You who will decide Killion's fate. In the end, we are accountable for our own actions and our actions alone. Again, God, keep us safe and show us the way. In Jesus name…amen."

Jamie shivered, overcome with sudden chills as they all said *amen* in unison. He was reminded of their prayer before going after Thirteen five years ago, when their path led them to a showdown at the old New York General Hospital. And now, five years later, he was amused at how similar their situation truly was.

Michael was overwhelmingly conflicted. Prayer was so foreign to him, but reverence was not. For his entire life, he'd been groomed to be reverent and mindful of the supernatural, to bow before the whims and leading of spirits, to channel their mysterious power through his mask. But know, he had the opportunity to be free from that bondage. For the more time he spent with his new friends, the more he realized just how deceived he'd been. Now his struggle was with the ever-growing hatred he felt for his father, Emeric Laurent: the Frenchman. This hate was a burden he could not bear.

Kayla's thoughts still lingered on the agreement she had made, to protect herself and Ashley first, to flee if things took a bad turn. The idea simply did not sit well with her. Five years ago, she'd never have settled for such an option. She'd have been one of the first to enter the fray. But the Kayla of old had been blessed with new responsibilities. She was a mother and she knew that her children had to come first.

Ashley hugged Gavin, so proud of the obvious turnaround in his life. As he'd tried to become what he thought was the perfect, responsible husband, he'd abandoned his past life including his identity. She realized now, how wrong that was, that he should have remained in service to God, even if it were in a different way. She knew they were both to blame. Though they worked jobs that kept them busy on many Sundays, had kept them out of church, she knew that they had let that become an excuse to miss church. And rather than make the necessary changes in jobs, they continued on, blaming their work schedules, rather than trusting that God would provide if they made the extremely difficult choice to simply follow Him, with no strings attached. She knew now that they were exactly where God needed them to be. Ashley realized that their real purpose in Paris was not really revenge, not really to save the world. God was using this opportunity to save them, to spare them from the path they were headed down, a path of superficial, uninvolved Christianity. But God was good and had other plans for Gavin and Ashley. He, the Lord, knew this all along and had shaped and prepared every step before they took it.

Jean Luc leaned against the counter, stroking his short gray and stubbly beard. He was no stranger to prayer, but did not speak so freely to God. He felt trapped in tradition, following monotonous and superstitious beliefs that bordered on rituals rather than worship. But in that moment, as Gavin was praying, he heard a small voice whisper inside his head.

I am the way, it told him. *No rite, no work will set you before My throne. I am the Alpha and Omega, the first and the last. Forget all you know and follow Me. I am forgiveness. I am redemption.*

He thought on these words even now, long after the prayer. After his time in the military, Jean Luc had lived a life of servant hood and penitence. But there was also misplaced homage. He had adored saints, prayed to Mary. Jean Luc had confessed his sins to priests and asked them for God's forgiveness. But he suddenly realized that those actions were not enough, not the real way. The voice had told him that *it* was the way. The Holy Spirit was making all things clear. Christianity, real Christianity, is not a religion, he realized, it's a relationship.

And Arthur, having excluded himself from the prayer, stood with an overwhelming pit of emptiness rotting in his gut. His mind churned with the words that Gavin had prayed as he wrestled with his thoughts and feelings. But, Arthur decided, rationalizing and defining his emotions, Gavin's prayer held no real power. His words were passionate, yes, and spoken from his heart, but they were meaningless because there was no God, no Savior, no great plan for them. Arthur rejected the Holy Spirit and shrugged off his convictions, choosing disbelief as his free will saw fit.

****

The hour grew late, the sun sinking into the west. Terrance Killion sat on a bench down on the promenade along the Seine River, angry and alone, a half-empty bottle of rich, strong Port wine in his hand, the beautiful cathedral of Notre Dame standing in the background. He was angry, sad, indignant: how could any of this have happened to him?

He reasoned through the day's events, trying to sort it all out and understand where he went wrong, how they could have gotten to this point, his brother being captured and facing certain death. Was it because he had left Edward all by himself? Edward was a man. He could handle himself. And, Killion convinced himself, he needed a break from his brother, needed the company of a woman to clear his mind. Maybe that was his mistake, maybe his desire for women, his unquenchable lust, was to blame? Perhaps, he reasoned, perhaps his desires that he thought he so well controlled, in all actuality, controlled him? He couldn't count the number of women he'd been with, couldn't remember all their faces. Seldom did he truly even bother with their names. All those poor women were nothing more to him than toys, playthings, and when *he* was satisfied, he cast them aside, never giving a second thought to *their* feelings, *their* desires.

But on the bench, alone beneath the orange sky, Killion understood what all those women he'd seduced must have felt like afterward, for he too now felt used and thrown away. He tried for the life of him to remember the name of the girl he'd been with that very day, the one that allowed him free reign over her as they gave in to their most basic desires. He remembered what they did, but *who* was she?

Killion took a long swig of wine and then leaned forward, his elbows resting on his knees. The more he thought about his mistakes, his lack of self control, the angrier he became. He blamed himself for the situation he and Edward were now in. And he was right. In the least, had he not run off with a girl and left Edward behind, drunk and unguarded, they could have possibly escaped, simply run from Paris and already have been back in London, money in hand, celebrating properly rather than drowning in cheap liquor in a French bar. Why hadn't they just left the city? What had kept them there?

Again, he drank more wine, unaware of the visitor who sat beside him. The creature had not revealed itself to Killion, but had been attached to him for days, whispering doubt, feeding him thoughts of lust and despair. It was the spirit who had encouraged the almost constant drunkenness that the Killion brothers experienced on their faux celebratory binge. It was this creature that guided them to the bar where Edward received the matchbook with the arms dealer's contact information. It too was the one responsible for Killion lashing out and killing the dealer after he acquired the weapons.

This demon was Killion's own, had been for decades: a secret companion. The two of them sat deathly still beneath the shadow of the haunting cathedral. This wasn't the first time, after plans seemingly went wrong, that Killion had found himself near a church, though he never managed to seek refuge within. He always seemed to get close, but never further. And here again, with his brother stolen away, now feeling drunk, helpless, and alone, he sat so close to a place of sanctuary, yet had no peace. The demon made sure of that.

"It's all your fault," the demon hissed through its razor sharp teeth. "You're so pathetic, Terrance. All you had to do was keep it in your pants for one day and you could have saved your brother, but instead, you did what you always do: you let him down. You're all balls and no brains, my friend."

Killion heard the words very clearly, but in his mind, they were uttered in his own voice.

"Shut it," he replied to the voice, replied to himself. "You don't know what you're talking about. I love my brother."

"Yeah," the demon whispered, "I see that. You flee for your life from the Frenchman's chateau, then end up abandoning Edward so you can bed some French bimbo? A standup man you are, a real gentleman."

Killion drank more wine.

"I bet she was good, but no Delilah," the demon laughed. "It's a shame you did her like that, but I get it, kill what you can't keep."

He tried for another drink, but couldn't manage, tears streaming down his face. Killion sat up and launched the bottle into the river, but it did little to relieve him.

"Now you've done it," the demon chided. "Edward will end up just like Delilah…and *you're* the one who's responsible. You've gone and killed the only two people you've ever loved!"

Killion burned with fury, but relented. He had no strength left, no will to fight.

"What should I do?" he asked the voice.

"You could take that gun you have holstered beneath your jacket and end it all, right here, right now, put the barrel in your mouth and blow it all away. Or, you can try to find your brother. Either way, this is the end for you. I'm certain, without a doubt, you will die, Terrance Killion, you deserve to."

Again, Killion leaned forward, his face buried in his hands as he sobbed. The voice was right: he didn't deserve to live.

****

The Frenchman stood in shock, the young, once innocent farm girl smiling at him in a way that made him more uncomfortable than he could fathom, "What have I done?"

"You set me free, Emeric," she explained. "No longer do I think of my parents or my sisters, no longer must I bother with meaningless chores and the folly of adolescence. I am alive!"

Laurent stared into her eyes, heartbroken. She threw her arms around him, trying desperately to force their lips to meet, but he resisted, pushing her to the floor.

"What's going on?" Sebastian exclaimed, hearing the scuffle as he returned to the room.

"She's out of her mind!" Laurent answered. "When she woke, she was like a different person."

"Do you know why?" Sebastian asked, helping the girl up from the floor and examining her pupils closely, spreading open her eyelids with his finger and thumb.

"I have no idea, she just *was*!"

"Hello, Sebastian," she said sweetly, placing her hands on his chest.

"The ritual did this to you?" he asked.

"Yes," she sighed aloofly.

"I thought she was dead," Sebastian said.

"I wish she was," Emeric admitted.

Without warning, the girl playfully touched her forefinger to the tip of Sebastian's nose, then spun and headed for the ritual chamber, "You boys can follow if you like."

"What are you doing?" Emeric questioned.

"It's almost sundown, I can feel it…it's time to reopen the portal."

****

After eating their humbly thrown-together supper, Gavin returned to the warehouse's rooftop. Black clouds had gathered overhead, blocking out what daylight was left. His eyes once more open to the spiritual world around him, he was tormented by the woops and howls of the thousands of demons that woke, stretching from their slumber, beating their leathery wings furiously.

"Would you have ever imagined such a sight?" a voice asked from over his shoulder, watching with him as the demons took flight, creeping from the shadows and blackening the sky along with the storm clouds.

"What's going to happen?" Gavin asked, his eyes never breaking from the horrible scene.

"I'll fight them," Joseph replied. "To my death if I must. I've assembled a host. They are prepared to die as well. We must hold them back!"

"How do you know this isn't the end?" Gavin asked in contemplation. "The signs are all there: wars and rumors of wars, earthquakes, famine...the world is falling apart, and now this!"

"You speak of the twenty-fourth chapter in the book of Matthew," Joseph smiled. "Indeed, what is plaguing the world seems to be what Jesus called *the beginning of sorrows*. There are nations rising against nations, world-wide persecution of Christians...everything just as Jesus said it would happen, all documented nearly two thousand years ago! But what does Jesus say about His warnings?"

"He warns us not to be deceived, that many will come claiming to be the messiah and that the wars and earthquakes *must* happen, but the end is still to come," Gavin said, recalling verses four through seven.

"But what did Jesus command?"

Gavin thought for a moment, the scripture still running through his head as he watched the swirling cyclone of demons, "Christ said not to be alarmed."

"Funny isn't it?" Joseph laughed. "Jesus already told you not to worry about what will happen here. Be still, my friend, and know that Christ is God."

"But what if we fail, if I fail?" Gavin argued.

"There is no failing in this matter, only fulfillment. All these things must come to pass in order for the promises in the Bible to be realized. We have already won. Don't forget that!"

Gavin whispered John 16:33 aloud, *"I have told you these things, so that in Me you may have peace. In this world you will have trouble. But take heart! I have overcome the world."*

"Exactly! We must now press on, unhindered by fear and doubt. With your eyes, you have seen terribly incredible things; terrible because of their nature, but indeed incredible, things that most people could not or would not accept, living their lives in oblivious wandering as the spiritual world rages on around them!"

As they spoke, the earth shook violently. Thunder clapped loudly, echoing through the streets as it started to rain.

"What was that?" Gavin asked.

"I fear the portal has once more been opened. I must go. Rest tonight, let *us* fight, then tomorrow, you need to end your business with Killion and focus on the real matter at hand: Laurent must be stopped, at all costs!"

26

Gavin stood on the rooftop, the rain pouring down on him. Joseph had left in a hurry, taking flight and leading the angelic warriors into battle. He thought of what transpired five short years ago outside of the Tri-Corp building in Manhattan, when the demon that lived within Triton was released by his death and confronted by Joseph, revealing to Gavin, Ashley, Jamie and Kayla his true form, not an elderly man, but a beautiful angel. Joseph's battle with the demon wrecked the street below, causing chaos and panic. What would happen now, with thousands of angels and demons trading blows?

Ashley joined Gavin at his side, her hand gripping his tightly. She'd found him there just after the earthquake. He'd explained to her what Joseph had said and now they stared, rain-soaked, off towards the Eiffel Tower.

The battle was epic, though Ashley could not see. Gavin smiled in awe: he simply could not help it, for the vision was both terrifying and inspiring. Every time the angels and demons would swing their swords, the meeting of the blades filled the sky with light, flashing and bright, the clanging of their weapons a thunderous composition that rumbled through the streets of Paris.

Closer to the mêlée where Joseph fought amongst the heavenly ranks, the war was furious. He chased demon after demon through the dark sky, parrying their attacks and running his sword through them, their bodies turning to crumbling ash. He swept his rain-slicked hair from his face and turned, an unexpected strike glancing off his silver blade. Again, he brushed off the attack and vanquished that demon to Hell with the rest.

Around him lingered the putrid smell of sulfur, lightning continued to flash as the angels pressed on. But the demons did not give up easily. With the portal still open, it seemed that every demon that fell was replaced by another and another, an endless stream of evil rising up from the churning water below.

Joseph watched as an angel was struck down, two particularly large demons besting him, their fiery scimitars slashing and stabbing. Three angels quickly ascended on the demons and avenged their fallen brother as it returned to Heaven in a flash of brilliant light.

The fighting continued for hours, growing more fierce as the demons began landing on the streets and rooftops, forcing the clash into the real world. Shattered glass sparkled as it flew through the air, glimmering with every flash of lightning as parked cars were smashed, the spiritual creatures flinging one another against them, resulting in blaring horns and screeching alarms as the vehicles reacted to the destruction.

Joseph continued directing the angels, guiding the heavenly forces to wherever the enemy's stronghold was the greatest. He had to get the evil creatures off the ground and drive them back into the sky, far away from where any people could get trapped in the conflict, leaving them hurt or even dead. But it seemed futile, as long as the portal was open, the wave of demons was unending.

****

The Frenchman cowered on the floor, crying over the body of his son. Sebastian lay perfectly still, his eyes staring into nothing, blood streaming from his nose.

The girl had begun the ritual by herself, without Laurent or the book. The solitary door stood wide open, light erupting from with its frame. Wind howled through the corridors of the crumbling chateau.

Engulfed in power, the girl faced the strange, spiritual doorway, her white clothing glowing, her face, arms, and bare feet awash in awesomely brilliant light. Her eyes were closed as her lips formed silent words over and again, chants and incantations: an invitation for evil to freely enter the world without inhibition.

It was as the power grew, that a shockwave had sent Sebastian falling backwards. He shook violently in convulsion before then entering the catatonic state in which Laurent held him. There was a pulse, albeit faint. The beloved son of the Frenchman was still alive, if only just a little.

Laurent cried, his tears a salty, fervent curse of the power he'd so willingly and joyously unleashed. But the girl had become something horrible, terribly horrible. She had assumed the role of the old and ancient key. No longer necessary was the relic, the door now freely opened by her will. She, in a sense, had become the doorway, a living, breathing gateway to Hell. Laurent was heartbroken. After all he'd done and sacrificed, after all his devotion; in the end, he was cast aside, left to mend his broken son, collateral damage of the cause.

True, he hadn't done any of this for his own glory. But he had foolishly assumed that the peace-bringer, as he liked to think of the antichrist, would soon rise to power, and he, Laurent, too would find a seat amongst the shapers of the New World. He counted himself a valuable member of The Collective, but feared, for the first time, his own death. Would this truly be the fate of such a pious believer?

Just as suddenly as it began, the droning wind fell silent and the bright light subsided. The girl collapsed to the stone floor, exhausted from the outpouring of power.

As soon as the ritual was complete, Sebastian blinked, raising his hand and wiping the blood from his face. "What happened, father?"

Laurent looked up, his eyes red and fearful, "You live! I thought she had killed you."

"How?"

"I don't know, my son; but clearly, she is more powerful than I could have ever imagined."

****

Joseph grew tired. The battle had gone on for most of the night. But there was hope. Another angel had decried that the portal had once more closed, the swirling water settling, the Seine returning to its peaceful state.

"We must make a push now," he shouted. "The sun will rise soon, do not let them disappear into the shadows!"

The angels made a valiant effort to destroy the remaining demons. With the portal closed, there were no new arrivals and they managed to thin the ranks by half.

But the sun, as it always does, peeked from beyond the eastern horizon. The angels cheered with swords pointing to Heaven as the demons slipped away into the remaining darkness, cursing and swearing that the war was far from over.

Joseph landed on the street below, surveying the damage and believing it could have been considerably worse. He wiped black and sooty ash from his sweaty brow. His muscles ached, his beautiful wings were heavy. Now the battle belonged to the humans. If Gavin and his companions were able to successfully stop the Frenchman from once more opening the gateway, then the angels could surely have victory in the coming night. Joseph was certain that this was God's will.

****

Jean Luc had woken early, wanting to prepare for their mission at the Louvre. He'd double checked their vehicles and ensured they were fueled and ready. The custom Remington 700 sniper rifle that Jamie would man was cleaned and function checked, then loaded with five .308 rounds. Jean Luc attached the large suppressor to the end of the barrel and raised the gun's stock to his shoulder, peering through the scope as he did.

The computer behind him blipped to life. Jean Luc turned to see what news had been delivered. Police had responded to a flood of strange reports over night. He read the online article, pausing at several points to reread and grasp what the reports claimed.

Witnesses watched as cars were seemingly crushed and crumpled at random, as if smashed by an unseen force. Street lights were toppled, buildings saw damage to stonework and rooftops. Several witnesses described what felt like an earthquake, but officials had yet to confirm or deny such activity as a likely cause for the disturbances.

There was a link to a video filmed by one of the responding officers, his phone capturing the strange imagery. Jean Luc moused over the link and turned the volume up slowly on the computer. He watched as the short video showed what appeared to be a whirlpool as it opened in the middle of the Seine river. Fierce winds had also been recorded by the phone's mic, but faintly heard amongst the howling was another sound, strange, sinister…maybe he was crazy, but Jean Luc was certain he heard laughter within the audio track.

"What are you watching?" Gavin asked with a yawn, coming down the stairs, coffee mug in hand, Ashley close behind.

"A video report from last night. It shows a strange occurrence in central Paris, near the Eiffel Tower."

"Really?!" Ashley asked excitedly. "Like what?"

"Cars mysteriously crumpling, odd sounds, a whirlpool in the Seine: I've never seen anything like this," Jean Luc admitted.

Jean Luc replayed the video. Gavin and Ashley watched in awe of the events.

"Was this the battle you said was coming?" Jean Luc questioned. "Was this a spiritual war?"

"I think so," Gavin agreed. "That whirlpool must be the portal that Joseph mentioned."

"So how do we keep it from opening?" Ashley asked.

"I'm not sure, but it has to be the Frenchman who is responsible. Joseph told me we have to stop Laurent. And in so doing, I would hope that the portal would remain closed."

"What kind of man has this sort of power?" Jean Luc wondered, rewatching the video once more.

"One that is deceived," Gavin replied.

"And how do you stop that man, when he can control the elements and bring chaos at will?"

"You don't, only God can. I have faith that this will work out. We just have to believe, follow the path that lies before us. We end this tonight!"

The three were joined by Jamie, Kayla, Michael and Arthur. The preparations had been made, the time set. This was it, the moment they'd all hoped for yet dreaded completely. If this were a game of chess, their next move would take the queen, leaving the king open and vulnerable. So many pawns had fallen in this devious game, so much had been threatened and lost, and for what? But they pushed such questions from their minds, focusing only on their next move: Killion must be dealt with; and then, the Frenchman.

****

The early morning sun glimmered off the peak of the glass pyramid architecture that marked the entrance to the Louvre, the rays refracting and glowing brilliantly. Michael pulled to a stop where Arthur specified, leaving the Range Rover running. Behind him, pulled off to the side of the rounding lane within the Louvre's courtyard, was the white van, driven by Jean Luc. Jamie, Kayla, Gavin and Ashley sat in the van's cargo area.

"Are you sure we can't help?" Kayla asked. "We could take up positions as lookouts. Killion wouldn't recognize me."

"Gavin and I agree," Jamie replied, "it would be better if you two waited for us to take him. We'll call and pick you up once he's secure. But if things go badly, you two must be able to escape!"

Kayla sighed. She didn't like the idea. Neither did Ashley, but she understood.

"For now, just go and enjoy the museum," Jamie continued. "It's currently a quarter past nine, leaving us less than three hours till the scheduled meet. Relax and don't worry. Jean Luc and Arthur won't let anything happen to us. After all, they're professionals."

Kayla and Ashley kissed their husbands goodbye and climbed out the back of the van, reluctantly, but also excitedly, heading for the famous museum. The men watched as their wives crossed the plaza, disappearing into the small crowd of tourists that had already grown.

"I hate sending them off alone like that," Gavin admitted. "I almost lost Ashley once, I can't imagine going through that again!"

Jamie understood perfectly, "I know. But it's all in God's hands. Kayla and Ashley are tough, they can handle themselves. Remember how well they did in New York? They held their own against the Tri-Six."

"That was five years ago," Gavin answered. "Kayla was an academy trained detective. Ashley was young and just naïve enough to be fearless. But now, after marriage and motherhood, and simply settling down, could they still do it, I mean honestly, could Kayla still pull the trigger if she had to?"

"I don't know," Jamie grinned, "but I'm praying we never get the chance to find out. Even after this, once we have Killion and we then set our focus on the Frenchman, I'm not so certain I want the girls coming along to the chateau."

"I agree. But how are we going to keep them from coming?" Gavin asked. "There's no way we'll get them to stay behind. They know we need all the help we can get. Plus, they've been here since the beginning. Don't forget that Ashley was targeted by Triton, their brother murdered by one of his associates!"

"I know," Jamie said, "I can hardly believe it all."

"If I might share my opinion with you both, I have something to say," Jean Luc interrupted, listening from the driver's seat as they spoke, his eyes reflecting in the rearview mirror as he glanced back at them.

"Absolutely," Gavin smiled.

"I know you men love your wives very much and you have this feeling of duty to protect them. But," he said, "you cannot shield them from everything. They must be free to choose for themselves how they will handle life and the many challenges we all face. I know you mean well, but do not let your love blind you to their strength. Your intentions are most definitely noble, but, as men of faith, *have* faith. That is just my humble opinion."

Jamie and Gavin looked at each other and smiled, both recognizing the truth in his words. Jean Luc was right.

****

Ashley could hardly contain her excitement as she and her sister walked the corridors of the famed Louvre. Occasionally, they would linger at an exhibit, Ashley giving a brief detailing of the painting, explaining the history and back-story behind many of the priceless works. Kayla listened, but feigned her interest. She still thought of the plan to capture Killion, her thoughts ever returning to the courtyard and the scene that would shortly unfold.

Kayla imagined the meet, envisioned Gavin and Arthur confronting Killion. Then, in her mind, things would go terribly wrong. She stared blankly at the portrait hanging on the wall as Ashley's voice seemed miles away. All Kayla could see was Killion pulling a gun and shooting both men, then finding the vehicles and ending Jamie and Michael. She nearly cried.

"Kay, are you with me?" Ashley asked. "Snap out of it!"

Kayla blinked, once more seeing the painting and not the imagined vision, "Yeah, sorry…just daydreaming."

"You look like you're going to cry."

"I'm not," Kayla smile. "I just have a lot of emotions hitting me right now. I'm scared, Ash. What if something happens to them?"

"Jean Luc won't let anything happen," Ashley smiled, taking her sister's hand and squeezing it tightly in reassurance. "Worst case, Michael has his mask. He's bulletproof right?"

"I guess," Kayla said, finding comfort in her sister's certainty, even if a little careless. "Let's go find the painting you were looking for."

The minutes that followed ticked away like seconds. Before they realized how long they'd walked the museum, the time had already passed eleven o' clock. Now, the sisters stood still in the Grande Galerie of the Salon Carré, staring on silently at the thirty inch by twenty-one inch, oil on poplar masterpiece that hung just feet away, smirking at them from behind its glass-cased, temperature-controlled housing, illuminated brilliantly by modern LED light.

"*La Joconde*," Kayla mused, reading the placard.

"The Mona Lisa," Ashley replied with tears in her eyes.

"Are you alright?" Kayla asked.

"I've just wanted to see this painting my whole life," Ashley explained. "I can't believe I'm standing in front of Leonardo da Vinci's greatest, most infamous work and all I can think about is Gavin. I wish he was here, sharing this moment with me, not waiting outside for a killer."

"I know," Kayla said, wrapping her arm around Ashley's shoulder as the crowd around them grew, slowly pushing them back as more onlookers tried to get their turn. "Come on, Ash. It's almost noon. We need to be ready for Jamie's call."

****

Jamie knelt as he stared out the back window of the van, the bolt-action rifle raised, looking through the scope as people wandered in and out of the crosshairs. Jean Luc remained in the driver's seat, scanning the crowd.

"How are you doing back there?" Jean Luc asked. "See him yet?"

"Nothing yet. But I have to say, with the suppressor on the end of the barrel, this thing gets heavy surprisingly quick."

"Rest the muzzle end of the suppressor on the edge of the window's frame. Use the window itself as a bipod," Jean Luc recommended. "You'll be able to hold steady longer and, if the need arises to fire, you will be more accurate."

Jamie tried using Jean Luc's advice. The man was right. With the end of the can resting on the window frame, Jamie could still swivel the long gun and he had greater control.

Jean Luc twisted in his seat and extended his hand out to Gavin, a small device in his palm, "Take this in-ear communicator. That way, you, Arthur, and I can keep in constant communication. It's almost noon. You should take position in the plaza, near the reflecting pool. Arthur will give you further instruction. I just watched him exit the Range Rover. He nodded at us which means he's heading for the cover of the crowd. Godspeed, Monsieur Dering."

****

Killion was tired and angry as he made the nearly two kilometer walk from Notre Dame to the Louvre. With nowhere else to go, he'd elected to sleep off his wine-induced drunkenness on the bench he'd occupied the night before, resting beneath the twinkling stars.

He crossed the Pont des Arts bridge and followed the flow of pedestrians across the Quai Françoise Mitterand, then left on Cour Carree. His jaw flinched in anger as he travelled anonymously amongst the happy gawkers who packed the museum grounds. Around him, cameras and cell phones clicked away, documenting the many tourists' visits to such a historical location. But he was in no mind to appreciate the art in this place.

Killion spotted the statue of the rider and horse and approached warily, scanning the sea of people for any familiar faces. He reached the sculpture, raised his hand high over his head as directed, waived, and then waited.

****

"There he is," Jean Luc said, his words transmitted by the earpiece.

"I've got him," Arthur confirmed, stalking through the crowd, stealthily slipping from one group of people to the next. "Gavin, you set, mate?"

"I am," he replied, moving along the southern edge of the plaza, keeping line-of-sight on his target.

"Alright, move now!" Arthur exclaimed. "I'm almost to him."

Jamie tracked their movement from the van, the Remington 700 trained on Killion, watching Gavin take cover behind the statue as Arthur appeared from within the vast crowd. Jean Luc looked on intently. Michael, from his vantage point in the Range Rover, clicked back the hammer on one of his matching 1911 pistols, just in case.

"Oi," Arthur called out as he approached his old friend.

"Arthur," Killion nodded in unhappy greeting. "Where's my brother?"

"Edward is safe. I'll take you to him if all goes fine."

"What do you mean?" Killion asked.

Gavin slipped from behind the statue and pulled his compact HK 9mm, pressing the barrel into the contract killer's spine, "Surprise. Remember me?"

"How could I forget," Killion snarled. "I should have killed you when I had the chance."

"Instead you killed Delilah, in cold blood," Arthur grunted. "Why, mate? She was one of us."

Jamie and Jean Luc listened with their earpieces. But as they watched, a large box truck with *Fleurs de Paris* printed on the side stopped right in front of them, blocking their view.

"No!" Jean Luc cried out.

"I lost them, I don't have a shot," Jamie said excitedly. "Do you hear me Gavin? I *don't* have a shot!"

Without warning, Killion's hand lurched back and found the short slide of the gun. He then violently twisted, locking Gavin's wrist in a terribly awkward and painful hold. Before the men could react, Killion had swept around them gracefully, now holding them at gunpoint.

The white box truck rumbled, then shook as the driver shifted into gear and began to lurch forward, traffic finally allowing him to move. Slowly, Jamie's and Jean Luc's field of view once more opened, but it was too late. As the truck crept on, they were horrified by the echoing boom of a gunshot reverberating across the congested plaza.

27

Screams filled the air as the panicked crowd scattered, ducking and trampling over one another. Killion whipped around, his eyes fiery with rage, the wound in his shoulder burning where the bullet had struck him. He aimed the gun in the direction from which he'd been shot, but was unsure of where his attacker was located. Another bang rang out, striking Killion in the thigh, piercing straight through, dropping him to his knees.

Kayla stood ready to fire once more if needed, her aim true, her finger waiting on the trigger of the Beretta held confidently in her hands. Killion focused in on her and raised the gun, trying to steady his shaky aim. She fired a third round, the bullet bursting through his abdomen and ripping through his stomach wall. He dropped the 9mm and raised his hands as best he could to signify surrender, his shoulder aching painfully as he did, blood spilling from the hole in his gut. Ashley came running up behind her sister, watching wide-eyed as the whole terrible scene unfolded.

Jean Luc started the van and yelled for Jamie to hold on as he floored the accelerator, pulling as closely to the action as the terrified onlookers would allow. Arthur took hold of Killion's arm and drug him to his feet, pulling the crippled killer along. Gavin snatched up the dropped HK pistol from the ground and he and the girls followed closely behind.

The van skidded to a stop. Jamie quickly opened the back doors and they all clambered in. Again, Jean Luc stepped on the gas. Michael trailed them in the Range Rover and kept close as Jean Luc merged into traffic.

"He's bleeding bad," Gavin announced as the van swerved and bounced as they raced away from the Louvre.

"Give me your belt," Jamie said looking up at Gavin, "quick now!"

Gavin unbuckled his black leather belt as fast as his fingers would allow and then tossed it to Jamie. Killion grimaced as the belt was wrapped around his leg and pulled tight to make a tourniquet just above the bullet wound.

"Ashley, put your hand on his stomach, keep pressure on the wound!" Jamie directed.

"Why are you trying to save me?" Killion asked wearily. "You want me dead don't you? Just let me bleed out."

"Shut up," Arthur commanded, his gun trained and ready if Killion tried anything.

Jean Luc slowed the van and managed to blend in with the other traffic as they returned to the warehouse. Police would of course be looking for a nondescript white cargo van, but it would take days, even weeks to narrow down a list of registrations and possible drivers. He knew there was no chance that the plates could be traced either, seeing as how he had them made, for just such occasions, by an old friend, a master forger who could provide everything from decoy license plates to passports and photo ID's.

Michael parked out front as Jean Luc waited for the garage door to open. He then quickly jumped out of the charcoal SUV and slipped through the door as it closed behind the van.

Killion looked terrible as they pulled him out of the van. He'd lost a lot of blood and didn't have long to live, they could see it in his eyes.

"Let's take him to Edward," Jamie said.

Jean Luc led the way, unlocking and opening the door that led to the storage room turned makeshift holding cell. As soon as Edward saw his bloodied brother, he stood from the chair, allowing for him to be gently lowered into the seat.

"What happened?!" Edward exclaimed.

"He tried to kill us," Arthur grunted in response, "what else?"

"Of course he did," Edward sighed.

"See Terrance, old boy," Arthur laughed, "your brother is alive and well, as promised."

Killion wheezed deep, labored breaths, his lungs beginning to fill with blood and fluid as he looked up into his younger brother's face, "Ed, I thought they'd killed you."

"Come along Edward," Jean Luc said, "you're free to leave."

Edward stared at his dying brother sadly, "Can we have just a moment alone before I go?"

Arthur nodded and he, Jean Luc, Gavin, and Jamie left the brothers alone.

"Don't do anything stupid," Arthur said, pulling the door shut as they gave them privacy.

"I won't," Edward agreed, never breaking eye contact with Terrance.

"Are you in pain?" he asked his brother.

"Not much anymore," Killion laughed, coughing and spitting blood onto the floor. "I'm numb all over."

They stared at each other for a moment.

"I'm glad they agreed to let you live," Killion said, managing a weak smile. "You deserve a happy life."

Edward didn't respond. He wasn't sure how to say what he wanted.

"Can I ask you something?" Edward continued.

Killion nodded and coughed again, the buildup in his chest thick and gagging.

"I want the truth. When you saved me at Laurent's, when those monsters nearly had me, did you come back for me or the bag of money I carried?"

Killion's gaze fell to the floor. He couldn't look his brother in the face anymore.

"I came back for the money," he said softly, shamed by his admission.

"That's what I thought."

"But I have always loved you, brother...*always*."

Edward stared at Killion, pained by his brother's words, both angered and moved, "I know you have. And I've loved you too."

Killion slowly nodded towards the left chest pocket of his blood stained suit jacket, "Take it, it's where we discussed. Live the life you've always wanted. Do it for me!"

Edward knelt and looked once more into his brother's drifting eyes, then reached carefully into his jacket and fished into the pocket. He removed a small slip of paper with two series of numbers written on it, one above the other.

"Gare du Nord...train station...find the lockers. Now, go."

Edward put the paper in his pocket and kissed his dying brother on the forehead, "I'll miss you, Terrance...goodbye."

He knocked on the door. Jean Luc opened it for him. Edward looked back at Terrance one last time.

Killion managed to look up, tears streaking his face, his chin quivering fearfully, "I love you, baby brother."

Edward nearly broke down, his eyes watery as Arthur grabbed him by the arm and pulled him away, leaving Terrance Killion at the mercy of his captors.

"I don't care where you go," Arthur said, "or what you do, but I never want to hear your name again. You disappear, savvy? And if I ever hear word you've gone after any of my new friends in a sorry whim of revenge, I'll kill you."

Edward agreed silently, nodding as he choked back his tears. Jamie escorted him to the front door and left him standing on the sidewalk, now all alone in the world.

"Are you ready to do this?" Arthur asked, unholstering his 1911 automatic and handing it to Gavin.

"It's time," Jean Luc urged.

Gavin locked eyes with Ashley. She stared at him sadly, feeling strangely sorry for Killion. Kayla watched as the five men headed for the storage room.

"Come on," Kayla said to her sister, taking Ashley by the hand, "let's go upstairs."

Gavin looked back to see Ashley once more before she and Kayla disappeared up the steps. He had to get a hold of himself. It was time for Killion to pay for all he'd done.

They entered the storage room, finding Killion much more alive than he had led his brother to believe. The Englishman glared at them resentfully, his bold gaze defiant to the end.

"I was afraid we'd find you dead,' Arthur smiled.

"I couldn't let Edward think I had a chance. He might have done something rash. By allowing him to think I was so close to death, I knew he would let me go and save himself."

"How nice of you," Jean Luc mocked.

"But you are close to death," Arthur laughed.

Killion coughed as he too laughed along, then spit a clump of thick, mucus and blood on Arthur's shirt.

"Go on," Arthur encouraged angrily, looking at the .45 in Gavin's hands.

"Yeah, go on," Killion smiled, blood trickling from the corner of his mouth. "Get it over with, make me pay. Exact your revenge!"

He clicked back the hammer on the stainless 1911 and raised the gun, pointing the five inch barrel straight at Killion's face. Jamie and Michael watched as Gavin readied to end Killion's life.

Gavin squeezed in on the grip safety, his finger ready on the trigger. He stared the murderous Killion in the eyes as he remembered how things played out on the wet and stormy pier at the lighthouse in the Chicago harbor. He imagined what life would be like had Killion done the unthinkable and hurt Ashley, even taking her life. He thought of how afraid she must have been when she awoke and found herself in a strange place and no idea where she'd been taken. She must have been terrified. Killion stared back, cold and unafraid.

"What are you waiting for?" Killion asked.

Jamie suddenly felt strange, like this wasn't the right thing to do. He wanted Delilah's death to be avenged, but this simply seemed wrong. Michael, too, felt very much the same way. He stepped forward and placed his hand on Gavin's shoulder.

"You don't have to do this," Michael said, his voice of reason comforting to Gavin. "We've got him, that's enough. He'll die from his injuries."

"Michael's right," Jamie added. "Kayla shot him in defense. He would have killed you if she hadn't. But this, you pointing that gun at him, if you kill him now, it's not self defense, it's murder."

"He killed Delilah!" Arthur argued as Jean Luc looked on silently.

"This is pathetic," Killion ridiculed. "Give me the gun, I'll do it myself."

Gavin's hand began to shake as he stared down the slide of the gun. All he had to do was squeeze the trigger and Delilah would be avenged. This was what he'd wanted to do this whole time, to catch Killion and make him suffer. But now, did he have what it would take? Again, he readied to shoot, steadying his aim. Gavin could feel the sweat as it gathered on his brow, his heart beating loudly in his chest.

Vengeance is mine, a voice spoke in his head.

Gavin lowered the gun and returned the hammer to half-cocked, "Your life is not mine to take. I am not the one to judge you. Only God has that responsibility. I'm sorry for what has happened, everything, that this is where we've all ended up."

He handed the gun back to Arthur who stood in stunned, jaw-opened silence. They all watched as Gavin left the small room.

"Gavin is right," Jamie agreed, following his brother-in-law's lead. "We've gone too far."

Michael stepped up to Killion and punched him squarely in the jaw, "You're lucky I've discovered a new path and I'm doing everything I can to atone for my sins. The old me would have made you suffer. Thirteen would never have let you live."

"Well then," Killion smirked, "Thank God for that."

Michael shook his head in pity and joined Gavin and Jamie in the main area of the warehouse. Killion was now alone with Jean Luc and Arthur.

"This has been a touching reunion," Killion said. "But since we've established that only God is able to judge me, what say we go ahead and settle this. If you would be so kind as to see me to a hospital right away, I'll be more than happy to share the small fortune awarded me by the Frenchman."

"That's enough, mate," Arthur said, reaching into his pocket for his cell phone.

Arthur quickly dialed a number on the touch screen and raised it to his ear, waiting for an answer on the other end. Jean Luc paced, anxiously waiting for what he knew was inevitable.

"Oi, mate," Arthur said as the call was answered, "we've got him."

Jean Luc stopped where he stood, his expression calm and sure. Arthur reached out and held the phone up to Killion's ear.

"Someone would like a word with you," Arthur said.

"How lovely," Killion winked, turning his attention to the person on the other end. "To whom am I speaking?"

"Hello, Terry," the voice replied coolly, "it's Solomon."

"Grier?!" Killion asked in surprise.

"That's right. So tell me Terry, before Arthur kills you, why did you do it, why did you murder Delilah? She was one of us. You loved her!"

"I had to," Killion sighed. "She didn't want me, mate. And, she wanted me dead. She and I were over. It was her or me and I chose me."

"Well, then, old friend, I guess this is goodbye," Solomon replied. "Put Arthur back on the phone.

"Goodbye, Sully," Killion said, looking up at Arthur. "Old Grier wants to speak to you now."

Arthur once again placed the phone at his own ear, "So shall I continue then?"

"Yes," Solomon answered. "End this game. I'll hang up when it's done."

Arthur held the phone at his side, Solomon still listening on the other end. He raised the gun, clicked back the hammer and frowned at the elusive Killion.

"I'll pray for your soul, Terrance," Jean Luc offered.

Killion smirked a blood-marred, toothy grin, "Don't bother."

There was a long silence as Jean Luc and Arthur stared Killion in his eyes, the anticipation growing. Their hearts raced as they readied to execute their old friend.

"Goodbye, mate," Arthur said, squeezing the trigger.

The hammer dropped and the .45 fired, the boom of the gun rattling the whole warehouse. Terrance Killion, the killer, the assassin, was dead.

****

Kayla and Ashley had returned downstairs when they'd heard the gunshot, not out of morbid curiosity, but because they wanted to be sure that everyone in their group was alright, that Killion hadn't somehow turned the tables, allowing for something terrible and unexpected to happen in his last moments alive. They were relieved to find Jamie, Michael, and Gavin waiting for Arthur and Jean Luc to exit the storage room; meaning, in the end, God had spared them from making the call and living with pulling the trigger. And certainly, though Gavin had wanted so desperately to be the one to avenge Delilah's murder, he knew he would not be justified in becoming a murderer himself.

"It's done," Arthur announced as he and Belesur stepped from the small room, blood droplets spattered on their clothing, the stainless steel automatic hanging at Blackwood's side.

"Terrance Killion will not harm another person," Jean Luc added, pulling the door shut to hide the gory mess

"I can't believe it," Ashley said, taking Gavin by the hand. "He's actually dead, we did it, we caught Killion."

"Let's not celebrate quite yet. We still have to deal with my father," Michael reminded.

"Yeah, but…he was going to kill me and Elizabeth. He deserved this!"

"Indeed he did," Michael replied. "But the real threat has yet to be faced. Killion was but a man. My father, well…let's just pray he isn't like Triton."

Ashley conceded. Michael was right. And celebrating anyone's murder, even a ruthless killer's, didn't sit well with her if she truly thought about it, for even a wasted life was still a life.

"We have to think about tonight," Michael continued, taking time to look each of his friends squarely in the eyes. "We need to know how we are going to end this."

"Edward said there were sleepwalkers," Kayla said.

"Hundreds of them," Jamie interjected.

"If they're protecting the Frenchman," Kayla continued, "then there's no getting around them. We'll have to go through them."

Gavin nodded in agreement. There didn't seem to be another way.

"So we'll use the full-auto guns," Gavin replied. "We hit them fast and we hit them hard. If we can weaken their numbers enough to clear a path, then maybe Michael and I can break free and confront his father. But make no miscalculations. We'll all be fighting for our lives, of that I'm certain!"

"Killion's brother marked the map for us," Jean Luc said, looking at his watch. Tours is nearly two hours from here and the Frenchman is yet further still. We will need to leave soon if we are to arrive before nightfall."

They all understood. There was little time to recover from their final showdown with Killion. If they were to successfully keep the Frenchman from once again opening the portal to Hell, then they would need to move quickly.

"I'm going to make us some sandwiches for the road," Kayla decided.

"I'm going to call mom and dad too. I want to hear the kids' voices before we go. "How about you, Jamie?"

He thought that was a great idea and followed his wife upstairs. Michael considered that this too could be his last chance to speak with Elizabeth and Cain, if the worst were to happen and they failed.

"I'm going to step outside and use my cell," Michael explained, turning towards the door.

Ashley, still holding her husband's hand, tugged at him and whispered that she loved him, happy that she was with him, even now at what could very well be their end. Gavin too, felt the same way.

"Are you certain you want to do this?" he asked. "Think of the baby, I just couldn't stand to lose both of you."

"And if I were to run away from this, what would happen if I lost you? Your baby would never know her father."

"*Her?*" Gavin smiled. "How do you know?"

"It's just a hunch, I guess," Ashley laughed. "We won't know for sure till like week twenty of the pregnancy, so we have a few months yet, but still."

Gavin grinned, imagining a perfect, happy, bubbling baby girl, "I hope she looks just like you."

"But with your eyes," Ashley added.

"Sorry to interrupt you two lovebirds," Jean Luc said, but we really must get the weapons ready and load the van.

"You're still coming with us?" Gavin asked.

"Of course," Jean Luc replied. "I will see you through to the end. I have realized that this is, what you would call, my destiny."

"How about you then, Arthur?" Ashley questioned.

"Sorry, love, but Killion was the end of the line for me. I'll stay here and clean up this mess. You should know that if you survive the chateau, I won't be here when you return. That's just how it is."

"We understand," Gavin nodded, stepping up to Blackwood and

shaking his hand firmly. "Thanks for all you've done."

"Of course, mate. Delilah deserved better than she got. It was right for Killion to pay. You lot need to come to terms with that. But, now, I'm certainly glad that I got to be the one who did it."

They packed a separate crate full of arms and ammunition, loading up with the HK UMP's, MP5's and G3's, and the M16's and AK-47's, as well as all the extra magazines they could find. Gavin was certain they would need every round they could get.

Soon, Jamie and Kayla returned, a paper sack full of road-sandwiches and a packed carton of bottled water in tow. They'd made their call, heard their children's sweet voices one more time. Clearly they'd been crying, their eyes red and puffy as they approached the van.

"Everything alright back home?" Ashley asked.

"Oh yeah," Kayla sighed, "just hard to think I might never see Marley and Ethan again."

"We'll be fine," Gavin assured. "God didn't bring us this far to fail."

The warehouse's entrance door opened. Michael had also just finished on the phone.

"How can I help make ready?"

"Grab the other end of this crate, but be careful. It's going to be heavy," Gavin warned.

With the weapons loaded into the van, they were ready to head for Les Trois-Moutiers and the Frenchman. They all once again thanked Arthur for his help, Jean Luc hugging his old friend, before they climbed into the van. The garage door hummed and shook as it opened, granting them access to the final step of their journey. Now, only a few hours' drive stood between them and possible death.

Jean Luc pulled out into the street, leaving Arthur and the dead Killion behind. There was no looking back: their path lay ahead.

28

Joseph beat his wings hard, shooting straight up into the sky above the warehouse. He'd tarried there for most of the day, but remaining hidden from them, anxiously waiting to see what choice Gavin would make in their dealing with Killion. The angel was proud of his former apprentice demon hunter. Joseph regretted even now, that Gavin and his friends had been placed in such circumstances, but for whatever reason, this was God's will. He had placed each of them, Jamie, Kayla, Ashley, Gavin, and even Michael, on this path. It was their choices that ultimately brought them to this moment, but in God's infinite wisdom, He saw the outcomes of each decision as they made it, allowing for them to be precisely where He would have wanted them in the first place. Jean Luc, for better or worse had become a part of the plan. Arthur too, had aligned with God's will, as executioner, the deliverer of God's wrath.

The hours would pass quickly now, Joseph knew this. He'd bolstered the angelic forces and developed a new strategy. The reinforcements, if the Frenchman reopened the portal, would be arranged as a perimeter around the whirlpool, striking down the demons as they arrived. If Gavin and his company were able to stop Laurent before he opened the gateway, then those angels would be able to join the rest of the host and wipe the remaining demons out. But even this new plan, was only a small bandage over a gaping wound. Eventually, unless Gavin succeeded, the constant flow of demons would overpower Joseph and his warriors, not in strength or cunning, but simply pure numbers. They'd be overrun and Paris would fall to their evil. And, Joseph feared, this same scenario would play out over and over again: London, Berlin, Madrid, Rome, then all of Europe, New York City, Boston, Washington DC, the eastern seaboard, then the Midwest, then the entire United States. From there, the demons would spread through Mexico and plague the continent of South America. Canada would fall as well. The path of destruction would follow then to Russia, across Asia and Africa, spreading like a cancer, till the whole world, every continent, was covered in a flood of demonic energy.

The world would be ravaged by chaos and war. The spread of famine and disease would reach new heights. Brother would kill brother, not even for survival, but because the voices in their head told them to. All the leaders of the world would cry out for the madness to end, pray to whatever gods they served for salvation.

And then, a man would ascend to power from the multitude of nations, a man like none before him, his handsomeness unmatched, his words flowing with a sweet elegance that no person can resist. This man will offer a solution, one that the entire world will beg for. He'll bring peace and food, provide shelter and cures. Then, he'll nearly die, struck down to the world's horror. But that will not be his end.

The man will live, miraculously healed from his fatal wounds. He will rise arrogant and unshakeable, reborn and baptized in bloodthirsty power. The whole world will bow to this man, will worship him for his greatness. And the evil which he held at bay, will once more, by his command, be set loose upon the earth.

Then, the end will come. Armageddon will shake every corner of the globe as the last great war will be fought. But the outcome has already been planned. Goodness will triumph. God's armies will be the victor. And when the man who fooled the entire world, the antichrist, is dead. Real, lasting peace will follow, as promised by God Himself.

Everything, that future which Joseph knew was inevitable, began there, now, in Paris. The Frenchman was not the first domino in the line to fall, but one of many. And as he toppled, the next domino would be struck, then the next, and again and again, till the day of judgment when all men and women must answer for the choices they've made.

Stopping the Frenchman would not avoid this future. Joseph was fully aware. But it would delay the coming plague of evil, allow mankind a little longer to seek God's truth and find salvation from the sure damnation that would follow. Regardless, he knew it was his place to fight. And that, same as the previous two nights, was what he would do.

Joseph landed on the very top of the Eiffel Tower, looking down at the battlefield, playing out the conflict before it actually took place. The angels had been divided into three groups: the ring surrounding the watery portal, a massive army who would fight the demons that awaited sundown in the shadows, and a large circular perimeter of warriors to keep demons from escaping the area. For their part, he believed the angels to be ready. They hovered even now, in their strategic placements, invisible to the human eye, but absolutely real and ready for the first demon to emerge in the coming darkness. They would fight to their death, and most certainly if Gavin failed to close the portal for good. Now, all Joseph could do was wait and see.

****

Jean Luc used every shortcut he knew and they were making great time. Paris was already far behind them. The van was travelling west of Orleans. Tours was less than an hour away.

"So answer this for me?" Jamie asked, his arm around Kayla as the van bounced along the highway, the hungry group eating the sandwiches that she had wisely prepared. "Where did you get the gun, the one you used to stop Killion?"

Kayla smiled, "Right before we left for the museum, I had this funny thought that it might be useful. So I quickly picked one I was familiar with and found the magazine was already loaded. I carried it in the back of my jeans, tucked in the waist. Thank God I did!"

"Yeah, thank God," Ashley grinned looking at Gavin.

They finished the simple sandwiches, glad for a moment of reprieve before the coming storm of certain violence.

"One more time," Gavin said. "We're all in agreement that we're going ahead with this? There will be lots of fighting and *everyone's* life will be in constant jeopardy!"

The positive replies in unison told Gavin that they all supported him, that they had his back.

"Alright then," he continued. "When we get there, Michael and I will scout and see what the property looks like, both layout and threats. You all stay with the van. Jamie, Jean Luc: you two will defend the van. Kayla, Ashley: if you choose to fight, make every bullet count. If there are sleepwalkers, remember to aim for their heads. That's the only way to bring them down. If we can find the Frenchman and get in and out quickly, we can save a lot of trouble. That's what Michael and I will do. The sooner this is over, the sooner we can all go home."

****

"Should we tell him?" a leathery demon hissed through his teeth, clinging to the ceiling of the candlelit chapel, it and another winged creature looking down on the careworn Emeric Laurent below.

"Tell him what?" the other asked in reply.

"That they're coming for him!"

"It'll be more fun to see the look of surprise on his face when they show up. I wouldn't miss that for the world."

"What about the war in Paris, did you hear about that?"

"Of course."

"Maybe we should, you know, go fight, help our brothers?" the demon considered.

"Are you kidding me?"

"What?!"

"Let them fight. We're perfectly safe right here. I don't have any reason to die at present. Do you?"

"No."

"Then it's settled. We'll watch the show from here."

****

The last leg of the drive was spent in quiet contemplation. Gavin and Ashley held hands and prayed softly. Jamie and Kayla shared fond memories of their life together, happy thoughts of their kids. Michael found himself talking to God, the silent words spoken in his mind as Jean Luc focused on the road ahead, the sun beginning to set.

Michael wasn't really praying, more having an informal, one-way discussion. But he was sure God heard his ramblings. He questioned the past and present. Asked God why him, why his family? Had he been chosen at birth to live a life of evil or had it been part of a destiny that would bring him to where he was here and now? Michael recalled all the evil he'd done, flashes of the haunting memories playing in his mind. He'd killed so many in service to Triton; and what was worse, through the dementia of the mask, he enjoyed the violence, even longed for killing. Could he ever be free of the mask, of Thirteen? Could Michael separate himself from the Laurent family's fate and find forgiveness in Christ Jesus?

On and on he went, speaking through thought, crying out to God, but there was no reply, no angelic choir or booming voice from the heavens. And so Michael found himself questioning if God was even listening. But if He wasn't, then why had Michael been awoken to his sin and broken by guilt?

Perhaps I'm not ready to hear God? he decided silently.

"We're here," Jean Luc announced, interrupting everyone's thoughts as he flipped off the van's headlights and cautiously turned onto the path leading into the densely overgrown property.

The entrance drive was short, opening into an open, gravel courtyard, outbuildings guarding either side. Ahead, rising up in the encroaching darkness, was the chateau, crumbling, decrepit, horrifying in the fading light.

Jean Luc parked along the outer wall of the building to the right of the drive, using the building itself to hide the van from direct line-of-sight from the chateau, "We should be alright here, at least for now."

"Alright," Gavin said, taking charge, "Michael, are you ready?"

"I am."

"Then let's go. You guys, keep watch. If there's trouble, well…shoot it in the head."

Gavin stepped from the van, the suppressed HK compact in hand, and disappeared into the overgrowth at the building's edge. Michael followed, reaching into his suit jacket's inner pocket as he followed into the darkness. Just out of sight of the others, he took out his mask, comforted by its familiarity, and pulled it down over his face, the eyes of the mask glowing white as Michael faded away, Thirteen taking over.

"You've never been here before?" Gavin asked in a low whisper.

"I'd remember a place such as this," Thirteen replied. "This property must have been Triton's."

The two crept in the shadows, stopping just short of the clearing that led up to the narrow stone crossing and the chateau itself. The wide ring of water stood deathly still as crickets chirped in long sustained song.

"Do you suppose the moat runs completely around the castle?" Gavin wondered.

Thirteen nodded, "Most certainly. There's power in water, supernatural energy. Running water can often provoke spirits and help with physical manifestations."

"But the water is stagnant."

"Didn't Joseph mention a whirlpool that opened in the Seine, a portal to Hell? Perhaps this water works the same way, when my father needs its power?"

"Could be," Gavin replied.

He began a slow , wary step onto the gravel ahead, but stopped and retreated to the cover of the bushes. Thirteen searched for the cause of Gavin's hesitation.

There, emerging from the trees that lined a narrow course into the woods, was an older man, his graying head down as he walked, obviously dejected, kicking at pebbles that laid in his path. His hands were thrust deeply in his pockets and his face bore the look of a man hard on his luck.

"Who's that?" Gavin questioned, assuming he must be another of Laurent's servants.

"That," Thirteen growled, "is the Frenchman."

They watched the old man pass on the walkway ahead, then turn up the stone bridge and disappear within the chateau. Gavin seemed perplexed.

"Not what you were expecting?" Thirteen mused, his crookedly stitched mask smiling for him.

"I thought the Frenchman would reek of power. Put a thicker beard and red suit on that guy and you'd have Santa Clause."

"Well, I'm not sure what's going on, but trust me, even like this, my father is more dangerous than you could imagine."

"We had a clear shot at him," Gavin realized. "We could have taken him right there!"

"It's better like this," Thirteen reasoned. "And, unless I'm mistaken, simply killing him won't destroy the power he's unleashed."

"How do you know that?"

"I can feel it, like a surging, over and over, a pulse of energy charging the air. My mask is tingling with power like I haven't felt in half a decade!" There's something unusual and special on this property. And…"

"What?!" Gavin asked, curious as to why Thirteen had suddenly stopped speaking.

"…the key, it's here. The Frenchman succeeded in using it. Of that, I'm certain."

Gavin turned his attention back to the ominous house, looking left and right along the walkway, "The coast is clear, let's move on."

Carefully and remaining as low to the ground as they could, Gavin and Thirteen hurried onto the gravel path and stealthily moved up to the chateau's once-grand entrance. Other than the sound of the gentle evening breeze stirring the tallest branches of the trees, the property seemed hauntingly empty and quiet. After a long moment of peering into the chateau from the cover of the heavy doorframe, they continued on into the entry hall.

The day's last light shone through the decrepit framework of the old castle, casting odd shadows. The overgrown interior, throttled by nature's devastation, also made spotting anyone in hiding difficult. A bizarre surrealism struck the men, the strange effect of trees and bushes growing up where furniture should be jarring, playing tricks with their minds.

"Look, up there," Thirteen pointed above the crumbling grand fireplace, a crest identical to the one on the ring found in Laurent's study still visible amongst the green vines and moss.

"Where did he go?" Gavin asked, nodding at the symbol, but focused on the Frenchman. "Your father wasn't that far ahead of us. It's like he disappeared!"

"Maybe there was a secret passage or something. We could have easily missed it in all this rubble and growth," Thirteen reasoned.

They lingered in the great hall, searching around the fallen stonework and crumbling walls, but there was nothing to find.

"This way," Gavin whispered, ready to head to the next room.

Thirteen followed and the men crossed into the great hall. A long, heavy and old wooden table with ornate chairs stood in front of them. Beyond the table, was Laurent's machine, the one used to draw blood in his rituals.

"Look," Gavin said, pointing at a dried bloodstain spattered on the wall next to them. "Something happened in here."

"Tell me, five years ago, when Jamie and Kayla were investigating the murders and Triton, did they ever figure out the strange markings on the bodies at the sacrifice, the event that started them down the path to where they are, here and now?"

"No, I explained the markings as part of a ritual."

"But do you know how the markings got there, the two holes in the victims' spines?"

"We're talking about this now?" Gavin asked, looking into the next room, his gun raised and ready.

"That machine over there, the huge mechanical chair, that is similar to what Triton used on the victims, though much smaller and modern. That chair must have been one of his early designs."

Gavin turned and stared at the maniacal device, "You mean that thing drains bodies of their blood?"

"Yeah, I've watched it in action, or at least Triton's machine in New York. He displayed it amongst his world-spanning trinkets in his office at the Tri-Corp building in Manhattan. You most likely saw it there and didn't even know it."

"Incredible," Gavin replied, pulling out his cell phone and capturing a picture. "Jamie needs to see this!"

"Come on then," Thirteen said, let's keep moving.

They turned to head through another doorway, but a faint noise pulled their attention back to the center courtyard. The sun had sank deep enough on the western horizon, that light was now scarce, leaving them in growing darkness.

"Arrêter où vous êtes," a bodiless voice called out. "That's far enough."

Thirteen turned to look back at Gavin, but was met by a heavy fist right to his jaw, sending him toppling backward, tripping over loose debris and falling to the ground. A man stood towering over him, a long, black, hooded trench coat exaggerating his large frame, cloaking his face. But Thirteen knew who the attacker was, the man overwhelmingly familiar.

"Hello, Sebastian," he said, looking up at his brother. "I thought you were dead. But I guess I was wrong."

Sebastian lunged at him, but Thirteen rolled out of reach, Sebastian's powerful fists missing and slamming into the floor, the impact cracking the softened stone tiles. Thirteen quickly stood and wasted no time in a counter attack, staggering his opponent.

"Get out of here!" Thirteen shouted at Gavin. "Go find my father!"

Gavin understood and raced down the nearest hall he could find, nearly tumbling down the dark stairway, unaware as the floor dropped out beneath him. In the courtyard above, Thirteen and Sebastian raged on.

A section of wall came crashing down as Thirteen was thrown against it, his body smashing through to the other side. Sebastian's attacks were relentless. His clenched fists glowed a radiant, supernatural blue, as if on fire, wisps of energy encasing his hands as the magic he channeled strengthened his already daunting strikes.

Thirteen climbed from the wreckage and summoned every evil spirit he could, the hideous mask fueling his hatred for his brother. Bloodlust coursed through his veins as he rushed forward in a flurry of thrusts and kicks, each blow finding its mark, leaving Sebastian staggered and bloody, his nose smashed by the heel of Thirteen's leather-soled shoe.

"I'll kill you," Thirteen growled, ready to strike again.

"Maybe, but I'll kill your friends first."

Sebastian tilted back his head and howled like a wolf. The floor beneath them began to rumble. The whole chateau shook, loose stones and dirt falling all around them. Outside, beyond their view, the still water of the moat began to churn and swell as bodies slowly surfaced , their leathery faces emerging from the dark murkiness. The creatures climbed out of the water by the dozens and slinked onto the outer pathway, skulking towards the gravel lot where the van was hidden, their soaked clothing dripping as they marched, leaving behind a watery trail.

"Jamie!" Thirteen screamed loud and shrill, his voice amplified by the demonic power he wielded.

Over one hundred yards away, the group huddled by the van looked up, surprised by the sudden call. Jean Luc peeked around the corner of the building, the oncoming terror clearly in view.

"This is it, what Gavin warned us about, get the guns ready," he cried, more panicked than he'd felt in all his life.

Loud pops of gunfire rattled off, echoing across the courtyard, bouncing back off the surrounding buildings. The muzzles of the guns flashed brilliantly as the friends defended their position.

They took aim at the oncoming wave of sleepwalkers, the spray of bullets ripping into them, sending black, oily blood spurting and bursting from their fiendish bodies.

"Remember their weakness," Kayla shouted over the ruckus, "aim for the head."

Within seconds, the bodies began piling up as the sleepwalkers fell, bullet wounds left where faces used to have been. The companions were amazingly accurate, their magazine reloads quick and expert-like. With such little time to train and prepare, even they were amazed by how well they meshed, covering one another and timing their attacks so that there was never a stop in the flurry of rounds.

Finally, and easier than expected, the last sleepwalker was brought down. They were slow and had a great distance to cover in a wide open area, this worked against them. Jean Luc smiled, glad for the tactical advantage.

"That was insane," he laughed, panting as he slapped Jamie on the back.

****

Gavin paused as the whole hallway shook from the fighting taking place upstairs. The hallway was pitch black and visibility was next to impossible. He felt along the wall for direction, his fingers dirtied by the mildew and soot covered stone. Trudging along in the dark reminded him very much of Triton's labyrinthine basement level in the bowels of the Tri-Corp tower. He mused at how similar Triton and the Frenchman were, but it made total sense: of course the apprentice would mirror the master.

Ahead, a flicker of candlelight drew his attention to the right. There was a room. Maybe that was where the Frenchman had gone? Carefully, Gavin peered around the old wooden doorframe, briefly taken aback. The small room appeared to be someone's quarters. There was a homely bed and a small table with a candle stand. Beyond that, another door, but to where? Gavin decided he must find out. He picked up the candle in his left hand and raised the pistol, aiming straight ahead as he kicked against the old door, sending it crashing open.

****

Joseph commanded the host of angels, pushing them harder and faster, watching as, one by one, the demons' ranks were thinned. Sadly, he'd lost some powerful warriors. But the battle was leaning in their favor. The demons were beginning to panic, their attacks becoming more and more haphazard as the angels remained calm and focused.

But then, just as it seemed the angels might put an end to the skirmish, the waters of the Seine began to twist and churn, then spin as the whirlpool began to form just as the two nights before. The portal suddenly opened as hundreds of demons pushed through the gateway from Hell.

Joseph knew right away: Gavin had yet to confront the Frenchman. The war was not over, it had only just begun.

29

Jamie stood next to the pile of dead sleepwalkers, studying the diverse dress and appearance of the fallen monsters. He kicked one of them as its hand flinched, then put another bullet in the leathery creatures head just in case.

"I still feel like that was too easy," Kayla muttered as she knelt down and checked several of the bodies for wallets or identification of any sort.

"Yeah," Jamie agreed.

"There's not a single ID here," Kayla said in surprise. "Who do you think they all were?"

"Casualties of an old man's game," Jamie answered in disgust.

"How on earth would you get people to follow along and let something like this happen to them, to be turned into one of these...*things*?"

"Something tells me they didn't have much of a choice, Kay."

Ashley watched from by near the van, pacing as she did, her every thought on Gavin and what must be happening inside the chateau. She turned to Jean Luc who also looked nervous.

"Should we go inside? Maybe they need our help?"

Jean Luc thought for a moment, wondering just what he'd gotten himself into, "For now, we must let this play out and have faith that we are all exactly where God needs us to be. Until we are told otherwise, I think we should begin reloading the empty magazines, just in case."

Ashley nodded. Belesur was right.

"I have a bad feeling about this," she said, pressing a 9mm round down into a Beretta mag.

****

"You must drive them back," Joseph shouted over the battle cries and rattling crashes of swords. "Hold them at the river. Do not let them beyond the perimeter. Paris must not fall!"

The angels did the best they could, fighting valiantly. But for every demon that fell, another took its place. They could not keep this up. The odds had changed, the scales tipping in the wrong direction.

****

Thirteen grew bored with physical combat. He pulled his guns from their holsters, a 1911 automatic in each hand, and blasted the rounds at his brother. Sebastian twisted and flipped, dodging each bullet as they slammed into the surrounding walls, sending plaster and stone flying, dust hanging in the stale air.

Sebastian, in turn, brandished his Sig Saur and fired back, but Thirteen stopped the 9mm rounds at will, the bullets dropping harmlessly to the ground as both men paused to reload.

"This is pointless," Sebastian laughed. "Our powers are too great. Maybe we should stop fighting and join together, rule the world as brothers. Our family deserves such a thing after enduring centuries of slavery at the hands of Triton."

"Do you have any idea what you've done?" Thirteen questioned, scolding his twin brother for his actions.

"Of course! Father and I have opened the path that will allow the world to come together and live in harmony. We've lit the lamp of discovery. Soon hunger will be no more and disease will be cured. Just imagine a world without war, without constant violence!"

"But at what cost, Sebastian?"

"If I die so that the stage will be set for the greatest leader the world has ever known, then I die a proud martyr, for my intentions are good, even if the methods are not."

"It's funny," Thirteen mused, "but I used to think the same way. When I killed Triton, I did not do it just because father had asked me to, but because I knew it would allow me a future, the means to care for my wife and son. But now I see the error in my thinking. A wrong can never be solved with a wrong. Killing Triton seemed right, but here we are, our own father taking the very place of the man we both despised."

"But there's a difference in the fact that Triton was not our father. My loyalty is in my blood."

"You've found loyalty," Thirteen laughed. "I've found forgiveness."

"How?"

"Washed in the blood of Christ," Thirteen replied.

"Look at you! How can you say such a thing, claim forgiveness, your words coming from behind that mask, powered by sin and pure evil. You cannot have both, brother."

"I don't need this mask anymore," Thirteen vowed.

"Then take it off," Sebastian grinned, "and we'll continue this face to face."

****

Gavin was stunned by what he saw, the soft light of the candle diminished by the bright luminescence of the energy escaping through the lone-standing doorway in the middle of the large, round room. Emeric Laurent trembled as he turned to find a gun pointed at him. The young girl was unmoved, facing the hellish gateway, her arms outstretched, her hair flowing freely in the energy that emanated from her.

"What are you doing here?" the Frenchman grunted at the intruder. "You have no business here. Leave us be!"

"Is this it," Gavin shouted over the pulsing drone of power. "Is this what you needed the key for?"

"Indeed," Laurent replied. "I have succeeded where Triton failed."

"Who's the girl?"

"She's a dreamer, essential to the ritual. I chose her and prepared her for this, fed her dreams and allowed her the vision to see the world like no one else."

"You called her a *dreamer*? Why is that important?"

"Dreamers," Laurent explained, "can view and commune with the supernatural. When asleep, their dreams are simply that: dreams. But when awake, when a dreamer dreams, there is incredible power. Unbridled, it can do things such as this. You know, Triton had chosen his dreamer and had begun grooming her for this very purpose."

"Ashley!" Gavin said angrily.

****

Joseph grew worried. His host was now outnumbered. He cried out for God to send help, but his shouts were drowned out by the wailing taunts of the army of darkness that covered the whole Eiffel Tower, scurrying along the steelwork, slinking along in the shadows.

He raised his mighty sword and flew headlong into the cloud of demons. He'd do everything he could to slow them, including sacrifice himself.

****

"If I were to remove the mask, I'd be at your mercy," Thirteen scoffed. "You'd strike me down without a second thought. Our blood means nothing to you."

"You're right, Michael. You abandoned us, turned your back on this family. Your son does not deserve the name of Laurent."

Thirteen struck out in anger, once more opening fire, unleashing a barrage of .45 caliber rage. But as before, the attack was meaningless. Neither brother able to kill the other.

****

"I'll give you one last opportunity to flee and save yourself," the Frenchman offered. "You need not die here tonight, demon hunter."

"If you kill me, then you'll have to answer to my friends outside. They'll come after you with vengeance. There's no way you can stop them."

"They're outside, you say?" Laurent winked. "Pity for them. I hope you said goodbye."

The ground rumbled beneath their feet. A shrill scream erupted from deep within the girl. And then, she collapsed to the floor, her skin white and pale.

****

"Did you hear that?" Kayla asked Jamie, jumping back from the pile of dead sleepwalkers. "That sounded like a scream!"

"It certainly did," he replied, scanning the chateau grounds for the source.

Ashley skidded to a stop on her heels as she raced to join her sister and brother-n-law, "Did that come from inside the castle?"

"Sounded like it," Jamie agreed.

The earth trembled. Then suddenly, the woods that guarded the property was disturbed. The darkness itself stirred, agitating the ancient growth. Branches snapped as something moved recklessly within the trees.

And then they saw what had made the noise. Emerging into the moonlight were more sleepwalkers than they could count, and worse, they were coming from all sides. They turned, but their way of escape was blocked. The sleepwalkers had them surrounded.

"I don't think we have enough bullets for all of them!" Jean Luc exclaimed.

"Let's pray we won't need them," Jamie said hopefully. "If Gavin can stop the Frenchman, then maybe we'll have a chance."

****

The war was incredible, the damage to the city of Paris extensive. But as long as Joseph still drew breath, he believed the demons could be stopped. His arms had been slashed as he fought, the wounds burning from the demons' flaming swords. Still, he pressed on. His sword grew heavy in his aching hands, yet he did not falter.

But the demons had led him into a trap. Now they circled him, whooping and hollering, mocking the angelic warrior. Joseph did all he could to defend himself, but there were just too many and he had grown weak from so much fighting.

A blazing sword swung by a lunging demon grazed Joseph's shoulder as he dodged the attack, parrying and countering masterfully, but another attack came from his side, slashing his wing. Crippled and unable to fly, Joseph fell, slamming into the grassy park below, broken and left for dead.

****

Gavin moved his aim from the Frenchman to the girl, "If I kill her, will it end this? Will it close the portal?"

"It's too late for that," Laurent admitted. "What's done is done. The power unleashed is irreversible."

"We'll see about that," Gavin said, squeezing the trigger.

The suppressor withheld the bang of the gun, but the bullet fired true, striking its mark. The girl's eyes flicked open as she gasped, suddenly aware of the burning in her chest.. She tried to stand from where she'd fallen to the floor, but her strength seemed to have gone. She no longer appeared the powerful monster the ritual had created, no. She was most certainly the young farm girl, scared and in pain.

"What have you done!" Laurent screamed, dropping to her side, brushing the hair from her young face as she gasped and coughed.

The Frenchman shakily jerked a pistol from beneath his suit coat, but Gavin was too quick. Before the gun was even leveled at him, Gavin fired again, the bullet striking Laurent in the arm, the gun dropping to his side.

"You've ruined everything!" the Frenchman sobbed, watching as the girl labored, clinging to the last strands of her young life.

Her eyes grew heavy and she blinked. As she did, Gavin realized that the white light coming from the door also dimmed.

"She's connected to the gateway, isn't she?" he understood, certain that he'd found a way to end this.

"Yes, but it doesn't matter now," Laurent said disdainfully. "You've killed us all. When she dies, we're all dead, all of us!"

Laurent turned his attention to the girl, gently touching her cheek as he held her in his arms. Her skin was growing cold as her pulse slowed. Tears streaming from his face, the Frenchman struggled to raise the pistol once more. But he did not take aim at Gavin.

"I'm so sorry," Emeric Laurent wept.

Gavin watched on in shock as the agonizing Frenchman placed the pistol against the girl's temple and fired, ending her misery, then turned the gun on himself, the barrel thrust into his mouth as he pulled the trigger and took his own life.

The light from the doorway began to hum and pulse, then a force began sucking the air from the room into the portal itself. Gavin fought to move. The vortex unimaginably strong. He managed to reach the smaller room, every step a little easier than the last, but the howl of the gateway was growing louder. Gavin turned just in time to see the Frenchman and the girl sucked into the doorway, spiraling into oblivion. The alter and the evil book followed. If Gavin didn't hurry, he knew his fate would be the same.

He raced out into the hall, hurrying in the darkness, trying to find the stairway leading up and away from the imposing doom. Gavin stumbled over debris hidden in the darkness, colliding with the stone wall as if the chateau itself tried to stop him, but he managed to find the steps, taking them three at a time.

The stairs led to the great hall, from there, a right turn through a tall doorway would bring him to the inner courtyard. Then, the exit would be so close, if he could just make it across the bridge.

Sebastian and Thirteen stood in stunned silence, the whole chateau shaking and shifting violently. Gavin ran as fast as he could, grabbing Michael by the arm as he sprinted between the brothers.

"Come on!"

They dodged and leapt over the fallen stones of the once beautiful castle, greeted by the moon's glow as they cleared the grand entrance. The bridge was just ahead. The water in the moat churned and bubbled. Beyond that, a dense wall of sleepwalkers stood in their path, the rapport of gun fire erupting from where the unrelenting wave of the terrifying creatures moved and groaned in a horrid dirge of death.

Within the ritual chamber, the free-standing frame of the doorway flexed and bowed under the immense strain of the vacuum pulling everything down into it. Finally, the old rotting wood itself gave in to the stress and splintered into pieces. A shockwave of energy blasted from the portal, toppling the walls, bringing down the ceiling.

The ground shook as the chateau, stone by stone, was sucked down into the hole, the vortex greedily devouring everything around it. Sebastian clawed his way from rock to rock, trying desperately to escape, but could not fight the pull, the chateau swallowing him alive.

In a last, devastating pulse, the whitest light imaginable shot from the closing portal, blinding Gavin and Michael, and leveling every sleepwalker and the companions fighting for their lives. The light faded; and then, silence.

****

Thirteen's eyes burned as they adjusted to the bright light that engulfed him. He looked around questioningly, finding himself not cast on the ground, but standing in absolute calm. Gone was the stone and grass of the chateau's grounds. The sleepwalkers and his friends were nowhere to be seen. Instead, he stood surrounded by pure white nothingness, no shadows, just light. There seemed to be no floor, no walls. He had nothing to gauge the scale of the space in which he found himself. Perhaps it was small or maybe it was infinitely large, its boundaries beyond time and space. Either way, it didn't really matter. He wondered if he was actually dead.

"Hello?" he called out, but there was no reply.

"Am I dead?"

A warm, jovial laugh suddenly rumbled all around him, from everywhere and nowhere at the very same time.

"Who's there?" Thirteen asked curiously. "Please show yourself."

"Tell me Michael," the voice replied, firm yet infinitely kind and understanding. "What do you see?"

"Nothing but light."

"Then you see Me. For I am light."

"Who are you?"

"I am. I am the word. I am the way, the truth, and the life. I am the alpha and the omega, the beginning in the end. Tell me Michael, who are you?"

"But you already know."

"Yes, but do you?"

Thirteen stood silent, pondering those words.

"Tell me Michael, do you know the story of Moses and the burning bush?"

"Of course."

"When Moses stood before the bush, in My presence, I asked him to do one thing. Do you remember?"

"He was asked to remove his sandals, for the ground on which he stood was holy."

"That's very good, Michael."

"So you want me to take my shoes off then?"

"No. You're mask, Michael. Remove the mask."

Michael slowly reached up and pulled the black cloth from his face, then looked down at the mask, stretching it out to view the evil grin.

"Are You really God?" he asked, feeling all the power of Thirteen drain from within him.

"I am."

"Then take this mask...*please*. I do not want it to be a part of my life anymore," Michael pleaded, holding the mask out in surrender.

"That's not how this works, Michael. That mask is your burden, your sin. I can forgive you of it, cleanse you if you repent and are sincere, but if I were to simply take it away, then I have ended your free will. Your sin will always be there to tempt you, to entice you, but it is your choice whether or not to give into that temptation or to rebuke it and follow Me."

"But the mask is evil, Thirteen is evil. I don't want to be him anymore."

"Then don't be," the strong voice laughed once more. "Do not let sin control you. If you give in to sin, then it has become your master and you are a slave to it. A man cannot serve two masters, but just because he chooses one over the other does not mean the other master is gone. In fact, the other master fiercely fights to keep his slave, making sin more difficult to overcome. That is why you must strengthen yourself in My word. Fill your mind with what is good and pure, and there will be no room for Thirteen. But, as long as you live, he will be with you, tempting you, pleading for you to return to him. Tell me, Michael. Who do you say that I am?"

"I believe you are God, though I don't understand how this is possible."

"With Me, nothing is impossible, Michael. Do you understand salvation?"

"I do," Michael replied. "I understand that Jesus Christ is Your son, the Messiah, and that His death on the cross was an atonement, once and for all, the fulfillment of the old covenant and the birth of the new covenant, that brings us freely to You, without need for priests or curtains.

By believing in You and asking Your forgiveness, You dwell in us, we ourselves becoming the Holy of Holies. I believe Jesus died for me, even for Thirteen."

"And are you sorry for all you've done in Thirteen's name? Do you repent of all the evil, all the wickedness, the vile actions and violations to My commandments?"

"I do," Michael answered, humbled by God's words.

"Then put away the mask of Thirteen, you are forgiven. I will count you amongst My sheep, the one that was lost and nearly gone forever, but you have once more become one of My flock. Be happy this day, Michael. Never part from these words or forget My promises. For today, you have found redemption."

30

Michael slowly opened his eyes, feeling his body violently shake as the wondrous light of God's presence faded to nothing but a memory. Gavin knelt over him, grasping his shoulders, trying desperately to wake his friend. Michael looked into Gavin's face, then up at the full moon glowing brightly in the night sky.

"I thought you were gone for a moment there," Gavin sighed.

"What happened?" Michael asked, sitting up, his body aching.

"There was a girl, a *dreamer*, as your father called her. She was the one opening the portal. You're father killed her, then killed himself. Then, for reasons beyond my understanding, the portal closed on itself, creating a vacuum of sorts, the energy pulling anything near it into itself."

"So my father is dead, what about my brother, what about Sebastian?"

Gavin pointed at the area behind Michael, the place where the chateau once stood. The entire structure had been consumed by the portal. After the portal closed, a deep well had sprung open, drowning the ruins and concealing it under water. Michael studied the moat, then the ring of grass and stone that was the foundation where the old castle stood; but now, a perfectly circular pool had formed, leaving nothing to show of the estate.

"Where's your mask?" Gavin questioned. "You were wearing it before the flash, but now, it's gone. I don't see it anywhere."

Michael reached up and touched his face, feeling not the cloth of the mask, but his own skin. And in his heart, he was truly happy, like all his burdens had been lifted. Perhaps the mask was gone as well?

"And the sleepwalkers? Is everyone else alright? Kayla, Jamie, Ashley?!" he said, his attention returning to his friends.

"The sleepwalkers are gone, just…*gone*. They disappeared in the flash of light. As for Ashley and the rest, they're all okay," Gavin smiled happily.

"Then it's all over?" Michael asked. "We did it!"

Gavin grinned as he helped Michael to his feet, the two men limping towards their astonished friends, "We did it."

Ashley threw her arms and around Gavin's neck and kissed him, happy tears streaming down her cheeks. Jamie and Kayla took turns hugging Michael. Jean Luc stood in awe, uncertain of just what miracle he witnessed, yet he knew that he had become part of something special.

"So what happened in there?" Jamie asked excitedly.

"I'll tell you on the plane," Gavin grinned, patting his brother-in-law on the shoulder. "It's a long flight back to the United States."

"Thank you for your help, Jean Luc, really, thank you," Kayla smiled, turning towards the still speechless man.

"But of course," he laughed deeply, accepting her handshake as he woke from his trance.

"So that's it then," Ashley sighed. "The Frenchman's terror has ended. Does that mean Triton's legacy has come to an end as well?"

"No," Gavin admitted. "The Frenchman told me, just before he died, what's done is done. The world will not recover from the events that took place here. But we all knew that going into this. No matter what we did, we can never stop the antichrist from coming. It's been prophesied, it will happen, just as the book of Revelation outlines. But what we did was set it back, if even for a day. And most importantly, we sent a message. Our actions boldly prove that there are still Christians out their ready to fight for our faith, to stand for God and speak out for truth. As long as people like us are here, proclaiming God's goodness and sharing the gospel of Jesus Christ, then the antichrist is powerless. It's up to us, as Christians, to show the world what God is really all about, to go beyond religion and *be* love, just as Jesus asks of His followers."

"And what do we do now?" Jamie asked.

Gavin again smiled, "It's written in the second book of John, verse six, *And this is love: that we walk in obedience to His commands. As you have heard from the beginning, His command is that you walk in love.*"

"Now, let's go home."

****

Joseph rested in the soft grass, smiling and laughing as he recalled the sudden shift in the battle, at a time when all seemed lost. He knew that Gavin had succeeded in his task, the whirlpool in the Seine not only closing, but actually drawing the demons back into it, dragging them back to Hell.

For three nights, he'd fought with his fellow angels, driving back the demonic horde, but fearing that victory was nearly impossible. Now, he couldn't stop laughing. The other angels might find him crazy and he mused that they'd be right. For that was proven most certain only a short time ago, when he'd flown headlong into the darkest stronghold and risked death for the sake of seemingly unattainable victory.

But Joseph was very much alive, beaten and wounded, but alive. He stretched out his battered wings, the pain almost unendurable. A section of feathers were missing on his right side, a demon's blade slicing them free. In time, the wound would heal, the butchered feathers replaced by new white growth.

He surveyed the battlefield. The area was nearly destroyed, rubble and debris everywhere. Smashed vehicles, crumbled buildings: it was a wonder the Eiffel Tower still stood. But the battle was over. And though he knew that it was only the beginning, that a constant and violent war loomed on the horizon, this victory proved something he'd believed in for so long, there was still hope for mankind.

SEVERAL MONTHS LATER

Edward Killion cruised along a wide open lane in the English countryside. The inline-six roared as he pushed the 1963 silver-birch Aston Martin DB5 along the winding, hilly road.

Beside him sat a pretty, but unremarkable woman, early thirties. She was quiet, reserved, nothing like the ladies his brother tried to push on him. Her hands were folded neatly in her lap and she sighed softly, loving the view from the classic coupe, even with the winter chill in the air.

As they drove along, Edward found himself recalling the day his brother, Terrance Killion, was judged and executed. He truly missed his brother, regretted that he had to die in a such a way, yet his brother made sure that Edward would be well provided for.

He pictured the slip of paper he'd retrieved from his brother just before looking into his cold, blue eyes for the last time. He remembered one phrase in particular, replaying in his mind the haunting words spoken to him by his brother, *Gare du Nord...train station...find the lockers*. And that's exactly what Edward did, he followed his brother's instructions.

No sooner had the door to the warehouse in Montmartre closed behind him, he had hailed a cab and requested transport to Gare du Nord, one of the busiest train hubs in all of France. There, blending into the troves of travelers, he searched for the locker marked with the number Terrance Killion had written on the paper. When he finally found it, he hesitated before punching in the pass code jotted just below, his finger lingering above the first digit in the series.

Though he loved his brother very much and knew that Killion did indeed reciprocate, he couldn't be certain that his brother truly wished him to live happily-ever-after without him. What if Killlion knew he was going to die and this was a trap, rigged to blow when Edward opened the locker, allowing Killion to take his brother with him to the grave?

Edward took a deep breath, exhaled, and punched in the code. The unit beeped, acknowledging the proper sequence, as the lock deactivated and the door swung open. He sighed in relief, hardly believing what he found. The large duffel bag they'd taken from the Frenchman was stuffed into the locker. Beneath it, Franklin's briefcase full of money, below that, his leather satchel containing his laptop. Killion, the sick and twisted killer, had left a gift for his brother, a token of his love and desire to see his brother happy.

He unzipped the black canvas bag and peered in. His fake passport was there, as were the guns taken from the dealer. Edward reached in and pocketed the ID, then carefully removed the FN P90 and the suppressed Sig Saur pistols, leaving them hidden in the locker. He wouldn't have any use for them now.

The duffel bag was slung over his left shoulder, the satchel over the other, in his hand he clung to the handle on the briefcase. Edward made his way to the ticket booth and waited in line, purchasing a one-way ticket to London.

And here he was, more Euros than he could spend in his lifetime, the proud owner of a vintage automobile dealership in central London, and a fine, honest English gentleman with a lovely young woman he loved and respected. If only Terrance could see him now.

****

Giant, wet flakes of snow fell lazily to the ground, covering the western Pennsylvania landscape in white Christmas cheer. Joyful carols and merry songs filled the air as Frank Sinatra serenaded the large group gathered at the Rose family homestead.

The kids played with their freshly opened presents in front of the warm, crackling fire. The tall, well-lit and heavily decorated tree towered over them, a tin star proudly atop the fur, as they celebrated life and family, their hearts filled with hope.

Michael sat with Elizabeth, sipping on hot cocoa as Gavin retold an old story they'd all heard a hundred times and would gladly hear a hundred times more. Ashley rested beside him on the couch, her festively red shirt stretched tight over her round, healthy, ever-growing belly. Kayla sat in Jamie's lap, the two nestled into an armchair, also drinking cocoa as they laughed, brought to happy tears by the expressions on Gavin's face. Kayla and Ashley's brother, Jake Rose, was their too, his pretty wife at his side, their two boys playing with Cain, Marley, and Ethan. Walter and Evelyn Rose couldn't help but smile, not because of their crack-up son-in-law, but because they were so proud of the kids they'd raised. And here they all were, the entire Rose extended family, warm and cozy, reunited as they celebrated the holiday.

"So honestly, Ashley," Jake's wife spoke up, finding the opportunity to change the subject as Gavin finished his exaggerated tale, "Are you going to tell us?"

"Yeah," Kayla chimed in, "what's it going to be, the baby. Is it a boy or a girl?"

Ashley squeezed Gavin's hand, her eyes sparkling in the soft light that reflected from the glowing strands on the Christmas tree as she smiled, "What do you think, babe. Should we tell them?"

"I think we should leave them in agonizing suspense," Gavin winked.

"Then it's settled," Ashley smirked. "You'll just have to wait and see."